Master of my Dreams

THE NOBLE LORDS: BOOK 1

DANELLE HARMON

More in This Series

THE NOBLE LORDS

Master of My Dreams

Taken by Storm

Scandal at Christmas

My Saving Grace

Prologue

IRELAND, 1762

The press gang was in.

One could tell by the way a thick pall had come over the land, like mist snuffing out the noonday sun. One could tell by the way the little village that clung to the sea's edge grew quiet and seemed to huddle within itself, the people slamming shut the doors of their whitewashed cottages and watching the roads from behind slitted curtains. One could tell by the way the taverns emptied and the young lads fled into the hills that climbed toward the majestic purple ridge of the twelve mountains, where they would hide until the threat had passed.

And one could tell by the big, three-masted man-of-war that filled the harbor.

England was still at war with France — and not everyone wanted to fight.

It was an infrequent threat, the Royal Navy seeking its unwilling recruits from this bleak, storm-tossed area of western Ireland that even God seemed to have forgotten. No able-bodied young man was safe from the press gang. And so it was that little Deirdre O'Devir, holding tightly to her mama's hand and clutching the ancient Celtic cross that hung from around her neck, solemnly bade her older brother good-bye. Roddy had blown her a careless, laughing kiss; then the door had banged shut behind him as he ran to join the steady stream of young lads who whistled and sang as they headed into hiding at the ruins of the old, haunted castle, far up in the hills where even the dreaded English would dare not go.

Then she and Mama had bolted the door and, huddling together beside the snapping, smoking peat fire, waited.

Roddy had said they had nothing to fear, for the press gang didn't take lassies. But as Deirdre stood at the window and looked off toward the sea, where she could see the towering masts of the man-of-war silhouetted against the brooding clouds, curiosity got the best of her. She had to see for herself just what was so terrible about the English and its Navy, which everyone so feared and hated.

After all, her dear cousin Brendan, who'd been raised right here in Connemara, was a midshipman in the Royal Navy, and despite having a British admiral for a daddy, was as much an Irishman as she or Roddy. Surely, if Brendan was in the Navy, it couldn't be as evil as everyone said it was ... could it?

Raising her chin, Deirdre made up her mind. Mama would never know if she sneaked out for just a bit. She was a wee mite, even for a seven-year-old; it was a simple thing to crawl out her window after she had made an excuse to steal off to her room. Once outside, she vaulted over the stone fence and rode away on Thunder, her own, well-loved pony.

She waited until she was well away from the cottage before she urged the pony into a gallop and raced him headlong toward the sea. The pungent scent of peat fires hung heavily on the air, mingling with the fresh, heady tang of the ocean. Drifting mist, cold, damp and penetrating, moved stealthily down from the mountains.

Night was coming on, and with it would come a storm.

Deirdre urged Thunder faster. Already the wind was picking up; now huge black clouds were filing in from the ocean, casting shifting shadows and colors over the rocky pastures, dragging patterns of light and dark over the sea. Recklessly, she pressed her heels to the pony's flanks, not pulling him up until they crested the last rocky hill.

There she sat, a pale little thing with thick, spiral-curling black hair whipping around a face dominated by the innocently wide eyes of a child. The wind gusted, promising rain. Far below, where the sea swapped kisses with the base of the hill, waves thundered and boomed and kicked up great sheets of spray that dewed her cheeks and tasted like salt.

A flock of rooks, shrieking, winged suddenly away, and in the distance she heard the mournful bleating of sheep. Behind her a stone, loosened by the pony's hooves, skittered down the hill, the sound cleaving the tense stillness. Deirdre gave a start and spun around, her skin crawling with the uncanny feeling that she was being watched.

But there was no one there.

Wind blew thick tangles of hair across her face. She clawed the wild tresses out of her eyes and looked anxiously toward the darkening sea.

There, a half mile out in the bay, the British warship lay, majestic in all its dread, frightening in all its beauty, the sky growing blacker by the moment behind its towering masts.

Deirdre's eyes grew huge. She reached up to touch the cross of hammered gold and inlaid emeralds that hung from around her neck, but the ancient heirloom was no comfort.

Beneath her, the pony tossed his head and pricked his ears forward, his attention caught by something out in the rising surf. Deirdre stared between his ears. A boat had been lowered from the ship and was headed toward shore, plunging through the rolling breakers and neatly avoiding the rocks, around which the surf boiled and foamed white in the gathering gloom.

Panic began to prickle up her spine.

Run, Deirdre, run! But she could do nothing except stare at the boat, forgetting the oncoming storm, forgetting the menace of the press gang, forgetting the fact that it would soon be dark and the banshees would come out.

Forgetting the awful feeling that she was being watched.

The boat was nearing shore now, its crew having a rough time of it in the rising seas as they steered it through the deadly rocks that reared out of the crashing surf. But even the rocks, which had guarded this ancient coast since time began, were helpless against invading Englishmen. Oars rose and fell in perfect rhythm, and every so often the boat's bow would nose up as it plowed a wave, drenching the men and the officer in the stern with spray. Deirdre felt sorry for them. But the oarsmen's smooth strokes never wavered, the boat wasn't dashed against the rocks, and steadily it drew closer.

A cold drop of rain hit her cheek. Another splashed upon her hand. Deirdre urged the pony to the very edge of the hill — and it was then that she noticed the officer in the boat had a telescope to his eye and was training it on *her*.

With a cry of fright, she wheeled Thunder around — and ran straight into a group of the most evil-looking men she'd ever seen in her life.

"And wot 'ave we 'ere, Jenkins? A wee Oirish lassie wi' purple eyes an' the fairest 'air ye ever did see!"

Deirdre's heart stopped, and bounced sickeningly down to her toes. Wildly, she looked behind her — but there was only the sea at her back, and nowhere to go.

She bit her lip and her eyes filled with tears.

"'Ere now, wot's this, tears on ol' Taggert 'ere?" One of them grabbed the pony's bridle, causing the animal to yank its head back and roll its eyes in fright. "Would ye lookee 'ere, Jenkins. Ye must've spooked her with that ugly face of yours."

Jenkins grinned, showing prominent teeth that only frightened her all the more. An oily braid hung down his back, tied at the end with a piece of leather, and tattoos competed for space on his thick, strapping arms.

"Let me go," she said, struggling to pull away.

But they simply laughed, fearsome and ugly men with hard eyes and menacing faces. Fumes of rum clung to their breath and some of them carried clubs; others had cudgels and one or two held cutlasses.

"Hold on to that nag's bridle, Taggert! With yer luck ye'll not be seein' another lass for some time to come!"

"Aye, she's the best ye're gonna do!"

Bursts of hearty guffaws followed their remarks, and their harsh English voices were foreign and frightening.

"Might as well take advantage of 'er before the lieutenant gets here!"

"Let me *go*!" Deirdre cried, kicking out at Jenkins's thigh with her foot.

He merely laughed, plucked her from the pony's back, and set her on the ground. His hand clamped around her wrist, holding her cruelly when she tried to fight and pull away. "Now, wot're ye doin' out here by yer lonesome when it's startin' to grow dark, eh? Ain't ye got a mother to watch over ye?"

Above, the clouds massed, stalled, and began to spit more rain. One drop. Another.

"'Sdeath, Jenkins, it's startin' to pour. We've work to do, and the lieutenant ain't gonna be too happy if he catches ye messing with a mere child."

"Indeed," said a cold, hard voice, "I damn well won't be."

Suddenly, the men behind Jenkins went still and stared with something like terror toward the hill's edge. Talk stopped abruptly. Faces paled. Eyes widened; gazes were cast down.

Far off in the distance, thunder rumbled.

There, a British sea officer stood silhouetted against the sky, watching them with eyes as cold and gray as the storm clouds that gathered behind him. His blue coat was soaked with spray, his lips were set in a severe line, and his features were as hard and uncompromising as stone.

"We've come here to press seamen, Jenkins, not frighten little girls. Unhand her this moment before you feel the bite of my anger — *and* my sword."

Jenkins released her so quickly she nearly fell. Recognizing the newcomer as the officer who'd watched her from the boat, Deirdre felt her knees begin to shake. She huddled closer to the pony's shoulder, her eyes huge with fright at the sight of the boat's crew gathering behind the officer, huffing and puffing as they came up the hill. They began to laugh as they caught sight of her and several exchanged smirks. But the officer did not seem amused at all. One sharp glance from him was all that was needed to instantly quell their grins. They looked down at the ground, obviously respectful of his authority and unwilling to displease him.

Even Jenkins backed away from the pony, his hands raised as though in truce. "Sorry, sir."

Pointing with his sword, the lieutenant snapped, "Get your carcass down that hill, drag the boats free of the surf, and mind that they're well hidden. We've King's business to conduct and no time to be dallying with diversions, damn you."

"Aye, aye, sir," Jenkins sputtered, and fled.

With a sharp and precise motion the officer sheathed his sword, the scrape of the blade against the scabbard sending shivers up Deirdre's spine. She stared at him, taking in the smart naval uniform and thinking that if he wasn't so frightening he might actually look handsome in it, even if he *was* a Briton. Not a speck of lint flecked the dark blue coat; not a smudge of dirt marred the whiteness of breeches and waistcoat—

But then he came forward, and Deirdre remembered her fear. The fearsome, rough-looking men parted, wordlessly letting the officer through their ranks. Cold sweat broke out along the length of Deirdre's spine and she trembled violently. A strange buzzing noise started in her ears, drowning out the crash of surf, the rising moan of the wind. Her fingers went numb and the feeling began to fade from her toes, her feet, her legs—

The lieutenant caught her when she would've fallen, his touch jerking her back to reality and stark, choking terror. She screamed in fright and struggled madly.

"Let me go!" she shrieked, kicking out at him. "Let me *go-o-ooo!*"

He let her struggle, her childish strength no match for his. Finally, she wore herself out and stood before him, frozen with fear and sobbing pathetically

"Poor little wren," he said, his voice deep and rich and soothing. He knelt down to her level, his thumbs coming up to brush away the tears that streaked her damp cheeks. She flinched, squeezing her eyes shut and trembling violently. "I daresay we've frightened you."

Deirdre opened her eyes. She stared at him, taking his measure from close range. His cocked hat covered bright, gilded hair that was caught at the nape with a black ribbon. He had long golden eyelashes, eyes the color of fog, and a sharp, clean profile that reminded her of a hawk.

Smiling, he took off his hat and tucked it beneath his elbow. His fair hair, contrasting sharply with the deep tan of his handsome face, was bleached and silvery at the ends, as though he spent a lot of time in the sun. His body was lean, his posture straighter than any she'd ever seen, and he had a firmness about his mouth that made her think he was well used to command. But then he smiled at her once more, and little crinkles appeared at the corners of his eyes, the sides of his mouth, and suddenly he didn't look quite so stern and frightening anymore.

She smiled back, hesitantly, childishly.

"Is this your pony?" he asked, still kneeling before her and inclining his head toward Thunder.

Her gaze still locked with his, she nodded, too afraid to speak.

"And what is his name?" He seemed heedless of the way his men were once more elbowing each other and grinning.

"Th-Thunder," she managed, her voice high with fright.

His brows drew together in bemusement as he caught sight of the Celtic cross hanging from around her neck. He reached out and hefted it in his hand, studying it while she went rigid with terror. "Thunder," he murmured absently, rubbing his thumb over the ornate design. Then, replacing the cross, he sat back on his heels and cast an admiring eye over the pony. "D'you know, I used to have a pony once, just like yours, except I called him Booley. He was a naughty fellow, though, full of mischief and pranks. Why, once he refused to take a fence and tossed me right off his back and broke my arm. Hurt like the devil, it did!" He smiled again, shot a glance toward the gathering storm clouds, and then his gaze grew serious once more. "So we have Thunder, here. And might I ask *your* name, little girl?"

Her gaze darted to the grinning seamen, then back at the handsome lieutenant, who didn't seem to care that the skies were about to open up. "Deirdre."

"Deirdre," he repeated, the name sounding strange on his foreign tongue. "That's a pretty name for a pretty lass." He was smiling at her, and for a moment she could almost imagine him as a knight from a fairy tale, so handsome was his face, so reassuring and kind were his gray eyes. Childishly wiping the back of her hand across her running nose, Deirdre gathered her courage and took a deep breath.

"And what's *yer* name?" she asked.

"Christian." He grinned. "Christian Lord."

"That's a funny name," she said, trying not to laugh.

"Indeed it is. My pious mother's idea of a joke, I suspect.

Would that I were a John. Or a Richard. Or even an Elliott, like my brother."

"But ye're in the Royal Navy."

"Aye, that I am, little wren."

"My mama says only pirates, thieves, and tyrants are in the Royal Navy." Frowning, she peered closely at him, searching the depths of his face for some proof of her mama's words. "But I think my mama might be wrong."

"Do you, now?" The corners of his mouth were twitching, as though he was trying awfully hard not to laugh. "And why d'you say that, foundling?"

"Because my cousin Brendan is in the Royal Navy, and he's the kindest, handsomest man in the whole wide world." His sudden laughter bolstered her courage, and she puffed out her chest importantly. "And he's not a thief, nor a pirate! His daddy was an admiral, and Mama says that someday Brendan will be, too."

"An admiral, you say?"

"Uh, Lieutenant?"

Beyond her new friend's broad shoulder, Deirdre could see another man leaning against his club and grinning crookedly. Without turning around, the lieutenant snapped, "For God's sake, Hendricks, don't just stand there. Go find O'Callahan so we can be about this devilish business."

"No need to, sir. I think I hear him coming now."

"As does the whole blighty village," muttered Jenkins.

Rising abruptly to his feet, the lieutenant donned his hat and turned toward the road. Deirdre stared at him in awe, but he seemed oblivious to her perusal. He cast a wistful glance toward the man o' war, as though he regretted being here and wanted nothing more than to be back aboard his ship. He looked once more toward the road. His mouth went hard, and when he looked down at her again, his mood had changed and his gray eyes had become determined and resolved.

"Time for you to run along, little wren."

"But don't ye want to hear about my cousin Brendan?"

"Next time, foundling." He reached down, put his hands around her waist, and lifted her up to the pony's back. The motion was quick and sure; the manner in which it was done brusque and businesslike. She allowed him to stuff the wet reins into her hands, noticing that he was no longer smiling, and that his mouth looked tight and strained. He gave her hair, damp now with mist and rain, one last tousle before turning away. "Now, off with you, before it gets any darker."

"'You can't let her go, Lieutenant, she'll spread the alarm!"

"A pox on you, Hendricks!" he barked with sudden anger. "'Tis too late for any alarm, they saw us coming long before we'd already lost the element of surprise. Hail O'Callahan's party and let's be done with this. By God, 'tis miserable enough business as it is, without having to spend the entire night in this godforsaken hellhole, damn you!"

Deirdre shrank back, the lieutenant's swift change of mood confusing and frightening her. The rain was falling steadily now, gathering momentum, growing colder by the minute and pulling little curls of steam from the pony's neck. She looked at the lieutenant, standing there in the rain, and waited for him to come back and talk to her again—but he did not. Why was he suddenly so angry?

Deirdre was just about to turn Thunder away when she heard men coming up the road. She couldn't see much through the rainy gloom, but the sounds that came to her were sharp and clear: the stamp of boots and rattle of muskets; dragging feet and angry shouts; the click of a flintlock, the dull thud of a club against flesh, and a man's howl of rage and pain. English laughter ... an Irishman's curses.

Another blue-and-white-clad officer was in the lead.

"Lieutenant!" he called, saluting. "I've got some for you, prime lads who'll do the ship proud!"

The fair-haired lieutenant cast a cold eye over the approaching group. "By God, that was quick."

"Aye, well, being born an' raised in this part o' the world sure has its advantages." The man's voice was Irish, familiar and dear among the strange tongue of the Englishmen. As the British seamen approached, Deirdre saw they had a smaller cluster of men with them, herding them like frightened sheep and threatening them with swords and clubs to keep them in line.

She frowned and craned her neck, her hands tightening on the wet reins. The rain was coming down hard now, pitter-pattering against the nearby rocks and heightening the scent of earth, grass and the pony's hide.

Somewhere out to sea, she heard the low rumble of thunder.

"And where were they hiding, O'Callahan?" The English officer strode toward the new arrivals, his long blue coattails dark against the back of his white-clad thighs.

"Just where I thought they'd be. Out in th' hills, and drinking themselves senseless in the ruins of an old castle."

"Splendid work, O'Callahan," the lieutenant said, yet there was an odd tonelessness in his words. "I shall make note of it to the captain."

But Deirdre's horrified gaze was not on the lieutenant, not on O'Callahan, not on the group of English seamen. She stared at the frightened, angry men whom the English tars surrounded. Their clothes were dirty and torn, their faces sullen, and some of them were cut and bleeding. Yet there was no mistaking who they were. Seamus Kelly ... Patrick O'Malley ... the brothers Kevin and Kenny Meeghan....

And Roddy.

It took a moment for the truth to hit. Before she knew it she was off the pony and racing across the wet grass. She slipped on a rock and went down hard, scraping her chin and knocking the breath from her lungs. "Roddy!" she cried. *"Roddy!"*

Her brother's head jerked up, and she saw horror in his eyes at the sight of her—horror that changed quickly to rage. Without a second's hesitation, he slammed his fist into the jaw of the nearest seaman and sent another sprawling with the deadly hook that had earned him many a free ale at the village tavern.

Chaos erupted.

Deirdre scrambled to get up. In a daze, she heard the shouts of the Englishmen, the barked commands of the lieutenant, the wild yells of her neighbors. Fists slammed against flesh; guttural groans and curses were all around. Managing to gain her feet, she resumed her flight toward her brother, only to be neatly snared by Hendricks. Sobbing wildly, she saw Roddy struggling between three burly seamen, spouting curses and kicking savagely out at their legs, their groins. A sharp cuff across the face stunned him; then, someone kicked him in the belly, and a cudgel's blow brought him to his knees.

With Roddy retching and coughing, the rest of the Irishmen quieted. They looked hatefully at O'Callahan, then at the fine English lieutenant. Their eyes were sullen, their backs rigid with pride.

'Take them to the boats and let's be off," the lieutenant commanded in a cold, toneless voice. "We're done here."

Deirdre felt Hendricks release her, and she stood frozen as the seamen hauled Roddy and his friends down the hill, slipping on wet rocks and cursing the Irish rain, the Irish cold, the Irish seas that awaited them. She stared dazedly at the proud profile of the English naval officer, suddenly realizing just what he had done.

No fair and handsome knight was he.

"My brother!" she wailed, throwing herself at him and beating her hands against his back. "Please, don't take my brother!"

He turned and caught her flailing fists. "I said go home, foundling."

"But ye can't take Roddy! Ye just *can't*! He's my brother!" She struggled madly against his iron grip. "Roddy!" she screamed as the last seaman disappeared over the far side of the hill. "*Roddy!*"

Her struggles quieted, and hanging from his grip, she collapsed in great, convulsing sobs of terror and grief. She heard the wind moaning across the dark pasture, and the voices of the seamen fading to a few barks of laughter, a curse, then nothing as they reached the beach far below. Her cheeks streaming tears and rain, her wet hair hanging in straggly spirals around her face, Deirdre raised desperate eyes to the lieutenant. He stared down at her, an anguished look on his handsome face, and for a moment she thought he was going to recall the men and release her brother. Then his jaw turned hard and unyielding, the set of his mouth resolute. "We are at war with France," he said harshly. "And while I despise the methods our Navy must employ to obtain its seamen, as an officer my loyalty and duty are with my country, not with my own inclinations." His eyes softened. "I'm sorry, little wren."

He abruptly released her and turned on his heel, striding down the hill without a backward glance. She watched him melt into the darkness, heard his footsteps fade, until she was all alone with nothing but the sad patter of falling rain and the mournful crash of waves against the beach far below.

Moments later, she saw lights bobbing out on the sea, fuzzy and dim in the mist, as the boat headed back toward the man-of-war and carried her brother away forever.

Deirdre stood there for a long time, the wind blowing her hair in wild, wet tangles around her shoulders as she watched the lights fade to tiny pinpricks in the foggy darkness and then to nothing. At seven years of age, she had just learned there were more frightening evils in this world than the banshees whose low moans could even now be heard through the darkness of the gathering night. She bit back one last sob. Then, wiping her eyes, she gripped in both hands the ancient cross that had once belonged to her formidable ancestress and raised her chin, her gaze fixed out to sea.

Someday, she'd be old enough to go to England by herself, seek her cousin Brendan, and obtain his help in getting her brother back.

Someday, she would find that English lieutenant and make him pay for what he'd done.

Someday, she vowed—she would see that English lieutenant *dead*.

Chapter One

The narrow, cobblestoned streets of Portsmouth were not the safest of places but Captain Christian Lord, Royal Navy, was well able to defend himself from the pickpockets, thugs, and other rabble that haunted the waterfront area. A heavy boat cloak hid his handsome blue-and-white uniform and protected it from the sleety drizzle, but, just as his demeanor made it obvious that he was a man of breeding and affluence—and therefore an attractive target—one would have to be stupid or blind not to recognize the military bearing that marked him as one capably employed in some service of the king. Indeed, he was well used to fighting bigger threats than those that lurked in the shadows around him, and the powerful breadth of his shoulders, the confident manner in which he carried himself, and the sword at his side were enough to deter any would-be assailants.

The streets, rimmed with filth and plagued by icy puddles, were polished by a cold rain that rode a bitter southeasterly out of skies gone leaden and gray. Buildings, huddled together as though for warmth, seemed to close in on either side of him, growing darker, seedier, sadder as he neared the waterfront. The wind blew hard, and he shifted the small white bundle he carried under his arm to protect it from the elements. Already he could smell the Solent; a moment later he could see its frothy expanse, and the anchored ships riding a chain of cruising whitecaps.

He pulled up the collar of his boat cloak, the harsh lines of his face unsoftened by the chilling drizzle. Standing two inches over six feet, he was an impressive figure, with wintry eyes and a mouth that rarely softened in a smile. But he hadn't always been like this. Tragedy and grief had extinguished the twinkle his eyes had once held and now, on the day before the Black Anniversary, they were bleak with suffering.

For a moment, he stared out to sea, his gaze traveling beyond the ships, the mist-shrouded Isle of Wight, the horizonless gray gloom of the Channel ... and into the past.

"Emily," he murmured, shutting his eyes against the sting of emotion.

Just as quickly the image was gone, and he was left standing alone in the rain, a forlorn, wind-whipped figure with nothing but memories.

And then his gaze fell upon the frigate he would soon command and anger swept in to drive the memories away.

Damn the admiral for ordering him to Boston, a sewer of malcontents and rabble-rousers if ever there was one. America, land of taxes, massacres, and dumped tea. Of discontent and rebellion left festering and unchecked. England was being far too lenient with those disobedient bumpkins across the Atlantic, and discipline needed enforcement before the situation over there got out of hand. He supposed he was to be part of that "discipline," but dear God, to think that Elliott was assigning him to a frigate — not just any frigate, but HMS *Bold Marauder* — after he'd commanded mighty ships of the line, served as flag captain for two admirals, and been proclaimed a hero for his actions in the Battle of Quiberon while still a lowly lieutenant during the Seven Years War....

But no, Elliott had insisted, nay, *ordered* him to take command of the thirty-eight-gun warship, with the excuse that he was the Admiralty's last hope of bringing law and order to a ship that everyone else in the Navy had all but given up on.

Bloody hell.

In his arms the little white dog whimpered and gently, very gently, he set her down, keeping a watchful eye on her as she did her business so she wouldn't run off. He had found her rifling through a pile of garbage some three streets back and immediately taken pity on her. Now she reared up on her hind legs and whining, licked the back of his hand, grateful that he had not abandoned her as someone else had obviously done.

The spaniel safely in his arms once more, he resumed his quick pace. No doubt, giving him command of the Hell-Ship was Rear Admiral Sir Elliott Lord's twisted idea of taking his mind off the Black Anniversary. But Christian was not grateful. In fact, he'd been downright furious to find, upon his arrival in Portsmouth yesterday, that his shrewd older brother had obviously had the thing planned for some time, for HMS *Bold Marauder* was already refitted and provisioned for sea.

Waiting for him — her new captain.

And there she was, distinctive, well-designed, and, if he were to allow himself a moment of romanticism long since blasted away by the realities of naval command, rather beautiful. She was anchored well out beyond the harbor, far away from the other vessels as though she carried the plague.

As *indeed she does,* he thought, blackly.

Her first captain, Richards, had been a lazy, drunken lout who'd allowed his crew the free rein to do just about anything they damn well pleased. Three men since the slovenly Richards had tried to turn her company into a fighting pack the king himself could be proud of. The first had come back insane, and it had required three marines to drag him from the cabin; the second had begged transfer to a seventy-four-gun ship of the line; and the third had quit the Navy altogether.

Of course, the fact that the frigate's officers were a tightly knit pack of wastrels — some the sons of peers of the realm, others the offspring of admirals ranked high on the Navy list — guaranteed the granting of their fondest desire. And that desire was that they were not to be separated and sent to different ships — a solution, Christian thought wryly, that would have solved the problem of HMS *Bold Marauder* immediately.

His eyes gleamed with determination. Well, the crew was in for a big surprise if they thought they could pull any nonsense on *him*. Cradling the spaniel in the crook of his arm, he drew his telescope and, lifting it to his eye, studied the frigate's decks with a seemingly detached stare that belied the steel in his frosty gray gaze. Sleet hit the glass lens, streaking the circular field, the frigate's dark form. He moved the glass, bringing it slowly down the length of the ship, his keen eyes seeing all and missing nothing — not even the figurehead, a brown-and-white bird dog crouched beneath the bowsprit, its foot raised to its chest in a rigid point as though seeking elusive game.

A hunter, Christian mused, but this particular ship had never fulfilled such promise. He trained the glass on her decks. What he saw only raised his ire all the more, for even from this distance it was frightfully obvious that HMS *Bold Marauder* fell short of the high standards of spit and polish that he, as an officer in the king's Navy, demanded of the vessels under his command.

He shut the telescope with a brisk snap.

A condition that would soon change, by God!

Grim-faced, he continued on, his long mariner's stride conveying his ill temper. The streets were nearly deserted, those who were wise, or able to afford it, taking shelter in drier places and huddling next to crackling hearths. But still, he was not alone. A group of seamen caught the glint in his cold gray eyes and respectfully touched their hats as he passed; a thug with a hanggallows look saw the sword peeping dangerously beneath his coattails and stepped aside; a pack of young boys engaged in a fistfight paused, then fell reverently into step behind him, trailing at a respectful distance, dodging into alleyways, hiding behind trash heaps, and trying in vain to keep up with him. But the captain paid them no heed. Straight to the quay he went — and came up short, his features darkening with rage.

The boys fled.

Captain Lord had every right to be furious. He had sent orders out to the frigate that its gig should be here, waiting to bring him to his new command — but the boat was nowhere in sight.

He was left embarrassingly stranded.

Either his orders had never been received or more likely, they had been blatantly ignored by the crew of rebellious rascals whom it would soon be his duty to command.

"Troubles already, Captain Lord?"

A young lieutenant stood there, nervously eyeing the tall and forbidding captain and correctly guessing the reason for his anger.

"Aye, but not for long. Lieutenant — *not for long!*"

His temper gone black, Captain Christian Lord turned on his heel and stormed down the quay. He would find a way out to the frigate, and when he stepped aboard her for the first time, there would be all hell to pay.

Chapter Two

C aptain Lord wasn't the only one on his way out to HMS
Bold Marauder. While he was trying to procure passage to
his new command, another had already done so and was waiting
to be rowed out to the warship.

Deirdre O'Devir had arrived in Portsmouth with nothing but
her name, her pride, her meager life savings, and a canvas bag
containing everything in the world that was most precious to her:
a miniature of her dead mother; a tiny model of a sailboat that
Roddy had made when he was a lad; and an old sliver of wood,
part of Papa's little boat, all that had washed ashore after the sea
storm in which the angels had taken him home so long ago.

Had those been the only revered occupants of Deirdre's
canvas bag, it would have been sadly empty. Carefully wrapped in
linen to guard against breakage was the vial of Irish seawater she'd
taken from the beach at Connemara the day she'd left for
England; a felt pouch containing sand and shells scooped from
that same shore; a pebble from the rocky pasture outside the
cottage that had been her family's home; a tuft of wool snipped
from a neighbor's sheep; a tightly corked glass flagon, seemingly
empty but full of Irish air, and of course, the loaf of bread—made

of wheat flour grown on Irish pastures and milk gleaned from Irish cows, and baked over the heat of a good, Irish peat fire.

It didn't matter that the bread had grown stale during her journey to England, for it was not to be eaten. Just as Deirdre O'Devir would never empty the water from the vial or the sand and shells from the pouch, just as she would never throw the pebble away or, God forbid, uncork the flagon of Irish air and let it escape, she would never eat the bread. Nor, she thought, reaching up to finger the ornate gold heirloom that hung from the chain around her neck, would she ever take Grace's cross off.

She stepped closer to the edge of the quay. Below, the old tar she had paid to take her out to the Boston-bound frigate was busy clearing space for her in his boat. Taking advantage of the moment, Deirdre raised a hand to shade her eyes from the watery sun that had just broken through the clouds. She peered across the water to the frigate. At the thought of her impending voyage, her heart jumped with fear, but she hid it well — just as she'd hidden the secret of her gender beneath a loose linen shirt, woolen jacket, and seaman's trousers. With her wildly curling tresses stuffed beneath a cap, there was little to give away the fact that the raw-boned lad with the fair complexion and bold black brows was actually a female.

Her face, a striking contrast of beauty and strength, denoted the courage of Celtic blood and showed none of the frailty that was often associated with her sex. Her nose was straight and bold, her lips full, her cheekbones high and proud. Only her eyes, a deep and mysterious purple, betrayed her fear and grief, for even here her mama's deathbed words, uttered not one month before, haunted her....

"Deirdre ... Go t' England and find my son. Go t' England ... go wherever ye have to, girl. But go, find my lad ... and bring him back home to Ireland so I can rest in peace."

Again she saw Mama, lying in bed with her eyes, once as deep a violet as her children's, faded like a piece of fabric left out in the sun for too long. She'd been dying — but then, Deirdre figured she'd been dying ever since the English lieutenant had come with the press gang and taken Roddy away from them. *I'll find that scoundrel, Mama,* she'd promised as she'd held her mother's small hand and felt the life fading out of her. *By all that's holy, I'll find him and kill him, destroy him like he did you and Roddy....*

She had gone first to London to enlist her cousin's help, only to learn that Brendan, a captain in the Royal Navy, had been sent to the American port of Boston. He and his younger sister Eveleen were all the family Deirdre had left — and Brendan with his naval connections was her only hope of finding Roddy. She would follow him to America, then — even if the thought of crossing the stormy Atlantic terrified her.

Again she reached up to touch the heavy cross that hung from a chain of beaten gold around her neck. It had belonged to her ancestress, the formidable Irish pirate queen Granuaile, known to the English as Grace O'Malley. Granuaile had lived during the time of Queen Elizabeth, and the cross had come down to Deirdre through her mother's people. To her, it not only symbolized her beloved homeland — it *was* her homeland.

"Ye ready there, mate?"

The old seaman was waiting for her, reaching up a gnarled hand to help her down into the boat. For a moment Deirdre hesitated, the wind blowing cold and lonely off the Solent and dragging a shiver of apprehension down her spine. But then she felt the reassuring presence of her canvas bag, the neck of which was clenched in her hand, and courage infused her again. As long as she had her precious bits of home with her she would never be alone. No matter where she went, no matter what lay ahead, they would always be with her to sustain and strengthen her, to remind her of who she was.

And what she was setting out to do.

One month ago, Deirdre had made a vow to her dying mama to find Roddy and bring him home to Ireland. Thirteen years ago she had made a vow to *herself* to find and kill the fair-haired English lieutenant who had stolen him from them.

And now the time had come to fulfill those vows.

Sustained by purpose, she crouched down and allowed the old seaman to help her into the boat. She sat clutching the gunwale and staring out at the countless lighters, barges, and ships of every size and shape that clogged Portsmouth Harbor and beyond it, the white-ruffled anchorage of Spithead.

And then her gaze found the frigate.

A seaman would have immediately noted the differences that set her apart from her neighbors. She was a warship, designed for striking hard and fast, a far cry from the tubby, bluff-bowed vessels that surrounded her. A seaman's trained eye would have admired the sleek lines that marked her as a fighter, the clean rake of her masts, the efficient and businesslike design of her hull, the row of gunports that ran along her sides. But Deirdre was oblivious to such details for to her the ship would serve only one purpose — and that was to take her to Boston and Brendan's help.

The mist had parted, leaving low-hanging clouds rolling across the leaden sky like giant white balls of dust. It would be a fine day after all even if it was cold, and the seaman whistled as he rowed, his wizened eyes scanning the harbor. He nodded at an acquaintance in a passing boat, then turned and caught her eye.

"Ye sure ye be wantin' to go out to *Marauder?*"

Deirdre shrugged. "Well, ye said she was goin' to Amerikay ... to Boston, and that I could get by in her without doin' much work."

"Aye, that ye can, lad." He stared over his shoulder, his eyes suddenly gleaming. "I reckon ye could certainly do worse fer yer first ship. Why, every jack's happy to serve on *that* frigate—most loosely run ship in the fleet!"

"But ... isn't she a King's ship? A Royal Navy vessel?"

"Aye, that she is," the old man wheezed, leaning on his oars, "but that don't matter none. She's the *Bold Marauder.*"

The way he said the vessel's name made it sound as though *that* explained everything. Was the *Marauder's* reputation for laxity so well known that she, Deirdre, was the only "sailor" on the wharves who was unaware of it?

Frowning, she gazed out across the rough Solent to the distant hump of the Isle of Wight —

— and nearly dropped her precious canvas bag in shock. Not a stone's throw away, a boat was ferrying a group of grinning, gaping tars out to *Bold Marauder,* and in their midst sat a painted, yellow-haired doxy whose breasts were the size of ale jugs. Deirdre's eyes widened. Sweet Jesus, not only were they *huge,* they were shockingly exposed, the flesh swelling above the low neckline of her gown, only the nipples hidden by the fabric. As Deirdre stared, gaping and appalled, the woman threw back her head with bawdy laughter, rested her hand on the thigh of one of the sailors, and leaned into the arms of another.

"Sweet God in heaven," Deirdre whispered. Then she blushed to the roots of her hair as one of the sailors shamelessly plunged his hand beneath the woman's hemline, only causing her to laugh harder. Mortified, Deirdre yanked her cap down over her eyes.

Noting her reaction, the old tar cackled with glee. "Better get used t' such sights, lad!" he wheezed. "This is the Navy yer goin' into!"

But there were no doxies being rowed with queenly splendor out to any of the *other* ships....

Swallowing hard, Deirdre wrapped her hands around her canvas bag and tried not to think of what horrors might await her aboard the vessel that would be her home for the next month. She had made a careful choice, hadn't she? After all, she *did* want a ship where she wouldn't arouse suspicion. *Bold Marauder,* with her obviously lax and indifferent captain, had seemed perfect...

But still, uneasiness began to nag at her, and the fear she had so bravely concealed was beginning to make itself felt in her damp palms and racing heart.

She stared at the approaching wall of the frigate's side.

Just what was she getting into?

♨

"SNIVELIN' blue blood, who the blighty 'ell does 'e think 'e is, any'ow? We ain't never 'ad to polish the bleedin' brasswork before!"

"You think that's bad? He had *our* watch out there swabbing the deck. Ye'd think he means for us to *eat* off it, so clean did he order it!"

"Scurvy bastard!"

"Imagine!"

"Ye didn't oblige 'im now, did ye, Skunk?"

"Christ, no! Ye'll see me rottin' in hell before I swab a bloody *deck!*"

"Well, he won't last. We've scared off three captains before him. Besides, if he's so lily-livered he won't even come aboard but has to send his orders through his bosun, you can bet your arse he'll not last out the day."

They stood huddled near the rail of His Majesty's frigate *Bold Marauder,* the officers high-born and privileged, the crew, a tough, evil-looking lot scraped from the worst of Bristol's streets, Cornwall's pastures, and just about every dockyard from London to Land's End. Some wore the garb of the Royal Navy seaman: loose-fitting trousers with red-and-white stripes, short blue coats, red vests, and carefully knotted kerchiefs. Others were clad in the blue-and-white uniforms that marked them as officers, and one — the frigate's first lieutenant — was even dressed in the manner of a Scotsman, with a bonnet, black-and-red-checked hose, buckled shoes, and a brightly colored plaid. The outfit might've looked striking had its wearer not thrown a blue-and-white lieutenant's coat over it in a halfhearted attempt to meet dress regulations.

The effect was totally ridiculous.

Above, the mist had cleared, leaving pale sunlight to poke down through the cold winter sky. The harbor was a mean, unfriendly blue, and a biting wind put caps on the waves, drove beneath heavy clothing and set teeth to chattering. But despite the cold, tempers were so hot they could have melted the ice in the water casks below.

The gunner, a hulking, malodorous, bear of a man with ribs like a ship's hull, folded his arms across his chest in defiance. "Well, all I know is that I ain't polishin' no bloody brass, nor decks, nor the buttons on 'is Highness's fancy bleedin' coat! If our new *Lord* and Master wants anything done, 'e can damn well do it himself!"

"Aye, ye can tell him that when he finally comes aboard, Skunk!" said the Scottish, red-bearded first lieutenant with a hearty guffaw. Brawny and tall, he had a jovial smile, a booming laugh, and no talent at all for playing the strange-looking instrument that was his most prized possession. Now he leaned against the bulwarks, carefully polishing it; it was called bagpipes, he'd told them, and it was supposed to make beautiful music—but so far, all that Ian MacDuff had managed to get out of the instrument was a horrible screeching noise that sounded like a cow in the throes of slaughter. That noise, however, had done wonders for driving the captain succeeding Richards into an insane asylum, and Ian — along with his shipmates — had high hopes of accomplishing the same with their new Lord and Master.

"Better yet," he said, "won't ye be getting Elwin tae do the scrubwork? Ye ken how, as surgeon, he is about cleanliness."

"On your life, Ian!" snapped Elwin Boyd, a gawky little man who walked with his neck out like a chicken waiting for the axe. He hefted a vinegar bottle and shoved it in the big Scotsman's ruddy face. "This is not for cleaning. I told you that long ago!"

"Here, now," snarled Skunk, "we're supposed to be discussin' 'is bloody Lordship and how we're gonna get rid of him, not brawlin' amongst ourselves!"

"Ah, yes, the *Ice Captain*," sneered Milton Lee, the purser, a bald little man with a stooping, lanky body and a nose like a parrot's beak. His eyes watering in the sharp wind, he glanced toward shore. Their new commanding officer, whom none of them had met, would soon find that the boat he had sent for would not be waiting for him, but was instead still snugged securely in the waist of the ship. It was the least they could do to irritate him. Already the new Lord and Master had had his belongings brought aboard *their* ship, as though he had every intention of staying; already he'd taken it upon himself to give *them* orders, as though he actually expected them to obey him!

Milton echoed the sentiments of his companions. "He's supposed to be the Navy's last hope of straightening us out. Ha! I give him one hour, Skunk, before we have him going over the side screamin' for mercy!"

"I give him ten minutes if Ian here hauls out those blasted bagpipes!"

'Ten minutes? He won't last five, I'm tellin' ye!"

"Here, now!" Ian protested, his Scots temper on the rise.

"Aw, piss off, Ian, we're just teasin' ye," Skunk said, waving his hand. "Hibbert! Ye made sure our sweet Delight was well hidden, didn't ye? We wouldn't want 'is bloody Lordship to find 'er and keep 'er all to 'imself, eh, mate?"

"Aye, I hid her in the brig," the midshipman said conspiratorially. His fourteen-year-old face was feral and sharp, his eyes beady and cunning, and despite the fact that his father was highly placed in the Admiralty, there wasn't a clean spot on the uniform that he wore with such disdain. "The captain'll never look there."

"Good job, m'boy!" Skunk hooted, clapping the youngster on the back. "And you, Russ! Ye're bein' awful quiet over there! Wot d'ye think of our new Royal Highness, eh?"

"What do I think?" Russell Rhodes said, taking off his hat to rake his hand through oily black hair gone silver at the temples. "Why, given his past record, I think our new Lord and Master's going to do his damnedest to succeed where his predecessors have failed."

"Won't never happen," growled Arthur Teach, just coming up from the brig, where he'd gone to check on the "welfare" of their lady passenger. At six and a half feet, Teach towered over even the burly Skunk and Ian MacDuff. Rumor had it that he was a grandson — illegitimate, of course — of the infamous Ned Teach, better known as Blackbeard. It was a fact that Arthur was exceedingly proud of, and one that he went out of his way to mention to anyone in the unenviable position of having to hear the story of how his illustrious pedigree had come about. With his bristly black hair and beard that tickled the belt of his trousers, he was hideous enough of both temperament and appearance that his presence alone had been enough to drive Captain Number Three from *Bold Marauder* with his tail between his legs.

Getting rid of Captain Number Four had been a collaborative effort on all of their parts — but this fifth one just might be a problem....

"Well, all's I know is that we ain't even *met* him yet and the bloody bugger's already overstepping his bounds," growled Skunk.

"Imagine what he'll be like once he gets aboard the ship!"

"Imagine what he'll be like once we put to *sea*!"

"Aw, 'tis cowing he'll be, just like the rest of them," Ian scoffed, tucking his bagpipes under his arm and ignoring the suddenly wary looks from his shipmates. "Anyone wantae hear the new tune I learned?"

"Spare us, *please*."

But Ian made a rude gesture, flipped his bagpipes over his shoulder, and put the blowpipe in his mouth.

Everyone backed up.

Ian grinned. "Ye sure, now?"

"Yeah, save it for his bloody Lordship!"

"Give 'im a concert he'll not likely forget!"

They howled with laughter until Ian, crestfallen, slammed his fist into Teach's jaw and Teach reacted with an equally hard punch to Ian's mouth that bloodied his lip. Fists flew, curses resounded, and in the ensuing chaos Elwin tossed the entire contents of his vinegar bottle at the big Scotsman.

"My pipes, damn ye!" Ian cried, going for Elwin's scrawny neck. Teach drew his knife and charged gleefully forward. Skunk began to bellow, Milton to howl, Hibbert to cheer—and at that moment, a frightened shriek split the air.

"What the hell was that?"

"Don't know. Shut up and maybe we'll hear it again!"

"Christ, Arthur, get that bloody knife out of my *face*!" bellowed Skunk.

The cry came again.

As one, they looked up and toward the entry port. There, pale and shaken and skinnier than a sea worm, stood a young lad. An oversize cap covered his head, his cheeks were white as fresh sailcloth, and he had that innocent, lost look that just *invited* abuse.

The lad's terrified gaze was fastened on Arthur Teach. "What're ye gawkin' at, ye snivelin' whelp?" Teach roared in his best pirate's voice. "Go on, hie yerself out of here before I carve out yer liver and toss it to the gulls!"

The youngster went whiter still, and glanced anxiously back toward the entry port. But his chin came up and resolutely, he came forward.

"I said, off with ye!"

The lad kept walking. He looked terrified but he came, and even the cool Russell Rhodes lifted a sardonic brow.

"Jesus," grumbled Skunk, "that one don't scare easy."

"He will. Let me have at him for a bit!" Teach stalked forward, hunching his shoulders and thrusting his great, hairy head down into the lad's face. He raised his cutlass and, in the best imitation of his grandfather, roared, "I said, get yer scrawny carcass off my ship, ye miserable pack of fish bones, before I—"

"Can ye help me find the captain o' this boat?"

They stared. They gawked. It grew so quiet one could hear the waves lapping gently at the hull so far below.

"*Boat?*" roared Skunk, his eyes bugging from his grimy face. "Ye bloody boglander, ye callin' this here fighting ship a *boat?*"

"Aye, that he did," said Ian, quirking a red brow and nodding sagely.

"I'm sorry." The lad gave a nervous grin. "Ye're absolutely right, sir. 'Tis not a boat, but a frigate of the sixth rate."

"*Fifth!*" roared Teach, with as much fury as he could muster.

Rhodes, who'd been watching the drama, finally shoved off from the railing and came forward. "What do you want?"

"To see the captain. Is he here?"

"Nay, he ain't come aboard yet, thank Christ. But I'm sure the Lord and Master'll be here shortly, just in time to weigh."

"Then I'll stay, as I'd like t' speak with him."

The piratical one reached out, grabbed her by her collar, and yanked her forward until his beard stabbed her tender cheek. Fumes of rum hit her in the face, and it was only by sheer will alone that Deirdre kept herself from fainting with fright. "Ye ain't no seaman, so ye got no business bein' on a king's ship! Now get your puny carcass off this here vessel before we toss ye to the sharks!"

"Aye! Toss him to the sharks!"

Deirdre's knees went weak. She shut her eyes, suddenly wishing she'd ignored the advice of the old sailor and found a different ship to take to Boston. Sweet Jesus, if the crew was such a pack of bloodthirsty brutes, what would their *captain* be like?

Then she felt the weight of Grace's cross, hidden beneath her shirt and lying against her pounding heart, and her courage returned. Her chin came up with stubborn purpose, and maintaining her brave front, she said, "Well, if the captain is not aboard, could I speak with his assistant?"

"*Assistant?*" the pirate roared.

"He means first lieutenant," said the other bearded one, who was almost as big and had a Scottish brogue that was oddly comforting amidst this collection of West Country and London dialects. He was carrying bagpipes, of all things, and Deirdre frowned as she noted his outrageous manner of dress. But the Scotsman merely cuffed the pirate away, grabbed her wrist, and said, "I'm Lieutenant Ian MacDuff, the man ye'll be wantin' tae see. Now, what is it I can be doin' for ye, laddie?"

She swallowed, carefully set her canvas bag down beside her foot, and tried very hard to look important. "I want to sign aboard."

"Sign aboard what?"

"Why, this boa—I mean, ship, o' course."

He stared at her as if she'd gone mad. "Ye mean, ye actually want to *volunteer?*"

"Isn't that the way it's done?"

The Scotsman glanced at his companions, took off his cap, and scratched his head. No one spoke, until at last the sinister-looking man in the officer's uniform cleared his throat. He moved with silken grace and had cold, sullen eyes containing about as much warmth as the bitter wind that cuffed the Solent into a mass of frothy white horses. "I'm Lieutenant Russell Rhodes. You want to sign aboard, eh?" He seized her canvas bag and, heedless of her frightened gasp, tossed it to the Scotsman before Deirdre had time to protest. "Well, then, let's see if you qualify. Climb that mast and don't stop till you reach the maintop — using the futtocks, of course."

"But ... but don't I have to sign somethin'?"

"Just get your arse up that pole!" roared the pirate, stepping forward and brandishing his cutlass.

"Aye, that's all the signing we'll ask of ye!" snarled a big, dirty hulk of a man covered with a mat of brown hair. His odor alone was bad enough to send Deirdre scurrying to the mast

"Jesus," said the Scotsman, slapping his broad forehead. "The tyke don't even know how to climb it!"

"Go to the gangway and use the shrouds, ye idiot!"

The pirate waved his cutlass in her face. Digging her nails into her palms, Deirdre looked up at the tall mast and choked back her fear, for it seemed to hold up the clouds themselves. Then the Scotsman shoved her toward the network of black, tarry ropes that ran skyward like narrow, tapering pyramids from the side of the ship.

"*Those* are the shrouds," he said gently. "Use them like a ladder. Ye ken, laddie?"

Deirdre pressed her hand to her shirt, seeking the comfort of the cross. Then, biting her lip, she nodded, grasped the tarry, ice-coated shrouds, and began to ascend. She climbed one step. Two. Three steps up, she looked down and, shivering, found the tip of the pirate's cutlass two inches from her nose. He was grinning evilly.

There was no going back. Not now.

Whimpering and nearing hysteria, Deirdre took a fourth step, clinging to the harsh ropes like a treed cat afraid to move. The deck was only a few feet beneath her, but she was off its solidness now, and she could feel the sway and movement of the big ship right through her hands and up through the soles of her feet.

"I can just see him in a storm," muttered the Scotsman, shaking his head.

"Hell, I can see him when our bloody Lord and Master makes us do sail drills."

"*Sail drills?* He wouldn't!"

"You doubt him?"

"No captain's *ever* made us do sail drills!"

"Well, from what *I've* heard, doona put it past this one." The Scotsman sneezed, pulled out an enormous handkerchief, and waved it at Deirdre. Raising his voice, he yelled, " 'Tis climbin' higher than that ye'll have tae be, laddie, if ye want tae reach the maintop!"

"I'm ... catchin' my breath."

The foul-smelling one stepped forward. "You ain't gonna have *time* to catch yer breath when you 'ave a storm howling up your arse and the bosun's mates laying the rattans across yer back! Now, *climb*!"

Deirdre pressed her face against the ice-encrusted ropes, smelling the pungent aroma of tar and sea salt. She was terrified. One slip, and she would fall into the water so far below. One slip, and she would be dead. Already the chill wind was singing in her ears, and she had a long way to go before she reached the maintop. *Oh, God,* she thought, digging her frozen fingers into the shrouds and fighting dizziness. *Oh, God, please help me.* She took a deep breath and pulled herself up a little farther.

But as she took another step, then another, she realized that the crew's attention was no longer on her. A boat was coming from shore, a feather of white at its bow, a militaristic figure dressed in blue and white in its stern.

Every man on the deck below had turned to stare at it.

"Christ, here comes the bloody captain now!"

"Quick, look busy!"

Deirdre flattened herself against the shrouds, shut her eyes, and swallowed the thick lump of dread. Oh, God. Oh, dear God. Now what? Stay here and be seen? Go back down and face the captain?

Or — her fingers bit into the shrouds as the ship swayed slightly, sickeningly, beneath her — go up?

She made up her mind, for there was no time to do otherwise. Desperate, Deirdre tilted back her head, scurried skyward, and didn't stop until she reached the hole that led into the maintop. She hauled herself through it and lay there on the platform, too terrified to look down.

And so it was that she missed Captain Christian Lord's arrival.

"Blind me, what the deuced hell is *wrong* with these people, Hendricks?" Christian snapped, his gray eyes hard with fury as he stared up at the gently curved tumblehome of *Bold Marauder*'s black-and-gold hull. "This is a king's ship, damn them, and as such they should bloody well know the meaning of *respect*!"

"Aye, sir," the dark-skinned Jamaican bosun said, a bit ashamed that he'd been away from the frigate when his friend and captain had sent the request for a gig. Had he been aboard, he would never have allowed such a thing to happen. Rico Hendricks, a former slave, had been with Christian since the captain's days as a midshipman, when the young boy-officer had rescued him from the gallows after Rico's involvement in a scheme to overthrow his cruel master in Jamaica. Christian had changed little over the years in *that* respect, Rico thought as he took the squirming, wet dog from his captain's arms. He might be harder, he might be harsher, he might be a hell of a lot sadder, but he still had a soft spot for the unfortunate and the abused.

And swift and fitting justice for the kind of pranks the new crew was up to.

Rico had been ashore, procuring some spare cordage, when he'd found Christian stalking the quay in a towering rage. From the interactions *he'd* had with the officers and crew of HMS *Bold Marauder,* Rico knew his captain was going to have his hands full with this bunch. Not only had his request for a gig been blatantly ignored, there was no one at the entry port to welcome him aboard his new command. And for a man who detested *any* slur on the king's Navy — be it a sloppy uniform, ungentlemanly behavior on the part of an officer, or any breach in discipline that would weaken the chain that was the Service — the simple denial of a welcoming party was a declaration of war on the part of a crew who had yet to learn just *whom* they were dealing with.

It was not a good beginning.

The boat's crew, a sloppy, sorry bunch of malcontents who looked like dregs out of Newgate, made several halfhearted attempts to hook onto *Bold Marauder's* main chains before finally succeeding. Furious, Christian looked up, still expecting the customary shrill of pipes, the smart rectangle of marines presenting arms, the roll of a drum and the organized fanfare a ship was supposed to give its captain.

But there was nothing. Not even a soul at the entry port.

Fuming, he scaled the ship's side, vowing that such nonsense would not be tolerated under *his* command. Behind him came Rico, cradling the captain's new pet in the crook of his arm, grinning to himself, and anticipating spectacular fireworks. At last, Christian reached the entry port and stepped smartly onto the frigate's deck.

There was no one there to receive him, just a seaman lounging against the bulwarks and watching him, picking his teeth with the blade of his knife.

Christian saluted the quarterdeck with tight efficiency, respectfully doffing his hat. Then he slammed it back atop his head and marched past a row of mutinous-looking men who sneered at him and spat on the deck in disdain after his passing. Straight up the ladder to the great, double-spoked wheel he went, his eyes blazing.

A seaman with black hair and a beard that reached to his waist stood at the rail nearby. He gave Christian an insolent glance. Then he went right on with what he was doing — nonchalantly carving his initials into the gunwale with a knife that could have skewered a cow from one end to another.

Without breaking stride, Christian reached out, spun him around, and, grabbing the man by the unsightly black growth that sprouted from his jaw, yanked him forward.

"Your name, sailor!"

"Arthur Teach," the seaman sneered. "*Sir.*"

"Well, Mr. Teach, fetch your first lieutenant and bring him to me."

"Don't know where he is."

"Then find him, you devilish bit of rabble! My patience has already been sorely tested and I warn you, the consequences of its being lost will not be pleasant for you or anyone else!" He yanked Teach forward by the beard until their eyes were inches apart, and snatched the knife from his hand. "Furthermore, I shall abide no defacing of property that doesn't belong to you, and I insist on a clean-shaven crew. Do I make myself clear?"

Teach made a rude gesture, tried to turn away — and had his neck nearly broken as the captain, still holding him by the beard, jerked his head around and hacked the evil growth off with one swoop of his own knife. Then he flung both the weapon and the beard to the deck, his eyes hard as he stared up into those of the stunned Teach.

"Now do I make myself clear?"

Teach stood gaping, his mouth opening and closing, his hands slowly coming up to feel his jaw. His face went white with shock, then red with fury, and Christian heard the hushed whispers from the group that was now gathering near the mainmast.

"Jee-zus, he just hacked off Teach's beard!"

"Holy Moses," another breathed.

Christian seized the seaman's sleeve and roughly shoved him forward. "I gave you an order to bring me your first lieutenant. Now, *move.*"

Teach staggered away, dazed, his hands cupping his shorn jaw. Out of the corner of his eye Christian saw Hendricks, still holding the little spaniel and watching him carefully, ready as always to step in and assist him should the need arise. But Christian was well able to take care of himself. He watched the men rushing up from below, gathering by the boats in the ship's waist, talking excitedly and staring at him in shock, disbelief, and sullen, open rebellion.

But he was in no mood to put up with further nonsense. "Now that I have your undivided attention," he began, raking them with his gray stare, "allow me to clarify something for you. This is a

King's ship and as such, is part of the most powerful Navy in the world. She was designed by a colleague of mine, a naval architect who is a master at his trade, and therefore should wear her name with pride, not disgrace. I intend to give her back that pride, and I intend to start here and now. Henceforth, you shall behave as seamen in the service of your king, honoring both this ship and her officers by showing them *respect.*"

The crew eyed him balefully. Someone spat. Someone else belched.

"The next time I come aboard this ship, I expect a proper and ceremonious welcome. You will pipe me aboard and you will stand at attention when I come through the entry port. As it should be a while before I have to do so again, you should have plenty of time in which to practice this simple ritual." Drawing his sword, he clasped his hands over the hilt and rested the point against the deck, his smile cold and forbidding. "Is that understood?"

Silence.

The wind played with his queue, was cold against his cheeks. "After I read myself in, we will weigh anchor and commence our journey to the American colonies, where *we* will lend our assistance to Vice Admiral Sir Geoffrey Lloyd in easing the mounting tension in Boston." He paused, feeling their hatred crackling through the air like lightning in an electrical storm. "Do I make myself clear?"

No one moved.

"Splendid!" He threw back his shoulders, his bright tone belying his cold, hard eyes. "I see that we have already arrived at an understanding. And I expect that we will *understand* each other even better by the end of this voyage. Should you demonstrate obedience and loyalty, you will find me a most agreeable comman-der. In the meantime, I warn you — do not test my patience, for you'll find it damnably short."

The crew, all one hundred and fifty of them, stared at him, their eyes filled with loathing.

"Any questions?"

No one moved. The seaman who'd spat did so again.

Without pause, Christian ordered, "Get a bucket and clean that up."

The seaman stared at him.

Christian locked gazes with him. "I'll not repeat myself."

The offender looked to Teach as though for permission — or, more likely, permission for refusal — and, finding no response from that quarter, walked slowly to one of the buckets lying near the bulwarks.

"Lively, now!" Christian prompted.

Every eye was on the seaman as, scowling, he picked up the bucket and swaggered back to his former spot. With a curse, he let it drop to the deck. Dirty water splashed out and made a pool at his feet.

"You may clean that up, too, sailor. And when you have finished you may give the mop and bucket to Mr. Teach so he can remove that ugly mess of black hair that is even now fouling my decks. This is a fighting ship, not a barbershop!"

With that he turned smartly on his heel, marched past them, and went below. There should have been a marine stationed outside his cabin door, and it didn't surprise him to find that there was not.

Another thing that would have to change, of course.

Entering the cabin, he slammed the door shut, but not before allowing the little spaniel, who had followed him belowdecks, to slip into his quarters. Christian released his pent-up breath, and willed his anger to abate. It would not do to be in such a black rage when the first lieutenant arrived. He picked up the little dog, who trembled and turned her face against his chest. He dipped his cheek to her fur and gently stroking her, went to the stern windows and looked out over the harbor. He was going to have his hands full with *this* crew. Already they had challenged his authority — but by God, when HMS *Bold Marauder* dropped anchor in Boston, Admiral Sir Geoffrey Lloyd would see a ship that the Navy would be proud of.

But as he stared out over the anchorage, the memories crept under his guard and drove away the troubles of his new command, for the rebellious crew was of little consequence when compared with the real devils that haunted him.

Tomorrow was the Black Anniversary, five years to the night since *she* had died.

He took a deep, shaky breath, hugging the little dog tight as he tried to block the memories, but they came flooding back — just as they sometimes did during his waking hours, just as they always did during his sleeping ones. But such hours weren't filled with dreams. They were filled with nightmares, nightmares that would haunt him for the rest of his life.

Emily. If only he'd stayed at home and been there for her, instead of off commanding ships of war, maybe things would have been different. If only he hadn't made a career out of the Navy, maybe she wouldn't have sought the arms of another. *If only....*

His cheeks were suddenly wet. He buried his face against the spaniel's soft ears, then raising his head, dragged his arm over his eyes. The proud captain's insignia on his sleeve blotted the tears, but not the memories. "Dear God, Emily, forgive me my failures. As a friend. As a lover. As—" He swallowed the thick, burning lump that caught suddenly in his throat. "As a husband."

Chapter Three

Deirdre couldn't stay up here forever.

Above, there was only a web of spars and lines and a sky smeared with clouds. Mustering her courage, she looked down — and immediately pressed herself back against the mast, her vision reeling and her hand clutching her stomach as she willed herself not to be sick.

She'd taken only one quick glance, but it had been enough. Far, far below, men scurried like ants on a deck that looked hideously narrow from this far up. Birds flew beneath her, not above. The waves on either side of the ship were tiny with distance, and she was so high up that she could look across, and down at, the rooftops of the buildings that framed the waterfront.

Shaking with both cold and fear, Deirdre shut her eyes. *Oh, God,* she thought, swallowing against the rise of bile in her throat and barely able to move her paralyzed throat muscles. *Oh, Jesus, Joseph, and Mary.* She wiped sweating hands on her trousers. Getting up here had been hard enough. *But how was she going to get down?*

And now someone was climbing skyward. Her terror mounting, Deirdre pressed her spine against the mast. A head appeared, capped by a great, oily mop of brown curls that looked as though it had never seen soap. The body that followed it looked — and smelled — no cleaner.

It was the man she'd heard the others refer to as Skunk. Grunting, he hoisted himself up beside her and frowned as he studied her anxious face. "I know it's always easier goin' up than gettin' down, so I've come up to retrieve ye. Best get yer arse down there before the bloody Lord 'n' Master finds ye slouchin' off."

'The Lord an' Master?" she squeaked. "D'ye mean our captain's a titled gentleman?"

"Damned if I know or care. Hell, I forgot, ye're a bloody land-lubber, aren't ye?" He shook his head. "Lord 'n' Master's a name we tars give to the captain of a ship," he explained. "But it especially fits that bastard below, given 'is surname. Ye'd think 'e's a bloody nobleman, the way 'e struts around here givin' orders an' expectin' 'em to be obeyed!"

"But isn't that what a captain's supposed to do? Give orders?"

"This here's *Bold Marauder*," Skunk said vehemently. "We don't take orders from *nobody*."

"Oh," Deirdre said in a small voice.

"Anyhow, I came up here to drag ye down. I knows yer scared, and 'is bloody Lordship'll be topside any moment. Pompous arse — we're all in for a hard pull with the likes o' that one in command. Why, I'll be bettin' my eyeteeth 'e don't know a damned thing about sailin' a ship; prob'ly got where 'e is by *who* 'e knows, not *wot* 'e knows, God rot his bloody, pampered hide!"

Deirdre said nothing, more concerned about the climb back down than she was the captain.

"Cruel bastard. Ye know what 'e did? Hacked off Teach's beard, right in front of the whole bloody crew. Hacked it right off! I'm tellin' ye, 'e'd better watch 'is back now, 'cause Teach'll be out for him. 'Course, we already got 'im good — ever hear of sabotage? — but he won't know 'bout that for a bit; besides, it ain't nothin' compared to what ol' Arthur's planning. Some night the captain'll wake up with 'is throat slit, and *that's* if 'e's lucky!" Skunk moved easily to the shrouds. "Here, gimme yer hand, lad. That's it, slide on up behind me, put yer hands around my neck and hold on tight. Not that tight; yer chokin' me. Watch yer head there. That's it."

Holding her breath, Deirdre shut her eyes and put her face against Skunk's broad back, wondering how long she could hold out before fainting — either from lack of air or from the strong odors coming from her savior's unscrubbed body. But they were going down, and that was all that mattered.

"He think's he's gonna impress his admiral by straightenin' us out, but he's got a thing or two to learn about us, and *we've* got a thing or two of our own to show the admiral! You just wait till we set sail, hee-hee-hee!" Skunk descended as easily as if he were going down a flight of stairs and Deirdre, opening her eyes the barest slit, breathed a prayer of relief as the faces of those below grew larger and larger. "Aye, you wait. We don't take no rubbish from no one, mark me well." He swung himself onto the deck and, kneeling, put her down. "Now, run along, boy, and don't let the Lord an' Master see ye, else he'll flay the skin off yer back and smile while doing it."

Deirdre needed no urging. Humiliated, and keenly aware of the smirks, sneers, and taunts of Skunk's shipmates, she snatched up her canvas bag and fled forward, where she melted safely into the group of seamen gathered near the ship's bell. They stared at her as though she had grown a horn in the middle of her forehead. Finally she found a hatch and ducked below. Dear God, the ship wasn't even out of port yet and she was already in trouble. How on earth would she last the passage to America?

But she had no choice.

Brendan was in America, and he was her only hope of finding her brother — and the hated British lieutenant who'd pressed him.

"Get the ship under way, please, Mr. MacDuff."

Captain Lord stood near *Bold Marauder*'s great, double-spoked wheel, his hands gripping the hilt of his sword and his eyes in shadow beneath the brim of his hat. He emanated authority and discipline, and the Royal Navy couldn't have boasted a more capable commander.

The men hated him.

His hat, turned up in the back, sporting a black cockade, and nearly spanning the width of his shoulders, was edged with gold lace and set smartly atop his head. His blue coat, its gold buttons winking in the sun, was open to show his meticulously clean white waistcoat and breeches. His neckcloth was smartly tied beneath his chin, his sleeves were frothed with lace, and not a speck of dust marred the black shine of his buckled shoes.

He looked every inch the naval captain that he was. But only he knew of his trepidation at the thought of his admiral and his peers watching from the shore, the signal tower, and the decks of other vessels. Some of them, he knew, had delayed their own departures, obviously unwilling to miss what promised to be quite the spectacle.

He tightened his jaw, vowing there would *be* no spectacle.

Beside him, his first lieutenant stood, anxiously watching the anchor party. Christian glanced up at the snapping masthead pennant and tried to ease the tension between himself and his first officer. "A fine day to put to sea, eh, Mr. MacDuff?"

The lieutenant looked nervous. "Aye, sir," he muttered, slinging something over his shoulder.

Christian turned, frowning. "Pray tell, what *is* that hellish contraption, Mr. MacDuff?"

"Bagpipes ... sir."

"And what is their purpose, Lieutenant?"

"Er, tae make music, sir."

"Have they any place in a battle?"

"No, sir. Not in a sea battle, that is—"

"Very well, then. I'd prefer that you leave them in your cabin when you are in the capacity of your command."

"But—"

"Mr. MacDuff, that is an order."

Christian tightened his lips. *Bagpipes?* By God, what the *devil* was the Navy coming to? Shaking his head, he glanced at the sailing master. A heavyset man, Tom Wenham had great, jutting ears that seemed to hold up his hat. Several fingers were missing from his left hand, and the tip of his bulbous nose was raw and sunburned. Beside him stood a feral-looking lad dressed in the dirty and stained uniform of a midshipman, a slate in one hand, a pencil in the other.

Christian put his hands behind his back and rocked on his heels. Out of the corner of his eye, he could see Ian MacDuff eyeing him nervously and stroking his beard, as though fearful that it would meet the same fate as Teach's. MacDuff had damned good reason to be nervous. As the frigate's second-in-command, he should be setting an example, not provoking more rebelliousness. Facial hair would *not* be tolerated — and neither would that outlandish Scottish garb.

Sudden anger inflamed Christian. By God, this was the *Navy*, not a damned circus show!

But he would wait until they were at sea before addressing the matter of Ian's beard — as well as Hibbert's filthy uniform and a score of other outrages he'd already noted in his log. Weighing anchor and getting the ship under way was a delicate enough operation without further complicating matters by alienating his first officer. And as for the crew itself ... they hated him now, yes, and they'd probably hate him even more once they got away from England and the ocean rolled beneath their keel.

Not that it bothered him, for he was not a man who courted friendship or popularity. For now, all that mattered was getting

Bold Marauder safely away from Portsmouth without mishap in sight of his acquaintances, his peers, or — God forbid — his admiral.

His apprehension built. The wind was blowing fresh, and it wouldn't take much to land *Bold Marauder* in trouble — literally. He laced his fingers together behind his back and took a deep breath. Forward, the anchor was nearly hove short, the men swearing and straining at the capstan, the great cable thundering and clanking through the hawseholes. A bosun's mate stood astride the bowsprit, his greasy pigtail whipping in the cold wind, one hand wrapped around a stay, the other circling in indication of how much cable was left to bring in.

Suddenly the man raised his hand, and Rhodes, who'd been supervising the capstan party, yelled, "Anchor's hove short, sir!"

Christian gave the barest perceptible nod. He glanced quickly at the signal tower on the shore, where flags fluttered in the wind, giving him permission to proceed.

Yes, they are all watching. The whole damned harbor.

"Bring it in," he commanded.

But something was wrong. He knew it even as the men at the capstan heaved, swore, and glanced in mock confusion at each other. He knew it even as he heard several amused guffaws. And he knew it even as he saw several seamen exchange glances and turn away to hide their sudden smirks.

Above, the wind blew impatiently, and out of the corner of his eye Christian saw the flash of sunlight against a telescope from shore.

"Is there a problem, Mr. Rhodes?"

Rhodes turned, a helpless look on his face that was directly at odds with the glint in his eye. "Uh, the anchor seems to be fouled, sir."

Bloody hell. Christian closed his eyes and mentally went through a vocabulary of much bluer naval language. "Are you certain, Mr. Rhodes?"

The lieutenant was peering over the bulwarks. Christian heard the crew snickering, and his apprehension turned to raw fury.

Sabotage.

Rhodes straightened up, feigning innocence. "Aye, sir," he called. "Seems to be caught on something."

Silence, with only the wind and the lap of the waves. Christian thought of those who were watching: Sir Elliott ... the men in the signal tower ... the hundreds of spectators, as well as other captains, officers, and seamen in and around Portsmouth Harbor and Spithead—

"Your orders, sir?" Rhodes called, with a falsely benign smile.

The embarrassment of losing an anchor couldn't have come at a worse time, and there were only two things he could do: either delay his departure and try to retrieve it, or cut the cable and get the hell out of there.

He thought of all the eyes watching from shore, from the other ships, and wasted no time on a decision.

"Hands aloft to loose tops'ls."

From below the quarterdeck rail, he heard fierce whispers that he did his best to ignore and vowed not to forget.

"This'll *really* make him look bad!"

"Aye, 'twill bring his bloody Lordship down a tuppence or two!"

His order was repeated through speaking trumpets. Men ran to the braces while others scrambled up the ratlines and out along the yards. Sail spilled down, rolling in the wind with a noise like thunder. The wind was blowing strong, and he knew he would have only a few short moments to get the sails properly set before the frigate was swept dangerously close to shore and the other anchored vessels. He would have to move fast, for once the cable was cut—

His heart began to hammer in his throat. From shore, another telescope glinted in the sunlight. Another, from an admiral's flagship....

He saw Rico, waiting for his next order; he felt the frigate trembling deep in her bones. He took a deep, steadying breath, stared nervously at the land, and snapped, "Prepare to lose the anchor."

The cable was cut. Like a bird trying out its wings for the first time, the frigate reeled drunkenly, her canvas flapping, her yards jumping, the men aloft yelling with alarm, and some with fear, as their precarious footholds jerked and bucked beneath them.

"Look alive on those braces!"

On deck, swearing, shouting men were laid nearly on their backs as they heaved and hauled at the braces. From above came a yell of alarm as a topman slipped on a foot-rope and nearly fell.

Christian stared at the land drawing closer and closer. *"Get those bloody tops'ls set!"* he roared.

The shore was now so close that he could see the people lining the docks and watching the magnificent sight of a King's ship getting under way; it was so close that he could hear the jeering hoots of ridicule from a moored sloop of war whose crew knew that the sight wasn't the least bit magnificent; it was so close that he could see the windows of an inn, and the glint of sun off another telescope. Another....

"Loose fore and main courses!"

Ian had been picking at a callus on his knuckle. "Huh?"

"Loose fore and main courses!"

"Oh. Aye. Uh, aye, *sir.*"

But just then the men, leaning on their heels and nearly horizontal to the deck as they hauled on the braces, sent up a great cry of distress and tumbled onto their backs.

A line had parted.

Another.

And then more cries of dismay as a brace gave way with a sound like a pistol shot.

Great God above!

Above, canvas flapped in out-of-control fury. Lines snapped to and fro like the tails of a whip, yards jerked and quivered—and HMS *Bold Marauder,* out of control, headed directly for shore.

"Assume the deck, Mr. MacDuff!" Christian yelled, already running down the quarterdeck stairs and racing forward to take control of the confusion.

But it was too late. Ian, standing dumbly beside the wheel, suddenly realized the magnitude of responsibility his commanding officer had just shoved on him. "Christ, laddies, *do something!* Where's Skunk? *Skunk!* Jesus, don't just stand there—"

Skunk stood just below the quarterdeck railing, grinning and idly picking at a tooth. "Piss off, Ian. Just because ye've been given a bit o' power, ye don't have to take it out on the rest of us!"

"Yeah, leave us out of it!" Teach yelled.

"Move!" Ian roared, seeing the shoreline coming closer and closer. "Saints alive — *Christ,* Wenham, there's a moored boat coming up off the larboard bows—"

"What boat?"

Ian grabbed the wheel and spun it hard, but with the sails flapping helplessly, it was no use. And the wheel—

"The steering's gone!" he cried, curling his hands into claws and raking at his hair. *"The bluidy steering's gone!"*

The little boat cringed beneath the shadow of the oncoming frigate, and Ian clapped his hands to his ears as it was helplessly smashed beneath the great bows.

"You tampered with the rudder!" Ian yelled, going for Wenham's throat, and the sailing master ducked as the Scot's huge fist swung. Ian didn't see his captain desperately shoving men aside as he fought his way back to the quarterdeck. He didn't see the crew tossing down what lines *hadn't* been tampered with and surging aft to view the fight.

And he didn't see old Admiral Burns's proud flagship looming up off the leeward bows, the admiral himself standing on the quarterdeck in horrified shock—

Sighing, the frigate sank her bowsprit into the flagship's

rigging, plunged through spars and lines, and then slammed hard against the massive hull with a stunning, grinding crash. The impact knocked everyone off his feet and sent seamen flying against pinrails, railings, and the deck itself.

Lieutenant Ian MacDuff's Scottish temper exploded and he came up swinging.

Skunk caught the first blow, dealt the second. Teach, seeing a good fight and furious at being left out, dove into the melee. Fists flew. Grunts and groans and curses split the air. And the new, rawboned little recruit raced up from below, saw her chance of escape from what she'd long since decided was the *wrong* ship to take to the colonies, and made a wild dive toward the rail.

"Get back here, ye miserable little worm! 'Tis all your fault we're gonna get in trouble!"

"His bloody Lordship's gonna have poor Ian's hide!"

Ian smashed a fist into Teach's jaw, raised his head, and bawled, "Damn right he is, and I'll nae suffer his temper alone, ye miserable pack of lazy, good-fer-nothing bastards!"

"Hell, don't take it out on us — it's that little pisser's fault!" howled the rat-faced midshipman, pointing at Deirdre.

"*My* fault?"

They came at her in a pack.

"No!"

Deirdre bolted for the railing, tripped over a coil of rope and went down hard, scraping her palms and smashing her chin against the deck. Her precious bag of Irish mementos skidded away. Stars exploded across her eyes. Her tooth cut into her lip. The coppery taste of blood filled her mouth and desperately she scrambled to regain her feet, only to fall once more as a booted foot caught her behind the knees. A hand yanked her to her feet; another shoved her violently toward the shrouds. "Get yourself up that mast and start cutting us loose — *now!*" shouted Hibbert, the rat-faced little midshipman.

There was no way in Satan's hell she was going up that mast

again — nor, since she was leaving, any reason to. "Get up it your-self, ye poxy, bleedin' bully!"

His fist crashed into her cheek. Dizzily, she swung back, lashing blindly out and managing to catch him in the mouth. Pain shot up her hand and mixed with blood — her blood, Hibbert's blood — and he came at her again, a stream of crimson pouring from his lip. Grabbing her wrist, he twisted it savagely behind her back. "He hit an officer!" the boy raged, his eyes wild. "He *hit me!*"

"Can't let such a crime go unpunished!"

"Aye, punish him! Lash him to the mast and give him Moses' Law!"

"Lash him good, I say!" Someone threw the middie a whip. "Strip the skin from 'is back!"

"Give 'im two dozen!"

"Give him three!"

Deirdre kicked and fought and twisted as they ripped her jacket from her, seized her wrists and tied them to the mast. Her teeth sank into someone's arm and she tasted grime and sweat. A hand cuffed her sharply across the jaw. Behind her the men were in a frenzy, desperate for a scapegoat so they wouldn't get the punishment their captain and his big Jamaican henchman would surely have in store for them.

"A dozen lashes, Hibbert!"

"Make it two!"

It became a chant. "Two! Two! Two!"

"No!" Her desperate cries rang in her ears as Hibbert grabbed up the cat-o'-nine-tails.

"No!" She writhed in terror, the rope biting into her wrists as she waited for the horrible, agonizing fire to slam between her shoulders and drive the breath from her lungs. Hibbert, his eyes maniacal, drew back his arm, and she screamed as someone slashed her shirt away and cold, bitter wind swept in against her back and the cloth with which she'd bound her breasts—

Hibbert's arm froze above his head.

"Holy God in heaven," someone breathed. "It's a *woman*."

Hibbert dropped the whip. A hush fell over the ship. Deirdre collapsed and hung by her wrists, breathing hard. Then, through the haze of fear, she saw the captain striding toward her, his jaw tight and angry, his face obscured by the shadow of his hat. This was the man they hated and feared. This was the man whose word was God's aboard the vessel. This was the man who controlled their lives, their actions, their destiny.

This was the Lord and Master.

The crew, silent and still, parted to let him pass. Straight up to her he came. She felt a knife sawing at her bound wrists. A uniform coat, warm with his bodily heat, being put around her. Strong hands lifting her, and a solid, hard chest against her cheek. Movement beneath her and faces passing, gaping, staring. She reached up, clutched his shirt and huddled against him, helpless to stop her tears that smeared his fine white linen waistcoat. His hand stroked her hair, held her protectively close. Then the sunlight was cut off as she was carried below.

"Easy, foundling." His voice was deep and rich and soothing, rumbling up out of his chest just beneath her cheek. " 'Twill be all right. Easy, now."

They passed bulkheads, alive with checkerboards of dark and light, and then the great, imposing door, where a grim-faced marine with a musket stood guard outside. Then they were through the door and into the cabin. He set her down upon the deck flooring and she stood there in a daze, shivering, tears of fear and shame coursing down her cheeks.

The Lord and Master's back was to her. He had height. Proud and capable shoulders. Gold lace on his cocked hat.

Then he turned, and the blood drained from Deirdre's face. She staggered backward, hit a table, and forgot to breathe.

It was the young lieutenant she'd vowed to find and kill.

Except he wasn't a lieutenant anymore.

He was the captain.

Chapter Four

She stared at him, denying the truth yet knowing there *was* no denying it.

He was broad through the shoulders, lean through the waist, and as tall as she remembered. It was impossible to know the color of his hair, as he wore a carefully powdered and rolled periwig, but there was no mistaking the haughty brows, taut mouth and hawkish profile that looked as though they'd been carved from stone. Unlike that long ago lieutenant she'd encountered on a stormy Irish beach, however, she sensed that if *this* man smiled, that rigid, disdainful face might crack.

"The devil take me," he murmured, raking her with cold gray eyes. Their color was that of the ocean beneath stormy skies. As he moved, sunlight slanted across the irises and brought out the barest hint of green. "A woman. Life is full of surprises, is it not?"

"*You...*" she breathed, yanking the hated coat from her shoulders. She hurled it to the deck flooring and as she did so, one breast slipped free from the binding — giving Christian an unobstructed view of the first female charms he'd seen in five years.

"Pray, madam, cover yourself!" he said hoarsely, picking up the coat and shoving it at her.

She yanked at the binding, trying to adjust it. "I'll rot in hell before I wear the King's coat!"

"You'll cover yourself, by God, or I'll put it on you myself!"

"You so much as touch me and I'll make ye regret the day ye were *whelped,* ye bleedin' English dog!"

Christian started toward her, his brow dark with fury, but just then the two ships slammed together with a stunning crash. The girl lost her balance, struck her thigh against his table as she fell to the deck, and cursed him roundly as again, Christian tried to cover her.

Outside the door came voices and the warning thump of Evans's musket against the deck.

"Don't you touch me, ye poxy wretch!" the girl raged, struggling to throw off the hated coat and fighting him all the harder when he attempted to snare her wrists. "Let me *go!*"

"Evans!" he yelled. "Keep your station at that door, mind you, and allow no one to enter, is that understood?"

"Uh—aye, sir. But—"

"No 'buts,' Evans. That is an order!"

"But, sir—"

The girl was shrieking at the top of her lungs. "I'll see ye in hell, ye rotten blackguard, ye worthless whelp of a stinkin cur, ye—"

"Captain, *sir!*" Evans cried urgently.

"Not now, Evans!"

"But, *Captain*—"

With a curse, Christian released the girl. "Damn you, Evans, *wait a moment!*" he roared, and ducked as she grabbed his water pitcher and hurled it at him. Behind him, glass crashed against the bulkhead and the girl, clutching at her binding in an unsuccessful attempt to preserve her modesty, bolted beneath his desk.

"Captain, sir!" Evans shouted from behind the door. "This is *most* urgent!"

"I said *in a moment!*" Christian shouted, reaching blindly

beneath the desk and trying to grab his quarry. He caught her hand, caught her other hand, and held on tight, her screams of rage piercing his head as he dragged her out from beneath the desk. She went wild, fighting him with all of her strength, shrieking, kicking, and cursing him in a scalding torrent of both Gaelic and English. Her foot lashed out, hit a chair, and sent it skidding across the deck to crash into the bulkhead. She twisted around, sank her teeth into his wrist, managed to free her hand and, slamming it into his jaw, lunged for the door.

He caught her before she could reach it and jerked her around, her bared breast coming up against his chest.

"Ye miserable knave, I'll see ye die if it's the last thing I do!"

Twisting against his grip, she lunged once more. His wig went askew, tumbling to the floor even as she brought her knee up and drove it savagely into his groin. Christian doubled over in agony, white-hot pain exploding behind his eyes, only to feel her fist smash into his jaw. He staggered backward, slipped in the shards of glass and water, and went down heavily on the deck.

"Sir, is everything all right in there?" Evans yelled.

"All is—*ouch!*—quite well indeed, thank you, Evans!" Christian grunted as the girl kicked him solidly in the shoulder; then, fighting his own pain, he lunged to his feet as she went for his pistol, deflecting her arm upward. She tumbled to the deck beneath him just as the gun went off—

And the door crashed open.

Christian froze and the girl went stiff beneath him. Evans stood there, sheepish, anxious, and wide-eyed. And with him, resplendent in a blue-and-white uniform glittering with gold lace, was an officer.

Not just any officer.

Elliott.

"Well, well. What do we have here? Really, Christian, I'd expected more from *you,* of all people."

The blood drained from Christian's face.

"What the devil *is* this, Captain Lord?"

The admiral stood with his weight slung on one hip, his hand resting against the door and his lids hooding dark gray eyes that were either amused or enraged. With Elliott, it was impossible to tell.

But then, with Elliott, it had always been impossible to tell.

Now his gaze took in the damning scene: the black-and-white canvas smeared with blood; the girl lying helpless beneath Christian, her lip bleeding and her cheek bruised—injuries apparently sustained when she'd tried to fend off her attacker's lust—and Christian himself, spread-eagled over her partially naked body in a *most* damning position.

Too late, Christian recovered himself. Burning with humiliation, he leapt to his feet, grabbed his hat, and bounced it off the top of his head in a hasty salute. The girl shot back beneath the desk and huddled there, her legs drawn up, her arms clasped around them to shield her breasts and her eyes glittering with fury.

Elliott put two and two together, and came up with five.

Behind him, several captains had gathered, craning their necks over their admiral's shoulder as they tried to peer into the cabin. Their brows shot clear to their hat lines, and exchanging glances, they began to snicker in amusement.

Christian, his ears burning, pulled himself up to stand rigidly at attention.

Elliott, as usual, was at his best—and enjoying himself immensely. "I say, Captain Lord, this is most humiliating—to the Royal Navy, to this ship, and, of course, to your name," he drawled. "Heathmore, would you please go topside and assist the first lieutenant in freeing this poor vessel from her hapless berth? God strike me, what is this world coming to!"

"Damn it, Elliott—" Christian said tersely, trying to explain.

"Really, Captain Lord, that is no way to address your admiral."

The corners of Elliott's mouth were twitching, and sheer will and years of discipline were all that kept Christian from leaping forward and strangling him. He bunched his fists at his sides and through clenched teeth, gritted, "Forgive me, *sir*, but what you saw was not what it appeared—"

"What I see, Captain Lord, is a young woman whose virtue has been sorely compromised, and a ship that has been abandoned by her commanding officer. I say, Admiral Burns is *most* upset. The impact knocked the old dog to his knees and he's howling for your head. Really, Christian, this is most unlike you. Neglecting your vessel so that you can molest a young girl ... *you*, a much-decorated sea officer! Tsk, tsk. Now, please come with me. I'm sure your poor victim will be quite safe until you return." He strode into the cabin, tall and elegant and astonishingly handsome, and bent down before her hiding-hole beneath the desk. "Won't you, my dear?"

She stared up at him, her face white and her arms locked protectively around her bosom.

The admiral removed his hat, revealing rich, sandy-gold hair that curled boyishly around his ears. "Too frightened to speak, are you? Poor little dear. Please, don't think that all of our officers behave thus. We do have our share of *gentlemen* as well."

He got to his feet and fixed Christian with a sharp look of reprimand. "Really, Christian, seducing innocent maids—"

"I didn't seduce her. I rescued her from a fate worse than—"

"Yes, yes, I'm sure you did," Elliott said, waving his hand in a gesture of dismissal. "Come along please, Captain Lord. You've much to answer to!"

Christian seized his coat and limping badly, slammed toward the door.

From beneath the desk, Deirdre watched him and the admiral with wary eyes. The door shut behind them. For a long moment, she didn't move as she listened to their receding footsteps and the angry protests of *Bold Marauder*'s captain. Serves him right, she thought angrily. She hoped he'd face a court-martial. She hoped he'd be demoted. She hoped he'd spend the rest of his days beached, miserable, and forgotten!

"Bastard," she whispered fiercely, hating him.

Above her head, she heard the shrill of pipes and thump of muskets upon the deck as the officers left the ship. She waited another moment, then crawled out from beneath the desk, surveying her surroundings and wondering what to do next.

He was the captain of this wretched vessel. Oh, Jesus, Joseph and Mary, that certainly complicated things.

She would have to kill him, of course. She'd made a vow, and there was no going back. But first, she needed clothes.

And a weapon.

She stood there looking around the cabin. Sunlight, reflecting from the water beyond the panoramic stern windows, shimmered against the white-painted beams and deckhead. A sea chest was snugged up against a bulkhead and opening the heavy lid, she found a clean lawn shirt that was far too large for her. Her modesty restored, she roved the cabin, looking for something with which to fend off the Lord and Master when — and if — he returned. He certainly seemed to live well, she thought bitterly. She looked at the green leather-backed chairs, grouped around a fine table; the small wine cabinet set into one corner; the desk of mahogany; and in a smaller, partitioned area off to the side, a bed that was smartly made — and contained a small, shivering, obviously pregnant dog who stared up at her with frightened eyes.

Deirdre stared back, wondering if she was seeing things. A *dog?*

Then she turned away — and her gaze fell upon the far bulkhead.

The captain's dress sword.

It rested there on two pegs. Mindful of the fact there was probably a marine stationed just outside the door, she crept across the cabin and pulled it down. Gently pushing the dog aside, she slid the weapon beneath the sheets, turned the sharp edge away from her body, and crawled carefully in beside it. Then she closed her eyes and reached up to touch the cross that rested comfortingly against her heart.

Granuaile, she thought as she stared up at the deckhead, *you'd be proud of me.*

And she'd be even more proud if Deirdre could slay her English enemy.

She lay back against the pillows, wrapped her fingers around the hilt of the sword, and listening to the rapid thumping of her heartbeat, waited.

Chapter Five

It had been several hours since *Bold Marauder*'s disastrous attempt to get under way. Now the frigate lay out in Portsmouth Harbor, her taffrail lantern glowing upon the water and making a beacon in the night. Heathmore had been successful in freeing her from the old admiral's flagship, but the damage done to her — and to the crew's respect for him as their new commanding officer — remained to be seen.

The crew he would deal with in his own time and way. It was the girl who had Christian most distressed; the girl, and his own passionate reaction to her.

At the edge of the wharf he slipped, bone-weary and exhausted, onto a bench to await the gig. Dropping his chin into his neckcloth, he wrapped his arms around himself against the cold wind and thought back over the afternoon. It had been a nightmare. Long hours spent undergoing rigorous questioning by a panel of five captains presided over by Sir Elliott himself; endless waiting, pacing the floor, while in the adjoining room his past was dissected and his future decided; anger with himself for trusting in an undeserving crew, and fury with his own vulnerability to poor, wretched souls in need of help, ranging from starving spaniels to Irish urchins.

That vulnerability had nearly cost him his career — not to mention his ship.

"Here comes the gig now, sir," Hendricks said, rousing him from his morose thoughts.

"Thank God." Christian opened his eyes and stared down at his feet, his mind many leagues away.

"I know you're thinking about *her,* sir," the bosun said, in reference to his captain's dead wife, "but maybe you ought to go out and get yourself soused tonight, if you don't mind me saying so."

"I *do* mind you saying so," Christian retorted, angry with himself that it had been the girl he'd been thinking about and not his dead wife — especially on this, of all nights. "And getting myself soused will not relieve the pain, or bring her back."

"Sorry, sir. It's just that — well, I hate to see you suffer."

"Hendricks—"

"And there *are* other women in this world."

"Hendricks!"

The bosun's teeth flashed white in the darkness. "Of course, if you *were* to interest yourself in that Irishwoman, no one has to know—"

Christian's sharp glance silenced him. "You have an impertinent tongue, Rico!"

The bosun bowed mockingly. "Thank you, sir."

"And one of these days I'm going to ship you out on another vessel and let someone else deal with it."

"After you've cut it out, sir?" Hendrick's eyes twinkled at the old joke.

"Aye, Rico. *After* I've cut it out."

Together, they watched the gig's approach in the darkness. Its presence boded no happiness for Christian. Soon it would carry him back to *Bold Marauder,* and he dreaded all that awaited him there — the girl, the crew, the humiliation, and always, the night-mares that would engulf him once he succumbed to the sleep his weary body so craved.

But tonight, he knew, those nightmares would be worse than they'd ever been — for tonight was the eve of the Black Anniversary.

The gig bumped against the wharf. Christian stared down at his buckled shoes and murmured, "Damn, what I wouldn't give for a tall glass of brandy and a warm bed."

"Don't know about the brandy, sir, but I'm sure the warm bed, at least, will be awaiting you...."

"Rico?"

"Aye, sir?"

"Shut up."

The bosun grinned. "So," he ventured, casually, "who do you think she is, anyhow? The Irish girl, that is?"

Why do I even bother? Christian thought, tipping his head back over the bench and staring up at the stars with increasing annoy-ance. "Damned if I know."

"I'll bet she's some doxy, brought aboard for the mutual amusement of herself and the crew."

"Well, she was anything but amused when I found her. If she's a doxy, she's an even better actress. She seems so—" He paused, frowning as he tried to find the right word.

"Innocent?" Hendricks offered, raising a brow.

"Aye, innocent."

"Well, next time you're tempted to believe that heap of rot, remember what she did to you. Then think of what her *innocence* nearly cost you, as far as your career goes. Why, if it weren't for your flawless record—"

"Hendricks—"

"And the fact that Sir Elliott is your own brother—"

"*Hendricks!* By God, man, do you *ever* give up?"

Grinning, the bosun jumped down into the boat as it bumped

against the wharf. As usual, not much perturbed the fellow and for that, Christian was grateful. Stuffing his cold-numbed hands deep into his pockets to warm them, he strode to the edge of the pier, carefully keeping any trace of emotion from his stony features. Again, the image of frightened purple eyes and a snarl of raven curls rose in his mind. Damn the girl! He ought to be planning the best way to handle that wretched lot of malcontents that awaited him, not thinking about a woman!

Still, his behavior today had been deplorable, and he couldn't blame Elliott for his anger. As a King's captain, he was expected to conduct himself accordingly; to behave as an officer and a gentleman; to exercise sound judgment, leadership, and diplomacy in his every action; to put his country before himself.

"Hendricks, are you bloody ready yet?" he snapped.

"Aye, sir," the bosun called up from below, his face glowing in the light of a lantern held by one of the gig's crew.

Thank God. Christian climbed down into the gig and settled in the stern. Aware of the speculative glances of the crew, he sat rigidly as the oarsmen shoved off, shivering with cold, wishing he had his heavy boat cloak, and being careful to keep his gaze on the moored frigate. They would get no hint of the day's rulings from him, by God.

Yet as the gig cut through the harbor's black water, he couldn't help but wonder why the Irish girl had even been *aboard* the frigate. Unlike Hendricks, he didn't believe her to be a paid doxy. No, she was probably some orphaned waif who'd accepted a coin or two from his crew in return for making his life hell.

No doubt, he thought on a sudden intuition, the "whipping" had been carefully staged, too!

His jaw tightened. Why hadn't he seen it before? She probably *was* working for the crew, a party to their malicious attempts to rid their happy ship of her newest commander. No doubt they'd all spent the day laughing their arses off over his complete and total humiliation!

Christian's fingers began an agitated tattoo against the gunwale. Laugh, would they? Bugger the lot of them! There'd be hell to pay after this, by God!

He had worked himself into a fine, fuming rage by the time the gig nudged against *Bold Marauder*'s hull, a dark wall that loomed above them like a small fortress. As the coxswain hailed the frigate, Christian looked up, saw the ship's yards and rigging silhouetted against the starlit sky, and — wonder of wonders! — movement near the entry port.

"The devil take me," he muttered. Finally, a proper ceremony for the captain as he boarded his command.

His spirits lifted, ever so slightly, and despite his aching leg, his sore groin, and his wounded pride, he almost smiled.

Until he hauled himself through the entry port and saw what awaited him.

No.

It couldn't be.

But it was. Lieutenant Ian MacDuff, garbed in that ridiculous Scottish cap and plaid, standing at attention with a single, foolishly grinning marine — Evans — smartly presenting arms.

"Welcome aboard, *sir!*" Ian beamed, and before Christian, flabbergasted and shocked, could call a halt to this lunacy, the Scotsman tucked his bagpipes under his arm, slammed his elbow into the bag, and, grinning at the loud, droning hum that blasted forth, shoved the mouthpiece between his lips.

"Dear God in heaven," Christian murmured. And then he forgot the events of the day, his dread of the inevitable nightmare, and even the girl who awaited him in his cabin as the first ear-shattering notes came bawling out of the bagpipes at a volume loud enough to drown out everything but his own agony.

"Enough, Mr. MacDuff!" he yelled, over the noise.

His face puffed up and red with effort, Ian, launching into a tune that might — with a little imagination and a lot of brandy — have been "Rule Britannia," never heard him.

"By the grace of Almighty God, *stop*!"

Christian waved his arms in a final attempt to get his lieutenant's attention — then swiftly turned and beat a hasty retreat aft.

Ian raced after him, crestfallen. Leaping over a coiled line, his eyes filled with despair, he cried, "Sir, wait! 'Tis trying I be, honestly!" He shoved the mouthpiece back between his lips and, catching the last sigh of raucous air as it exited the bag, took up where he had left off.

"Hendricks!" Christian yelled over his shoulder. "I cannot for the life of me imagine a more ghastly sound!"

"What?"

"I said — oh, go on with you. I'm going below!"

"What? I can't *hear* you!"

There was no point in trying to be heard. His ears ringing, his head pounding, Christian grabbed for the hatch, ducked beneath the low deckhead beams, flung open his door—

— and was nearly decapitated by the sword that came swinging out of the darkness to slam into the bulkhead just beside his ear.

Chapter Six

She'd missed.

Oh, dear, I've done it now, Deirdre thought wildly.

In the faint glow of moonlight she saw the English captain stumble back against the bulkhead, momentarily dazed by the viciousness of her unexpected attack.

Then he came for her.

Deirdre fled behind the table. "Get away from me!"

"Come here, foundling."

"I said, *get away from me!*"

He stood unmoving, every muscle tensed to spring, his face almost unholy in the glow of the lantern. Raw terror paralyzed her, for even in the gloom she could see the glint in his eyes, the harsh set of his unforgiving mouth, and the anger in his stance—anger he held barely in check.

Deirdre's gaze cut to the door, looking for escape.

"Really, my dear, I have no intention of doing you the harm you mean me."

He feinted to one side, Deirdre dove to her right—and smashed directly into his chest. It was like hitting a solid wall. She panicked as his arms closed around her. With a cry, she drove her foot down on his toe and lunged for the door, knowing she'd never make it in time.

He caught her as her hand hit the latch.

"Filthy English *dog*!" she raged, fighting him. "I'll see ye *dead*!"

"And I'll have some answers from you if it damn well kills me!"

"Good, I hope it does!" She kicked out at him, but he only hauled her, kicking and screaming, across the cabin. His face was an icy mask of determination, and he didn't stop until he'd dragged her into the separate sleeping compartment. There, with a lack of dignity that stung her already wounded pride, he picked her up and tossed her across the bed, his eyes blazing as her shirt, far too big for her, gapped open, baring her binding and far too much flesh.

Angrily, he grabbed a blanket and flung it over her. "Cover yourself, doxy!"

Deirdre, unwilling to accept anything from this man, flung the blanket aside. "I am Irish," she said proudly, her eyes glittering and defiant, *"but I am no doxy."*

"You will forgive me if evidence leads me to conclude otherwise." His eyes narrowed. "Now tell me, which of my crew of reprobates and rogues is responsible for smuggling you aboard this ship in an attempt to beguile and irritate me?"

"None of them! I came of my own accord!"

"You lie."

"Even if I did, I'd see ye in hell before I'd tell you!"

"Then have a good look, because I've *been* in hell these past five years, and now—" his gaze dropped to her exposed skin —"I might like a taste of heaven."

She froze. Christian leaned down and lifted one black, spiraling curl. Despite himself and his efforts to prevent it, his gaze dropped again to her skewed shirt and the bare curve of her breast, pale in the lantern light, that the bindings refused to contain. Something stirred deep inside of himself, and he took a deep and steadying breath—

But then Emily's face appeared in his mind's eye, her eyes accusing, and the fire in his blood cooled as quickly as it had flared to life. Anger, swift and savage, filled him, and, desperate to hold on to something he hadn't felt in over five years, he plunged his fingers into the doxy's snarled hair and lowered his mouth toward hers. She tried to twist away, but his thumb caught her jaw, forcing her to still, and before he could help himself he was claiming her lips in a hard kiss that was meant to prove something to himself far more than it was ever meant to do the same for her. She whimpered deep in her throat, her struggles only fanning his determination to drive away the devils that had tormented him for so long—and to affirm that he could still, by God, function as a man.

Her struggles increased. Christian was no brute. He abruptly released her, shaken to his depths by what she had awakened in him and turning his back, wanting only to put distance between himself and her, stalked away.

It was a mistake, and he knew it even as something slammed into the nape of his neck with an impact that sent him to his knees; a moment later, he found himself on his back, the girl's knee driving into his belly and the short black nose of his own pistol just inches from his startled eyes.

His blood turned cold.

There was an ominous click as she brought the gun to half-cock. *This can't be happening to me*, he thought. He, who'd survived Quiberon and countless naval battles, storms at sea, and other perils that made up the everyday life of any sea officer. He—about to die at the hands of an insane young woman? But no, this was all too real. It was, indeed, happening. He swallowed, not daring, even, to breathe.

Her hand shaking, she brought the gun closer to his face. Behind it, now so close that he could smell the spent powder from previous firings, he could see that her eyes were cold and hard.

"For thirteen long years," she said, pushing her hair off her forehead with trembling fingers, "I've waited for this moment. Thirteen long years, I've waited for the chance to kill ye."

Christian stared into the deadly black mouth of the pistol, his mind racing over a short list of long-forgotten paramours whom he must have unwittingly spurned. He wasn't in the business of breaking hearts, but then, maybe his memory wasn't as sound as he'd thought it to be. Not surprising, given his current predicament—

"Thirteen long years, *Lieutenant,* to avenge the terrible wrong ye did me and me family."

Cold metal touched his forehead—and then he heard the mad skitter of nails as Tildy shot from off the bed and across the cabin toward him. In a single, swift movement, the girl jerked the pistol around—

"Don't!" Christian cried hoarsely.

—and swung back to face him, her eyes panicky.

He swallowed hard and shut his eyes. "....Hurt my dog."

"What?"

"Please ... don't hurt my dog."

The girl's mouth fell open and she stared down at him in confusion and astonishment. Slowly, shakily, she lowered the gun.

Christian let out his breath and closed his eyes.

And Deirdre, still straddling the English captain with her knee deep in his abdomen, felt her blood go cold as the awful reality of what she's been about to do, flooded her.

I almost killed a man.

The gun was suddenly a horrible, wretched thing, and she put it down, recoiling from it and feeling suddenly sick. The dog, whining, had fallen upon the captain, licking his face in a frenzied display of love and devotion. He did nothing to push the animal away, instead wrapping his arms around the squirming little body and hugging it close, apparently more concerned with the dog's welfare than his own. Deirdre stared down at him in frustration, confusion, and self-disgust. She had failed miserably in her self-appointed mission to avenge her brother, make good on her promise to her mother, and do honor to the proud blood that ran in her veins.

Granuaile, who would have had no trouble dispatching an enemy, especially a hated English one, wouldn't be proud of her, now.

"Thank you," she heard him say, beneath the dog's soft whines.

"For what?" she spat scathingly. "Not killin' ye?"

"No ... for not hurting my dog."

Hysteria, insane and unexpected, rose up in her and it was all she could do not to let out a bark of laughter as she got to her feet. "I was wrong to come here," she said, as the captain also rose, the little dog cradled in his arms. "I'm leavin'."

"It is nearly midnight, madam. Despite your seeming appetite for violence, I am adverse to setting a young woman loose in the streets of Portsmouth at this hour. You will remain here until the morning, at which time I will gladly see to your request."

"I will not stay here with ye!"

"That choice is not yours to make. But you are quite safe, I can assure you. You have my word as a gentleman that I will not avail myself of your charms, delightful and dangerous though they may be."

"You think I'd believe the word of an Englishman?"

"Probably not." He eyed her dubiously, retrieved the blanket he'd tried to give her earlier, and offered it to her once more. This time, she grudgingly accepted it. "Oh, don't get me wrong," he added. "I would *like* to see what you offer, if only to prove to myself that I can still enjoy a kiss, a touch, a tryst, as much as the next fellow ... but I daresay that would be a most ill-conceived idea, given our present feelings toward each other." His voice was suddenly rough and unguarded, and he turned abruptly away. "You see, I loved a woman once ... but she was taken from me in the cruelest way imaginable. Love has no place in my dead heart, and lust, no place in the disciplined order of my life." He looked at her then, his eyes dark and haunted. "Therefore, you are quite safe with me."

He moved away from her, cold and aloof once more, and she wondered if the brief vulnerability she had seen—or thought she'd seen—in his eyes, had been nothing more than a trick of the lantern light. "Tomorrow I will set you ashore," he said. "But tonight, you will sleep in my bed. Alone. I will take my rest on the bench seat in my main cabin. Do not hesitate to summon me if you need me for any reason."

He picked up the little dog and moved behind the canvas screen.

Leaving Deirdre alone.

Chapter Seven

It was nearly midnight, several hours later.

While their captain had faced his admiral's wrath, the crew had worked all day to replace the damaged spars and rigging suffered by the collision with Admiral Burns's flagship and now, exhausted but triumphant over the earlier debacle, sat around a table in the wardroom, laughing over the embarrassment they had caused their new Lord and Master.

The door opened.

"Mr. MacDuff, sir?" The youngest of the frigate's three midshipmen poked his head into the crowded wardroom and then darted inside, shoving through seaman and officers until he came to Ian. The big Scotsman sat on a sea chest, polishing his bagpipes with a square of linen and half watching a card game that took up the entire table.

Ian glanced up, scowling. "Hugh, laddie! 'Tis past your bedtime, and there be things in here ye shouldnae be seein'!"

But young Hugh's eyes had already found the thing they shouldn't be seeing, and gaping at the scantily clad woman who sat atop Milton Lee's knee, he managed to blurt, "Captain's compliments, and he requests your presence in his day cabin!"

"Uh-oh, you're in for it now," Milton Lee predicted darkly, sliding a hand up the doxy's thigh. "The admiral's probably taken the Lord and Master down a peg or two and now he's looking for someone to put the blame on."

Skunk roared with laughter and dealt a new hand of cards, the movements of his arm sending a cloud of stench across the table and making those nearest to him gag. "An' looks like yer that someone, Ian!"

"Aye, fine job you did, getting us under way this afternoon," said Russell Rhodes, smirking as he leaned against one of the big guns that competed for space in the wardroom.

"And a fine job *you* did, my handsome lieutenant," the woman purred, sliding from Lee's lap and sauntering across the cabin to Rhodes. She touched his arm, letting her nails drag up his sleeve while she tilted her head flirtatiously and stared into his eyes. "Hiding me down there in your brig ... such a perfect place for a friendly liaison, no? Why, I can't wait"—her husky voice dropped to a rich, throaty whisper—"to have you *all* to myself."

"Delight, please, have me first!" cried Midshipman Hibbert, grinning foolishly and sweeping off his stained and dirty hat.

As the room erupted into laughter, the woman turned her bold gaze on the fourteen-year-old, letting it drift slowly down his filthy, wrinkled uniform and toward his groin, until young Hibbert's pink cheeks began to turn red. "Why, Hibbert, *cheri,* I just love young boys ... their energy is so tireless, their enthusiasm so refreshing, no? But I think I shall wait till tomorrow ... and then eat you for breakfast!"

Hibbert went scarlet. Raucous guffaws split the small room and Skunk clapped the midshipman across the back. Only the beardless Arthur Teach, who'd spent the better part of the evening sulking in the corner, did not join in their laughter. Now he sat sullenly polishing a tomahawk, taken in trade from an Indian chief he'd once met in the American colonies. The blade glittered dangerously in the lantern light.

"What, have ye no comment tae make, Arthur?" Ian prodded, getting to his feet and twirling his bonnet on his thumb. "Nothing tae say about our new Lord and Master?"

The seaman looked up, his eyes black with menace. Slowly, he ran his finger down the flat of the tomahawk's blade.

"I'll kill him," he vowed softly.

Nobody moved. Skunk exchanged nervous glances with Ian. Hibbert paled and looked at his feet. Even the yellow-haired woman paused, her hand going still on Rhodes's arm.

Outside, the winter wind blew ominously around the hull.

The young midshipman finally broke the heavy silence. "Er, Mr. MacDuff, sir?" he said, moving fearfully away from Teach. "The captain's waiting. And, begging your pardon, sir, but he's in a foul temper."

"Aye, as I expect he would be," Ian murmured, frowning. He raked a hand through his thick red hair, donned his cap, and prepared to face the music.

UNABLE—AND unwilling—to sleep, Captain Christian Lord sat in his day cabin, thinking about the girl in his bed such a short distance away. He was trying, unsuccessfully, to take his mind off her by reading *Bold Marauder*'s log under her previous captain when the thump of Evans's musket on the deck outside announced the arrival of Ian MacDuff.

He shut the leather-bound book with a snap and looked up. The Scotsman, silhouetted by the swinging deckhead lantern behind him, stood at the door, nervously twisting his bonnet in his hands.

"Do come in, Mr. MacDuff."

Bobbing his head, the Scot entered the cabin, aware of the raw disapproval on his captain's face as he took in his outlandish attire. Ian had worn his plaid in defiance of Navy regulations and in proud display of his heritage, but now, under that frigid scrutiny and without the backup of his fellow miscreants, he felt rather silly. Especially with his blue uniform coat thrown haphazardly over the whole thing and his knees, sprouting red hair, peeping out from beneath.

"I do trust you will discard that ridiculous attire and dress yourself appropriately," Christian remarked dryly. "You test the limits of my patience with the beard, but I cannot abide both. Choose one or the other, Mr. MacDuff, and we will get on famously."

Taken aback, Ian stared at him, for he'd expected a sharp reprimand for both the beard and the plaid. Eyeing the captain warily, he pulled out a chair, his gaze falling upon the screen that divided the day cabin from the captain's sleeping area. Was the Lord and Master keeping the young Irishwoman in there? He grinned slyly; if so, the knowledge would be good fodder for the lads back in the wardroom....

Ian glanced up—and found the gray eyes quietly assessing him. His grin promptly faded. He returned the stare with innocent defiance, trying in vain to discern the strengths and weaknesses behind the captain's cold eyes. The Lord and Master was a handsome man, but Ian was not jaded into thinking that was all he was. He recognized, and respected, the power in his new captain's shoulders, the intelligence behind his eyes, the determination in the set of his mouth, the discipline reflected in the scrupulously neat and clean state of his uniform.

As for weaknesses, Ian MacDuff could discern none.

He felt the first twinges of alarm. He and the crew might not have an easy time of it, winning their ship back from such a man as this.

"Despite the debacle of this afternoon, I appreciate that you managed to restore the ship to sailing condition in such a timely manner," the captain said. "It was more than I expected of any of you."

"Why ... thank you, sir."

The captain smiled faintly, but his gaze remained cold as it settled unnervingly on Ian. "Mistakes do happen, do they not?"

"Aye, sir."

"Of course, they only happen once. Twice, and they are put down to incompetence—and incompetence, we all know, has no place on a fighting ship."

"Aye, sir," Ian said again.

"I am sensible to the fact that this afternoon's doings were no accident, Mr. MacDuff. I know you would all be quite happy to see the last of me, but I can assure you that I won't be as easy to dislodge as my predecessors have been."

"But sir, we don't—"

"However, I am willing to forgive what happened earlier. The mistake, of course, was mine and mine alone for trusting my command to a crew whose strengths and weaknesses I've yet to discern—and whose loyalty I've yet to secure. But mark me, I will not make that mistake again. Tomorrow I will carry out a complete inspection of this vessel before we weigh. We will leave Portsmouth under *my* hand"—he eyed Ian coldly—"and I expect your cooperation in seeing that our people behave in an organized, well-disciplined fashion."

"Aye, sir," Ian repeated, beginning to squirm.

The captain leaned across the table, poured brandy into two glasses, and pushed one toward Ian. "In any case, I did not summon you here to chide you for the events of this afternoon."

Ian bolted the brandy, growing more and more nervous under the captain's flinty stare.

"I summoned you, by God, because I would like an explanation as to who is responsible for bringing that trollop aboard my command!"

Ian nearly choked on the liquor. "T-trollop, sir?"

"That deuced Irishwoman, damn you!"

Thank the gods he hadn't been referring to Delight, Ian thought in dizzy relief. Surely he would've confiscated her and put her aboard a proper merchantman for the passage back to America—

"Answer me, Lieutenant!"

"I, uh ... doona ken, sir."

The captain only glared at him, a muscle ticking in his jaw.

"Honestly, sir, 'tis tellin' ye the truth I be! I doona ken who the lassie is! Ye see, sir, we was havin' an argument when all of a sudden there she was, all dressed as a laddie and begging for us tae let her sign aboard!" Quailing beneath the captain's icy stare, Ian grabbed the brandy bottle and dosed himself with more of the liquor. "I didnae ken she was a 'she,' sir!"

The gray eyes narrowed.

Ian gulped his brandy. "Next thing I know, ye was wantin' tae get the ship under way, and, well, with all the, um, accidents, sir, things got a wee bit tense. The steerin' went, a fight broke out, and we hit the admiral's flagship—" He grabbed the brandy bottle. "The lad—I mean, the lassie—well, they just needed a scapegoat tae blame for it, so they turned on her—"

"And I suppose you don't know her identity either, eh, Mr. MacDuff?"

"No, sir, never saw her before in my life!"

"And, to your knowledge, has anyone else aboard this vessel?"

"I doona think so, sir. She's as much a mystery to us, sir, as she is tae you."

The Lord and Master stared at him for a long time. Finally he blew out his breath, refilled the brandy glasses, and leaned back in his chair. "I'll likely regret it, but I daresay I believe you," he said quietly.

"I wouldnae lie tae ye, sir."

"No, Mr. MacDuff ... I don't think that you would." He took a sip of his own brandy, then continued. "Tomorrow, we weigh. But before we do, you will remove that girl from this ship and see that she is safely put into the care of the fellow who owns the Spindrift Tavern." He shoved a purse across the table. "This should see her on her way handsomely, I should think."

Ian looked down at the money, stunned by the Lord and Master's generosity. "Ye be wantin' me tae do that tonight, sir?"

'Tomorrow morning, Mr. MacDuff."

"But I have the watch then—"

"Then see that Mr. Rhodes escorts her ashore. Perhaps, as an officer, he'll even find a way to behave like one." He rose to his feet, the interview concluded. "That is all, Mr. MacDuff."

BEHIND THE CANVAS partition that divided the sleeping area from the main cabin, a very homesick Deirdre O'Devir lay unmoving in the bed, fiercely clutching her canvas bag of Irish mementos that the sailor named Skunk had returned to her. The ship, tugging at her anchor, rocked gently beneath her.

He had kissed her. He, her enemy, had put his wretched English lips against hers and *kissed* her.

And she had allowed it.

Maybe, in some odd and awful way, even ... enjoyed it.

She put her hands over her eyes and pressed hard, as if she could banish the memory. In the other part of the cabin, she could hear the captain speaking quietly to his nervous lieutenant. Damn him! Damn his poxy hide to hell and back! Why did he have to go and be nice to her, when she was trying her best to kill him?

She wiped her hand across her lips, but it could not erase the hard, masculine feel of him, the taste of him, the answering fire in her blood that even the memory evoked.

"I hate ye," she murmured, staring up into the shadows. "I should've killed ye when I had the chance."

But she had not been able to do it. She remembered his face, calm and unflinching behind the mouth of the pistol as she'd prepared to put a ball between those steady gray eyes. Thirteen years of fantasizing about the moment—and she hadn't had the courage to pull the trigger when that chance had finally come.

Coward!

Steady and calm, those eyes ... until she'd swung the weapon on his little dog. She would never have harmed the spaniel, of course, and her reaction had been one of startled surprise. But what shook her to her very core, what confused her past all understanding, was the fact that the Lord and Master seemed to care more for his pet's life than for his own. What sort of man was he?

She was growing more confused by the moment. If only she had never left Ireland. If only she were back home right now, safe in the little cottage she'd known since birth.

If only *he* wasn't out there, she could get up and go to the stern windows and find the North Star.

Then, at least, she might know which direction home lay in.

Beyond the screen, she heard the slam of the door as the Scottish lieutenant took his leave ... the sounds of the captain moving about ... the murmur of his deep voice as he spoke to the little spaniel ... the sound of him moving across the cabin.

He was standing directly over her.

Deirdre froze, feigning sleep and hoping he couldn't hear the sudden, wild thump of her heart. That thump seemed to crash to a stop as he lifted a thick tress of her hair, then gently placed it back across her shoulder. He stood there for what seemed a long time; then he gave a deep, ragged sigh and she heard him moving back through the darkness toward his day cabin.

Trembling, she rolled onto her back and stared up into the gloom. Her heart was beating so hard she could barely hear her thoughts over it.

Ye have to kill him, ye know. He'll go back on his word and touch ye with his dirty English hands ... again and again and again.

Her hand crept out, seeking the canvas bag, and finding

within it her flagon of Irish air. She pulled it out and held it close to her heart, taking comfort from its nearness.

He'll touch ye ... and ye won't deny him.

She swallowed tightly, suddenly cold and afraid. *Kill him?* She had already bungled the first two attempts. But the pistol would've been too merciful, the sword too bloody. There were other, less gruesome methods of disposing of an enemy....

Yes, that was it. She just hadn't found the right method of carrying out her vow. That was why she hadn't been able to kill him.

Wasn't it?

From the darkness, she heard the rustle of clothing as he shed his clothes and readied himself for bed. A sudden wicked image of what he must look like, naked, surged into her mind and horrified at the direction of her thoughts, she squeezed her eyes shut. From the near darkness came a squeak of leather as he lowered himself down on the bench seat at the window, the murmur of a quick prayer, and the snap of his fingers.

She frowned. Snap of his fingers?

Then she heard the skitter of claws upon the deck, a happy bark—and the captain's soft crooning as he comforted the little animal and the two of them settled down for the night.

He sleeps with the bleedin' dog?

She lay back against the pillows, listening to him toss and turn until his breathing grew heavy and rhythmic in the darkness.

She had never been more confused in her life.

Chapter Eight

L ieutenant Ian MacDuff returned to the wardroom, feeling flattered, confused, guilty—and torn.

They pounced on him like a school of piranhas.

"So wot did 'is bloidy Lordship say, eh?"

"Did ye get yer comeuppance, Ian?"

"C'mon, man, out with it! What'd the bastard say?"

Ian waved them off. Troubled, he turned and picked up his bagpipes. Oh, how he wanted to tell them all about his meeting with the Lord and Master! How he wanted to bask in all the attention it would get him! But a sobering thought kept him from doing so.

Lieutenant Ian MacDuff did not want to betray his new captain.

The man had given him what no other commanding officer aboard HMS *Bold Marauder* ever had—forgiveness.

And, the chance to redeem himself after making a serious mistake.

Ian's chin went up a notch higher. He, Ian, was the frigate's first lieutenant, and his captain *needed* him.

The others pressed close, their faces eager and their eyes bright with excitement.

"C'mon, Ian, what did the bastard say to ye, eh?"

"Did the admiral knock him down a peg or two?"

Even Delight raised a perfect golden brow, her silky gaze sliding down the length of his torso, pausing at his groin, and making him feel as though she could see right through his plaid. "Yes, Ian, sweet," she purred seductively, "*do* tell us...."

But Ian turned away. "Aw, shear off, all of ye!" he muttered, the good-natured tone of his voice belying his troubled eyes. "He just wanted tae find out who the boglander lassie was, 'tis all."

"Aw, Ian, there must be more to it than that! What did 'e *say?*" Skunk persisted with a toothy grin.

But the big lieutenant was already on his way out the door, taking his bagpipes with him.

"Well, now, what d'ye make of that, eh?" Skunk said, frowning and shaking his head.

"I don't know, but I sure don't like the looks of it."

"Emily ... Dear God, Emily, no.... *No!*"

The tortured cry penetrated Deirdre's sleep, bringing her quickly awake. For a moment she lay staring into the darkness, confused and disoriented, the sheets fisted in her hands, her bag of Irish keepsakes pressing comfortingly against her thigh. Then she remembered. She was on the king's frigate *Bold Marauder,* and lying in its captain's bed.

The Lord and Master.

He didn't sound so high-and-mighty now. In the darkness she could hear his harsh breathing, the sound of his tossing and turning, and the little dog's soft whimpers—whimpers that the captain never heard, whimpers that he never heeded.

"Poxy, bleedin' bastard," she muttered, flinging herself onto her side and clapping her hands over her ears. But it was no use. She could still hear the sounds of his torment. And now even the little dog was growing distraught, her whimpers progressing into nervous whines until there was a light thump, the sound of claws against the decking, and a cold wet nose against Deirdre's arm.

The animal's plea for her help was unmistakable.

Tight-lipped, Deirdre pushed aside her canvas bag, swung her legs out of the bed and, grabbing a blanket to ward off the cold, marched through the darkness and into the day cabin. The spaniel followed her, pressing anxiously at her heels. Moonlight streamed in from the stern windows. Shapes materialized from out of the gloom: the desk ... a bowl and pitcher set on a little stand ... the captain's cocked hat, resting beside it—

And the captain himself.

There were dreams, and then there were nightmares. This was a nightmare and a bad one, too, by the looks of it. He lay on the bench seat, one arm flung over his eyes, his chest, as formidable and strong as she'd figured it would be, bare and damp with sweat in the moonlight. He looked vulnerable, and all too human in that vulnerability, and as she stared down at him Deirdre felt an unwelcome softening within herself, because enemies were not supposed to look human.

"Emily ... please, come out.... You can't die.... I won't let you die!"

Deirdre took a step back.

"Emily, dear God, where are you? Emily!"

Never had she heard such raw, broken anguish in a man's voice. It was awful to listen to, terrible to witness, and in that moment Deirdre wanted nothing more than to flee the cabin and the ship and run all the way back to Ireland. But she couldn't move. Couldn't take her eyes off this wretched picture of suffering as his head thrashed on the pillow and he writhed in a torment only he could know. Finally, he flung his arm over his eyes once more, and his hoarse cries faded until only his lips moved, mouthing words that were known only to him.

Slowly, silence returned to the cabin. Then, from beneath his broad wrist, Deirdre saw a silver, glistening track of moisture leading down his cheek.

Another, and barely discernible in the silence, the sounds of his weeping.

She pushed her fist against her mouth. She had never heard a man cry before. It was an awful sound, one of agony and suffering.

And she hoped to never hear it again.

Stricken, Deirdre stood there until the awful sobs finally began to fade. His fist clenched once, twice, the knuckles showing white in the darkness. Then his hand opened, and something dropped to the deck flooring with a dull thud.

Deirdre leaned down to pick it up, and saw that it was a tiny portrait of a woman.

This Emily person?

Then he kicked his feet, and the sheets dragged down his torso.

Jesus, Joseph, and Mary—

He wore no shirt, and beneath the breeches he'd worn to bed, she could see an unholy ... bulge.

Her eyes widened and she abruptly dropped the miniature, her face flaming, before fleeing back to her bed. There she lay staring up in the darkness, her mind stamped with the image of what she had seen. She heard his breathing grow deep and rhythmic once again; she heard the little dog jump back up to join her master, and she should have been able to finally get back to sleep. But no. There was no way she could sleep, when all she could see was that last, wicked picture of the captain's strong and handsome body, helplessly caught in the throes of a nightmare that only he could see.

That strong, handsome, and splendidly *male* body.

She swallowed tightly, once, twice, again. She flipped onto her stomach, dragged the pillow over her head, and tried in vain to block out the sound of his breathing ... and the thought of that powerful body, sprawled in the darkness such a short distance away.

Nearly naked.

Deirdre punched the pillow, hoping the noise would rouse him enough that he might cover himself. He didn't stir. She punched it again, muttered an oath into the warm stuffing, and bit back a scream of frustration.

Nothing.

Finally she tossed back her coverlet and stormed across the cabin. Reaching down, she picked up the sheets he'd kicked off and flung them over his body.

He bolted upright, blinking.

Oh, Almighty God.

"What are you doing?" he asked.

Suddenly afraid, Deirdre backed up. "Nothing!"

He raked a hand through his rumpled hair. "Do you always make it a habit to watch a gentleman while he sleeps?"

"Do *you* always make it a habit to wake people up with yer nightmares?"

Wordlessly, he swung his legs from the cushion, gained his feet and straightened to his full height, completely awake now, tall, forbidding, and most definitely dangerous. Any vulnerability he'd shown in the grip of his nightmare was long gone; this man was angry, he was formidable, and Deirdre was suddenly very, very afraid.

She crept backward, toward the door.

"Come here," he murmured softly.

Deirdre took another step back. Her hand groped behind her —and came up against his desk and a half-full pitcher of water atop it.

Her fingers closed around the handle. With all her strength, she hurled it at his head.

Too late, his arm came up to fend it off. There was a loud crash, but Deirdre didn't stay to see the results of her actions. She bolted from the cabin, hearing behind her his groan of pain and the sound of his heavy body hitting the desk, then the deck flooring.

She was past the drunken Marine and halfway across the moonlit deck when unseen hands caught her roughly by the shoulders and yanked her around. Instinctively, her hand came up to defend herself, and was caught in a meaty fist.

Skunk.

"Hush, girlie, before ye wake up the whole ship! Christ, I ain't never heard such a racket in my life! Wot the hell is goin' on down there, eh?"

"Get yer hands off o' me!" Deirdre cried, wrenching free and away from him. Already, others were melting out of the darkness: Teach, not quite so fearsome without his beard; Elwin the surgeon, stretching his chicken-neck as he tried to see around him; Hibbert, the midshipman she'd scrapped with earlier; Russell Rhodes, dark and sinister in the moonlight; and several others whose names she didn't know, and didn't care to know—including the voluptuous, well-endowed doxy.

"Where's 'is bloody Lordship?" the big gunner demanded, his eyes narrowing. Beside him, Hibbert stood gawking at Deirdre's bare legs until Skunk cuffed him sharply in reprimand.

"Sleepin'," Deirdre shot back, with a fearful glance behind her. "What else would a body be doing in the middle o' the night?"

"I might ask you the same question," murmured Ian MacDuff, emerging from below and holding up a large fragment of the pitcher that Deirdre had just hurled.

She paled and would have fled if not for Skunk's restraining hand on her arm.

"What's this all about, Ian?"

"I doona ken, Skunk," Ian said, frowning. "Found our commanding officer in a rather sorry state."

"Sleepin'?"

"Aye, most definitely," Ian returned, taking off his cap and scratching his head. He pointed an accusatory finger at Deirdre. "For such a wee kitten, lassie, 'tis one hell of a wildcat ye be!"

"I was only tryin' to protect myself!"

Skunk wrapped a large, grimy arm around Deirdre's thin shoulders. "What's yer name, girlie?"

Ian stepped forward, scowling. "Skunk—"

"Aw, piss off, Ian," Skunk said, waving him away. "This is important!"

"Deirdre. Deirdre O'Devir."

"Well, Miss Deirdre, we already got us one lady stowaway, might as well 'ave two. Ye can keep each other company on the passage over. This here's Dolores Ann Foley—"

"But I go by the name of Delight," the woman purred, flirtatiously touching Ian's arm.

Deirdre stared at her. "Delight *Foley?*"

The woman gave a husky laugh. "*Oui, cherie.* As in *delight-fully*."

"*Skunk*—" Ian tried again.

Skunk ignored him. "We knows Rhodes here has orders t' put ye ashore tomorrow, but we figure we can just hide ye down below with Delight 'til we're a ways out to sea, then bring ye both out when it's too late to head back to England. Ought to rile the new captain nicely, eh? Hell, 'e's gonna make our lives hell for the next month, might as well return the favor!" The big gunner laughed, elbowed his grinning mates, and leered down at Deirdre. "By the way, we really admire yer attempts to end his Lordship's life, though ye *could* use some advice on how to kill someone." He grinned. 'Teach here can help ye with that, eh, Arthur?"

A chorus of guffaws went up.

"So, girlie, what d' ye say?" Skunk prompted. "Ye want t' stay with us or go back ashore?"

Deirdre thought of her cousin Brendan, whose help she so desperately needed if she were to find her brother. "I do have to get to America," she said slowly. Then her eyes narrowed. "But I'll be warnin' ye. If ye be thinkin' to see me at the same trade as Delight *Foley,* ye'll find out I don't need lessons from Teach or anyone else about how to kill someone!"

"Nah, nah, ye're quite safe. We won't be touching ye," Skunk said, boxing Hibbert's ears as the boy tried to see down Deirdre's shirt. "Now, if we can only get Ian here to quit being such an old fart, we'd be all set."

"I willnae be a part of this conspiracy!" Ian raged, clenching his fists at his sides. "Ye hear me? Ye keep yer bluidy schemes tae yerselves!"

With that he stormed away, leaving a confused silence behind him.

"What's up with him?"

"Don't know. He ain't been 'imself since the captain had that private meetin' with him."

"He'll come 'round," Skunk muttered dismissively. "So what do ye say, girlie? Ye got anythin' better to be doin' for the next month? We told ye *our* purposes. Now why don't ye come down to the wardroom and tell us *yours,* eh? You help us"—he grinned—"and we'll help you."

Deirdre stood unmoving. They were offering protection and safe passage.

"Well?" Skunk said.

Far beyond the harbor, the first streaks of dawn lit the cold eastern sky in a band of pink. Deirdre thought of her cousin Brendan, a shining vision of hope, somewhere across the sea in a distant land called America. She thought of her promise to her dying mother and of her beloved, long-lost brother.

Then she thought of the English captain, strong, virile and dangerous.

She swallowed hard. Next time, he would not go easy on her. But getting to America was worth the risk. And in the meantime, this rebellious crew would protect her.

"Can I go back to the cabin so I can get me belongings?"

"Don't need to." Milton Lee stood there, holding up her bag of Irish mementos. "It's already been done."

"And you can borrow one of my gowns, *cherie*," Delight offered.

Deirdre raised her chin. "Well, then, just lead the way," she said and, hugging her arms to herself to preserve her modesty, followed her escorts below.

Chapter Nine

Given the ship's history, the brig of HMS *Bold Marauder* had never been used for its intended purposes and indeed, if the vessel's builders could have seen what it was being used for now, they would have fainted dead away in shock.

A floor-length mirror was set up against one bulkhead, bottles of fragrance covered the top of an ornate dresser, and an exotic screen of black lacquer portioned off a corner of the small space. The cloying scent of perfume choked the air, and a light dusting of powder coated the deck planking, imbuing it with the scent of lilac, lavender and rose.

The room was dominated by a bed.

Deirdre wanted nothing more than to flee this chamber of sin, but she'd gotten herself into this predicament, and now she could only stand helplessly as Delight, her hands on her voluptuously curving hips, eyed her up and down while thoughtfully tapping a nail against the corner of her mouth. Finally, she nodded, turned, and pulled a stunning velvet gown from the trunk at the foot of the bed. It had a beauty and elegance about it that the Irish girl had never before seen in her life.

It was also of a color that Deirdre had never before *worn* in her life—deep, shocking, blood-red scarlet.

The shade alone was enough to make her blush.

"You like, *cherie?*" Delight asked, tilting her head to one side and smiling.

"I—I can't be wearin' *that*!"

"Lo, you have the most *delightful* brogue! You'll just *have* to teach it to me, no? Ah, yes, the gown. Let's see what else I have." Delight tossed the rich garment over the bed, pawed through her trunk once more and with an exclamation of triumph, lifted another, her eyes dancing.

"Aha!"

The blood drained from Deirdre's face. "I can't be wearin' *that*, either," she cried, shocked. 'There's ... there's no *bodice* on it!"

"Oh, there's a bodice. See? It's just—transparent."

Deirdre hugged her arms to herself. In comparison, the red gown didn't look so bad after all. Echoing her thoughts, Delight tossed the second dress back into the trunk and grinned. "These two are my most modest, honey. Personally, with that black hair and white skin of yours, I think you'd look devastating in the scarlet."

The scarlet it was. Moments later, Deirdre found herself wrapped in the sinful, wickedly seductive gown as Delight, with a needle and thread, took in the bodice to accommodate Deirdre's significantly smaller bosom. At last she stood back, and clapped her hands in glee. "Aah, you are *magnifique*—here, have a look!" she cried, and hauled Deirdre to the mirror.

Deirdre's mouth gaped open. Never had she worn, or expected to wear, such a beautiful gown in her life. Its color was a striking complement to her black wildly curling hair, setting off the fine translucency of her skin just as Delight had predicted it would. The neckline was cut shockingly low, flaunting her bosom; the waist was tightly nipped. In style, design, and color, it was not a dress that any respectable woman would wear, and thoughts of being seen in it brought the blood flooding back to Deirdre's cheeks.

Thoughts of the Lord and Master seeing her in it deepened that blush to a scalding crimson.

"Aah, you will melt our handsome Ice Captain for sure with this, *cherie*! Perhaps your hair should be up ... no, no, let's leave it down. Oh, this is great fun. I never dreamed such a dreary passage might have such wonderful possibilities! And look at you." She lifted one of Deirdre's spiraling curls. "Aah, to have hair like that! And that cross you wear is the *perfect* complement to your loveliness, rather pagan, just like you, no? Wherever did you get it?"

"It belonged to my grandmother," Deirdre said, "who lived some two hundred years ago. She was a pirate queen."

"A pirate queen?"

"Aye. Grace O'Malley," Deirdre said proudly.

"Do forgive me, sweetie, but I've never heard of her. The only pirate queen *we've* ever had is Anne Bonney."

"Where in France was she from?"

"France?" The vivacious Delight threw back her head and laughed, her voice full-throated and gleeful. "Sweetie, I'm *American*. French by marriage, and a short and unhappy one at that, but widowed now these many months and now, on my way back home to live once again"—she gave a theatrical sigh— "with my parents."

Deirdre stared at her, confused.

"Ye're not French?"

"Nay, and I'm no courtesan, either, though I *am* trying to hone my skills as one. Don't look so shocked, *cherie*! The French are the world's greatest lovers—where else would I learn the best ways to pleasure a man? It's all in the technique, sweetie, getting a man's body to harden with passion and respond to you with all the lust of an untamed stallion."

Deirdre was shocked into speechlessness.

"My parents expected me to sail home to America months

ago, but you see, I wanted to stay in France for a while longer to further my *education*." Delight touched her generous bosom and affected a stern look that was totally out of character with her vivacious behavior. "Such scandalous ambitions would never be tolerated back home, and certainly not by *my* papa! In fact, if he had known what I've been up to these past many months, he would've moved heaven and earth to drag me back!"

"And what were you up to?" Deirdre asked, certain that she didn't want to know.

"Why, learning how to seduce and net me the Irish Pirate."

"The ... Irish Pirate?"

Delight cast her eyes heavenward and touched her heart. "Aah, *there* is a *man!* A hero back home, you know, and the sooner I can get him into my bed, the better chance I have of winning him for myself! Hair as black as yours and a face to die for ... like our Lord and Master's, no? Once, when I was younger, he kissed me ... but I was inexperienced, clumsy, and not enough woman for him. Well, no more! Now, he won't be able to resist me! I went to Paris to learn my skills as a *woman,* to London to learn my skills as a *lady,* and to Portsmouth to practice everything I'd learned on some of the most notoriously wicked and wonderfully lusty seamen on the planet! And we all *know* that there is no one more lusty than a sailor, no? Aah, it sets my hot blood on fire just to think about it!"

Deirdre's head was reeling.

"Lo, I simply can't *wait* for this voyage to begin! Just think, Deirdre, I've a whole ship of sailors to practice my new skills on before I get home. *This* time, when I get my claws into the Irish Pirate, he won't be able to resist me. And, my time in France has given me a perfect accent. Do you like it? I've worked so hard at perfecting it. Men just *love* this throaty, nasal sound, and if you lower your voice to a whisper—like *this*—and touch your man a lot while talking to him and stripping him with your eyes, why, it'll just set him on fire! The combination is lethal!"

Deirdre was at a loss for words. Her thoughts, unfortunately, were not so impaired. Unbidden, Captain Lord's handsome face flashed before her eyes and she found herself blushing once more. Then she thought of Delight, practicing her *skills* on him, and she felt a stab of something that was dark, ugly, and not at all pleasant.

That *something* dismayed her greatly, for she instantly recognized it for what it was.

Jealousy.

Totally unwarranted, of course, but there it was.

"What are ye goin' to do when the captain ... finds out ye're aboard?"

Delight laughed, her voice rich and sultry. "Oh, I have a few things in mind, *cherie*! But 'til then, I doubt I'll have a problem hiding myself away from him. Ah, too involved in his own affairs is our handsome commander, no?" Laughing gaily, she hooked her arm through Deirdre's and guided her to the door. "Now, you go find one of the lieutenants and get yourself hidden away somewhere. We'll be weighing soon, and you need to be out of sight!"

TOPSIDE, Captain Lord was just coming on deck to take command of His Majesty's frigate *Bold Marauder*.

Dawn was a new visitor to the day, touching the harbor with pale salmon light. It reflected itself in a million little diamonds over the water's surface as the cold wind arrived with it. But the frigate's crew was heedless of the dawn. They were too busy staring at the Lord and Master.

With no outward sign of the injury that had felled him earlier, he looked terribly proper, well groomed, and the epitome of what a naval officer should be. His uniform was meticulously clean, the gold buttons and gilded lace bright in the early sunlight. His periwig was carefully rolled and tied beneath his cocked hat and his face was freshly shaved. His coat was as blue as the ocean, and his waistcoat, breeches, and stockings were whiter than sea foam.

"*Holy Moses,*" Skunk muttered, exchanging puzzled glances with Rhodes.

No emotion touched the hard set of the captain's mouth nor softened the harsh lines of his face, and the expression in his eyes was guardedly aloof. He made a quick tour of the decks, checking the rigging, the furled sails, the guns lashed in double rows along the frigate's sides. Mounting the stairs to the quarterdeck, he solemnly doffed his hat, then strode abruptly to the helm, where Wenham stood beside the wheel, the tips of his jutting ears already red with cold.

Wenham's shocked gaze roved his captain's face. "Er, how ye feeling this morning, sir?"

"Fine and proper, thank you, Mr. Wenham. We shall be getting under way shortly, so please see to it that *Bold Marauder* does us proud this day."

On the gun deck below, Skunk and Rhodes swapped puzzled glances. Aside from a tiredness around his eyes and a slight swelling on his cheek, their commanding officer looked right as rain.

"Now what?" Elwin hissed from the rail.

"Shut up and look busy, else ye rouse his suspicions. He'll be lookin' for the girl soon enough," snapped Rhodes.

"Why would he? He gave the order for you to put her ashore."

Rhodes just smirked and caught the eye of several nearby seamen, who also were hard pressed to contain their guffaws.

But the Lord and Master seemed more concerned about his frigate than he did about the hellion who'd laid him out cold on the deck of his own cabin. He glanced up at the wind-whipped pennant, then at the feral-faced midshipman, Hibbert, standing faithfully beside Wenham.

The middie's uniform was stained and filthy, as if it had never been washed. Christian eyed it flatly, then pulled out a chart tucked near the binnacle.

"I trust you have another uniform, Mr. Hibbert?"

"Several." The youth's tone was impertinent, his eyes challenging, for he hadn't recognized the dangerous, silky tone of his captain's words. "Down in my sea chest ... *sir*."

The tone in which he said the last word was as insulting as if he hadn't used the respectful form of address at all, and the boy, snickering, glanced slyly at Skunk for approval.

Christian was still unrolling the chart, his gaze moving over it. "Then pray, go change out of those rags and into something clean, and report back to me immediately." He looked up, his eyes now cold and angry. "By God, this is a king's ship, damn you. Take some pride in that fact—and in yourself, for that matter!"

He looked back down at the chart. "Mr. Rhodes? A moment, please."

The second lieutenant, very aware of the suddenly anxious looks of his shipmates, strode to the helm. He touched his hat. "Sir?"

"That—*Irishwoman*." The Lord and Master did not look up. "Did you see her safely ashore this morning?"

"Aye, sir," Rhodes lied, without the slightest twitch of an eyelid.

"Very well, then." The captain ran his finger over the chart, his hat casting the paper in shadow. "Go forward and take charge of the capstan, please. And, Mr. MacDuff? I would like you to man the mizzenmast with those who are the least nimble—the older fellows, the new recruits, and, of course"—he grinned fleetingly—"the terrified. There is also a sloppily coiled line on the gun deck that is sure to foul itself. See to it, please."

Ian bobbed his head and rushed away, but his companions were not so genial. Out of the corner of his eye Christian could see them gathering in groups, muttering amongst themselves and casting rebellious glances his way. Towering over the lot of the buggers was Arthur Teach.

Christian marked his place on the chart and glanced up, his gaze steady and unwavering as he met the hostile eyes of the big seaman. "Mr. Teach? We are not in engagement with an enemy. Therefore, I see no need for three pistols, five knives, a cutlass, and"—his eyes narrowed and he lost his place on the chart—"pray, what *is* that ghastly thing you are carrying?"

Without warning, that "ghastly thing" came hurtling through the air with vicious intent. The Lord and Master ducked a moment before the tomahawk would have taken off his head, and the weapon slammed into the mizzenmast behind him.

The ship went dangerously still. Even the gulls overhead fell silent.

"Jesus," someone whispered.

The captain straightened up. For a long, terrifying moment he said nothing, though he'd gone white around the mouth and his eyes began to blaze. With trembling hands, he slowly, carefully, set a pair of navigational dividers atop the chart.

Then he turned his gray stare on his assailant.

Teach looked away.

The big Jamaican bosun, faithful as ever, was suddenly there at his captain's side. Christian lowered his gaze to the chart, his expression carefully veiled, though inside he was shaking. "Hendricks," he said tightly, without looking up, "please have one of your mates escort Mr. Teach to the brig, and station a marine at the door." Cool and detached, he took a pencil from Wenham and made a notation on the chart. "As soon as we're well under way, I shall require all hands to lay aft to witness punishment."

"The *brig*?" someone yelled.

"Hell, that ain't fair!"

"How come he gets to go and not me?"

Christian lifted his head, wondering if the girl had knocked something awry inside it with the force of the blow. They *wanted* to go to the brig?

What the devil was wrong with these people?

He shook his head, trying to appear unfazed. The movement only reminded him of the headache that raged behind his eyes and the jagged cut high on his temple, carefully hidden beneath the periwig.

He felt the sailing master staring at him. "Is there a problem, Mr. Wenham?"

"Er ... no, sir."

"Then prepare to loose topsails," he snapped.

Rico Hendricks, wearing a silver whistle around his thick neck, had returned and now stood several feet away. "I checked everything, sir," he said respectfully. "No signs of foul play this time."

"Thank you, Hendricks." He turned to the sailing master. "Get the ship under way, Mr. Wenham."

Moments later, the frigate came alive as pipes shrilled, orders were passed, and the seamen, goaded by Hendricks's threats and the reminders of the rattan, scurried to carry out their captain's order. And if they hustled so, it was not in deference to their captain's authority, but in hopes of being the first from their watch to escape below—where Delight waited in the "brig."

"Heave short."

Forward, men gathered around the capstan, throwing their weight against it to the song of a chanteyman. Slowly the cable leashing *Bold Marauder* to the land began to chink and clank as it came up through the hawseholes, dripping mud, water, and weeds.

Christian's eyes narrowed.

"Anchor's hove short, sir."

He tensed, remembering yesterday's debacle. "Loose topsails, Mr. Wenham. Smartly, please."

The orders were repeated. Again came the shrill of pipes, the drum of pounding feet, and then the flapping thunder of canvas dropping from aloft.

So far, so good.

"Man the braces, please."

Christian set his jaw, keenly assessing the crew's efforts. *Frightfully incompetent,* he thought grimly. But men were scurrying aloft, sails were filling with wind, and the frigate was beginning to fidget. He nodded smartly to the sailing master.

"Up and down, sir!" came the cry from forward.

"Break her out," Christian snapped.

The anchor came wearily free of the sea, dripping mud and water and glistening in the sun. *Bold Marauder,* impatient, heeled over and began to thread her way carefully between the other vessels, her shadow sliding over them with stately grace. In the near distance, buildings shone in the morning sun, their windows glowing with pale, lemony light.

Christian gripped his sword hilt, waiting for something to break, something to foul, something to go awry. But the frigate continued slowly forward, finding speed, finding confidence, and he began to relax. Elliott would find no fault with him this day.

He glanced up at the masthead pennant, wincing as pain stabbed through his aching head. The urge to slide his fingers up and touch the gash at his temple was hard to resist, but he was determined not to show even that bit of weakness in front of the crew. The blow had been a nasty one, but soap and water, his periwig, and the shadow of his hat hid such things from inquiring eyes whose owners would be quick to mock and snicker.

They were almost out of the harbor now.

"Hold her steady, Mr. Wenham."

High above, the canvas made great, billowing curves that stole wind and sunlight both as *Bold Marauder* pushed toward the mouth of the harbor, where Christian could see several spectators standing on the headland.

Beside him, Wenham was also staring ashore, grinning and waving his hand in farewell to a group of doxies.

"See to your ship, Mr. Wenham!"

The sailing master looked at him, his eyes blank.

Firmly, Christian said, "In future, I would prefer to see more speed and skill in setting the sails. Starting tomorrow, I intend to make you all practice it until such maneuvers are performed to and beyond my satisfaction."

He thought he heard the master groan.

"I beg your pardon, Mr. Wenham?"

"Er, nothing, sir. Just a frog in my throat."

Some of the crew began filing below. Others moved out along the yards, coiled lines, sheeted sails home, or yelled encouragement to each other. His eyes critical, Christian watched them, finding their performance sloppy but acceptable. Perhaps they could do better; in all likelihood, they could not. But at least the bloody buggers hadn't dared to sabotage the ship today. A hard smile touched his mouth. Perhaps there was hope for them after all. And when they returned to England, the crew of HMS *Bold Marauder* would be something the king himself would be proud of.

That, he vowed on his very life.

Forward, the anchor was catted amidst a chorus of blasphemous oaths, and Christian sighed in relief as *Bold Marauder* showed her heels to Portsmouth.

They were free. On their way.

His smile broke into a downright grin.

And then he saw the tomahawk still impaled in the mast, and the smile faded abruptly from his lips.

AT THE APPEARANCE of the first tar—a blushing boatswain's mate holding his hat in his hands while Arthur Teach towered impatiently behind him—Deirdre decided that the brig was the last place she wanted to be.

Embarrassingly aware of the hot stares that she herself, clad in the scarlet gown of crushed velvet, was receiving, Deirdre hastily made her excuses and fled into the bowels of the ship. She stumbled through gloomy darkness, and finally ducked into a small chamber that could only be the surgeon's domain, where she sat huddled against the curved timbers of the hull.

Beneath her, she felt the ship moving. They were leaving, about to cross an ocean under nothing but God's will and Captain Lord's command, and she would probably never see Ireland again. Tears stung her eyes, and swallowing hard, she hugged her arms around her legs and bent her brow to her knees.

Ireland.

But she was not alone. She had her bag of Irish mementos beside her. She had her cross, a powerful reminder of the courage that had been *Granuaile*'s. And, she thought, running her fingers over the sensual red velvet of the gown, she had her pride.

Just touching the lush fabric reminded her of how wanton it made her look. Unbidden, she thought of the English captain.

What would *he* think if he saw her in it?

She made a noise of despair, wishing she'd killed him while she had the chance—as she had vowed, for thirteen long years, to do. Maybe she didn't have her ancestress's warrior blood in her veins after all. Maybe the dog had distracted her from her purpose when it had skittered to the captain's aid. Maybe she'd misjudged it when she'd tried to take his head off with his own sword. After all, it *had* been dark in the cabin ... it was easy to miss what should have been an easy target.

But then that other thought came to her, cold, unwelcome, and rebellious.

Maybe she hadn't really *wanted* to kill him.

No, no, no, nothing could be further from the truth! For thirteen long years she'd kept his face alive in her memory, only so that she could destroy him. Of course she wanted to kill him! She just hadn't had the chance.

But she *had* had the chance. While she'd stood over him, watching him toss in the fitful throes of a nightmare, he'd never been so vulnerable. She could have plunged his sword into his black heart and ended it right then and there. She could have gone back after knocking him senseless with the pitcher and shot him with his own pistol.

But she had not.

And in her heart, she knew that she didn't have it in her to murder anyone.

Maybe she didn't have Grace O'Malley's strength after all.

She stared morosely into the gloom of the small space in which she found herself. Beneath her, and around her, the motion of the ship grew more pronounced and she tried not to think about it leaving the relative safety of the harbor and heading out into the Channel. She tried not to think about the fact that she was about to cross three thousand miles of ocean. And she tried not to think about the fact that she might never see her beloved Ireland ever again.

Ireland.

She took a deep, steadying breath, reached into her canvas bag and withdrew the little bottle of seawater, taken from the beach at Connemara.

From home.

She set it down at her feet, drawing courage from its nearness.

Yes, they must definitely be into open sea now. The frigate's movements were no longer gentle and rocking, but a longer, deeper surge as it began to meet the long, rolling combers coming in off the ocean. Moments later, the deck tilted over as the vessel tacked, and the little bottle of water went rolling across the deck into the darkness. Deirdre, panicking, scrambled to find it. Then the ship righted herself, slowly, sickeningly, and she was flung hard against the hull, banging her elbow in the process.

She swore roundly, trying to find the bottle.

And froze.

From somewhere had come a noise. Not the squeak of a rat. Not the steady creak and groan of timbers.

But footsteps.

Her head jerked up, her curses ceasing abruptly. "Skunk?"

The footsteps were coming closer. They were not heavy enough to be Skunk's footsteps. Not heavy enough to be Ian's, even.

These were different. Precise, measured, and purposeful.

A door opened somewhere, and the dim glow of a lantern touched the dank timbers around her. She pressed back against the curve of the hull.

The footsteps came closer, steady, determined. The light grew brighter. The footsteps stopped a few feet away, and looking up, Deirdre saw only the lantern.

She couldn't see a face. She couldn't see a form. She couldn't see anything—just that raised lantern and, below it, a dark blue coat and long, hard-muscled thighs clad in white breeches.

The lantern lowered, and a man's face shone cold above it.

Captain Lord's.

Chapter Ten

"I suppose," he murmured, "that I should have known better than to trust my crew to carry out the simple order of removing you from this vessel."

Deirdre froze, unable to speak. Raw terror tingled up her spine. Her every muscle tensed for flight, but she was frozen, pinned beneath that chilling gray stare.

His face glowed amber in the flickering light of the lantern, and he looked impossibly tall and frightening from where she sat huddled against the hull. She saw his gaze moving over her, taking in the wild black curls that lay in disarray over her shoulders, the swell of her breasts, the cut of the scarlet gown—and the gown itself.

He stared at it, his eyes narrowing, as though the sight of her in it displeased him, and displeased him greatly. She didn't like the look in those eyes. There was no heat there. No warmth. And certainly no admiration for the seductive picture Delight assured her she'd make in it. Nothing but coldness, and a controlled lack of emotion that frightened her.

Somewhere in the darkness, a rat scurried.

"You are fortunate, dear girl, that my conduct is dictated by the high esteem I have for the phrase 'officer and a gentleman.' Were it not, I can assure you that you would be a very sorry creature indeed."

Deirdre wished she could shrink up in a little ball and roll into a crack in the deck flooring.

"Why are you still here?" he demanded. "This is a warship. No place for an Irish harlot."

"I may be Irish, but I'm no harlot!"

He was still staring at her gown as though it was something that had crawled out of the bilge and wrapped itself about her body. "Are you not?"

"How I despise ye," she murmured. "I wish I'd killed ye when I'd had the chance."

"Ah, yes, that. I am trying very hard to discern the reasons for your hatred of me. My crew's, I understand—they have no wish to abide by my strict codes of discipline and authority. Because I know the cause of their enmity, I can address it. Yours"—he finally lifted his gaze from her much-revealed bosom and impaled her with his glacial stare—"I don't understand. That's exceedingly unfair, don't you think?"

Her hand came up, unconsciously, to touch the cross.

"When I address you, I expect an answer," he said coldly.

"I'm a guest on this ship, not one of your crew that you can order around!"

"Guests are invited. You, dear girl, are nothing but a stowaway, and a damned troublesome one at that."

"Then turn the ship around and take me back to Portsmouth!"

"And chance a repeat of yesterday's debacle? Certainly not. We're underway, and the next landfall we make, God willing, will be Boston. In the meantime, you will come with me."

He reached down to haul her to her feet, and Deirdre, panicking, shrank back against the curve of the hull.

For a long moment he simply stared at her—then he withdrew

his hand. "Do you honestly think that I intend to harm you?" he asked harshly.

The way he said it touched something deep inside her, shamed her, and Deirdre turned her head away, refusing to meet the captain's eyes. He remained unmoving; then, slowly, he lowered his tall body down to the deck across from her, wincing a bit as he stretched his legs before him and leaned his back against the stout leg of the surgeon's operating table.

"Forgive me," he said quietly.

Suddenly he was no longer frightening. Suddenly he was no longer her worst nightmare. Suddenly, she was more confused than ever. Deirdre refused to look at him. She could feel his gaze upon her, though he said nothing.

"I may be many things," he continued, "but I am not a man who would ever harm a female."

Out of the corner of her eye, she saw him slowly, carefully, reach up and remove his hat. She saw something else out of the corner of her eye, too, and horrified, she turned her head to look. Lantern light caught the purple swelling at his temple, the cruel gash, and the dark area of newly dried blood that made a stark contrast to the whiteness of his periwig.

The sight of the wound filled her with guilt and self-loathing. She'd be damned, though, if she'd let him know it.

"So, did ye come down here to punish me?"

A smile, faint with warmth, perhaps even humor, touched his lips, and in that fleeting instant, Deirdre saw again the man who had bent down and soothed the frightened little girl she'd been thirteen years ago; she saw a man who, without that stuffy periwig and harsh demeanor, might actually be quite handsome.

Quite handsome indeed.

"You're a poor excuse for a murderess, you know. Perhaps you should take lessons from Mr. Teach."

"Why? It doesn't look like he's been successful, either."

"True enough. And *he* will have to be punished, I'm afraid."

Unbidden, her gaze traveled up the proud breadth of his chest and shoulders, the handsome planes of his face ... the purple-and-red gash at his temple. She winced, and it was all she could do not to reach out and soothe the wound with her finger. "If Mr. Teach is to be punished ... why not *I*?"

"You were frightened. You acted in self defense. Mr. Teach, I'm afraid, was far more determined and calculated in his efforts to dispatch me."

"Ye think the sword nearly taking yer head off wasn't determined or calculated?"

"I think, foundling, that had you truly wanted to kill me, you would have found a way to succeed."

"I'm going to try again," she vowed, trying to convince herself. "And again and again."

"In that case, I will consider myself duly warned."

"I mean it! I *will* kill ye!"

"Well, then, I guess I *will* have to punish you."

"You can't punish me if ye're dead."

He sat there on the deck flooring watching her, his eyes inscrutable. She held his gaze, trying to hold on to her anger and failing miserably. Something passed between them, something deep and gentle and unspoken.

Deirdre looked down, finding a sudden interest in a knot of wood near her knee.

The captain remained silent.

"Does yer head hurt so very much?" she ventured, at last.

"I daresay I'll survive."

"I nearly *did* kill ye. Any other man would be angry. Vengeful. Why not you?"

"Vengeance serves no noble purpose. And besides, how could I be angry with you?" He gave a fleeting smile, as though humor was something to which he was unaccustomed. At her confused look, he added, somewhat jokingly, "My dear girl, I am plagued by nightmares. They make it hard for me to find rest, let alone sleep.

Thanks to you, this was the first time in five years that I've slept so soundly."

"Do ye want me to be hitting ye again, then?"

He actually laughed. "The rest is not worth the headache, thank you. And the next attempt on my life will have to merit a punishment, I'm afraid. Poor Mr. Teach is already in the brig, awaiting his."

She made a sudden choking noise.

"Did I say something wrong?"

"He's in the *brig?*"

The captain frowned. "Pray, what is it about this brig—"

"Nothing!" she cried too hastily. "Nothing a'tall!"

The gray eyes narrowed.

"'Tis where the crew hid all of my—my personal belongings," she sputtered. "Ye don't want to be going in there. Ye see, I—I—" She cast about quickly for the first thing to come to mind and colored furiously. "I have my ... menses."

His face went as crimson as her gown. *"And Mr. Teach has been brought there?"*

He jumped to his feet, his long stride already carrying him across the room. Too late, Deirdre saw the bottle of precious Irish seawater, rolling back, now, across the deck flooring. Too late, she saw that his path would take him straight toward it. Too late, she knew that he would never see it—

She cried out just as his foot crunched down on the glass.

"What the devil—"

Deirdre scurried across the little room on her hands and knees, her hair spilling over her shoulders. "My *water!*" she said brokenly, desperately smearing her hands into the spreading pool of moisture as though she could scoop it back up. But it was too late. She turned anguished eyes upon the captain. "Look what ye did! That was my *water!*"

"What?"

"Ye broke my water!"

Christian stared at her, thinking she was quite mad. He clenched his hands at his sides in confusion.

"I'm sorry," he bit out, not knowing what he was apologizing for.

"Ye don't understand!"

"You are correct, I do not. But I can assure you, we have plenty of water both inside and outside of this ship, I can certainly procure more for you—"

"*It's not the same!*" She swiped at a tear. Another. "That was seawater ... from ... from—" She turned away before he could see her tears beginning to fall— "*Ireland.* "

Christian stood helplessly. He had never felt more awkward, confused and taken aback in his life. And as he stared at her unruly curls, his gaze fell again upon the cross—a heathenish ornament etched with a Celtic design and studded with emeralds. His frown deepened, became a scowl. Something tickled his memory, something distant yet near, something he was very close to recalling but couldn't quite grasp....

That cross. That hair. Those eyes—

Ireland.

Dear God above.

He stepped backward, horrified as the realization of just who this young woman was—

Thirteen long years, she had said yesterday, and he hadn't picked up on it.

Thirteen long years, she had said, and he'd thought she had been an old paramour that he'd unwittingly jilted.

Thirteen long years—and she had come back to settle the old score between them.

"Dear God, forgive me." He moved toward her, one arm outstretched, disgusted with himself for not having recognized her earlier.

"Get away from me, ye filthy English *dog.* Just *get away from me!*"

In a flash, his hand snaked out and plunged into her hair, anchoring her head so that she couldn't move. He forced her head up, studying her intently. *Yes,* he thought, in stricken dismay, *it is she. That same little Irish girl whose brother I press-ganged.*

No wonder her animosity

No wonder her vow to kill him.

She glared at him, trembling beneath his hand but unwilling to back down.

"Now, I understand," he said softly.

"What?"

"I know who you are, foundling."

Her eyes defied him.

"You're the little Irish girl from Connemara. The one with the pony ... Thunder, I believe his name was? The same little girl whose brother we took with the press gang, the same little girl who—I see—has not forgiven me these many years, but has returned to avenge that wrong."

She shut her eyes as though she couldn't bear to look at him. Thirteen long years dropped away, and he was once again the anguished lieutenant, doing a deed he had no stomach for, following an order he had no choice but to obey. Thirteen long years dropped away, and she was once again the frightened, grief-stricken little girl. Thirteen years dropped away—and came full circle.

"Why didn't you tell me?" he asked harshly.

She only opened her eyes and glared at him accusingly.

"I never quite forgave myself for what I did to you that day. It has been a source of great torment for me."

"Torment? Ye lie! I've heard yer nightmares, I've heard ye call out in his sleep, and it isn't the memory of what ye did to my family back in Connemara that tortures ye."

He stared at her, taken aback. "I beg your pardon?"

"I've *seen* the miniature of some red-haired hussy that ye keep like a shrine on yer desk! 'Tis not yer despicable deeds toward an innocent Irish family that torture ye, but yer dear, darlin' *Emily*!"

The color drained from his face. "Do not speak her name."

"Emily, Emily, *Emily*!" she spat, taking twisted pleasure in hurting him and cruelly mimicking the tortured words of his nightmare. "'I didn't mean it, Emily. Dear God, please don't take her—'"

He stepped back, away from her.

"Emily ... oh, God, Emily, *please* don't die—'"

He remained frozen, and she saw raw anguish in his eyes before the cold, frosty mask of indifference was in place once more. "It would seem," he ground out, his voice harsh and emotionless, "that my sympathy toward you was grossly misguided. My apologies."

And with that, he picked up the lantern and moved toward the door.

"Don't come near me again, or I *will* kill ye!"

He paused, turned, and regarded her for a long moment. "As you wish, my dear." His eyes were carefully veiled, the long, pale lashes masking any emotion he might have felt. "I will gladly stay away from you. In fact, the next time I consider doing you a kindness, I will resist that urge."

She glared up at him, angry, confused, and upset. "A kindness? What possible *kindness* could ye possibly think to bestow upon me?"

The English captain picked up his hat and set it down atop his periwig, covering the bruise at his temple once more. "The coast of Ireland will soon pass far off our starboard beam." His voice turned hard. "Forgive me, but I merely thought you'd like to see it a final time."

Then he turned smartly on his heel, tromped through the sad puddle on the floor, and was gone.

Chapter Eleven

Topside, every mouth slammed shut as the Lord and Master reappeared. Every eye followed him as he mounted the quarterdeck ladder, crossed the deck, and strode to the frigate's big, double-spoked wheel.

And every man knew just what had him so riled.

He had found the Irish girl.

The sailing master, standing beside him, took one look at the fury in those cold gray eyes and said carefully, "Course west by southwest, sir. Full and by."

"Very well, Mr. Wenham. We will remain on this tack until the end of the watch."

"So, er, we're not going to ... uh, head back to England?"

Christian raised a pale brow and regarded him flatly. "Pray, Mr. Wenham, whatever for? Does your little Irish stowaway rate so highly that she would interfere with the business of a *king*'s ship? I think not." He pulled out a chart of Boston Harbor, laid it on the binnacle, spread the damp paper flat with his palms and stared down at it, his gaze roving over the carefully drawn figures. "Since you are all so eager to keep her here, you can begin inconveniencing yourselves by making accommodations for her immediately. In fact, Mr. Rhodes may move himself out of his cabin so the girl may move herself in."

"H-his cabin, sir?"

Christian glanced up. "Yes, Mr. Wenham, his cabin—the one next to mine, in case you don't remember." He let the chart snap shut. "Now, where the devil is the bosun's mate?"

Ian was just coming aft, his red beard blowing in the wind. "I believe he went down to get Mr. Teach, sir—like ye asked."

"That was twenty damned minutes ago. Where the bloody hell did he *go*?"

Ian flushed and looked away. "Uh ... the brig, sir."

"Send Midshipman Hibbert to fetch the both of them this instant. In the meantime, please have all hands lay aft to witness punishment."

His words stunned the deck into silence.

"P-punishment, sir?"

"Pray, does everyone on this ship have a damned speech problem today? Yes, *punishment!*"

Ian's ruddy face paled. "But, sir, we've never had a whipping aboard *Bold Marauder* before—'tis not well the men will take tae it, sir!"

Christian gave a hard smile. "I do believe, Mr. MacDuff, that is *my* problem, not yours."

"But, *sir,* 'tis startin' a mutiny ye'll be! I beg of ye tae reconsider!"

"Do not challenge my orders, Mr. MacDuff."

Christian swung away and went to the weather side of the quarterdeck, his head pounding, his mouth tight. He had no right to take out his anger on the crew, especially not on Ian. It was the girl who deserved it, that bedeviled, wretched, *Irish* girl. It was bad enough she'd had the audacity to stow herself aboard a king's ship, *his* ship; it was bad enough that she'd tried twice to kill him. But she had insulted the memory of his dead wife—and worse, had awakened feelings he'd thought he no longer had. Even now his loins throbbed as he thought of her in that obscenely low-cut, vulgar, form-fitting, scarlet ... *gown.*

Damn her, she had no business making him feel such things. *No one* did. It was Emily he'd loved, Emily he would *always* love!

Behind him, he heard the shrill of pipes and the sudden roar of angry protest as the crew, herded by Evans's nervous marines, began to head aft. Even from here, with the wind in his face and half a deck to separate them, he heard their words.

"Bloody son of a bitch, just who the hell does he think he is?"

"We ain't never had no one whipped before!"

"So much for yer damned hero worship of him, Ian!" he heard Skunk yell. "And so much for yer damned praise for Admiralty for sending us Captain Christian Bleedin' Lord! He's a damned *fool*!"

"Cruel, high-bred, spawn of a whore! How dare he think to whip one of ours, lads! 'Tis cause for mutiny, I say! *Mutiny*!"

The word caught like flame set to black powder. "Mutiny!"

"Mutiny!"

Christian remained unmoving, even as cold fingers of dread touched his heart. Their resentment was a live thing, a rippling undercurrent of loathing that intensified with each sweep through the men now gathering aft.

Calmly, he took one last look out to sea and turning abruptly, returned to the helm. "How fares the weather, Mr. Wenham?"

The wind had risen, teasing the waves and coaxing them high; now, white foam was breaking at their crests, the spray flinging itself high over the frigate's decks with every dip and plunge of her bows. But the sailing master, his nervous gaze darting to the angry, shouting mob, appeared not to have heard the captain.

"Mr. Wenham, the weather, please!"

The big man was still staring at the massing crew. "We'll be in for a blow before nightfall, sir."

Where the devil was Hendricks? His hand sliding beneath his coat to touch his pistol, Christian looked up at the masthead pennant streaming so far above, then down at the binnacle where the needle held steady on the compass card. He nodded curtly, his eyes as gray and forbidding as the sky above. "Thank you, Mr. Wenham. I shall keep that in mind."

The bellowing of the seamen had reached a deafening roar.

"Mutiny, lads, mutiny!"

"We'll not let no captain get away with this, Hero of Quiberon or not!"

"String 'im up to the yardarm and let 'im swing!"

"Off with his bleedin' head!"

"Mutiny! Mutiny! *MUTINY!*"

Ian was there at his elbow again, his eyes desperate. The big Scot took off his cap and held it nervously in his hands, tiny beads of sweat beading on his brow. "Sir, 'tis a-beggin' ye I be tae reconsider the wisdom of having Arthur whipped! We've nae had a murder aboard this ship, but if you insist on going through with this"—he gulped and swallowed—"this—"

"*Folly,* Mr. MacDuff? Pray, do not think to deny me the one bright spot in what has turned out to be a hellish nightmare of a day."

Ian exchanged a desperate glance at Wenham. In Captain Lord, he had thought he'd finally found a commanding officer he could look up to, a commander he could *respect*—but he'd been wrong.

As one, the two officers glanced at the aloof face of the man who was about to sign his own death warrant, both knowing that the moment the dreaded cat-'o-nine-tails slashed down across Teach's back, it would be all over.

Not for Teach—but for the Lord and Master.

HEARING the rising uproar on the deck above, Deirdre, frightened, grabbed a knife from Elwin Boyd's box of instruments, picked up her skirts and fled topside, emerging breathless onto the frigid, wind-whipped deck.

Fighting to keep her balance against the ship's roll, she made her way to Midshipman Hibbert's side and grabbed his dirty sleeve.

"Hibbert! What's happenin'?"

The youth swung around, gaping and flushing at the sight of her in the blood-red dress. He saw the gooseflesh on her arms and gallantly handed her his coat. Then, regaining his composure, he said, "Our Lord and Master is about to prove his stupidity, that's what!" He watched as two frightened bosun's mates rigged a grating, their eyes darting between the captain and the swelling masses assembled aft. "You wait, he'll have a mutiny on his hands before the hour's up!"

Rhodes, passing, snapped, "He won't last that hour, mark my words! Soon's that whip comes down on Arthur's back, it's all over for him."

Gasping, Deirdre turned toward the quarterdeck. *Bold Marauder*'s captain stood at the rail, detached, aloof, and alone. Sudden unwanted fear for him drove through her heart, but she willed it away. Bleedin' wretched bastard, he deserved whatever he got!

He turned his head and saw her. Their eyes met and held. She saw pain and anger in those cold depths, detachment, and a total lack of warmth. There was no forgiveness in those eyes. None at all.

Then he turned away, leaving something awful and empty coiling in the deepest chambers of her heart.

A young midshipman, white with fear, came running up from the hatch, a leather book in his hands. He pounded up the ladder to the quarterdeck, remembered to salute it at the last minute, and handed the book to his captain.

"The Articles of War," Hibbert murmured reverently as the

Lord and Master's deep, clipped voice began reciting the unfamiliar words.

Aft, a man lunged forward, shouting, to be quickly subdued by a marine.

The captain, unfazed, never looked up. At last he closed the book with a sound like a coffin being shut for the last time, and handed it back to the nervous boy. Above, dark clouds began to gather above the mastheads but the captain seemed oblivious to the threatening storm. His gaze met Hendricks's. "Bind the prisoner, please," he ordered.

A roar came up from the crew. Teach went wild as he was dragged kicking and screaming to the grating. He twisted, his black eyes boring into the cool gray ones of the captain. "You're the scum of the earth, you vicious, bleedin' pig! So help me God, I'll have your black heart on a platter to feed to the sharks! I'll have your head on a pole to parade through the streets! I'll have—"

Christian nodded to Hendricks. "You may commence punishment."

Teach was lashed to the grating—not by the wrists as was customary, but by the ankles, in what looked to be a new method of torture.

Hendricks loosened the red baize bag and gave it to his mate.

Teach went ashen, the sweat rolling down his brow.

And the captain, leaning on his sword with his hands crossed loosely over the hilt, said nothing as the bosun's mate reached into the bag, shook it upside down, and stared at that which came slithering out to fall upon the deck.

"What the hell...." the man said, looking up as though he'd been the butt of a cruel joke.

For it was not the dreaded cat-o'-nine-tails that lay there, but an oily pile of rags.

The crew, confused, instantly quieted. There was no sound but the hiss of spray at the bows, the whine of wind through the shrouds. In the shocked, ensuing silence, Rico Hendricks threw back his head in laughter, bent, and casually tossed one of the rags to a stunned Arthur Teach. Then he turned as two bosun's mates, sweating and swearing, dragged a huge chest across the deck and up to Teach's bound feet. With his foot, Hendricks broke the latch and kicked the lid wide.

The crew stood frozen, motionless, silent.

"God strike me," someone murmured.

In the chest was a collection of axes, pistols, knives, and boarding pikes. As the crew stared, gaping with shock, the big Jamaican reached inside and handed the first weapon he found—a boarding axe—to a bug-eyed and gaping Teach.

Several feet away, the Lord and Master leaned casually on his sword and watched with faintly smiling eyes.

And then the crew of HMS *Bold Marauder* witnessed the most unorthodox—and effective—punishment the Royal Navy had ever doled out as, with each roll of the drum, an oiled rag and a weapon from the chest were given to Blackbeard's hapless grandson, and he was forced to clean every axe, knife, tomahawk, and pike it contained.

Two hours later, Teach was finally finished. Wearily, he oiled the last pistol, tossed it back into the chest, and, wiping his brow, glared up at his new captain. But in his black eyes was something that hadn't been there before—a wary gratitude, a grudging respect.

The Lord and Master had not whipped him.

The captain met his gaze. Then he picked up his fat little dog, who had come waddling up on deck to join him and, cradling her to his chest, swept the crew, staring at him in amazement and shock, with his hard gray eyes.

"I cannot abide abuse," he snapped, his voice rising over the wind. "But I *will*, by God, have obedience and respect from the lot of you. Test my patience, and I promise you that punishment will be swift—*and* fitting to the crime."

Overhead, black storm clouds came together and the first raindrops began to fall as if they, too, had obeyed the will of the Lord and Master.

His flinty gaze swept over Deirdre, passed on.

"You are all dismissed," he said coldly and, touching his hat to them, went below to his cabin.

Chapter Twelve

"Twenty-two years at sea and I ain't never seen anything like it!"

"Bloody bastard the captain is," Skunk said, putting his mug down atop the wardroom's scrubbed mess table. "Arthur'd've been better off with a whippin'! At least there's *dignity* in that!"

"Aye, dignity," Russell Rhodes muttered as he dealt a fresh hand of cards to his shipmates. He slapped his palm down atop them, holding them as the ship tilted in a steep swell and then crashed down into the trough. "'Twas a humiliation, making Arthur clean all those weapons ... Wasn't it, Arthur?"

Teach, sitting moodily in the corner with his back propped against a bulkhead, looked away, unwilling to take a stand for or against what the Lord and Master had done to him.

Or, more correctly, what he had *not* done to him. Rhodes glanced sideways at Teach. "Well, don't forget what he did to your beard, Arthur."

The big seaman looked down, his thumbs grazing the blade of his knife. But the fury had gone out of his eyes, and that had Rhodes, Skunk, and the rest of the troublemakers more than a little worried, for Teach, normally full of fire, was behaving like a tame bear in a traveling fair.

And he wasn't the only one. Ian MacDuff, still topside with the watch, had shed his Scots garb and donned a proper lieutenant's coat for the first time in anyone's memory, and the Irish girl, who'd come aboard vowing to kill their new captain, was strangely quiet, her lovely eyes troubled.

No, things were not going well at all. The Lord and Master was proving to be a cunning strategist—and no one knew quite what to do about it.

Skunk, who'd been leering at—and down—the bodice of Delight's gown, leaned over and leered down Deirdre's instead. She flushed, yanked the warm woolen shawl that Delight had given her around her shoulders and leaned away, trying to escape both his eyes and his scent. But Skunk only laughed and laid a grimy paw over her hand. "Yer lookin' a bit pale around the gills, girlie. Scared? Sick? Now, don't ye worry none 'bout this little storm. 'Tis just a mere blow and it's gonna get worse before it gets better. The ship'll be all right. After all, the Lord and Master *commands* it, eh, lads?"

Laughter met his remark but it was guarded, and Deirdre sensed that something had changed about the crew's feelings toward the captain.

Something that was changing within herself as well.

The thunder rolled again and she said a silent prayer as the ship began to climb the next towering swell, there to hang suspended before thundering down into a trough.

The captain. She closed her eyes and wiped damp palms on her skirts. Sweet Jesus, she'd feel a lot safer if she were in his presence right now, secure in his assurance that *Bold Marauder* would not go down—

Her head snapped up. Dear God, what was she *thinking*?

"The Lord an' Master," she spat, in defiance of her thoughts. "A curse on that poxy blackguard!"

"Well, I'm glad to see that not *all* of us've taken leave of our senses," Rhodes said, with a sidelong glance at Teach. "By the way, Deirdre"—his gaze dropped to her bodice, then back up again—"Elwin tells me you helped yourself to one of his knives. You wouldn't be thinking of using it for your next murder attempt, now, would you?"

"Murder attempt?" Skunk cried gleefully. "On his bloody Lordship? Why, show us the knife, girlie!"

"Aye, show us the knife!"

Slowly, she picked up her canvas bag, which she'd put protectively beside her leg. One by one, the objects came out and were carefully, reverently, placed upon the table. The loaf of Irish bread. The flagon of Irish air. The pouch of Irish sand and shells. The wool of an Irish sheep. The pebble from Irish land. Trying not to think about the jar of Irish water—which *he* had so heartlessly broken—Deirdre at last found the knife. "Here," she said, shoving it across the table toward Skunk.

"Murder weapons?" Delight asked, staring at the odd collection and grinning as her hand roved down Teach's side and over his thighs.

"No. Keepsakes from home." Deirdre said tightly, her tone of voice forbidding further discussion about the curious items she was quickly stuffing back in the bag.

Skunk grabbed the knife and held it up for all to see. "Now, have ye ever seen a finer weapon, lads?" He swung around, his raised arm overpowering them with fresh stench. Then he pressed the blade's hilt into Deirdre's hand. "Now, when his bloody Lordship comes down from the deck, ye'll be waitin' fer him in the cabin, just like ye did before. But this time ye won't fail, girlie. When he opens that door, bring yer arm back, like this." He gripped her wrist and pulled her hand up and back. "A real vicious chop to the throat oughtta do it."

"Go for his jugular," Elwin hissed, grinning.

"Aye, don't stop till he's dead and twitchin' at yer feet!"

Hibbert added, hiding a grin as he elbowed Edgar Hartness, a freckle-faced midshipman who was making his first cruise on *Bold Marauder*.

"Then plunge it into his heart for good measure!"

"But first, *do* avail yourself of his handsome body," Delight purred, smiling. "'Twould be a shame to let such a fine specimen of a man go to waste, no?"

Deirdre stared at her, temporarily forgetting her fear.

"Of course, if *you* don't want to, I'd be happy to oblige," Delight added with a wink. "I'd find great *delight* in melting our Ice Captain!"

Again thunder boomed outside, echoing up through the timbers of the ship and drowning out the sounds of their laughter. Deirdre swallowed hard, picturing hundreds, maybe thousands, of feet of cold, merciless ocean beneath them. If *Bold Marauder* went down, the sea would swallow them up like the whale had with Jonah. *Dear God,* she thought, shivering. Her very life depended on the sturdiness of a scant bit of wood and canvas, the seamanship of a crew whose competence she was already beginning to doubt, and the leadership, intelligence, and ability of a man they did not trust, did not respect, and certainly did not like.

It was his will alone that kept *Bold Marauder* from going down. His—and God's.

The ship rolled atop a particularly long swell, and Deirdre felt cold sweat prickle up her spine.

"Ye forget one tiny important detail," she said, trying to keep the terror out of her voice. "The Lord an' Master has banned me from his cabin and put me in the one next t' him. There's no way I can ambush him."

Skunk braced himself against a steep, rolling plunge and gave a dismissive wave of his hand. "That's all taken care of, girlie. Our carpenter here—where are ye, Bernie?— chopped a secret hole in the bulkhead screen between your cabin and the Lord 'n' Master's, just this afternoon. It's deck-level and just big enough for ye to crawl through, not that our fearless leader's ever gonna notice it anyhow— right, Bernie?" He clapped the beaming carpenter on the back. "Bernie here fixed it so the door opens beneath his Lordship's desk. You ought to be able to crawl in and out between the two cabins with him bein' none the wiser!"

Deirdre's mouth went slack.

"Why, that sounds like something *I'd* enjoy doing," Delight mused. "Imagine, if our bold captain happened to be sitting at his desk at the time ... I suppose that being deck-level, that would make me come out at just about the level of his love-organ. Lo, I can just *imagine* his surprise to feel slow fingers stroking his more *sensitive* parts as he was trying to work...."

Every man in the room flushed. Young Hibbert clawed at his throat, his eyes bulging as he put his hands over his groin to hide his sudden arousal.

"Here, now, Delight, ye're disturbin' the children!" Skunk cried, hooting with laughter.

"Perhaps, then, some children ought to be in *bed,* no?" Delight returned with a wicked smile and a pointed glance at young Hibbert's groin.

Her face flaming, Deirdre got up to leave.

"Here now, girlie, get back here," Skunk said, grabbing her arm. "Poor Bernie didn't go through all that trouble fer nothin'"

"Fine, then, *let* Delight do it. I despise the man, but I can't kill him. I've already tried twice."

"Ain't nothing to it," Skunk said, still gripping her arm. His eyes gleamed with mischief. "All ye gotta do is crawl through the hole, wait for yer victim, and then stick yer knife squarely in the middle of his gut—"

"Aye, carve his liver out and bring it up on a platter!"

"And his heart, too! Don't forget his blackened heart!"

Sudden, awful images crowded Deirdre's mind. Of the captain dying in a pool of blood. Of his cold eyes staring up at her in death, accusing, unforgiving.

Is that what ye really want, Deirdre?

She stared at the glittering blade in horror.

"The coast of Ireland will soon pass far off our starboard beam. Forgive me, but I merely thought you'd like to see it a final time."

"Aw, don't look so scared, Deirdre. He won't feel a thing," Skunk said, picking up the knife and forcing it between her stiff fingers. She stared at it, bracing herself against the roll of the ship and therefore missing the mischievous glance he exchanged with his shipmates. "Now, c'mon. Let's get you up there and into his cabin before he retires for the night. Hibbert, take her up, would ye?"

The middie, still staring at Delight's bosom, got up.

"I told ye, I don't think I have it in me t' commit *murder*—"

The door crashed open and Ian MacDuff poked his head inside. Water streamed from his ruddy face, his beard, his hat. "I couldnae help hearing your conversation," he said desperately. "Listen, laddies, perhaps we can reach a peace with the captain—"

"Aw, Ian, don't go gettin' all soft on us," Skunk complained, waving his hand in a gesture that released a fresh cloud of stench from beneath his armpit. "Hibbert, get the girlie up there, would ye?"

Hibbert, still staring at Delight, grabbed Deirdre's arm and bolted from the room.

Ian turned angrily toward his shipmate. "Skunk, ye go too far. I cannae permit this, ye ken?"

"Piss off, Ian. Ye know as well as the rest of us that the girlie hasn't the will or the guts to kill his bloody Lordship. We're just havin' a bit of sport and ye know it. Hell, if'n I was serious about wanting 'im dead, I'd do away with 'im myself." He clapped a big, meaty hand across Ian's back. "Besides, ye know none of us really want to *kill* the bastard ... we just wanna shake him up a bit. Ye know, make him a little aggravated."

"Oh, ye'll aggravate him, tae be sure. At the wee lassie's expense!"

With that, Ian stormed from the wardroom, slamming the door behind him.

At the wee lassie's expense.

He couldn't have issued a more prophetic statement.

LEAVING a master's mate and four experienced hands at the helm, Christian, exhausted, made his way through the stormy darkness toward the hatch.

He was shivering and soaked to the skin. His hat dripped a steady stream of seawater that trickled down his face and neck. His neckcloth was damp, tight and itchy against his throat, his uniform was wet beneath his oilcloth greatcoat, and he felt as though he would never get warm again.

His thoughts were as dark as the night.

Damn her, he thought, ducking beneath the hatch and clawing at his stock. How dare she taunt him with that vulgar gown fit for a prostitute? He rued the years that had turned the innocent Irish girl with the huge purple eyes into the soiled creature she'd become.

Emily's face rose up in his memory, and he was suddenly ashamed of himself for thinking of the Irishwoman. For feeling the resultant stab of lust. His eyes hard, he stalked through the darkness, hating himself for such carnal desires, resenting the girl for causing them. She had no right. She *had no right*!

The storm sounded furious down here, the tattoo of rain thrumming against the quarterdeck nearly deafening him. The frigate rolled beneath his feet, lurched upright. But his steps were sure, his balance secure—until he reached the door of his cabin and nearly tripped over Evans.

He stared down at the marine, his crossbelt a dim white X in the darkness. Obviously, the thundering rain did nothing to disturb Evans's sleep. Or, his sweet dreams.

"Ah, Delight," the man murmured on a sigh.

Christian frowned, and resisted the urge to rouse the marine with a toe to his ribs. "Bugger the lot of you," he muttered. Then he stepped over the marine and stood staring at his cabin door.

It loomed ominously in front of him.

He rubbed his chin, thinking.

Then, taking a deep breath, he drove his foot savagely against the wood and instinctively jumped back.

Thwaaack!

The knife slammed harmlessly into the doorframe.

Evans shot to his feet, blinking in confusion. Ignoring him, Christian entered his dimly lit cabin. Nonchalantly, he removed his wet hat, tossed it aside, and pried the knife—a wicked, curving blade of death—from the wood.

"Really, now. Is that the best you can do?"

The girl stood in the middle of the cabin, gaping at him. Her hair hung about her shoulders and her eyes were huge pools of violet in her chalk-white face. Predictably, she reached up and curled her fingers around the cross.

"I ... I missed."

Shedding his dripping oilcloth, Christian brushed past her, went to his table, and poured a hefty measure of brandy into a glass. He raised it to his lips, watching her. "Indeed."

Deirdre saw no anger in those frosty depths. Nothing but a strange, dark heat, and a flicker of something that might have been amusement.

"Next time I won't miss!"

"Oh?"

"Next time I'll ... I'll—"

"Save it," he said, pulling a blanket off his bed and wrapping it around himself before settling wearily into a chair. As he raised his glass and took another sip of the brandy, Deirdre saw that his hands were red and raw with cold.

She bit her lower lip, staring at those hands.

"It saddens me," he said at length, "that in the thirteen years since our last encounter, you seem to have turned into a woman who sees no better outlet for her charms than a ship full of men who do not know the meaning of the term *gentleman*. I have tried to conduct my actions, and my thoughts, in a gallant and honorable way, but it appears that you are determined to break me."

"I don't know what ye're talkin' about."

"Do you not?" He made a noise of disgust. "What woman wears a whore's gown and pretends such ignorance as to its purpose?"

"It's not *my* gown," Deirdre muttered, looking away. "One of the um ... crew, gave it to me since all I had were the boy's clothes I came aboard in." She looked up at him then, her eyes defiant. "I'm sure ye'd be even more disdainful if I donned shirt and breeches."

The captain just raised a brow and took another sip of his brandy.

She stared mutinously back at him, saying nothing.

Finally, he sighed and put his glass down. "I think it's time you tell me exactly why you're on this ship. Surely it's not just to avenge your brother's press-ganging by murdering me. That could have been safely accomplished ashore without your having to subject yourself to an ocean crossing. Therefore, it must be the ocean crossing itself that you sought, not my demise." His gaze was steady, gray, penetrating. Why?"

"I need to get to America."

"And what could one homesick Irishwoman possibly expect to find in the colonies?"

"My cousin, Brendan."

"America is a big place, Miss...."

"O' Devir. Deirdre O' Devir." She watched as the fat little dog suddenly appeared and jumped up into the captain's lap, turning once, twice, around before settling herself into a ball atop his blanketed legs. It didn't escape Deirdre's notice that he slid a hand beneath the dog's body, trying, perhaps unobtrusively, to warm it. "America may be big, but I already know that Brendan is in Boston. Like you, he serves with the Royal Navy. He's the only family I have left ... I'm hopin' he can help me find my brother."

At mention of Roddy, a shadow passed across the captain's stark face and he reached again for his glass.

"I hate to disappoint, Miss O' Devir, but it will not be so easy for your cousin to just leave his ship in order to assist you in your endeavors. Common seamen and crew cannot just come and go at will—"

"Brendan's no common seaman. He's a captain, and he can come and go as he pleases."

The captain raised a pale brow. "A captain, you say? What ship does he command?"

"I don't know. But he's in Boston, and he'll help me."

The captain pulled his hand out from beneath the dog's body and began stroking her fur. "Perhaps," he said, gazing down at the spaniel, "I may be of some assistance, myself. "

"You?" She gave a bitter laugh. "You were the cause of all this to begin with, I don't need or want yer help, Captain Lord."

"That is a pity. I am quite happy to give it."

"I bet ye don't even remember me brother. Or what might've happened to him."

"We pressed a lot of men over the years, Miss O' Devir. You are correct in that I don't remember the fate of one Irishman taken into the service well over a decade ago. Some desert. Some fall overboard. Some succumb to disease or the rigors of life at sea, some end up beached following injury. Forgive me, but I have no recollection of your brother, especially as I was transferred from that ship to another within a month of our trip to Connemara."

"So ye're sayin' it's a lost cause?" she asked, unwilling to admit defeat.

"Not at all, but finding your brother, or what has become of him, will present certain challenges that may require more than just the well-meaning help of your cousin. I know you loathe the sight of me, but three officers, one of them highly placed, have a far greater chance of successfully locating your brother than just one Boston-based captain alone."

"Three?"

"Well, do not forget, Miss O' Devir," he said, with a little smile. "My brother is an admiral. He has access to information that your cousin and I do not."

Deirdre eyed him with suspicion and the faintest beginning of hope. He was making it awfully hard to maintain her hatred toward him, and even harder to remember her vow to kill him. She pursed her lip, watching him quietly petting the spaniel. "Ye'd really help me, then?"

"It would be the least I could do to atone for my insult against your family, Miss O' Devir."

He was still stroking the spaniel's fur. Swallowing hard, Deirdre looked down at that hand, the chapped skin and raw, red knuckles that were a quiet testimony to the hours he had spent up on the wet, open deck, in a storm, in the middle of winter on the open Atlantic, trying to keep this ship and all who were aboard it safe. Before she could stop herself, she reached out and gently placed her own hand over his.

"Maybe I won't kill ye after all," she murmured with a little smile of her own, and on an equally dangerous impulse that surprised herself as much as it did him, leaned down and dropped a kiss on his harsh cheek.

He stiffened and shut his eyes, and for the briefest moment, his hand, still cold and sticky with sea-salt, closed over hers in something like desperation. For an equally brief moment, Deirdre felt sure that he was going to kiss her.

But no. He released her, the moment was—thankfully—gone, and Deirdre, confused and shaken, fled the cabin for the safety of her own.

Chapter Thirteen

She awoke in Rhodes's cabin, in Rhodes's bunk, and in total darkness.

Alone.

Outside, the storm rumbled, the deep, reverberating tremors of thunder shaking the very timbers of the ship.

Deirdre couldn't see the lightning, and somehow, that was worse. Against her shoulder the bulkhead pressed, cold and damp, and she realized, in the disorienting darkness, that the frigate was heeled hard over on her side.

She could hear fresh torrents of rain whipping across the deck above. Beneath her the ship rolled heavily, creaking, groaning, and straining in the pounding seas. Shivering with cold and fighting panic, Deirdre groped for her canvas bag and, pulling it close, wrapped her arms around it and pressed it to her madly pounding heart.

Thunder crashed again, close, very close, and the bunk vibrated eerily against the bulkhead.

In pitch blackness, she swung out of bed and, gripping the bunk, balanced herself as the frigate rose, seeming to hang suspended before crashing down into a seemingly bottomless trough with a force that nearly knocked her off her feet.

Terror filled her. Wind screamed, and the ocean roared just outside and she decided that if she were going to die, it wasn't going to be down here, trapped all alone in a tiny cabin in the dark. Timing her movements with the violent ones of the ship, she stumbled toward the door, sick with fear and desperate for the comfort of someone, anyone—

Him.

It opened just before her hand hit the latch.

He stood there, holding a lantern, his eyes panicky, his face pale.

"Thank God you're awake."

For one brief, crazy moment she almost flung herself into his arms with relief; instead, she braced herself as the frigate rolled and crashed yet again into another trough, making Deirdre wonder how much of a beating the ship could take before she broke apart and sent them all to the bottom of the Atlantic. "Of course I'm awake," she snapped. "If we're all goin' to die, I'm not about to meet me maker with my eyes closed."

"It's Tildy," he said, seizing her wrist with an urgency that scared her. "Will you come have a look at her?"

"Tildy?"

"My dog." He glanced anxiously over his shoulder, back toward his cabin. "There's something wrong with her. She's hiding in the corner, panting ... she's staring into space and whining—" His throat worked and for a brief moment, she wondered if this cold, taciturn Englishman who had himself so tightly under control, was going to fall apart before her eyes. "Forgive me, but I did not know who else to summon."

"Let me get my coat."

She tossed the heavy garment over her gown and clung to his arm as, with a sure-footedness that she herself lacked, he guided her back to his cabin. The wind shrieked in demonic fury outside, and why he wasn't terrified that they were all going to die was beyond Deirdre's comprehension. Then he pushed open the door to his cabin and held the lantern aloft, and in its dim glow, Deirdre saw the little dog lying wedged into a corner, her eyes large, dark pools of fear and pain.

The instant Deirdre saw her, she knew what was wrong.

"She's dying, isn't she?" the captain said, his voice hoarse with emotion. "My God, I knew I should never have subjected her to the rigors of a ship—"

"She be whelpin'," Deirdre said flatly.

"What?"

"Havin' puppies."

"Puppies?"

"Aye, puppies." Despite herself, she couldn't help but grin at his stricken, helpless look. "Animals often pick storms to be birthin' their wee ones," she said, kneeling down to stroke the spaniel's heaving sides. "Why don't ye be gettin' me some blankets so I can make her comfortable?"

"Puppies...."

"The blankets, Captain?"

He stumbled as the ship pitched violently beneath him and suddenly seemed to recover. "We can't have puppies here! *This is a King's ship!*"

"I don't think ye have a choice, and neither does yer bleedin' king. Now get me the blankets," she commanded, sliding her arms beneath the dog and lifting her gently as the captain grabbed a blanket from his bed and hastily spread it on the deck against the bulkhead.

Deirdre petted the spaniel, trying to soothe her. She was aware of the captain's gaze on her back, grateful, worried, and yes, relieved. He, proud commander of a warship, had turned to *her* in his hour of need, humbling himself and placing his trust in her abilities. *Hers.* She was suddenly assailed by feelings she couldn't explain, and as he came to stand behind her, leaning over her like a protective father, she felt the searing heat of his body against her own and flushed hotly.

Turning, she snapped, "Really, Captain,. this won't be a pretty sight. Go have yerself a tot o' rum or somethin'."

He pressed closer, his worried gaze on the laboring dog. "I've seen plenty of blood in my life."

But when Tildy's whimpers progressed to sharp cries of pain and the first tiny puppy emerged some ten minutes later, pink and bulging in its sac, the mighty Lord and Master went as white as his shirt.

Deirdre glanced behind her to see him leaning heavily against the bulkhead.

"If yer goin' to be faintin', I'd appreciate it if ye'd do it elsewhere," she said, cleaning the pup's mouth and nose with a corner of the blanket and placing it against one of Tildy's swollen teats. But he didn't move, and when Deirdre looked up at him, she saw something unguarded and vulnerable in his eyes that swept in under her guard and went straight to her heart.

She was suddenly warm, too warm, beneath her clothes.

Something caught in her chest and she looked down at the pup, recognizing the feeling for what it was. A thawing. A sudden rush of feeling for this man who was her enemy, this man she had professed to hate, this man who was causing her more confusion than she had thought a body could possibly hold.

"Aye," he murmured. "Perhaps I shall go relieve the officer of the watch."

She tried to hold on to her resentment toward him. But it was no use. She gazed down at the little white dog and softly, murmured, "Yes, do. And perhaps when ye come back ye'll have a whole new family to welcome."

He said nothing, just looking at her for a long, quiet, moment; then he picked up his coat and left the cabin, his footsteps quickly lost to the howl of rain and wind and storm. Deirdre took a deep, shaky breath and shut her eyes, and beneath the frenzied shriek of the wind outside, she heard the soft, kitten-like mews of the tiny puppy, this stalwart evidence of new and abiding life oddly comforting and reassuring in the midst of the tempest that roared around them. She had witnessed the miracle of birth before—many times, in fact—but never had it seemed so precious, so holy, so achingly beautiful.

A sudden warmth flooded her and she hugged her arms to her breasts, thinking again of Captain Lord, and the way he had looked at her just before he had left the cabin. But just then, Tildy stiffened in pain and crying, began to push out another tiny form, leaving Deirdre no time to ponder the new and confusing feelings of her heart.

An hour later it was over and the spaniel, exhausted, was quietly licking the three little newborns who sucked greedily at their mother's teats. Deirdre, her eyes misty with emotion, reached out and touched each tiny, squirming body. For a brief moment Tildy lifted her head and seemed to smile in gratitude; then the little dog's head fell back to the blanket, and with a heavy, satisfied sigh, she closed her eyes.

Deirdre rose to her feet. Her work here was done. Fighting the violent tilt of the deck, she staggered to the door, opened it, and in the gloom, permeated only by a crazily swinging lantern, saw Evans blinking sleepily.

"Summon yer captain and tell him he's the proud da o' three wee babes," Deirdre said. Then, with a last glance over her shoulder at Tildy, she turned and stumbled back to her cabin where she fell, exhausted, into her bunk.

THE STORM CONTINUED FOR A WEEK, pounding the frigate and battering her beneath mountainous waves and blinding sheets of rain, snow, and sleet. The pumps labored day and night to rid the bilge of water that streamed down through the hatches and came in through seams that were hard-pressed to stay tight against such an onslaught; some of the men got seasick, and the crew, still wrapped in their drenched clothes, tumbled into their damp hammocks after their watches, cold, wet, and unable to do more than close their eyes and succumb to exhaustion.

As for the captain himself, he was grateful for the storm. It kept his tormented mind occupied, for with the ship demanding every bit of his attention, he had little time to think of the girl he no longer trusted himself around, the girl whose eyes followed him wherever he went, the girl who was managing, somehow, to vie with his beloved Emily for the affections of his tightly guarded heart. Such feelings unnerved him and he began to go out of his way to avoid her, until the dark purple eyes grew confused, and then angry with hurt.

But he had no choice. She was too young for him. She was too innocent for him. He had done her a grievous wrong thirteen years ago, and it was far better for them both if she hated him. He *preferred* that she hate him. But as the second week dragged by, he found himself pausing for long moments outside her cabin in the dead of night, laying his palm against the wood as though he could reach inside and touch her warm skin, her hair, her softly beating heart.

Then he would turn away and stumble wearily to the loneliness of his own cabin—and the nightmares that haunted his troubled sleep—never knowing that, only several feet away, the Irish girl pined for him as much as he did for her.

THE STORM DID NOTHING, however, to put a damper on Delight Foley's *business*; indeed, she found such twisted and convoluted motions on the frigate's part a boon to her inventiveness when it came to sexual pleasure—and positions. A connoisseur of carnal ecstasy, Delight loved her adoring flock of lusty seamen, though she insisted that she would only allow Skunk near her if he dragged a bar of soap on deck with him during a particularly violent bout of rain.

Two and a half weeks after they'd left Portsmouth, Deirdre finally sought out Delight.

"Deirdre, *cherie*!" The girl grinned and flung the door open wide. A pungent blast of French perfume hit Deirdre in the face, nearly suffocating her. "Do come in! I was just reading about a new position in my manual—here, have a look!" Blushing, Deirdre pushed the book away, for lately her own thoughts had been dominated by the captain—and with strange, wicked notions that brought odd sensations to her womanly parts.

"Delight, I have to talk to ye."

"Lo, Deirdre, I just *knew* something was troubling you. You've been so quiet lately. Sit down right here," she said, patting her bed, "and tell Delight what the problem is."

Deirdre eyed the scented sheets, the spread of red satin— and took the chair instead. She hung her head and twisted her hands together, suddenly uncomfortable and shy.

The other woman came to her, put her hands on her hips, and tilted her head to one side. "Let me guess," she said brightly, tapping a nail against a pearly tooth. "It's our handsome Lord and Master, no?"

Deirdre's cheeks flamed and she looked away. "Is it that obvious?" she asked wretchedly.

"Lo, Deirdre, when you're older you will learn how to hide the lust in your eyes. It's plain as day that you feel for the man."

Deirdre stared down at the floor. "I don't want to feel for him. He's English. He press-ganged my brother and brought years of pain to my family. He's cold and emotionless and he has nightmares that keep me awake half the night. I want nothin' more than to hate him, but I can't." She made a helpless motion with her hands. "Saints alive, Delight, what am I goin' to do? I can't stop thinkin' about him."

Even now, she thought of her reaction when he'd come into his cabin as she'd been feeding Tildy the night before. The lantern light had shone down on each glimmering strand of his hair, making the damp, slightly wavy locks so pure and pale a gold they were almost silver. His hair was the color of beach sand on a hot day, curling boyishly behind his ears and at his nape, and she had almost forgotten herself and reached out to touch it just to see if it was as soft and crisp as it had looked.

She looked up to find Delight gazing at her with a knowing expression on her face. "You're in love with him, aren't you?"

"*Love?*"

"There's no use denying it, sweetie. He's a fine man, strong and chivalrous, though a bit too righteous and noble for his own good. But mark me, there are none finer on this vessel, perhaps none finer, even, in England. You want *my* advice?" She laughed. "Set your sights on him, *cherie*. He is a good catch, your man."

Deirdre dragged her head up. "But, Delight, he's not interested in me. I'm Irish. A commoner. He's an English gentleman, master of a king's ship, well learned an' educated."

"So?"

"He avoids me."

"So?"

"He ... he's got rules he lives by, Delight. He's ... he's an officer and a gentleman. I'm just—"

"The woman he could fall in love with."

Miserably, Deirdre shook her head. "Nay. He's in love with someone else. Someone called Emily."

"Aaah," Delight nodded, knowingly. "His dead wife." She raised a brow at Deirdre's surprised look. "Oh, don't look so shocked! Rico told Ian, who told me. Happened five years ago, it did. The poor dear died in a fire. But really, Deirdre, do not let *that* stop you. Whatever his thoughts are toward his dead wife, she can't warm his bed at night. You, on the other hand—"

Deirdre, her face hot, was already reaching for the door.

"Thank ye, Delight. Ye made some things clear in my mind, ye did."

Delight just shrugged and smiled brightly. "Well, anytime you want advice, you come here to me. And when the time comes for you to lure the Lord and Master into your bed, you just let me know. I have all kinds of *devices* to make the task go easy for you, no?"

On that note, Deirdre went scarlet and fled the brig, Delight's amused laughter ringing in her ears.

EMILY.

His wife came to him as she had nearly every night for the past five years, waiting until he was asleep before inflicting this same hell upon him that he was doomed, it seemed, to never escape.

Christian's blood went cold and he trembled, curling himself beneath the blankets and hearing himself whimpering deep in his throat. But there was no hiding. No escaping.

"Emily?" He was dreaming, he *knew* he was dreaming, but nevertheless it was all happening again, just as it had that long-ago night in the distant English countryside, and there was nothing, absolutely nothing, he could do to change it. He reached out for her in the darkness, knowing, of course, that he would find her side of the bed empty.

He swung himself out of bed, the floor cold against his feet. After so many months at sea, he was used to a rolling deck, not cold marble, plush Persian rugs, and a solid floor that did not move. But no, he was not aboard his ship, but at home at the fine country estate in Hampshire that had been in the Lord family for centuries.

He stood for a moment, swaying in the darkness and getting his bearings. Everything about this room felt cold—not unlike the way *she* had behaved toward him since he'd dropped anchor in Portsmouth a week before.

"Emily?"

He stumbled along, slightly disoriented, the ornate furniture with which she had filled their bedroom looming as huge, dark shapes in the gloom. The furniture was ugly and far too grand for his tastes, but she had wanted it, and it wasn't in his heart to deny her.

"Emily?" he said again, beginning to grow worried. With her legs crippled from a childhood illness, she couldn't have gone far. He paused, listening. From downstairs came the steady *tick, tock* of a clock; from beyond the window, the shriek of a night bird. Land sounds, unfamiliar to his mariner's ears. Outside, an owl hooted, once, twice.

Dread snaked up his spine. Where the devil *was* she?

It was as his hand groped for a flint that he heard it: from downstairs, the tinkle of her laughter.

He froze, the blood chilling in his veins.

His hands were shaking as he tried to light a candle. Shielding the flame and gripping the candle so hard that his knuckles went white, he crept out of the room and down the twisting marble staircase.

Voices came drifting through the hall. "Really, James, I prefer it when you touch me there ... oh, yes, *there*. Oh ... *oh, yes...*"

Shock paralyzed him. And then, anger that blinded him to all thought, all reason, all caution. He rushed forward. His foot slammed into the parlor door and sent it crashing back against the wall.

By the dim glow of candlelight, he saw it all. Emily on the sofa, her hair spread beneath her, her long, frail legs opened wide, her thighs wrapped around her lover's back as he pumped and strained madly above her.

With a hoarse cry, Christian charged forward.

❧

DEIRDRE O'DEVIR AWOKE WITH A START.

Something had roused her. She sat up in bed, her heart pounding

The Lord and Master.

Through the canvas screen, she heard him thrashing in his bunk, his hoarse cries blotting out even the moans of the wind and sea outside.

Deirdre flung the covers aside, left her cabin, and stepping over the snoring sentry posted just outside the captain's door, padded on silent feet across the checked canvas that covered the deck planking.

This cabin offered the only windows on the ship, and through them, she could see that the storm clouds were parting. The full moon shone brightly, and by its silver glow she saw the English captain writhing in torment in his bed. The sheets were twined around his legs, sweat sheened his chest and his mouth was open in a silent scream.

She stared down at him, the barely remembered face of her brother rising up before her eyes to remind her of her forgotten vow.

Kill him, Deirdre. Kill him ... remember what he did to us. To you and our mam ... Remember your vow, *Deirdre!*

"No!"

She clapped her hands to her ears, squeezing her eyes shut and shaking her head as she tried to push the images away, to block them out.

Kill him.

Never would she find the Lord and Master more vulnerable.

"I *won't!*" she cried, clawing at her cheeks.

"Emily," he moaned, his voice deteriorating into awful, choking sobs that tore at her heart. "Dear God, Emily...."

Her hands shaking, Deirdre took a deep breath and picked up the brass dividers that lay glinting in the moonlight on his desk.

Then she moved toward the bed.

"I'LL SEE you in hell, by God!"

Christian dove forward, hearing his wife's scream as her lover lunged to his feet and fled from the room. Blinded by rage, Christian pounded after him, her desperate voice echoing behind him.

"If you weren't at sea all the time, you wouldn't have forced me to take a lover! If you were half the husband you ought to be, I would never have strayed! Dammit, Christian, *don't do it!*"

Black rage. His breath roaring through his lungs. The man's pale, naked form rounding the corner into the hall, racing through the elegant drawing room, stopping only long enough to snatch a lamp from the wall and hurl it at Christian with all his strength—

The room exploded into flames. Fire whooshed up the curtains in a deafening roar, sending Christian reeling back, away from the wall of intense heat. The rugs went up in an inferno, and flames charged up the fine paper that covered the walls.

In minutes, the house was ablaze.

Servants, clad only in their nightgowns, raced past, screaming. Christian pounded back down the hall, hearing the roar of the fire behind him. *"Emily!* Emily, dear God, where *are* you?"

The parlor was empty.

Thick black smoke blinded him, driving the breath from his lungs. Heat blasted against his skin, his eyes, singing his hair. Coughing, he stumbled and raced on, the flames chasing him as he tore madly through the house in a desperate search for his wife.

"Emily!"

Pounding up the stairs, he crashed into the bedroom and

found nothing. He half ran, half fell, down the spiraling staircase, and it was only then that he heard her screams of terror.

"Christian! *Christia-a-a-a-an!*"

Where was she? Frantically, he kicked open doors that were already in flames. He bolted through rooms crackling with heat and engulfed in fire. The acrid stench of burning fabric, plaster, and wood seared his nose and the flames clawed at him like a live thing.

Her voice rose to a shrill scream. *"Christia-a-a-an!"*

There, huddled in a heap at the far end of the hall, he saw her, her frightened face glowing orange in the leaping flames, her frail body lying where her crippled legs had finally given out.

He raced headlong down the burning hall, her screams of terror guiding him through flames that tore at his face, smoke that stung his eyes and filled his lungs.

"Christian!"

He was almost there. *Almost there!* Another few feet and—

With a roar, a wall crashed down around him in an inferno of showering sparks and leaping flame, forever separating them.

Emily!

He heard her unholy, dying screams.

Then nothing.

DEIRDRE STOOD ABOVE THE CAPTAIN, helpless, the brass dividers forgotten. Any thoughts of avenging Roddy fled her mind as his writhing body finally quieted and he curled himself up amidst the twisted sheets, his arms over his face, his broad, strong, back to her. She was about to flee back to her own cabin when she realized that an awful sound was coming from him: harsh, racking sobs that were so desolate, so full of raw anguish that her own heart felt like it was being torn asunder.

Tears welled up in her own eyes and she stared down at him

for a long moment, seeing the Lord and Master as none of the others aboard the frigate had seen him.

Alone, tortured—and defenseless.

And suffering in a way that no person should ever have to suffer.

Deirdre bit down hard on her lower lip. Then, her heart aching for him, she peeled back the blankets, slid gently in beside him, and wrapped her arms around his heaving shoulders, holding him tightly. At last his breathing steadied, his muscles relaxed, and his anguished sobs faded until there was nothing but the sheen of tears upon harsh cheeks that shone silver in the moonlight.

Chapter Fourteen

Dawn's pink light shone through the stern windows and probed the expanse of the cabin.

Christian opened his eyes.

The deckhead beams glowed softly in the morning light. He heard footsteps just above and Ian MacDuff's gruff orders to lay the frigate over onto the other tack. Everything was well. Everything was as it should be.

Except for the woman asleep in the bed with him.

He sat up with a start and stared down at her, sudden heat pulsing through his blood. "What the devil?"

He reached out a hand to wake her and froze, stricken by her beauty, unwilling to disturb her even as he wondered what on earth had possessed her to crawl into bed with him. Thick black curls framed her face, webbed her cheeks, tangled in lashes the color of charcoal. They tumbled around her neck, swirled around pale white shoulders, and danced across the pillow. Beneath the blankets, he could see the curves of her figure blatantly outlined, and his throat went dry.

He pushed the blankets back and tried to crawl out and away, but he could not do so without waking her. The narrowness of the bunk only made the endeavor that much more difficult, and the Irish girl seemed determined, even in slumber, to capitalize on that fact. Her arm lay curled at her side, her fingers only inches from his nakedness. In dismay, he felt himself stirring.

The Lord and Master swallowed hard, as helpless as a square-rigger caught all aback.

She was wearing nothing but baggy trousers and a long shirt, probably borrowed from one of the midshipmen. It had ridden up during the night; now it lay bunched and twined around her waist, exposing a flat belly and more of her bosom than was decent. He had thought the scarlet gown to be vulgar. Now he realized that with such a shape as hers, it wouldn't matter *what* she wore.

Desire. It tore through his loins, cruel, uninvited, unwanted. It caused him to grow stiff and swollen, and he heard his breathing coming faster, felt himself breaking out in a fine sheen of sweat that wilted the sheets where they touched his skin.

The girl sighed softly in her sleep, unconsciously nestling closer to him until her fingers, resting in the pale, wiry hair between his legs, lay a mere two inches from his throbbing shaft.

He froze.

Tried to get his breathing under control.

Lust. It was nothing but lust, he told himself. Emily might have done him wrong, but *she* was his love, his only love, and always would be. He would not betray his wife by allowing his head to be turned by this Irish girl, who probably *wasn't* a doxy after all—but who could definitely mean the swift and sorry ruin of his career if he got tangled up with her.

The girl moved again, and her fingers brushed his nakedness. Christian clenched his teeth together, biting back the groan that rose in his throat. The sensation filled him with longing—and with despair, for he alone knew that he could not carry out the love act itself.

Not with Emily still coming to him every night. Not with Emily's face still rising up before his eyes at the first hint of desire for another. Not with Emily's death still filling him with raw, torturous guilt that he had been unable to save her....

But his wife's long-dead face did not appear in the haunted rooms of his mind as he tentatively reached out and, holding his breath, touched the girl's black, spiral-curling hair. It was coarse, wiry, as willful as her spirit and just as wild. His thumb began a gentle caress, crushing the lock in his fist, as something huge and painful welled up in his chest. He gently laid the long curl over her shoulder, his gaze straying down her softly rising bosom to follow the chain that lay slackly around her neck. The cross, glinting in the dawn's light, rested atop the swell of one breast, mocking him with its blatant reminder of their differences in religion.

He was Anglican.

She was Irish Catholic.

There were those who would frown upon a highly respected naval officer taking a papist to wife. There were those who would think her coarse and unsuitable as the bride of an English nobleman. There were those who would have nothing but contempt for her. Christian tightened his lips. Damn them, damn all of them who would put her, the only woman he'd so much as even *looked* at since Emily, out of his reach.

And then he realized where his thoughts had been leading.

Wife.

"Dear God," he murmured, dragging a hand through his rumpled hair.

Bride.

He shut his eyes, and broke out in fresh sweat. *Control yourself, Christian. You are an officer.*

An officer. A gentleman. As such, he was supposed to conduct himself in a stellar manner. To do otherwise would be to bring disgrace upon his king, his country, and the uniform he wore with such pride. The embarrassing debacle of Portsmouth, and being found in such a compromising position, still rankled—

and rankled deeply. Another such incident could bring about his ruin.

Desperately, he glanced at the box beneath the stern windows that the ship's carpenter had made for Tildy and her puppies. The babies were still asleep, but sensing her master's stare, Tildy raised her head and looked at him, her eyes bright.

"Ha, ha," the little spaniel seemed to say. *"Now what are you going to do?"*

His swollen arousal now lay stiff and hard against the sleeping girl's knuckles. He tensed and shut his eyes, hating himself for not getting up and making a swift exit from this bunk, this cabin. How he wished she'd move that little hand closer; how he longed to feel her soft, whispery touch moving over his aching length, stroking it, coaxing it harder and higher, until—

Sudden, violent anger slammed through him.

What the devil was he thinking? Cursing, he crawled out and away from her, no longer caring whether or not he woke her. She remained asleep. Breathing hard, he stood naked on the slightly angled deck and tried to rein in his thoughts.

His desires.

He stared out the stern windows. The sea was deep and blue and ruffled by wind, its reflection dancing against the deckhead like sunlight through a thousand diamonds. He passed the back of his wrist across his brow, then clenched his fists at his sides as his gaze crept, unbidden, back to the girl.

He was damned, he thought, damned to hell and beyond. Turning, he rushed through his morning ablutions, cursing when the razor caught his chin and raised a trickle of blood. He grabbed his wig, arranged the rolled curls over his still faintly bruised temple, and donned his uniform with a haste he hadn't shown since he'd been a fourteen-year-old midshipman who, cocky after his first night with a cheap doxy, had shown the bad sense to arrive late for his watch.

His mood black, Christian stuffed his shirttails into his

breeches, grabbed his coat, and slammed out of the cabin without a backward glance.

***

"Er, Ian? I really think you ought to have let her go for another hour or so before tacking," Wenham said, scratching his ear as he peered up at the set of the sails with a critical eye. *Bold Marauder* was quite comfortable, driving along on a larboard tack under reefed topsails and courses, but he knew that the Lord and Master would have the hands piped for sail drill as soon as he came on deck.

That would mean, of course, that the men would have to go aloft to reset the sails for the second time this morning. Wenham groaned. Why work the crew any more than needed? he thought, watching the thin curl of smoke that rose tantalizingly from the galley funnel as his stomach growled in anticipation of breakfast.

Ian puffed out his chest. "The captain left *me* in charge, Thomas," he said, hoisting his bagpipes and squeezing the bag beneath his brawny elbow. The big Scot missed the looks of alarm that spread amongst those standing nearby, for Ian's talents at playing his instrument had not improved in the slightest. "And *I* think it was time tae tack, so doona question my wishes!"

Rhodes, leaning against the rail, rolled his eyes as Ian stormed off. "The captain!" he sneered with a derisive glance at the hatch. "If he were any sort of commanding *officer,* he'd be up here on deck, seeing to his ship!"

"Prob'ly fussin' with that stupid wig," Skunk remarked.

"Or feeding treats to that sap-eyed dog," Elwin spat.

Hibbert, who'd spent a very educational hour in the company of Delight Foley, gave a sly grin. "Or tumbling the Irish girl."

A dark shadow fell over the deck. "That will be all, Mr. Hibbert."

Hibbert's head shot up, the blood draining from his face at

the sound of that icy, dangerous voice. Abruptly, the officers snapped off guilty salutes; then all turned hastily away and pretended to be engrossed in their duties.

Christian wasted no time in pleasantries. His jaw hard, and the very wig they were ridiculing carefully combed and tied at his nape beneath the wide brim of his cocked hat, he crossed to the weather side of the ship and stared out over the brilliant azure sea. The wind was cold and biting. Spray was almost crystalline. Foam rode high on the tumbling waves and flecked the ocean for as far as the eye could see. He stared up at the masthead pennant, licking like a serpent against fluffy white clouds that raced high above the frigate's yards.

The ship nosed into a swell, and a huge sheet of spray drove over the rail and drenched his coat. He heard someone howl with laughter before Ian's sharp reprimand abruptly silenced him.

He ignored them, though his eyes narrowed and a vein throbbed at his temple. Let them have their little fun. They'd learn, soon enough, that his patience for putting up with nonsense was limited. Squaring his shoulders, he strode to the wheel, keenly aware of the hostile glances the two helmsmen bestowed on him as he studied the compass.

Wenham was right. Ian *could* have left the frigate on the starboard tack for another hour.

He glanced at his first lieutenant, thinking to mention the matter to him. But there was such a hopeful look in Ian's eyes, such an anxious look about his mouth, that Christian, despite his black mood and better judgment, decided to let the matter go.

He saw Skunk, his grimy hair caught in a long pigtail at his nape and hanging between his beefy, tattooed shoulders. Several of the other troublemakers—Teach among them—stood nearby, carefully upwind of the big gunner. Skunk's gaze was on Christian. So was Teach's, Wenham's, and that of every tar from bowsprit to taffrail.

Watching him. Judging him. Searching for some flaw in his

character, some weakness they could exploit. Christian smiled, though his jaw tightened and his sharp gaze raked over them with the keenness of a well-honed blade. They would find no flaw to attack, no weakness to exploit.

And, he thought wryly, no blemish upon his behavior. Regardless of how or why the Irish girl had ended up in his cabin, he had not taken advantage of her.

He cast an appraising eye over his command. Ian had seen fit to at least *try* to make the frigate look smart after the buffeting she'd taken during the past two and a half weeks; her sails were drawing well; the guns were lashed down tightly and sparkling with spray; the men were bright-eyed and ruddy-cheeked, and all turned out in proper uniform, and the decks—

Christian's jaw fell open and his eyes widened in shock.

"Mr. MacDuff!"

The big Scotsman's head jerked up at the sharp tone of the Lord and Master's voice and instinctively he tightened his elbow over the bagpipes. "Yes, sir?"

Christian was staring, incredulously, around him. "Who had the morning watch?"

Ian paled. "Er ... uh, no one, sir...."

"No one? And who has the watch now, Mr. MacDuff?"

"Er, Mr. Rhodes, sir," Ian said lamely. "Why?"

The crew exchanged nervous glances, wondering what had so riled their captain.

They soon found out. "By God, *look* at these decks! Torn cordage, seaweed, slime—why, this is an *embarrassment,* not only to me, but to this ship!"

Nobody moved.

He glared at his officers, the anger in his eyes causing them to take an involuntary step backward. "What the bloody deuce is the matter with you all? This is a *king's vessel!* Take some pride in that fact, and in yourselves!"

They stared at him, totally uncomprehending.

"This is a king's vessel!" Hibbert mimicked, smirking.

"Silence, the lot of you!" Christian roared, his eyes hard beneath the shadow of his cocked hat. He took a deep breath and willed control into his tone. "Mr. Rhodes, set your people to scrubbing, and when they have finished, have them wash down the deck with seawater and vinegar."

A low grumble of protest swept through the crew as the sharp scents of frying pork wafted up from the galley and drifted on the wind. "But, sir," Ian ventured, trying to intervene, "what about breakfast?"

"Breakfast will keep, Mr. MacDuff. In future, perhaps the crew will remember that if they wish to break their fast on time, such *mundane* tasks as scrubbing the deck are to be performed before sunup!"

Such a threat was enough to send even Skunk running for a mop. Christian watched the crew attack the job with a vengeance. *Another small victory in this little war,* he thought smugly. And he hadn't even had to enlist the help of his bosun.

Speaking of Rico....

He descended the quarterdeck companionway and strode among the men, moving upwind of Skunk. The gunner was attacking the grime from beneath the hulking shadow of a cannon, grumbling as he scrubbed. Rhodes looked over at Christian, his eyes contemptuous. Hibbert, his back toward him, was supervising a group of swearing, laboring seamen, his hands on his hips, his uniform unacceptably filthy. Christian set his jaw and, coming up behind the youth, clapped a hand over his scrawny shoulder.

"Mr. Hibbert?"

The midshipman whirled, paled, and shrank back.

"Have you seen my bosun?"

Hibbert's face changed, becoming smug. "Aye."

"That's aye, *sir,* and don't you forget it lest I box your ears and send you to the damned brig!"

"The brig? I would like that, sir—"

Too late, Hibbert realized his mistake. The Lord and Master's cold gray eyes narrowed. The ship quieted, the mops stopped, and only the hiss of spray at the bows broke the sudden silence.

"The *brig.* 'Twould seem that is a most *popular* area of the ship, is it not, Mr. Hibbert? Pray, is there something down there that is escaping my attention?"

"N-no, sir! Not at all!"

"We shall see," Christian said coldly, and abruptly turned on his heel.

The crew froze. As one, every sailor, every officer, and every marine watched him go, each man's eyes desperate, anxious, and stricken.

The Lord and Master was headed for the hatch. The Lord and Master was going to find Delight. The Lord and Master was going to put a swift and abrupt end to any chance of enjoyment this cruise might harbor.

For the crew of HMS *Bold Marauder,* it was the beginning of the end.

DOWN INTO THE bowels of the frigate he went, descending hatches, moving down companionways, his stride never faltering.

The brig. It loomed in front of him, its door shut tight. Without pausing, the Lord and Master drew his pistol, lifted the latch, and, placing a palm carefully against the door, pushed it open.

He blinked once, twice.

The pistol fell from his hand and glanced painfully off his toe.

On the bulkheads were enough mirrors to send his reflection back at him from every point of the compass. On the deck was a rich purple-and-red carpet strewn with pillows. In the middle of the space, draped in sheets of dark red satin, was a bed.

And reclining on the bed was a woman.

She was reading aloud, in French, and appeared not to see him. But he saw her. Wickedly long, shapely legs, bent at the knees and lazily spread to reveal enough of her to make his face flame. Black garters that disappeared beneath the hem of a short shift. Long fingernails tapping the book and a sultry, husky voice that was meant to be felt, not heard.

If Captain Christian Lord was stunned by the discovery of what the "brig" contained, he was downright shocked by the discovery of what its occupant was reading. For he understood French, and understood it well, and what the woman was reading was no dignified work of an educated scholar.

"'....After tying your man up, preferably to all four posts of your bed with a length of rope'—hmm, being a ship, *that* should be an easy commodity to come by!—'move your tongue over every square inch of his skin, thoroughly wetting him and then blowing coolly upon the wet areas until he is hot and hard and begging for release. Work every area of his body, moving your tongue slowly into the folds of his ears, sucking on his earlobes, and then letting your tongue drag down his neck, over his shoulders, lapping his nipples, even the inside of his navel. It is very important to pay particular attention to this area before proceeding to his—'" She stopped, lowered the book, and without faltering, purred, "Why, hello, Captain Lord. *Do* come in and join me. I've been waiting for you."

He stared, slack-jawed and unable to move.

"What, is our bold and handsome commanding officer shy and inhibited?" She laughed, a rich, husky sound, then set the book aside and came to her feet.

She crossed the room in a slinky, sinuous float, her eyes never leaving his. In their blue depths was an invitation that had his heart pounding long before her nails even touched his waistcoat, his shoulders. She dragged them seductively down his chest, flicking them around each gold button and undoing them as she went. "Aah, such a handsome uniform ... a sea warrior you are, no? Such a brave and noble man you must be ... here, darling, let Delight show you how much she *appreciates* brave and noble men...."

Christian recovered enough to shove her away. "How the bloody *hell* did you get aboard my ship?" he thundered.

"Lo, I just *love* a man when he's angry," she purred, sauntering around behind him and letting her hand rove down his spine. "Makes my love-juices flow, no? Here, darling, take my hand and let me lead you to my bed ... I do need someone on whom to practice my new techniques...."

"Get away from me!"

"Ta, Captain, you hurt poor Delight's feelings with such words! You do not have to act the part of a gentleman with me, you know? Let me touch you ... let me taste you ... let me do things to you with my tongue that you wouldn't dream could be done. Wouldn't you enjoy the feel of my lips around your cock, Captain? I know *just* how much pressure to exert in order to give you the most enjoyable release. Do you know, I have sent lesser men than you to the *petite morte*. Come, let me play with you ... I'm very good, you know."

The Lord and Master was turning purple. *"Rico!"* he bellowed as her hand slid over his breeches and flickered suggestively, boldly, across his groin.

"Dear Rico, you just missed him ... he left here quite, quite exhausted ... do you know, I have *just* the lady for him when we reach home."

"Home? Damn you, we're going to the colonies, not France!" He caught her hand and stared, horrified, at her probing fingers. "By God, this is *a king's ship*!"

She wrestled her hand free. "Yes, darling, I know ... but the king's proud officers need their just rewards, too, no?"

Long, skillful fingers toyed with him through the breeches,

and angrily he caught her wrist once more. "Damn you, I asked you how you got aboard this ship!"

"Why, Captain, I merely asked and your men brought me aboard. They took pity on me, you see, because I needed passage home to Boston."

"Boston?" he roared, shoving her hand away from his groin.

"Yes, darling, Boston. Had you fooled, no? I'm not French, I'm American, though I've lived in a little village in Normandy with my husband, God rest his soul, for these past three years ... after his death I went to Paris, where I spent the past eight months learning the finer techniques of pleasuring a man, though if dear Papa knew, he'd surely get apoplexy, if not something far worse. *He* thinks I've been in mourning, so if you run into him when we get to Boston, please, do not tell him."

He gaped at her, unable to move as her fingers moved toward his slowly rising tumescence.

"You see, Captain, furthering my *education* was the only way I could think of to make myself competitive, as all the ladies back home want the same man I mean to snare for myself. I *had* to learn things they did not, so that I would have the advantage over them."

"Advantage?"

"Yes, darling, *advantage....* You see, I was once kissed by a dashing rogue there, a handsome scoundrel who calls himself the Irish Pirate, and I will do anything, *anything,* to get him into my bed and firmly entrenched between my legs. Captain Lord? Captain Lord, are you all right?"

His mouth had gone slack with shock.

"Come, my handsome captain, you simply must lie down, no? You have grown pale, and if you fall here, you may hurt yourself. Lo, you are so big and strong I do not think I could lift you ... though if you prefer, I would be most happy to practice a little something right here. Have you ever heard of *pattes d'araignee,*

Captain? Most do it only with their fingers, but I have grown most skillful with my toes....

"My God," he said, coming to his senses and shoving her away once more. "This—this is madness!"

"Madness? Ah, Captain, you won't know *madness* until you spend an hour with *me*." Her hand was moving toward him once more. "And let me tell you, it's an hour you'll not soon forget."

He backed up, trying desperately to escape. "You cannot stay here, by God!"

"Then by all means, my sweet, let us go to your cabin instead. Surely, 'twill take the pressure off our poor little Irish girl, no? She is so innocent and naive, why, you should have seen the shock on her face when I gave her that gown to wear ... poor little thing, I thought she would faint dead away!"

I have to get out of here, Christian thought, not liking his body's reaction to her and beginning to panic. Desperately, he caught her hand and yanked it up and away from him, wincing as her other hand slid out to run dangerously up the inside of his thigh. Swearing, he caught that one, too, and set her forcefully away. "This is a *king's* ship, madam, and I will not tolerate such lascivious behavior! I give you ten minutes to get out of that ridiculous attire and into a proper gown, and if I don't see you up on deck within the hour, so help me God, I'll make you rue the day you met me!"

She pressed her body against him, rubbed her bare foot up the back of his calf, and, tilting her head back, allowed her lips to curve into a sensual, feline smile. "I should dearly *love* to come on deck, Captain ... I *do* need to find myself some rope...."

"And furthermore," he thundered, forcibly holding her at arms' length, "you can collect your belongings and prepare to move them! I'll not have a floating *brothel* aboard my command, do you understand? This is a—"

"Yes, darling, I know. It is a *king's ship* and you simply *must* uphold the standards that are set for you."

"Do not try my patience, woman!" Releasing her, he moved

toward the door. "And do not think to toy with me, do you understand? I've had a damned bellyful of conniving women! For the rest of this hellish voyage, you will confine yourself to the cabin next to mine, and the Irish girl whose innocence you so obviously disdain!"

He snatched up his pistol, spun on his heel, and stormed off, more angry—and aroused—than he'd ever been in his life.

A crew who was determined to make his life hell, an Irish girl who crept into his bed, and now, an American brat aspiring to be a French whore.

Hell and damnation, would this bloody voyage end soon enough?

CRUNCH, crunch ... snuffle, crunch, crunch....

Deirdre O'Devir yawned and stretched as soft whines and strange noises slowly penetrated the blissful haze of her slumber.

She turned over and drew the blankets up over her shoulders. Her hand slid across the sheet, where dim memories of a hard, warm body still lingered. There vas no warmth there now, and slowly, lazily, her eyes drifted open.

Crunch, crunch ... snuffle, crunch....

The dog, she thought. No doubt Tildy was gobbling up one of the treats the captain was fond of giving her, a fact that would soon have her even fatter than she'd been prior to whelping her litter.

"Go away," Deirdre mumbled sleepily, her fingers tracing the sheet where the captain's powerful shoulders had left an indentation. A smile of contentment curved her lips as she gazed drowsily at the spot. Then she jolted awake as the memory of last night drove through her.

"Dear God," she breathed, suddenly horrified. "I spent a night in the Lord and Master's bed ... with *him*...."

Her face grew feverish. Her nipples tingled unexpectedly, shocking her.

Crunch, crunch. Snuffle, snuffle. Crunch....

Taking a deep, shuddering breath, Deirdre rolled onto her back and stared up at the deckhead. Sudden, shameful images drifted into her mind and she shut her eyes against them. She had grown up in the countryside; she knew what stallions did to mares, what roosters did to hens. What had the captain done to *her* during the night, after she'd fallen asleep? Or, worse, this morning when he woke and found her nestled in his arms?

What if he—she gulped and swallowed—*took* me?

Surely she would have woken ... wouldn't she?

Biting her lip, she shut her eyes and drove trembling hands beneath her shirt, touching her breasts and running her palms over her ribs, the crests of her hips, down the outsides of her thighs. Everything seemed as it should be. She didn't hurt anywhere, and if he had done *that* to her, surely she'd be aching somewhere ... wouldn't she?

Heat burned her face and caused her heart to slam a wild tattoo against her ribs.

"Oh, sweet Mary," she murmured, clasping the cross in atonement for a sin she didn't know if she'd even committed.

But the dream images were there, vivid, colorful, and erotic. Dreams, or—she gulped, the blood beating hot in her face— *memories?* Dampness gathered between her thighs as the wicked images burned through her mind ... of the captain's hands skimming her breasts, cupping them ... his fingers grazing the swollen nipples, and squeezing the soft mounds as his mouth came down to suck at one hard crest, then the other....

She shut her eyes and bit down on her lower lip.

.... Of his hands, fanning down the curves of her waist, the tautness of her belly, the supple flesh of her inner thighs, the dark junction of moist curls between them—

She pressed her hands against her eyes, trying to block the

images. *Had the Lord and Master taken advantage of her while she'd slept?*

Horror swept through her.

Crunch, crunch, crunch....

She flung herself onto her side and saw Tildy's head and shoulders buried in the canvas bag that contained all she had left of her beloved Ireland.

The bread.

"Tildy!" she screeched, jumping out of bed and lunging for the furry white rump.

With a startled yelp, the spaniel shot out of the bag and beneath the desk, the bread still in her mouth. The bag lay on its side, a sad fan of crumbs on the floor around it.

"Give it back!" Deirdre howled, reaching blindly under the desk. "'Tis mine, d'ye hear me, *mine*!" Kneeling, Deirdre got down on her elbows and crawled under the desk. "You come out of there right now, ye miserable, mangy, cur!"

Suddenly the cabin door banged open, a hand grasped her by the arm, and she was hauled forcibly out from beneath the desk.

It was the Lord and Master, his face dark with fury. "What the devil is all that shouting about? You've got the whole ship in an uproar!"

"Yer bleedin' dog ate my bread!"

"What?"

"I said, yer dog ate my *bread*!"

"The bread? Dear God, what was wrong with it?"

She only yanked herself free of his grip, snatched up the canvas bag, and stormed toward the door.

Terrified for his dog, he made a grab for her, his fingers biting into her shoulders. *"What was wrong with it?"*

Deirdre spun around. "It was from *Ireland*!"

He stared at her, gaping—and then understanding swept in. *Ireland.*

"Bloody deuced hell," he swore, turning away in disgust. "All that carrying-on over a piece of stale bread just because it came from *Ireland?* By God, if it makes you feel better, you can have a whole confounded *bag* of ship's biscuit, and with my blessing!" His voice softened as he saw the sudden hurt in her eyes, and damning himself for his insensitivity, he reached out to take her hands. "Hang it, girl, you really know how to frighten someone, you know that? Here I thought something dreadful had happened to you—"

She tore free of him, her eyes blazing. "Somethin' *did!*" she cried, diving into the opening he'd so unwittingly provided. "And maybe you can tell me just what it was!"

"What?"

"Ye heard me, ye stiff-lipped paragon of honor an' conceit! Last night! Don't be actin' like ye don't know what I'm talkin' about! Ye did somethin' to me, somethin' vile, unspeakable, *sinful,* and I want to know just what it was!"

He stared at her in confusion.

"How dare ye stand there and pretend ye don't know what I'm talkin' about, when all I can remember is—is—"

Her face went crimson at the thought of putting those vivid images into words.

"Is what?" he demanded.

"Shameful things.... Such as yer hands touch—" She flushed and choked out, *"Touchin'* me when I was sleepin'!"

"Touching you?" Sudden understanding darkened his features and he made a noise of frustration. "Perhaps you'd like to know where *your* hand was, dear girl, when I opened my eyes this morning. To say nothing of your body itself, which I distinctly remember having assigned to the adjacent cabin."

Humiliation burned her cheeks. "Only the worst sort of person would take advantage of a lass in her sleep!"

"And only the worst sort of person would consider taking a man's life in *his,* Miss O'Devir."

"What are ye talkin' about?"

He inclined his head toward the floor, where the brass navigational dividers gleamed in the sunlight. "I suppose they just crawled off my desk and ended up there under their own power? Or let me guess. The dog did it."

"So maybe I *did* think of killin' ye. Or maybe I didn't! I don't have to be remindin' ye that yer list of enemies on this boat is rather long!"

"So, you admit it."

"I admit nothin', except the fact that I could've ended yer miserable life and didn't, a fact I now regret with all my heart after the vile things ye did to me last night——"

"I did nothing to you," he snapped, furious that she could stand there and accuse him of something he *knew* he hadn't done, something he knew he *couldn't* do.

"Ye *touched* me!"

"You flatter yourself to think I even *dreamed* of it."

"Oh? And what *did* ye dream about that had ye so torn with grief, eh? Who is it that lays the Lord an' Master so low every night, huh?" She glared up into his harsh face, now turning white with anger. "*Emily?*"

The gray eyes went cold.

"Did ye envision yer precious *wife* beneath ye when ye touched me, kissed me——"

He grabbed her wrists and yanked her up against him, his mouth a slash of pain. *"I did not touch you,"* he ground out, his voice tight with rage, "and I will make something very clear to you, once and for all. I have no intention of touching you, not now, not *ever."* He drew her so close that her frightened eyes were a mere inch from his nose. "And as for your precious virtue, you needn't worry about me compromising it, Miss O' Devir. I have been unable to feel anything for any woman since my wife died, and you, I can assure you, haven't a prayer of stirring lusts I no longer have."

He pushed her away and turned to go, his shoulders stiff with fury.

"Unable to feel anythin'? Lusts ye no longer have? What's the matter, doesn't yer wedding tackle work?"

He froze, turned, and Deirdre, stung to the quick by his words of rejection, knew that her reciprocal barb had hit home.

"So that's it, isn't it?" she spat, her eyes glinting with triumph, her heart sinking even as she railed against the truth revealed so blatantly in his stricken face. "The haughty Lord and Master— decorated hero of Quiberon, pride o' Britain's Navy, and master of its swiftest warship—is *useless* as a man!"

"Silence," he said, his face paling as he stumbled backward, away from her.

"Useless!" she repeated, swiping viciously at a tear that had leaked from one eye, then another. "He cannot function! He's less than a man! He doesn't *work*!"

She threw back her head and laughed, overcome with hysteria and a strange, inexplicable grief that blinded her to the unforgivable and awful thing she had just done— stripped him of every shred of his masculine pride.

He turned on his heel and all but fled the cabin, her wild laughter following him, mocking him, and chasing him into the depths of hell itself.

Chapter Fifteen

"I tell ye, this is turnin' out to be the voyage from *hell*," Skunk spat, kicking viciously at a neatly coiled line and sending it snaking across the deck. "First he has us cleanin' the decks, then he has us practicing sail drills, then he takes our Delight from us —Christ, I'd as soon stayed in bloody England!"

It had been more than three long, miserable weeks since HMS *Bold Marauder* had shown her heels to Spithead—and things weren't getting any better. Although the marine who guarded the cabin where the two girls now stayed was easily *coerced*—by a very manipulative Delight—into admitting "visitors" while Deirdre was absent, the rebellious spirit with which the ship had left England was sadly lacking. Sail drills had everyone's backs and arms aching. Gun practice had them all exhausted and half deaf. Strict observation of quarterdeck rules and Navy protocol had everyone wishing he'd taken duty on another ship. Only Delight maintained her bright and bubbly spirit, and she alone kept the men smiling when they found nothing to smile about.

The Irish girl, however, was another matter. She spent her time standing at the stern rail with her canvas bag clenched in one hand, her sad face turned toward an Ireland that was now nearly three thousand miles away.

And the aloof and unapproachable Lord and Master spent *his* time watching her.

Neither spoke to the other, both went out of their way to avoid each other, and the tension between them escaped nobody's notice.

Now the men, just finishing their morning task of scrubbing the decks, watched their captain with mutinous eyes. As usual, they were full of complaints—but that was the extent of it, for none dared to cross him. His unorthodox punishments, beginning that awful day he had forced Teach to clean all the objects in the weapons chest, were doled out swiftly and mercilessly. Hibbert, having been caught once too often in his filthy uniform, had been forced to soap and scrub the uniform of every officer on the frigate. Skunk, caught swearing in front of the ladies, had been made to stand before his shipmates for an entire hour and read from the Lord and Master's big leather Bible. Worse, all punishments were carried out to the slow beat of the marine drummer's drum, with the entire crew and officers assembled to watch. Such humiliation was enough to make even the most recalcitrant of *Bold Marauder's* men think twice about raising the Lord and Master's ire.

But it did nothing to make them like him.

"Aye, Skunk, it just ain't fair," Teach grumbled, scratching at the chin he kept clean and well shaven—not to please his commanding officer but Delight, who happened to prefer smooth faces. He turned toward his shipmates, his huge, burly arms outstretched in a silent plea. "Why the hell did *we* have to end up with the stuffy prig, anyhow? Ain't he a ship-o'-the-line captain? What's he doing on a mere frigate?"

"Dunno, Teach, but I don't believe all that rot about him being a decorated hero for one bloody minute," Wenham muttered, staring up at the set of the topsails and sullenly tugging at his ear with the stubs of his missing fingers. He risked a glance at the bosun, for Rico Hendricks was usually within earshot. "Probably made one too many embarrassing mistakes somewhere and the Admiralty thought they could squirrel him away on *Bold Marauder*—at *our* expense!"

"Decorated hero, my arse! Besides, whoever heard of a naval captain who wears a *wig* aboard ship!"

"Maybe he's got a big bald spot he's tryin' to cover up!"

"Maybe 'e's afraid wot little brains 'e has'll leak out if 'e don't keep a top on 'em!"

"Maybe he thinks he looks right handsome in it and is trying to impress the girl!"

"Ha, he's doin' a fine job of *that*, ain't 'e!"

They howled with glee, remembering the now-faded bruise that the wig couldn't quite conceal. Every man on the ship had heard about the latest falling-out between the Irish girl and the Lord and Master, but only Delight knew what it was about and she, as Deirdre's cabin-mate and friend, wasn't telling.

"Hero or not. I'll bet my last shilling he ain't never seen action in his life! Prob'ly *bought* all those fancy medals!"

"Here, now, Skunk, ye be mindin' your tongue," Ian chided, frowning. "Ye canna put doon the mon when ye've never seen battle yersel'!"

"None of us have, Ian, but *we* ain't the ones wearin' the rank of a post captain or carryin' a fancy dress sword, an' we ain't the ones with medals of valor affixed to our best coat! I *still* bet he bought 'em off someone, or stole 'em off some corpse. Why, I'll bet when this here ship gets into a battle—not that I think she ever will—our fearless leader'll go running below with his tail between his legs!"

"Aye, and leave *us* to do the fighting!" Rhodes spat, detaching himself from his place by the pinrail. "Why, it wouldn't surprise me a bit to find his Lordship hiding down in his cabin, fussing with his wig and taking tea!"

Hibbert, who'd been watching with a gleam in his eye, swaggered out from Wenham's shadow, smirking. "Aye, taking *tea*," he sniffed, striking an exaggeratedly dandified pose, flaring his nostrils, and making a big show over smoothing his rumpled uniform.

The crew roared with laughter.

"Aah, ye show 'em, laddie!"

To windward, far off over the leaping wave crests that rolled endlessly toward the frigate's bows, tiny splotches of white hung suspended from the clouds that lay piled on the horizon.

But no one saw them, nor heard the distant echo of gunfire—not even the lookout, who, at the moment, was lying flat on his back on the maintop, with a boyishly disguised Delight straddling his belly and putting his mind on other things.

"Keep it up, Hibbert!" Skunk roared, slapping his thigh. "'Sdeath, we could do with some amusement to brighten these decks!"

Laughing, Hibbert primped his ill-kempt queue and pranced across the deck in a exaggerated caricature of his commanding officer. Pinching his nostrils shut to affect an exaggerated nasal drawl that sounded nothing like the clipped, educated tone of their captain, he sniffed, "Mr. MacDuff, I daresay we're in for a *devilish* blow ... would you please put a reef in the forecourse?"

A burst of raucous laughter went up from his mates, and several threw wary glances forward, where Ian had gone off to use the head. Their first lieutenant was no fun anymore, refusing to join his shipmates in making jokes about the Lord and Master.

Grinning, Hibbert pushed his hat back, primped and preened some more, and then, clasping his hands behind his back, strode slowly across the deck. He sank his chin into his neckcloth and drew his brows close in a threatening scowl. "Oh, and, Mr. Skunk, please see to it that the deck is scrubbed and clean before I come topside!"

Skunk threw back his grimy head, roaring with laughter. "Ye've got it, boy! Ye look just like the blasted blueblood!"

"Aye, just like 'im!"

"More, Hibbert, more!"

On the horizon, the triangles of white began to take on distinct shapes as they detached themselves from the cloud mass.

The midshipman grabbed a boarding pike from the rack at the mainmast and leaned his weight on it in imitation of the captain with his sword. His eyes half-shut, Hibbert stiffened his back and drawled, "Oh, and Mr. Teach, please remove that *growth* from your face. This is a fighting ship, not a barbershop!"

"Not *fighting* ship," Skunk cried, "A *king's* ship! If yer gonna do it, do it right!"

Hibbert struck a pose. "This is a *king's* ship!"

"Ha, ha, ha!"

Someone coughed.

But Hibbert, lost in the game, never saw the object of his ridicule standing behind him, silently watching him and cradling three tiny puppies in the broad shelter of his arm. Primping his hair, the youth swaggered to the wheel and stared haughtily down at the compass. "I *daresay,* Mr. Wenham, the forecourse is not in proper trim for this wind. Pray, do see to the matter!"

"Er, Hibbert—"

"Mr. Rhodes, please do not interrupt your commanding officer," Hibbert said, with an imperious wave of his hand. He turned to face the second lieutenant. "You *know* how it grieves—"

He broke off abruptly and dropped the pike on his toe. The Lord and Master was standing a mere ten feet away, coldly watching him.

"Are you quite finished, *Mr.* Hibbert?" The frosty gray eyes, hard with anger, raked the boy's face. "Pray, remind me to purchase tickets next time you decide to stage such an amusing performance."

Hibbert paled, gulped, and stared down at his shoes. "Aye."

"Aye, *sir.* And get your damned hide below and change out of that miserable excuse for a uniform and into something presentable!"

Hibbert fled, nearly colliding with the returning Ian MacDuff in his haste to escape.

"Hey, watch it, ye imperious wee upstart!" Ian roared, raising his fist. But the midshipman was gone.

Christian strode to the rail that separated the quarterdeck from the waist of the ship. His cold gaze swept the sea of smirking faces beneath him, noting the exchanged glances, the quickly muffled guffaws, the twitching lips. He let the silence build, knowing that their attention was on him and him alone. Then he cleared his throat and, cradling the three puppies to his chest, stared down at them.

"It is a pity," he said coldly, "that here we are, only a few days out from Boston and you, as a company, are no closer to doing your Navy proud than you were when we left England. I had truly hoped to make a favorable impression upon the admiral there, but I'm afraid that I shall be ashamed, not proud, to bring this vessel into that harbor and present her to my superior."

Skunk and Rhodes exchanged smirks.

"You think that having me as your commanding officer is the worst thing you could have imagined, don't you?"

Skunk opened his mouth to reply in the positive, but a quick jab in the ribs from Rhodes silenced him.

The action was not wasted on the captain. "Why must you comply to discipline and tradition? you ask. What reason is there for saluting the quarterdeck, for touching your hat to your commanding or superior officers, for manning the side when your captain leaves the ship?" Christian's hand tightened around the rail. "Do *you* think me so pompous that I ask your compliance for *my* sake? Do you think me so arrogant and conceited that I demand it for *myself?*"

They stared at him, uncomprehending. No one spoke. Above,

wind sighed softly in the shrouds and made the sails taut and hard against the blue, blue sky.

"Death at sea can come swiftly, in any form, at any time. A sudden squall. A battle. A mistake in interpreting a chart, a position, an enemy's strength. At such times, when chaos may reign, there is one thing and one thing alone that will keep a ship together, and *that* is called *discipline*."

He stared hard at them, letting them absorb his words. "Our Navy is the most powerful sea power in the world, with possibly only the French to challenge it. That strength does not arise out of the independence of each vessel, but out of unity amongst them all, and the men who serve them. That strength is rooted in discipline and strict allegiance to tradition—they are the glue that holds our Navy together, not something to be sneered at, scoffed at, ridiculed. Now, if everyone decided not to respect their seniors, and they in turn did not respect the flag that flies above their heads, where, then, would this Navy be? Indeed, where would *England* be?"

Nobody was smirking anymore. A few men looked down at their feet, visibly ashamed.

"I do not chastise you for your impertinence and disrespect to *me;* I chastise you for your impertinence and disrespect for *Britain.* Your blatant disrespect of me is not an insult to *me*—it is an insult to your *country*."

More men stared down at their toes, their faces reddening with shame. Even Deirdre had turned away from the rail to listen.

Christian gazed up at the pennant that streamed proudly above. "When you salute me, or the quarterdeck, you are partaking of a ceremony that is far older than you are and one which shall persevere long after you are gone. Since you are representatives of your king and country, your conduct as seamen is representative of England. By seeking to anger *me*, you disgrace not only your country, but your ship and the men you may someday fight beside.

"Tradition, ceremony, discipline, and obedience are the essential glue that holds a fighting ship together. A fighting ship is the essence of a fleet; a fleet, the pride and guardian of a nation. Remove one chink in the armor, one link in the chain, and it is weakened. Do *you* want to be remembered by those you love and protect back home as being that weak link?"

No one moved.

"*Do* you?"

They stared at him while high above, the pennant undulated with majestic grace in the wind.

"I have nothing more to say." Turning his back on them, the Lord and Master touched his hat to those proud colors above his head and, passing his shame-faced officers, his strangely silent crew, went below.

But even he did not see the distant puffs of white far off the starboard bows—puffs that might have been clouds, but were no clouds at all.

"Lo, Deirdre, I wish you'd come to me earlier," Delight said, plopping down on her bed as the Irish girl came miserably into the cabin. "I told you before, there are ways of bringing a man to his knees. Surely, whatever damage you've done is repairable, no?"

"I accused him of havin' faulty weddin' tackle," she blurted out.

"You *what?*"

"And then I laughed at him."

"Oh, dear."

Deirdre twisted her hands. "But ye say that all insults can be forgiven, right?"

"All, I'm afraid, except *that* one. Lo, Deirdre, you've sorely wounded the man's pride! 'Twill take a lot to make him forgive you."

Deirdre put her face in her hands and sank down on her bunk. "Oh, Delight, I didn't mean it, I was just so *angry*. I woke up that mornin'—I mean, I got in bed with him the night before because he was havin' that awful, *awful* nightmare ... and I felt bad, and just ... well, I wanted to comfort him, so I got in bed with him. The next mornin' I woke up and he was gone, and I had all these thoughts that maybe he touched me, that maybe he might've stolen me virginity—"

"You mean, you didn't know?"

"How *would* I? I was sleepin'!"

Delight threw back her head and laughed. "Lo, child, if he'd taken your maidenhood, I can *assure* you that you'd know it!"

"*Maybe* he did," she replied stubbornly.

"And besides, you would've found your maiden's blood on the sheets, no?"

Deirdre looked down, her face beginning to redden.

"Ah, you are more innocent than even I would've thought. What you must do, Deirdre, is win your man back to you. He carries more scars than a battle warrior, no? Scars of the heart, that is. Someone has hurt him deeply, probably this Emily. You have a formidable opponent in this dead wife, but *she* is dead, and you are not, and our Lord and Master cannot make love to a dead woman, no?"

"But, Delight, it's wrong that I have such feelings. He took my brother from me—"

"No, Deirdre." The other woman placed her hands on Deirdre's shoulders and looked her in the eye. "The *Royal Navy* took your brother from you, not Captain Lord."

"Besides," Deirdre persisted, "he's English."

"I know, a stuffy, pompous race, but we cannot dictate the direction of our hearts."

"Ye make it sound like I'm in love with him!"

"No, Deirdre, *you* make it sound like you're in love with him."

She smiled patiently. "My advice to you is to get to work *immediately* on proving to him just how you feel."

"How? He hates me, he does, and with good reason after what I said to him."

"No, he does not hate you. He merely thinks he loves another. And you have sorely wounded his male pride. But *you* are a woman, Deirdre. A living, breathing woman. He will not stand a chance against you once you put your mind to it to go after him, no?" She grinned, curved an arm around Deirdre's shoulders and guiding her to the door, scooped a gown out of her armoire. "Now here, put this on and make sure you tug the bodice down so that the top of your nipples show just above the lace."

"Delight!"

"Don't be a ninny. 'Tis time you started thawing our handsome Ice Captain! Lord knows *I* cannot! Now go," she said, grinning. "We'll be in Boston in a few days, and the ladies there will all be falling over each other to get their claws into your man. Make an effort to have the advantage over them!"

Deirdre clutched the gown to her chest, thinking of the captain's reaction to the tame, by comparison, scarlet one that he had so despised. But at that moment sudden cries drove down from above.

"Two sail off the starboard bows! And another, fine off the starboard beam! She's an English ship—and she's being attacked!"

Chapter Sixteen

On deck, the crew of HMS *Bold Marauder* wasted no time in summoning their commanding officer. Now they stood anxiously beside him, glancing at his harsh face for reassurance as he took a spyglass from Midshipman Hartness and trained it on the three ships.

"What do ye make of it, sir?" Ian murmured, as each distant explosion of gunfire came rolling back to them from over the water.

The Lord and Master studied the three vessels for a moment longer, then closed the glass with a snap. He turned and walked toward the wheel. "One is a French corvette, Ian."

The big Scotsman lifted a brow at the captain's use of his first name, but Christian continued as if the familiarity were of no consequence. "The second is a sloop, flying no colors at all. And the one they are attacking"—he looked at him gravely—"is an English cutter."

"But it's *peacetime,* sir!"

"I know that, Ian."

Young Edgar Hartness was pointing at the flags being run up

from the English ship. "The cutter is signaling for our assistance, sir!"

Teach, scowling, had climbed into the shrouds and now called over to the quarterdeck. "The sloop—the one flyin' no flags—I've seen her before, sir. It was on my last voyage to the colonies. She's a smuggler, mark my words."

Christian put the glass to his eye once more. Through it, he saw a fox-featured, laughing rogue with high cheekbones and glossy black curls caught in a length of purple velvet, standing at the tiller of the sloop. Probably its captain, judging by the fine cut of his clothes and his stance of command. The absence of a flag confirmed Teach's words, and Christian felt a wave of contempt. "Bloody freebooter," he snapped. "I have no stomach for smugglers, and even less for one who would attack a lone English ship!"

"What'll we do, sir?" Ian asked anxiously.

"Send the women below to the surgeon, where they will be safe. Then clear for action and beat to quarters."

"B-beat to quarters, sir?"

The crew exchanged glances, their faces white with horror. Then they stared at their captain, and saw the cool detachment and resolution in the steady gray eyes.

"Yes, that is what I said, Mr. MacDuff. *Beat to quarters.*" He handed the glass back to the midshipman. "We are going to fight."

BELOWDECKS, the two women heard it all: the urgent tattoo of the marine drummer, the shrill of bosuns' pipes, the feet pounding up the companionways and across the decks, and the ominous rumblings from above as the frigate's big guns were moved into place.

Deirdre, watching Delight roll bandages under Elwin's instruction, didn't need the surgeon to tell her what was happening up there. "They're clearing for action now," he said bleakly, as though taking comfort from the sound of his own voice. His bony hands shook as he laid out an array of saws, knives, tourniquets, and bandages on the table.

Deirdre stared at the gleaming instruments, at the bottles of rum that, when the wounded were brought down, would be the only respite from the pain as Elwin dug and cut and—

Her blood went cold, and she hugged Tildy close, trying to still the pounding of her heart. Then she put the dog down with her puppies, safely nestled in their box that one of the crewmen had brought down.

"Is it goin' to be that bad, Elwin?" she whispered.

Even Delight paused, her eyes wide and frightened.

"Might be." He tied on his surgeon's apron, then positioned a wooden bucket beneath the table. Moments before, that same table had been where the midshipmen took their meals; now it might be seeing horrors she could only guess at. Above, the swinging deckhead lanterns threw shadows over the operating table, the deck flooring, and Elwin's tense face.

"What will happen, d'ye think?"

"Hopefully, nothing. This here ship's never been in a fight and I doubt today'll be any different." His lips thinned and he swung away, busying himself at tearing bandages from a fresh piece of linen. "But then, she's never had a captain like this one, either."

Cannonfire boomed somewhere outside as *Bold Marauder* drew closer to the fight.

She's never had a captain like this one.

"Elwin, I'm scared."

The small man glanced around to see if anyone was within earshot. "So am I, girl." He perused the space, assuring he'd done all he could to prepare for what looked like the inevitable. "I have friends up there. This could be bad."

Outside, more gunfire boomed out from the other ships, rolling like thunder across the water. Deirdre shut her eyes and wrapped unsteady hands around Granuaile's cross. But there was no strength to be had there, no comfort.

Think of Ireland. Stone fences and misty skies ... whitewashed cottages and rocky pastures ... sheep bleating on twilit hills....

Ireland.

With a start of horror, she realized she'd left her precious canvas bag in the Lord and Master's cabin. More big guns boomed from somewhere beyond the hull, deep and reverberating and awful. Tildy whined with fear and Deirdre picked her up once more, cuddling her. Beneath Deirdre's chin, the spaniel buried her face against her chest, shaking in terror.

Please, God, be with us. Please, Mother Mary, keep us safe. Be with this ship, and ... and be with our Lord an' Master. Please, oh heavenly Father, guide him, let the crew follow him, help him to get us out of this and keep everyone safe. She squeezed her eyes shut, feeling the misty sting of tears behind her lids. *And please, dear Jesus, I beg of ye, please, please, please keep him safe.*

Here she was, praying for the safety of a man she had once vowed to kill.

Dear God.

From above came another resounding crash, and a chorus of shouts and yells. *Bold Marauder* was getting close now. Very close.

"I hope Captain Lord knows what he's doing," Delight said nervously.

"They say he's been captain of many ships," Elwin murmured. "That he saved the day at Quiberon. That his last command was a mighty first-rate man-of-war carrying one hundred guns. Ever see a hundred-gunner, girls? It's so big, it'd make this here ship look like a sailboat."

They heard a low, menacing rumble as a gun was hauled across the deck, a shout, and then *Bold Marauder's* own bellowing voice as one of the nine-pounders in her bow was fired. The deep rever-beration sent thunder echoing through the small space. Two bottles of rum clinked together, and Delight paled.

"No." Deirdre murmured. "I've never seen a hundred-gunner, Elwin. After this, I don't think I ever want to."

Another cannon boomed out from above, sounding like a thunderclap striking too close. Deirdre tightened her arms around Tildy, while Delight hastily gathered the three puppies up into her arms.

Oh, dear God, please be with our Lord and Master.

What went through a man's mind at a time like this? What must he be thinking? Feeling?

She thought of the hateful words she had last spoken to him. She wished with all her heart she could take them back.

"I don't hate him, Elwin."

"Eh?"

"I don't hate him ... I said awful things to him, and if something were to happen to him—"

She couldn't complete the thought. Couldn't bear to think of him injured or dead. She bit her lip, and felt the comforting touch of Delight's hand upon her shoulder.

Another gun banged out, making the instruments shake and rattle atop the table. "Soon now," Elwin said nervously, wiping his palms on his apron.

More pipes shrilled, bare feet stamped across the deck overhead, and then the deck beneath them began to tilt upright, leveling out for a brief moment before the ship angled over onto the other tack. A pair of forceps slid down the table and clattered to the deck. They heard wild shouts from above, then felt the frigate pulling herself up out of the water, the hungry, surging motion as she gathered speed ....

Elwin shut his eyes. "The Lord and Master's sending her in now."

From above came shouts, rumblings ... then an expectant silence as the ship tensed for the overwhelming might of its own impending broadside.

Deirdre clapped her hand over her ears, hearing her heartbeat thundering against her palms. And then the world erupted as *Bold Marauder* engaged the enemy.

❧

"TOPMEN ALOFT, and men to the braces! Stand by, Mr. Wenham, and prepare to come about!"

Pipes shrilled, and men swarmed up the shrouds and out along the frigate's yards. Moments later, *Bold Marauder* was nose-up to the wind, fighting her crew and trying desperately to fall off.

"Now, Mr. Wenham!"

The deck seemed to drop away beneath them as the frigate flung herself onto the other tack and charged down toward the battle.

"Steady as you go, Mr. Wenham!"

"Course south by southwest, full and by!"

Christian stood at the quarterdeck rail, watching the ships drawing closer and closer through the heavy smoke. His mouth was tense and set, his eyes emotionless. Yet he was aware of Ian, standing beside him and gripping a huge Scottish claymore, his red beard blowing in the wind and his eyes fierce. He was aware of Rhodes, in place beside Skunk and the larboard battery of guns; he was aware of the frigate's lively response, and he was aware of the nervous crew, their stares fixated ahead toward the fight. Thick, roiling smoke hung above the three ships, broken topmasts and streaming pendants poking up through the acrid gray cloud.

Christian tugged at his sleeve. There had been one or two snickers of disdain about his "primped" appearance, but only he and Rico Hendricks, whose black eyes met his from some thirty feet away, knew the real reason he'd donned a fresh shirt and his finest coat, and clipped his best sword to his belt frog—he was a king's officer, and if he fell today, he would do so with honor.

If he fell.

How many times had he sent ships into battle with that same thought running through his mind? How many times had he counted on the strength and loyalty of men who would blindly follow him into hell itself?

But *these* men....

Fiercely gripping the quarterdeck rail, he peered across the double batteries of guns and their anxious, crouching crews. Faces ran with nervous sweat. A few men looked ready to bolt. Only Rhodes seemed calm. Christian met his gaze and gave the briefest of nods, then stared over the lieutenant's head. Just beyond, *Bold Marauder*'s plunging jib-boom seemed to swallow up the sea as she charged down toward the three smoke-cloaked ships.

"The sloop's makin' off," Ian yelled, pointing at the ship that flew no colors.

Christian took the glass from the midshipman. The little one-masted vessel swam into view, and his eyes narrowed as he trained the glass toward its helm. There was her captain, looking back at him with a hand raised in mocking farewell, and Christian frowned for somewhere, at some time, he knew he'd seen the man before—

"Shall we chase him, sir?" Ian asked, pointing at the fleeing ship.

"No." Christian snapped the glass closed. "The cutter has requested our assistance, and I'll not desert her to a damned Frenchman."

Gunfire echoed across the water. Christian saw the ornate stern of the French corvette showing dimly through the smoke, her masts poking up through the thick cloud that engulfed her. More guns boomed out in flashes of orange against black, and there was a splitting crash as the English cutter's single mast toppled, dragging spars, rigging and screaming men with it down into the sea. A great cry went up from *Bold Marauder*'s crew at the sight of their fellow countrymen floundering in the waves.

"By the saints," Ian gasped, with a desperate glance at his captain.

"Mr. Hibbert!" Christian caught the midshipman's scrawny arm, his gaze on the men struggling pitifully in the swells. "Bring up some hammocks from below, make sure they're tightly rolled, and toss them to those people out there so they have something to hold onto until we can send boats to rescue them."

The middie, terrified, just stared at him.

"Damn you, *move*!" Christian shouted, shoving the boy into action. "Bring her up a point, Mr. Wenham, right up around that Frog's stern. With a bit of luck, I daresay we can strip the guts from her with a broadside or two."

Cold spray hissed and dashed over the frigate's bowsprit, soaking the decks, the men, the guns.

"Starboard battery, run out!" Christian yelled.

All along the deck, men strained and heaved, muscling the big guns into position.

Not fast enough, Christian thought, in despair.

"All run out, sir!"

Christian stepped forward, his face in shadow beneath his hat. He saw the gun captains staring aft, awaiting his signal, and beyond them *Bold Marauder's* jib-boom, just thrusting into the frayed edges of the thick cloud of smoke.

Drawing his sword, he raised his arm, the Irish girl's face swimming into his memory once more, her words coming back to haunt him.

Useless as a man.

Savagely, he brought the sword down. *"Fire!"*

The world exploded.

IT WAS a scene from hell itself. Midshipmen racing through the smoke to relay orders; flashes of musket fire from the French ship as her marksmen tried to pick off *Bold Marauder*'s blue-and-white-clad officers; iron shrieking overhead, spars and pieces of burning rigging bouncing off the nettings spread above the deck, guns belching death and destruction, and men falling, only to be dragged, screaming, away to the surgeon's knife below.

And the Lord and Master, steady, aloof, and unruffled, veteran of countless sea fights and the one, the only, force holding *Bold Marauder's* frightened crew together.

"Starboard broadside, *fire!*"

The big guns roared out one by one, leaving his ears ringing and thunder vibrating up through the deck and into the soles of his shoes. It wasn't a timed broadside; it wasn't even close. *By God, we have to do better, or we're all done for!*

An answering boom from the French corvette roared through the smoke, and a cannonball screamed across the deck, smashed against one of the starboard guns, and exploded. Several gunners, grimy with smoke and sweat, fell screaming, blood streaming from their broken bodies and their legs kicking in death.

Through the smoke and haze, Christian saw the French ship's yards turning as she abandoned the English cutter and came about, the water glistening from her side, her ports open and her guns poking their black snouts toward them—

"Reload and run out!" he shouted, gripping his sword. "Give them a good drubbing, lads!"

Beside him, one of the helmsmen cried out, and clutching his side, crumpled to his knees.

"Fire!"

Guns belched smoke and flame, recoiling against their tackles. The raw scent of sulfur singed the air. Several feet away, Teach, cursing, stumbled back in horror as his nine-pounder slammed inboard, nearly crushing him.

Christian shut his eyes, clenching his sword hilt.

"For God's sake, sir!" Hibbert raced back to the quarterdeck. "They're killing us!"

"We'll nae win this fight, sir; they be too strong for us!" Ian yelled desperately.

Christian turned on them, his eyes fierce. "I'll be damned if I lower my colors to a bloody *Frenchman!* Mr. Wenham!" Cupping his hands over his mouth, he yelled, "Hard-a-lee, and prepare to ram ... *now!*"

"R-ram, sir?"

"Yes, Wenham, *ram!*"

Several feet away, a pigtailed seaman, slamming a fresh charge down one of the starboard guns, suddenly threw his hand over his eyes and fell to the deck, a musket ball buried in his brain. Guns roared from the corvette, and a nearby pinrail exploded in a shower of wood. Then the helm went over, and with slow, stately purpose, *Bold Marauder* drove her jib-boom into the French ship's rigging. The jarring smash of hull against hull hurled men to their knees, the Lord and Master against the wheel, guns onto their sides.

"Stand fast, lads, and prepare to repel boarders!" Christian yelled, his voice raw with smoke as he fought to pull himself up from the deck.

Slowly, the two vessels pivoted, locked nose to shoulder as their guns pounded each other at close range with vicious fury. The English cutter drifted away, her battered crew trying to bring her under control. Then Ian grabbed his captain's arm and pointed at the stream of yelling, cutlass-wielding Frenchmen leaping across to *Bold Marauder*'s deck.

"They're boarding us, sir!"

Shot whined past, and Wenham gasped and slumped over the wheel. From above came a high, terrified scream and a marine fell, spiraling and kicking, to the deck. Somewhere forward, one of *Bold Marauder*'s guns banged out, and Christian heard the pop of muskets as his marines fired across at the enemy.

"They're onto us, sir!"

Thank God, Christian thought insanely. He took one look at his men—dirty, ragged, untrained, and defiant—and in that fleeting instant, knew that his decision to ram the other ship had been the right one, the only one. They were inexperienced at fighting the guns of their frigate, yes; they were quarrelsome and rebellious, yes; but they were English sailors, and as such, there were none on God's earth who would fight harder, nor more fiercely, when it came to defending their home.

And *Bold Marauder* was their home.

Drawing his sword, he leaped down the quarterdeck ladder and into their midst. "To me, lads!" he heard himself shout, his blade coming up to clash with the steel of the first wild-eyed intruders as they swarmed over the side like a horde of angry wasps.

For one awful moment, the crew did not move, stunned by the courage of the man they'd thought to be nothing but an aristocratic fop.

Then they reacted.

"Holy hell," Skunk cried, his eyes bulging as the Lord and Master swung his sword against a Frenchman's with a ringing clash, and then disarmed the man with a mighty blow. Rico Hendricks had already run toward his captain to help defend him and now Ian, his claymore high, charged toward the pair, instinctively placing his back to his captain's as the three single-handedly took on the yelling, screaming boarders.

And now more and more of the French devils were leaping over *Bold Marauder*'s rails, *their* rails, their swords slashing.

Bold Marauder's crew began grabbing pikes, pistols, and axes, and yelling in fury, raced to join the bosun and their two senior officers. Not to be left behind, Skunk seized a cutlass and threw himself into the fray. And then, with a wild, rushing roar, the rest of the men abandoned their guns and, howling like Indians, charged into the melee, fighting as they fought best—hand to hand, in bloody, ruthless combat.

Christian, parrying an enemy's sword, saw flashes of red

streak past as his marines joined the fight, their bayonets gleaming, thrusting, stabbing. A gun, then another, banged out from forward as some levelheaded soul fired into the corvette's hull. He felt a brief swell of relief, but there was no time to thank God that his plan had worked, that his men were finally behind him. He knocked aside an attacker's sword, chopped his own blade into the man's ribs and jerked it free, only to stumble over a sprawled body. He fell heavily to the deck. A shadow filled his vision, and momentarily helpless, he stared up into the maniacal eyes of a Frenchman leaping down at him from out of the smoke.

Christian saw his life flash before his eyes as the Frenchman, his face wild and triumphant as he stood over the fallen English captain, raised his sword with a yell—

Then Teach was there, bellowing with fury, his massive arm knocking aside the Frenchman's cutlass, his sword impaling the man through the heart.

Christian's eyes met his for the briefest of seconds. "Well done, Mr. Teach—"

But Teach was gone, pounding across the deck to take on another.

Dazed, Christian felt Skunk hauling him roughly to his feet. "You all right, sir?"

"Hibbert...."

Swinging around, Skunk saw the young midshipman raising his pitiful dirk against the charging might of a boarder's pike. With a howl of rage, Skunk knocked the pike aside. The full weight of his big body was behind the impact and as the Frenchman fell to the deck, Skunk turned back to the Lord and Master, only to see him flinch, drag off his hat, and clap it to his shoulder.

"Bloody captain," Skunk said, knocking aside an enemy musket with the ease of a child fending off a stick. "Now isn't the time to stand on ceremony by doffin' 'is hat!"

"Shut up, Skunk. The *bloody captain*'s the only hope we have of surviving this"—stab, thrust, stab—*"massacre!"* Ian yelled, beating back a boarder with vicious swings of his claymore.

But even Ian was too crazed with excitement and bloodlust to notice the color draining from his captain's face. All he saw was that they were steadily driving the enemy back onto its own decks as, whooping in triumph and glee, *Bold Marauder's* men, now joined by those from the English cutter, leaped over the side and dropped from the jib-boom as they took the fight to the French ship.

The tide had turned.

Tiring rapidly and still holding his hat to his shoulder, Christian jumped for the gangway. Someone on the corvette had already chopped away the spars and lines tangled in *Bold Marauder's* bowsprit and now the French ship, freed, was beginning to draw away, her officers screaming encouragement to the retreating sailors as the gap of blue sea between them grew wider and wider. Gauging the expanding distance between the two ships, Christian leapt, hearing Skunk, Ian, and Teach yelling in triumph behind him.

Protecting my back, he thought dazedly.

His feet hit the enemy's deck and he almost went down. Shouting, their swords flashing, his men rushed past him, nearly knocking him to his knees. Then Hendricks was there, lifting him by his elbow, and he was carried forward on the tide of English seamen.

His vision swam, and he pressed his hat to his shoulder, not wanting his men to see the seriousness of the wound and lose heart.

Pray God, let me hold out just a bit longer, he thought. Then he slashed and fought his way toward the corvette's quarterdeck even as its colors tumbled to the deck in surrender.

A great cheer went up from *Bold Marauder's* men as Skunk and Teach grabbed the corvette's commander and hauled him unceremoniously toward Christian.

"Huzzah! Huzzah! Huzzah!"

"Three cheers for our Lord and Master!"

"Here ye go, sir, the bleedin' bastard 'imself!"

Dirty, cut, and bleeding, Christian wearily accepted the other captain's sword. Then, still holding his hat, he lowered his arm and for the first time his men saw the perfect, round hole punched neatly below his shoulder and the spreading blood that turned the blue coat around it to purple.

"Well done, lads," he said, with a faint smile. "Well done."

Then his knees buckled and he fell heavily to the deck.

Chapter Seventeen

In the surgeon's area, Deirdre choked back nausea as the wounded were dragged below. Above, the guns boomed, making conversation nearly impossible, making her ears ring with pain, making her fear the very deck was going to come crashing down atop them—

"The captain!" she cried, overcome by sudden terror as a seaman dragged a moaning Wenham into the little room and laid him on Elwin's table beneath the swinging lantern.

"Huh?"

"The *captain*!" she shouted, trying to be heard over the unholy roar of cannon.

Wenham shut his eyes. "Leading a boarding party onto the enemy. Ain't seen nothing like it." He groaned in pain as Elwin, aided by two assistants, positioned him on the bloodied table and tore off his shirt.

"Nothing but a scratch," snapped Elwin. He slapped a needle and thread into Deirdre's hand as another seaman was dragged below, this one with a gash across his arm. "If you're going to stand there, then get busy, girl! Sew up that man's arm before he bleeds to death!"

From above came more firing, then a deafening cheer.

"We must be beatin' 'em, lads!" yelled the injured man, sitting upright. "The Lord and Master must be driving the bloody Frogs back onto their own ship!"

Christian, Deirdre thought wildly, her hands shaking as she tried desperately to thread the needle. Beside her Delight, tight-lipped, washed the blood from the man's wound with a wet rag. Steeling herself, Deirdre pinched the ragged edges of flesh together and slowly pushed the needle into the man's flesh. He went white with pain and as the moments dragged on, the only way Deirdre was able to hold her breakfast down was to imagine the scene above, her lips moving in a desperate prayer for the captain's safety.

There was no use lying to herself anymore. She, who had spent years dreaming of killing him in revenge, was terrified for his safety, his welfare, his life—

Through ringing ears, she realized the firing had stopped. Another cheer came from above and then Hibbert came running in, his face dirty and streaked with sweat. "We saved the English cutter, the sloop fled, and we took the Frenchie!" he gasped, swiping at his brow. His eyes were wild with pride. "They surrendered to our captain! To *us!*"

Ian crowded the space behind him, his ruddy face bleak. "Aye, but at what cost." He met their gazes and in the sudden, awful hush said solemnly, "The Lord and Master's down."

Deirdre was dimly aware of Delight's hand upon her arm; then the blood faded from her face as she looked past the midshipman, past Ian and the milling, silent, crew, and to the huge man who suddenly filled the doorway.

It was Arthur Teach.

He was carrying the body of an officer in his great, muscled arms. Blood darkened the officer's shoulder, soaked his sleeve, followed the curve of his lax fingers, and dripped silently to the deck flooring.

Deirdre uttered a silent cry. She didn't have to see the man's face to know just which officer he was.

❧

CHRISTIAN CLAWED his way up through the darkness and opened his eyes to the sight of Rico Hendricks standing protectively over him. Elwin Boyd stood at the big Jamaican's shoulder, his face, silhouetted by a swinging lantern, strained. The pungent scents of blood and death lay thickly around him, and Christian realized that he was laid out on a table in the surgeon's quarters, its surface hard beneath his spine.

With a gasp, he sat up.

"Don't move, sir," Elwin muttered, pushing against his chest and trying to force him back down.

"Let me up, damn you, I've a ship to see to, wounded to care for—"

"The Frogs've surrendered, sir, don't ye remember? And Ian and Rhodes are seeing to the ship."

"How many dead?"

"Twelve. Now, lie back and relax. You've got a musket ball in your shoulder, and if I don't get it out, you'll be joining them before the day is out."

Christian tried again to rise. "I don't have time for this—"

"Sir, I *must* insist!" Roughly, the surgeon shoved him back down on the table.

A voice exploded above Christian's head like a cannon blast. "Ye be easy with him, Elwin, or I'll have yer head on a pike!"

"Look, just get the hell out of here, all of ye!" Elwin spat, waving his bloodied hands to push away the group of seamen that were clustered around the table. He picked up a rag and doused it with vinegar. "How's a man supposed to do his work if ye're all—"

Skunk lunged forward and grabbed the surgeon's wrist. "You

put that on the cap'n's wound and you'll be answering to me, ye hear me, Elwin?"

"For Christ's sake, Skunk, I'm merely cleaning my instruments in it—"

"What's this?" Ian barged in, his Scottish cap askew. "Is Elwin mistreating the captain? So help me God, Elwin—"

"Damn you, damn all of you, just clear out and let me do what needs to be done!" Elwin raged, angrily wiping his bloodied hands on his apron. He snatched up a metal probe and, waving it at them, snarled, "Pack of useless, good-for-nothing loafers! Now, *get out!*"

Christian saw that long, wicked piece of metal coming toward his shoulder and went stiff, bracing himself for the pain. Fierce but gentle pressure tightened around his fingers, and rolling his head sideways, he saw that someone was standing on the other side of the table and holding his hand, someone he now realized had been standing there and holding his hand all along.

Deirdre O' Devir.

Tears sparkled on her lashes, and her eyes were huge pools of sorrow in a face that was pale and strained. She squeezed his hand, and the moisture in her eyes spilled over and traced a glistening track down her cheek.

He stared at her, confused. "Miss O'Devir?"

"Teach carried ye down," she whispered. She bent her head, and he felt the brush of her hair against his face. The heavy cross that hung from her neck dangled near his nose, and he closed his eyes as she reached up and laid a soft hand against his cheek. "The whole crew's bragging about how ye led 'em to victory and saved the ship."

"Damn right he did!" Skunk snarled. "If it weren't for his bleedin' Lordship, we'd all be at the bottom of the sea!"

"Or at the mercy of those Frenchies!" Teach thundered.

"Gentlemen," Elwin warned, lowering a knife to the bullet hole in his patient's coat and deftly thrusting its tip beneath the

bloody fabric, "if you don't let me attend to my business, your captain won't live to see the next sunrise. That ball is lodged in a vascular area, and if I don't get it out.... "

With a flick of his wrist he jerked upward, slicing through the blood-soaked uniform coat.

Christian turned his head to look, but the girl loomed above, her eyes dark with compassion ... and something else. Her hand still cupped his jaw, and now she gently coaxed him to look toward her so that he couldn't see Elwin's ministrations. He closed his eyes, relaxing under her gentle touch as the surgeon's knife ripped through his coat. "Elwin's right," she said quietly. 'The ball has to come out. But I'll be here, holdin' yer hand through it ... Christian."

Christian.

He swallowed hard, several times, against the sudden sting of emotion.

She called me by my name.

He took a deep, shaky breath, his pain, and apprehension of what Elwin was about to do to him, suddenly forgotten. Skunk and Teach came forward, sliding their hands beneath his shoulders and lifting him up so that Rico could remove his blood-soaked uniform, waistcoat and shirt. He tried to move and could not, and was alarmed at how weak he'd grown.

Christian, she'd said.

As they lowered him back to the table, he shut his eyes against the raw emotion. Then cool air swept against the exposed wound, and he didn't have to hear Delight's soft cry, or the collective gasps of dismay, to know how serious it was.

Rolling his head, he looked up at the girl and managed a smile. "That bad, eh?"

She was pure white. The fierce pressure of her fingers around his was answer enough.

"You're lucky to be alive," the surgeon muttered, wiping his hands on his bloodied apron and picking up the needle-like metal probe once more. "And you'd be luckier still if you hadn't woken up, because I can tell you right now, you're going to feel this."

"I'm warnin' ye, Elwin!" Teach snarled, pushing forward. "Ye make one slip and yer going to be eating steel and shittin' bullets, you hear me?"

Pushing past Teach and ignoring the crowd anxiously gathering in the cramped space, Elwin offered a mug of rum to Christian. "Drink this, sir," he urged. "It'll dull the pain somewhat."

"And have the men see me helpless beneath a haze of alcohol? Thank you, Mr. Boyd, but I happen to value my coherence." He steeled himself for the inevitable. "Now get on with it, please."

Elwin gave a noncommittal shrug. "As you wish, sir."

Christian shut his eyes, and only the girl, fiercely holding his hand, felt the tension in his grip. Then she brought her other hand down to his lips, her fingers gently coaxing him to take and bite down on a strip of leather. He gazed up into her eyes, knowing that he could endure anything as long as she looked at him like that. He saw apology in their depths, kindness, and yes, even forgiveness.

Forgiveness.

Beyond her, the three young midshipmen stood with the anxious crew. Christian gave them an encouraging smile. Then Elwin moved close, and he tensed in expectation of the first touch of cold steel against his flesh.

Pulling the girl's hand close, he pressed her fingers to his lips.

"Don't leave me," he murmured.

Her eyes were soft, luminous, and damp with tears. "'Tis a ... a wonderful smile ye have," she said, her voice breaking. "I wish I'd noticed it before."

The knife touched the raw edge of the wound and Christian shut his eyes.

The girl bent close, her hair hanging over one shoulder and brushing his cheek. "And I'm sorry for everything I said to ye that day Tildy ate my bread," she whispered, her lips moving against his temple. "Ye're a good man, Christian, a fine man, and I think ye're very brave an' worthy."

Elwin was digging around in his wound now. Nausea flared in his stomach, and his shoulder throbbed with fresh agony, the pain radiating into his neck and down his back as the surgeon probed the wound in an unsuccessful attempt to locate the musket ball. Christian gripped the girl's hand like a lifeline; from far away he felt her breath against his face, her soft hand stroking his cheek, his hair.

"Damn," the surgeon snapped, holding the edge of the wound aside with a two-pronged retractor as he dug and probed the hole. "I can't find this godforsaken thing—"

Christian sank his teeth into the leather, hearing the girl's voice fading in and out, coming from a great distance away.

"And I was wrong about Englishmen ... some of ye can actually be quite nice...."

The probe, deep in the wound now, scraped against raw bone, and his testicles seemed to shrivel in agony. The girl's grip on his hand tightened. His molars grinding into the leather, Christian rasped, "I have not forgotten my promise, Miss O' Devir ... when we reach Boston, I shall do all in my power to ... find your brother. So help me God."

Elwin was going deeper, and pain was exploding in great sheets of agony behind his eyes, throbbing in time with his pulse. Christian shuddered, felt the sweat breaking out along his brow and neck. He breathed deeply, trying not to faint as again, the probe scraped against the raw underside of his collarbone.

"Let go," the girl was saying, her lips close to his ear. "Let go, Christian. Succumb to the darkness ... I'll watch over ye."

But the surgeon straightened up, wiping bloody hands on his apron. "I can't get it out," he muttered, glaring at his gathered shipmates as though daring them to defy him. "I can't even *find* the damned thing."

"You've got to get it out," Ian insisted.

"*Now,*" Teach threatened.

"Ye heard what Elwin said! He's going t' bleed t' death if ye don't!"

Elwin swept up the probe once more and with his scalpel, opened the wound further. Fresh blood bubbled out, the captain went rigid and the Irish girl rounded on him. "Jesus, Joseph, an' Mary, ye're *hurtin'* him, Elwin!"

In a fit of temper, Elwin flung the scalpel down and raged, "What do you want? He won't take rum, I can't get the ball out, and there's nothing else to do!"

"Ye'd give up just like that? What kind o' surgeon *are* ye?"

Elwin ripped off his apron and flung it to the floor. "Fine, then —if you think you can do better, do it yourself!"

He shoved past the stunned officers and crew, pushed through the marines, and slammed out.

In the ensuing silence, only the deckhead lantern moved, swinging eerily in the gloom.

Deirdre stood there, shocked, and for a startled moment, she could only stare at those around her. Her stricken gaze moved from Teach to Skunk to Ian to Hendricks to a pale and green-looking Hibbert, to the seamen and red-coated marines pressing against the doorway, and finally to Delight, standing quietly beside her.

They were staring at her. Every last one of them.

"It's your decision, *cherie*," Delight said softly.

Deirdre looked down. The captain was fading fast, the blood, obscene and purple in the glare of the lantern light, pulsing down his chest with every beat of his heart. His eyes, glazed with pain, were half closed.

"You can do it, foundling," he murmured. Then he dragged his eyes open to gaze up at her face. "That is ... if you want to."

The others looked at her, holding their breath.

You can do it.

She stared down at the raw, ominous hole just beneath the ridge of the captain's collarbone, and swallowed hard.

They were waiting. All of them.

She glanced about, but there was no help to be found. The small space was suddenly too hot, the air too thick to breathe, her heart pounding too loudly in her ears. "I—I don't know what to do."

"Just dig the thing out," Skunk said. "Here, we'll all hold him down. Get over here, lads—"

"No," the captain said quietly, his voice now so faint that Deirdre had to bend down to catch his words. "There ... there is no need. Just get on with it, girl." He gave a strained smile. "I have a ship to run, you know."

Aware of every eye in the room, she nodded and, taking a deep, shaky breath, bent over the wound.

Christian closed his eyes as he felt the heavy cross brushing, then resting upon, his bloody chest. Her fingers touched his shoulder. They were gentle, warm, perhaps, if he allowed his mind to drift, even loving. He let out his breath on a long sigh, the tension leaving his body as she held his shoulder with one hand and gently slipped her fingers into the ragged hole of the wound.

Her fingers.

It came to him that she would not use the steel probe, the knife, or any of the other wicked instruments of torture in the surgeon's collection.

She would use her fingers.

He studied her face as she worked, watching her lovely features tighten with concentration. Once, she glanced up at Hendricks as though for reassurance; he nodded, and Christian felt her fingers in his flesh once more. Pain began to throb up into his neck, down his back. He shut his eyes and bit down on the leather, the inside of his cheek, until he tasted blood.

"Easy, Christian," she whispered, her face so close to his shoulder he could feel the warmth of her breath against his skin, the torn flesh itself. Her fingers pushed in deeper, and he bit back a flood of nausea as she touched the raw edge of his collarbone.

Deirdre, however, was nearing despair. She looked up and caught the anxious gazes of the crew. "I can't find it."

"Go deeper," Skunk commanded harshly, pressing closer and blocking the lantern light.

Biting her lip, Deirdre pushed her forefinger back into the hole, feeling the warm embrace of muscle, sinew, and tissue.

The captain moved beneath her, the sweat beginning to roll down his temples. "Keep going," he rasped. "Deeper."

Hot blood pulsed over her fingers. She felt bone, muscle ... and then something round and hard—

"I found it—I think I have it!"

But the ball was slippery, and eluded her.

"Oh, dear God, sweet Mary—"

She glanced down at the captain. Mercifully, he had fainted.

"Quick, girl, get it now, while he can't feel it!" Hendricks urged, shoving forward with the crowd.

"And mind ye doona miss any pieces of his clothing that might be in there, too!"

Her lips tight with concentration, Deirdre pushed her finger back into the hole. Fresh blood welled up and flooded over her knuckles. Holding her breath, she explored deeper—and found the musket ball.

She gripped it between thumb and forefinger and pulled.

"I lost it!"

Teach was there, his hands against the captain's powerful chest to hold him down. "Quick, Deirdre, he's coming to—"

Desperately, she gripped the slick ball once more and, with a cry of triumph, pulled it free.

The room erupted in wild, deafening cheers as Teach grabbed the bloodied bullet and held it up for all to see. "She did it! The lass did it, by God!"

"Three cheers for our Deirdre!"

"Hip, hip, huzzah!"

"Hip, hip, huzzah!"

"Hip, hip, huzzah!"

The pent up sobs came at last. She bent her head to the captain's chest, uncaring that his blood was warm against her cheek and mixing with the tears she could no longer hold back. She felt his wet, wiry chest hair beneath her cheek, his hand resting weakly upon her head—and heard the beat of his heart beneath her ear.

"Thank you," he whispered.

He was alive.

And that was all that mattered.

Chapter Eighteen

Through careful questioning of its captain, Lieutenants MacDuff and Rhodes learned that the French corvette and its consort, the sloop, had happened upon the lone English cutter while transferring arms ... easy prey, they had both thought, until HMS *Bold Marauder* had come upon the scene. But even the combined menace of Arthur Teach, Ian MacDuff, Rico Hendricks, and Skunk could not convince the Frenchman to disclose the name of the sloop, which had promptly fled as the powerful English frigate had closed in.

As for the corvette herself, she now lay far astern, her crew confined in her hold. Manned by survivors from the cutter, they would sail her on to Boston, where the admiral there would decide her fate.

Deirdre, however, was only concerned with her patient, whose side she had not left since she'd extracted the musket ball six days before. She had carefully packed and bandaged his shoulder, walked beside him as Teach and Hendricks had carried him back to his cabin, and held his hand until he had finally succumbed to a strong draught of laudanum. In the days since, she had maintained a faithful vigil beside his bed.

Now, on this night nearly a week after the battle, she stood on deck, gripping the salt-sticky rail and gazing up at the panorama of stars twinkling in the vast sky above. The ocean merged with the night around her. Moonlight frosted the sails, the guns, the deck planking; a harsh wind gusted off the North Atlantic and drove through her clothes, chilling her to the bone.

But she felt alive, exhilarated, and strangely ... *free.*

Beneath her feet, the frigate rose and plunged and rose again in a timeless rhythm that brought with it a sense of eternity. From around her came the sounds of masts creaking and groaning, the hiss of spray at the bows, waves breaking against the hull. She drew the sea air deeply into her lungs. Then she gazed out over the blackened waters, where the reflection of moon and stars coasted atop the restless swells.

"Christian," she said softly.

She felt strange and new, as though her heart had been flushed clean of the bitterness, hatred, and need for revenge that it had carried for so long and now ached to be filled with something good, something joyous, something wonderful.

Below, the sea fell away in great sheets of foam that glinted in the darkness as the frigate smashed down on each heavy swell. Above, the stars were so close she could reach up and touch them. "Christian," she said again, her voice carried away by the breeze. "It doesn't matter anymore that ye're an Englishman, one of the enemy. I'm tired of fightin' what I feel for ye in my heart. I know now that what ye did to me brother all those years ago was somethin' ye didn't want to be doin'. Ye was just followin' orders. That's what ye do. Ye're an officer, who knows no other way of life but discipline and servin' yer country."

The wind snapped the pennants high above.

"It was the *Navy's* fault, Christian. Not yers. And to think of all these years I hated *you*...."

She didn't hate him now. But just when had she begun to love him?

Perhaps when he had discovered her aboard the frigate, intervened on her behalf, and carried her to safety in his powerful arms. Perhaps with that first unforgettable meeting thirteen long years ago. She did not know. She did not care. But the seeds had been sown, somewhere, sometime, and that love had grown with each act of kindness and patience he'd shown her, each time she'd watched him tending his little canine family, each instance he would have been justified in punishing his crew with the harsh and brutal discipline for which the Royal Navy was famous—but had instead reacted with compassion, inventiveness, and yes, *humanity*.

Love.

The final revelation had come during those terrible moments in the surgeon's bay—when Teach had carried him down and she had thought him dead. When fate in the form of a Frenchman's musket ball had placed him in her hands. When he had gazed up at her, his calm gray eyes reflecting trust and confidence that she, Deirdre O'Devir, could succeed where the surgeon had failed.

When he had trusted her with his life.

Love.

Above, the stars grew brilliant, sparkling like chips of crystal in a vast and inky sky. The ocean took on a mysterious beauty, and the frigate's lights spread searching fingers of gold across the waves, as though the ship was reaching out across forever toward her own destiny.

But the frigate, all alone on the sea as she drove steadily on toward Boston, had no one but the lonely helmsman and the bow watch with whom to share the beauty of the night.

The spot at the rail where Deirdre O'Devir had stood was empty.

He had beautiful hair.

With trembling fingers, she reached out and touched it.

The Lord and Master was deeply asleep, thanks to a strong draught of laudanum that Hendricks had slipped into his tea. But it gave Deirdre the opportunity to study this enigmatic man without those cold gray eyes taking her measure. In sleep, and softened by the glow of the single lantern, his face wasn't quite so austere and forbidding; in sleep, it was handsome and youthful, the years dropping away until he was once again the fair-haired lieutenant who'd bent down to calm and reassure a frightened little girl.

Somewhere in a darkened corner of the cabin, she heard the sounds of the puppies in their box, of Tildy quietly licking their tiny bodies. Beside her, the captain's steady, rhythmic breathing was the only other sound. Deirdre sighed, her heart suffused with warmth, and suddenly she wished that *she* had a family, too. A man to love her, care for her, cherish her.

Christian.

By the light of the lantern swinging from the beams above, she pulled up a chair and sat beside him, taking his hand. Her gaze moved over his face. Yes, he had beautiful hair. It was thick and pale and wavy, the color of sunlight at the hottest part of the day, though in the soft light of the lantern, it was almost amber. Leaning forward, she reached out to touch it, and found it soft and springy to the touch.

She looked at him, seeing him as though for the first time. At the haughty, well-shaped brows ... the nose that was straight and proud; his lashes, thick and pale, bleached at the tips and lying heavily against high and prominent cheekbones. She'd never realized that a man could have such long lashes, that a man could have such beautiful hair; she'd never realized how handsome and vulnerable a man could look in sleep; and never, ever, in a thousand years had she thought to apply any of those words—*handsome, beautiful, vulnerable*—to the cold and enigmatic captain of His Majesty's Ship *Bold Marauder*.

The cabin seemed suddenly stuffy, the air cloying and still. Mesmerized, Deirdre let her fingers drift to the pale locks that swept back from his temple, and then the faded bruise just beneath. Her touch lingered there, feeling the fragile pulse that beat beneath her fingertips.

Her eyes filled with wonder.

He was an Englishman. The enemy. Part of that hated race that had been tramping on the rights and land of her people for centuries. But enemies were supposed to be cold and alien, monstrous and inhuman—weren't they? Yet this man's skin was as warm as her own. His pulse beat just as strongly as hers did, his chest rose and fell with the same breath, and the blood that had flowed so freely from his shoulder was just as red as hers.

Her throat tightened as she remembered his agony during the surgery. As stoic as he had been, he had felt pain as acutely as any Irishman she'd ever known.

Weren't enemies supposed to be ... *different?*

But no. He was human, warm and alive and breathing. He had hopes and fears, dreams and visions, and somewhere, people who cared about and loved him. *He was no different than she was*—except he'd been born in a different place.

Deirdre swallowed against the lump in her throat.

"I'm sorry, Christian," she whispered, her heart aching. "God help me, I'm so sorry."

She lifted his hand and held it to her cheek, seeing his face, the pulse beating at his throat, the magnificent, muscled expanse of his chest—and remembering how safe she'd felt when he'd gathered her against it and let her cry all those weeks ago when the men had been about to whip her.

She touched his bandaged shoulder, then placed her hand directly over his heart, feeling it beating steadily beneath her palm. Then, unbidden, her gaze moved downward, to the covers that draped his hips.

Heat flooded her cheeks. She did not have to lift the blankets to know he was naked beneath.

His tortured confession—that he was unable to function as a man—suddenly came back to her.

And as for your precious virtue, you needn't worry about me compromising it, Miss O' Devir. I have been unable to feel anything for any woman since my wife died, and you, I can assure you, haven't a prayer of stirring lusts I no longer have.

What was wrong with him that he lacked this ... ability? What possible defect could he have? And who, God help her, would ever know if she lifted the blanket for a mere second, just to see for herself what this horrible defect was?

She bit her lip and shot a nervous glance toward the door. What if Hendricks came? What if Evans looked in on them? What if—

No. It was late. No one would come. It was just her and Captain Lord.

Go ahead. Look. He'll never know.

Swallowing hard, Deirdre reached down and gingerly gripping the blanket between her thumb and forefinger, lifted it.

EMILY.

He braced himself, even though he knew it was the nightmare in all its horrifying familiarity; he heard the same noises downstairs, crept from the empty bed, descended the stairs, and paused behind the door. He heard her laughter and saw the two bodies entwined; he heard his own howl of rage and saw the intruder, terrified and cowardly, fleeing.

This time, Christian vowed, he'd bloody well kill the bastard.

But this time, the nightmare was different.

Her voice rang out behind him, pleading and desperate. "Christian, no! Let it go! You know what will happen if you don't!

He'll throw the lantern and there'll be a fire! I'll *die,* Christian, and this nightmare will haunt you for the rest of your days!"

She *knew* about the nightmare? Confusion drove through him. The hall seemed unreal and fantastic, and beneath his feet, the cold marble floor surged back and forth, not unlike the deck of a ship. Yes, it was a dream. But if he kept going, it would become the nightmare.

"Don't *do* it, Christian!"

He paused, hearing her lover fleeing the house; then, with a fierce cry, Christian turned and ran back to that closed door, knowing this would be the only chance he would ever have to forgive her, put an end to the nightmare—

He flung open the door and saw her.

"Christian," she said in a husky dream-voice.

His mouth fell open and the breath caught in his throat. He stumbled back against the doorframe, shaking badly.

She was lying on the sofa. Her legs were open, her eyes were hungry, and she was naked.

Waiting for him.

❧

DEIRDRE HADN'T MEANT to do more than just *peek* at him, and briefly at that. She hadn't meant to do more than just *look* at his maleness for a moment, to see what it was about it that made him unable to function.

Unable to function, he'd implied.

And her words: *Useless as a man.*

Now, gazing down, she saw that he'd been right.

There was no big secret beneath the covers, nothing to hold one's breath over, and with an odd, empty feeling of sadness, she stared at the limp and flaccid flesh that lay nestled in the patch of hair between his thighs.

Useless as a man.

She felt pity for Captain Lord, and then anger that she felt the pity. He had told her the truth. There was no way that this sad bit of pale flesh could ever do a man's work, like a proud stallion with a mare. What lay beneath her gaze was slack and still.

Her breath came out on a sigh. Slowly, she peeled the blanket back, farther and farther, finally laying it across his knees and exposing the whole of his loins to her blushing gaze. Pity, that such a proud and handsome specimen of a man—even if he *was* English—was so ... deformed.

But here was the proof.

She reached down, thinking to pull the covers back up over his groin, but instead, her fingers strayed to the limp curve of flesh.

It was warm; quite so, in fact. Holding her breath, she nervously glanced at its owner's face. He didn't move. Bolder now, she looked back at the thicket of springy hair, slid her fingers into it and then, carefully, beneath the male flesh. She stared at it; then she stared up at his still face; then she stared back at the warm flesh in her hand, and felt it give a little quiver.

She gave a little start and glanced at his face, her own cheeks flaming red. He was deeply asleep; no doubt the tremor she'd felt against her suddenly moist palm was nothing more than some perfectly normal body function or, perhaps, a twitch from a dream.

Her heart began to pound loud enough to echo in her ears. She bit her lip, held her breath, and touched the limp flesh again, wondering at its soft and velvety texture.

Again that involuntary tremor.

"Oh, my," she breathed, frowning. It felt different; a bit warmer, maybe a bit firmer. She stared hard at it, wondering, in the lantern-lit gloom, if there was something suddenly different about it; then her eyes widened.

Heat washed over her face. She wasn't imagining things. That alien bit of anatomy was not only warmer, not only firmer—it was *bigger*.

The captain sighed softly in his sleep, and then groaned. But Deirdre was no longer looking at his face. Frozen, she cupped the growing—yes, it *was* growing—length of him in her hand and watched, mesmerized, as it began to transform itself before her very eyes, growing stiff and hard and hot in her hand.

And large.

Very large.

Replace the covers. Get out of here before he wakes up. Now, before, before—

But transfixed, she couldn't move.

EMILY.

Her hair was dark and glorious, spread out over the arm of the sofa, trailing halfway to the floor. Her thighs were open with invitation, the dark patch of hair at their center glistening, eager, and damp; her arms were raised, her eyes hungry.

His felt himself stirring.

"Come to me, Christian ... you know he never meant anything to me ... it is *you* I love, you I *want* ... this is your only chance, darling. Your only chance to say goodbye before I leave you forever."

"No, please ... *Don't go.*"

"Christian, darling, you *know* this is a dream. I'm dead, remember?"

No, not dead. No dead woman looked like she did. Tears stung his eyes, that he should be given this chance to make things right after all these years, even if it was a dream, even if the woman on the sofa was not the shy Emily he had married, but a sultry vixen with the eyes of a courtesan. With a helpless groan he went to her, shedding his robe and letting it slip to the floor as he joined her on the sofa.

Wake up, Christian. It's a dream.

No. He fought the tug, the pull, to awaken.

His body hardened in response to her. Her arms came up to touch his shoulders, rove down his back, skim over his buttocks. "There now," she breathed, her voice warm against the curve of his shoulder. "Aren't you glad you didn't chase after him? Aren't you glad you came back to *me*?"

"You're — this is a dream."

Her hands were on him, sweet and gentle yet confident where they needed to be, *when* they needed to be. One moment feathery and grazing; the next, bold and exploring. Desire rocked him and he sprang to life in her hands, tightening in soundless pleasure, his breathing harsh, his heartbeat filling his ears.

Such gentle hands. Such *soft* hands.

He groaned, and broke out in a sweat. He felt the fog swirling around him, and in that weird way of dreams, the scene shifted and she was suddenly above him, no longer Emily but someone else. He couldn't see her face, but that didn't matter, for his eyes were closed. He couldn't hear her voice but that didn't matter either, because it was a dream. The only thing that mattered was that she was loving him and he, tortured, hardened and alone, had not been loved by anyone for so very, very long....

He gritted his teeth, and his eyes rolled up behind tightly clenched lids.

"Dear God," he said roughly, one hand gripping the sheets. "Dear God, please don't stop."

"I WON'T," Deirdre said.

Her cheeks burned hot. Her eyes were wide and staring, her breathing thick and measured. Strange feelings gathered in the pit of her belly, burned between her legs, and she felt a spreading moisture there that only increased with each movement the captain made on the bed beneath her, with every rasp of his tortured breath, with every twitch of his legs, his hands, his—

No limp and flaccid piece of sorry flesh, this! Dear heavens, the thing filled her hand and defied the span of her encircling fingers; it was hard as marble, proud and stiff and tall, and with every brush of her thumb across the engorged head, it jumped.

A pearl drop had gathered on the blunted tip, gleaming in the lantern light. Deirdre stared at it for a moment, then recklessly smudged it over the velvety cap.

He moaned, still in the throes of sleep, and his head moved restlessly on the pillow.

Heady excitement surged through her. *She* had brought him to this state. She would give him this gift of confidence, and prove to him that there was nothing wrong with him, despite what he believed. She would show him, make him understand, that he was far from being "useless as a man."

Encircling him between thumb and forefinger, she squeezed him gently. His breathing quickened, and a fine sheen of sweat glistened on his brow.

"Yes," he murmured thickly.

Deirdre smiled, watching his face, the harsh mouth that was now slack with passion, the eyes that moved rapidly beneath his lids.

"Please, don't stop."

She tightened the circle of her fingers, feeling the answering heat in her own blood, in the thundering of her heart against her ribs, the flooding dampness between her thighs.

"Don't stop ... *please.*"

She couldn't stop even if she wanted to. Breathing as hard as he, she stroked harder ... faster ... velvet over steel, up and down, faster, faster—

He suddenly stiffened and cried out in his sleep, his body

convulsing in great, mighty shudders, and as she froze in terror, wondering if she'd killed him, something warm and wet spurted over her hand, her wrist, her arm, his belly.

The gray eyes shot open.

Her heart was thundering. Her blood was racing. She jumped up and took an involuntary step backward, away from that confused stare—a stare that reflected horror and then, raw, bone-chilling fury.

Chapter Nineteen

"**B**y God, woman, have you no shame?" Christian roared, mortified, as he came suddenly and rudely awake. Snatching the blanket, he hauled it up over his thighs and snarled, "Go, *leave me!*"

"But you asked me to—"

"*I said leave me!*"

"Ye can order me to leave, Captain Lord, but I doubt ye're as strong as ye'd like to think ye are," she said, with a pointed glance at his bandaged shoulder. "I'm staying."

"You will leave now, by God, or I'll toss you out on your bloody ear!"

"I only looked because I wanted to see what ye meant when ye said ye were *useless* as a man—"

"*You* said I was useless as a man—I merely said I couldn't function as one!"

"—and I did what I did because ye *asked* me to!"

He froze, his eyes narrowing. "*Asked* you to?"

"Aye. Ye not only *asked* me to, ye told me not to stop."

He set his jaw and turned his face away, his lips a slash of anger. Deirdre pushed the chair aside, moved closer to the bed, and sat down beside him. "I'm sorry," she murmured. Her chin came up and she met his angry, accusing glare. "But I thought I could help ye, especially since ye've been goin' on so about how deformed ye are—"

"*Deformed?*" he thundered, bolting upright. "Deprived, madam, but, I can assure you, not *deformed*!"

"Ye don't have to be yellin' at me! I just wanted to see what was wrong with ye so I could ... so I could help ye to get over it. And now I think there be somethin' wrong with *me,* because my— my—oh, I ache in funny places, and—"

Christian swore roundly. Then, damning himself for a fool, he gathered her close, his fingers tangling in her curls. "I'm sorry," he muttered.

"No, I am. I never meant to make ye feel bad, Christian."

"You didn't. You made me feel ... good." He felt her arms going hesitantly around his neck, and shut his eyes in defeat. "There is nothing wrong with you, Deirdre. What you are feeling is simply a healthy female attraction and response to the male species, a feeling no doubt exacerbated by the shocking spectacle your virgin eyes have just witnessed."

Against his neck, she whispered, "Do you ... do you have these feelings, too?"

"Yes, I have them, too ... for all the good they do me," he said bitterly.

"I don't understand."

"They do me no good, Deirdre, because I ... because I—" He set her back and looked away, too ashamed to meet her questing gaze. "Oh, the devil take it, *because I cannot function as a man*!"

She stared at him, at the proud, hawkish profile, the sharp cast of his nose, the lips that were compressed in a slash of pain and humiliation. "But wasn't that a manly thing ye just did while ye was sleepin'?"

"Aye," he said tightly.

"Then ye must be able to function quite *well* as a man."

"I was asleep!" he snapped, as though that explained everything. "Awake, I fear I cannot sustain that—that *state* long enough to—" He looked away, unable to meet her gaze. "This is most uncomfortable for me to discuss. I have my pride, and you are making a shambles of it by forcing me to admit that I am ... that I am ... impotent."

"But what just happened—"

"I told you, I was *asleep*!"

"Why can't ye do such a thing awake?"

"Because a certain jealous specter of my past—*my dead wife*—will not allow it." His eyes were raw with anguish and shame. Then he saw the confusion on her face, and his manner softened. He took a deep, steadying breath. "You see, Deirdre, there is nothing *anatomically* wrong with me." He sighed, and pointed to his temple. "It's all in *here*. My ... my jealous specter, if you will. As long as I blame myself for the death of my wife, I am of no use to any woman."

The silence hung heavily between them. Voices drifted down to them from above, and the deck began to slant as the frigate leaned hard over onto the opposite tack. Deirdre looked down at his hand, lying stiffly atop the blanket, and reached out to take it in her own.

He did not pull away.

"Ye are of use to *me*, Captain Lord, whether or not ye can ... *function*." Against her hip, she felt the hard ridge of his thigh, and it took all of her will not to reach out and touch it, just to see how hard and muscled it was.

He didn't answer, only the sudden tightening of his fingers over her own indicating that he'd heard.

"Christian?" she said softly.

He looked up, his eyes tortured, his mouth a grim line of pain. "You are too young, too innocent, to speak of such things," he said sharply. "Now go, leave me, while I still have my pride and you, the remains of your innocence. This discussion should not be taking place. It is … it is improper."

"Nay, Christian, it *should* be takin' place. It should've taken place a long time ago."

"By God, just *go,* before I lose my patience as well as my damned dignity."

Her chin came up and she faced him defiantly. "And yer heart, Captain? 'Tis innocent I may be, but I'm not stupid. I know the look a man gets in his eyes when he sees a woman he fancies. D'ye think yer Emily has robbed ye of even *that*? No, the only thing she's robbed ye of is yer confidence. I don't believe for an instant that she's made ye as *useless* as ye've led yerself—and, for a while, me—to believe. Oh, no, I think ye can function as well as any man."

"This is not a subject I care to discuss."

"What, are ye afraid, then?"

"Do not challenge me, girl. You may find yourself in waters over your head."

"No, Christian, 'tis *you,* I think, who's afraid. Afraid of settin' yerself free to love another. Afraid of followin' the wants of yer heart, yer body, for fear of discoverin' that ye *can* love someone else—someone who's not yer dear Emily. And that scares ye, doesn't it?"

His face hardened.

"Doesn't it?"

"By God—"

"The good Lord didn't put us on this earth to suffer. Maybe ye think it'll atone for whatever happened to yer wife, but torturin' yerself isn't going to bring her back."

He looked away.

"What happened to her, Christian? What happened, that smiling comes hard to ye, and ye can't sleep without nightmares that are so terrible that they frighten even those of us who're on the outside lookin' in?"

"Isn't it obvious? She died." His mouth hardened. "Because of me."

Deirdre said nothing, and waited for him to continue.

He looked up at the deckhead, his eyes distant. "It was five years ago. I had been away at sea. I came home, and was awakened in the night by an empty bed and voices downstairs. Hers ... and a man's." He swallowed, hard. "I got up to investigate, of course, and found that she'd taken a lover in my absence. *Because* of my absence. I chased the fellow ... he threw a lantern and in moments, the house was in flames. He escaped. Emily did not. I was unable to save her, and she—she died in the fire."

From outside, came the hum of wind in the rigging, the endless creaks and moans of a wooden ship at sea.

The clang of the ship's bell, the sound of the watch being changed.

"I'm sorry, Christian," Deirdre said quietly. "And I'm sorrier, still, that ye blame yerself for what happened. That's a heavy burden to bear, but don't ye think five years is a long enough time to be pullin' it?"

He turned his face away, blinking. "You should go, Deirdre."

His hand gripped hers, belying his words.

"Nay, Christian. I cannot, and I will not. Ye need me."

"I don't need you. I don't need *anyone*."

"Well, I need *you*." She took both his hands in her own. "I need that fair-haired lieutenant who came to Connemara, a man who laughed and smiled and took the time to calm a frightened child. Where is that man now, Christian?"

"He is long gone," he said harshly, his face still averted.

"Nay, I see him still. I see him in the captain who tries so hard to appear cold and distant, yet who croons to and cuddles a little dog when he thinks no one is lookin'. I see him in the man who cannot stand to see anything helpless and hurt. I see him in the officer who follows Royal Navy customs and rules to the letter, but who hasn't the heart to have an offender whipped. Oh, no.

That man's still in there." She laid her palm across his heart. "Right *here*. He just needs someone to show him out o' the prison he's locked himself in."

"Why should you care? After what I've done to you?"

"Christian ... ye didn't *want* to do what ye did to me brother those thirteen years ago. I didn't know it then, but after watchin' ye, and gettin' to know ye these past weeks, I know it now. Ye're a product of the Navy. Ye live by its rules, its traditions, its principles. If I blame anyone for taking me brother, 'tis them, not you." She reached out and touched his jaw, his cheek. "I forgive ye, Christian."

He shut his eyes, unable to speak.

She leaned down and, ever so gently, placed her lips against his brow. He trembled violently. The cross slipped free of her shirt and lay heavily upon his chest. She felt him blink his eyes, the tips of his lashes grazing the underside of her throat, and gently kissed the faded bruise at his temple. Then she drew back, cupped his face in her hands, and looked deeply into his eyes, pretending not to notice the tell-tale glassiness of unshed tears, the rising emotion he was desperate to contain.

"For an Englishman, ye're very handsome," she said. "'Specially when ye smile. Ye just need someone to make ye do it more often."

He took a deep, measured breath.

"And ye need someone to bring ye laughter and joy, someone to be making a big fuss over ye and tellin' ye how special ye are."

He trembled with the supreme amount of will it took to control his emotion.

"And ye need someone to ... to love ye." She gathered her thick, curly fall of hair, draped it over one shoulder, and pulling back the covers once more, climbed into the narrow bed beside him.

Her arm went around his chest, holding him close to her own

body, and answering heat began to beat in his blood even as the dimly lit cabin went blurry with unshed tears.

Don't do this to me, he thought desperately as she drew him close, her tiny hand warm against his ribs, gently stroking him with overwhelming tenderness. *Don't shatter these defenses ... they're all I have.*

The back of his throat began to ache, and he fought to control himself. He did not trust himself to touch her in kind, to respond to her, to even push her away. He did not trust himself to move. He did not trust himself to—

"I love ye, Christian," she said.

He shuddered and shut his eyes, hoping that in the gloom, she would not see the wetness that was spreading down his cheek.

"And ye don't have to suffer this alone."

He began to shake, and a single, desperate sob caught in his throat.

"I'm here for ye, Christian. For as long as ye want me to be."

He couldn't move. His heart's final defenses were slowly crumbling.

Tumbling.

Crashing to the feet of this young woman.

She had saved his life, when she'd had every reason to hate him enough to see him dead. She had dug a musket ball out of his shoulder—not with the steel probe, not with the harshness of a cold piece of metal, but with the loving gentleness of her bare fingers.

She had said she loved him.

"Nobody should live in the kind of hell ye put yerself in every night, Christian. It's time to let it all go. Time to forgive yourself. To live the life that God set before ye."

He took a deep, shuddering breath.

"Hug me, Christian."

He needed no encouragement. He turned toward her, and she was suddenly crushed against him with a desperation that nearly broke her ribs. She felt his big body begin to quake with deep, awful sobs that shook him to the core.

"It's all right, Christian," she whispered, holding him close. "It's all right...."

He clung to her, and her own arm went around his shoulders, holding him close.

"Go ahead and let it out," she murmured, hugging him, rocking him, holding him, loving him. "No wound's ever healed till the poison comes out. Yers has been festerin' for five long years. There's no shame in lettin' it go."

"She haunts my dreams every night. I see her face in the flames ... I hear her screams as she's dying ... *dear God, I smell her burning*." Harsh sobs racked him, and she felt his pain as her own, felt her own tears running hotly down her cheeks and splashing upon his proud shoulder.

"She's dead, Christian, and nothin' ye say or do can bring her back," she said gently, feeling dwarfed by his size and strength as she held him close and her own tears mixed with his. "Ye've given five years to torturin' yerself about it. Do ye want to sacrifice the rest of yer life to sufferin' as well? Ye're healthy and whole. If the good Lord didn't want ye to live, he'd have taken you, too. Such decisions aren't ours to question, merely to accept."

Her hands, gently and soothing, roved down his back. Christian clung to her, ashamed that she should see him thus: he, a proud and decorated sea warrior, veteran of countless battles, laid low and sobbing in the arms of a woman.

She's dead, Christian.

The words pierced him.

Dead. Powerless. Unable to give him nightmares unless he allowed it. Unable to torment him unless he permitted it. Unable to harm him, hurt him, haunt him. For five long years he had allowed it, yes, perhaps even *wanted* it, as atonement for his failure to get her out of the burning house, as punishment for leaving her for so long while he was away at sea. The nightmares, the guilt, the grief—Emily had not done that to him; he had done it to himself.

In the quiet darkness, lit only by the soft glow of the lantern, he felt something open in his soul, like huge black clouds filing out after a heavy storm, and the pain and grief that had been his sole companions for so long began to file out with it. He saw Emily's face, lingering briefly; then she began to fade, until there was nothing left but a quiet exhaustion and a tremulous, fragile hope.

Through the stern windows, dawn's pink light began to glow against the sea.

Christian cupped the wet cheeks of the woman who held him so tightly. "Deirdre," he breathed, and on a broken, victorious sob, claimed her lips with his own.

Chapter Twenty

Deirdre melted against him, feeling the hard strength of his arm behind her back, sighing as his lips drove against hers and his tongue slipped out to coax her lips apart. She pushed closer to him. His tongue pressed against her teeth and she opened her mouth to him, touching her own tongue to his, hesitantly at first, then with growing confidence. Her heart began to pound. Her clothes began to feel too warm, too tight, too constricting. The strange heat between her thighs began to thread its way up her belly. *Breathe*, she thought, somewhat dizzily. She sucked in a great lungful of air through her nose. She had it now. She was breathing all right, and breathing hard.

So was he.

He dragged his mouth away from hers and when she looked up into his face, she saw that his eyes were dark, heavy-lidded and intense—and that he was smiling. *Smiling.* For her, and at her, in relief, in triumph ... in wonder.

"Deirdre," he said simply, and touched her cheek.

He was looking at her as though he had just discovered something beautiful and revered. His gaze roved over every detail of her face and she blushed, feeling suddenly shy. He reached out and cupped her jaw against his palm, his thumb gently rubbing her cheek as he studied her with an intensity that brought a swirl of heat to her insides.

"Thank you," he murmured. "Thank you ... for not leaving me, even when I asked it."

His hand slid through her hair, cradling the back of her head and pulling her close. She closed her eyes as his lips, so hard, so warm, found her own once more. She moaned deep in her throat and pressed against him, feeling his other hand come up to gently touch the rise of her breast, and then, the gold chain that hung around her neck, following it down until he came to the cross.

Slowly he pulled away, his head bent and his pale hair falling over his brow as he gazed down at the talisman in his hand.

"It never leaves me," Deirdre said, feeling a need to explain.

"I know."

"'Tis part of me ... part o' me heritage ... but if it disturbs ye for me to be wearin' it in light of what's about to happen between us, well ... I suppose I can take it off."

"Do you wish, uh, something to happen between us?" he asked, with a little smile.

"I don't think I'd be lyin' here in a narrow bed with a man as naked as the day he was born, if I didn't."

He looked up then, smiled, and gently let the cross fall back against her shirt. Then he leaned close. His lips touched her brow, and his breath warmed her temple. "Leave it on, then," he murmured. "It is as much a part of you as that bottle of Irish seawater, or the bread that Tildy ate."

"Aye, Christian," she said soberly. "'Tis more than a part o' me. 'Tis a part of *Ireland*."

He gathered her close, clasping her tightly to his chest. She shut her eyes again, her chin just touching his bandaged shoulder, every nerve in her body jumping, every inch of her skin tingling. Neither spoke. The silence stretched on until it became awkward for both of them; he, knowing what he wanted but afraid of failing himself and her; she, knowing what she wanted but innocent, unsure, and afraid to push him too far, too fast. The cabin began to glow pink in the light of the strengthening dawn, and tiny orange diamonds began to glint off the waves beyond the stern windows as the sun slowly heaved itself above the horizon. But neither noticed. They were aware only of each other: he, of her soft, soapy scent, a strand of hair that was tangled in his eyelashes, the swell of her breasts pushing against his bare chest; she, of the hard muscles of his shoulder, the little scar on the side of his neck only an inch from her nose, the scent of his skin and the thump of his heartbeat against her own.

"I"—he took a deep breath—"I do not know if I ... if I can do this, Deirdre."

She pulled back slightly and looked into his eyes. Gently, she said, "If ye can't, Christian ... only the two of us will ever know."

He tightened his mouth and stared down at the deck flooring. Long moments went by, and she sensed the inner war he was waging; for him, the courage he had to muster for this most manly of acts, this most supreme test of his masculinity, must be far more than that of sending a ship into battle.

And then he raised his head and looked at her, his voice commanding and direct.

"Go lock the door, Deirdre."

Her heart began to race. She slid from the bed and did as he bade. It took her a moment to accomplish the task, so badly was her hand shaking. Then, taking a deep breath, she turned and slowly faced him, suddenly aware of the sensuous feel of her hair falling in thick, riotous disarray around her shoulders and back and breasts.

He smiled, looking unbearably handsome in the warm pink and orange light.

"Come here, Deirdre."

She wrapped her arms around herself and moved back across the cabin to where he lay, her gaze never leaving his. Every sensation was heightened, acute: the scent of the sea outside, the taste of nervous anticipation in her mouth; the fear and eagerness of the unknown; the chill of the air, the hard deck beneath her feet, the thunderous echo of her heartbeat in her ears.

He raised his hand, stopping her several feet away from the bed.

"Deirdre—" His voice was hoarse, shaky, a direct contrast to the boldness of his eye. "I want you to be sure this is what you want. This might be your last chance to leave."

She hugged herself tighter, knowing that despite his injured shoulder, his fears, and his tenuous, slipping grasp on his standards of behavior as an officer and a gentleman, he did not want her to go.

She walked straight up to him and into his arms. "I don't *want* to leave, Christian. Not now ... not ever."

"Ah, Deirdre," he murmured, pulling her down with him. "Against every principle I hold dear, against every rule I enforce, against every shred of my conscience, my morals, my better judgment ... you have broken me."

She cradled his face in her hands, shamelessly kissing his lightly-stubbled cheek, his jaw, the corners of his mouth.

"You're shivering," he said.

"I haven't done this before."

"Slide under the covers with me."

She did so, wrapping her arms around his neck as he kissed her once more, his mouth moving urgently against her own. Beneath her shirt, his hands—big and warm, the palms rough with callous—cradled her breasts, teased the nipples, burned a path over her skin. She kicked off her shoes, heard them thump on the deck flooring, and broke the kiss long enough for him to coax her shirt over her head, the trousers following it on its way to the floor. Cold air swept against her skin; his palm roved over her bottom, down her thighs, and then he pulled her protectively close and back under the blankets with him.

The heat of his powerful body was like a furnace. She molded herself to it, delighting in the roughness of his chest against her breasts, the feel of his arms pulling her close. There, that stab of sensation deep in the pit of her belly again; there, a flood of dampness between her legs. Her toes curled with pleasure, and she quivered in eagerness as he drew the blanket up to their chins, encasing them in warmth and making her feel delightfully wicked and wanton in the knowledge that they were both shamelessly naked beneath.

His breath was warm against her nose and cheeks and brow. She moved restlessly as sensation built within her and her nipples tingled with a gnawing ache. Anticipation rocked her body, and suddenly she realized that now it was she who was shaking, he whose hands were confident and masterful.

"Yer shoulder," she said weakly, pushing back a bit so that they lay side-by-side, facing each other.

"Bugger my shoulder." Beneath the blanket, his palm trailed down her arm and over the concave dip of her hip. "I know what it is capable of."

Face-to-face on the pillow, they gazed into each other's eyes, touching and exploring. Never had Deirdre experienced the sensation of a male body against hers and the feeling left her deliciously weak. She was aware of his chest hair against her breasts; the heaviness of one hard, muscled leg thrown possessively over her thigh; the scrape of his foot as it moved up and down her calf....

And the feel of his manhood—strong, rigid, hot, and pulsing with life—against her belly.

She reached down beneath the covers and touched it, feeling it throb with response; but he gently pulled her hand away, guiding it upward and murmuring that she must not rush things. Her fingers splayed against his chest, tangling in the mat of crisp hair as his hand moved over her skin. Her breathing grew harsh, raspy, erratic with each new spot he touched, each previously unexplored inch of flesh.

Gently he coaxed her onto her back and, supporting his weight on his good side, pushed the blanket down her belly, leaving it bunched above her knees. She shut her eyes, trembling as he rained gentle kisses over her face, her lips, her eyelids.

"Relax," he murmured, remembering that she was an innocent virgin. "You have taught me how to hug, how to smile, encouraged me to live again. Now let me show you what it feels like to be cherished, adored, worshipped ... loved."

Deirdre melted inside.

Unsure what to do, she settled back, quaking at the vibrant bursts of sensation each touch of his hand, each press of his lips, brought her. She felt his fingers moving over her collarbone, her breasts, the rise of her ribs and the curve of her hips. His mouth grazed her cheek, leaving hot kisses in its wake; then he kissed her, gently at first, then fiercely, drawing the very breath and soul from her with the searing intensity of his desire. Fear filled her, fear that she was not behaving the way she was supposed to, that she might do something wrong, that in doing so she might upset the delicate balance that he was so afraid he would lose.

But he did not seem to share her concern.

He lifted his head again, his breath coming harder. "I am going to kiss you now, Deirdre."

"But ... wasn't that what ye were just doin'?"

"I have only just *begun* kissing you."

She shut her eyes tightly, quivering and hot inside as his mouth roved deliciously over hers once more. And then, kiss her he did—her forehead, the base of her nose, her cheeks, her fluttering lashes, the coarse spirals of her hair. He lifted each of her hands and kissed her palms; he kissed the inside of her elbow, her forearm, and touched his tongue to the underside of her wrist until gooseflesh puckered her skin and feathers of sensation darted through her belly. He bent to take her mouth once more, and she felt his thumb grazing the wildly beating pulse at the base of her throat as she met his kiss with building need and a hunger she was only just beginning to understand.

His head lowered, and she threaded her fingers in his hair, holding him close. His lips were warm against the side of her neck, her collarbone. He nuzzled the cross aside and she heard herself making little noises in her throat as his mouth brushed across her breasts, warm and gentle and leaving her wanting more. She felt his lips against one aching peak. Wetness as his tongue slipped out to touch and taste the erect and hardening nipple. Deirdre caught her breath and sat up with a gasp.

"Lie back, foundling."

"Are ye *supposed* to kiss me there?"

"Yes, love. I'm supposed to kiss you *everywhere*."

"But, Christian, I don't know if ye should. I mean it's been a long time, and ye might be forgettin' just where ye're supposed to be kissin'—"

His lips twitched and he bent his head once more, hefting her breast in one hand and kissing his way around her nipple. "I can assure you, dearest, that I've not forgotten a single, blessed thing." He looked up, touched her cheek to reassure her, and pressed firmly against her shoulder to coax her back down to the bed. "Now, relax ... or do you not enjoy this?"

"I ... I'm scared, Christian."

"Shall I stop?"

"N-no!"

He smiled then, and never had she thought a man could be more handsome than the Lord and Master. And then she forgot all else as his head lowered once more, his lips, and then his tongue, playing with her tightened nipple until the fire between her thighs became unbearable. She sucked her lips between her teeth and touched tremulous fingers to his hair, crushing the pale locks in her fist as the pressure of his lips became a little less gentle, a little less hesitant, a little less restrained.

His mouth moved to the other breast, and she gasped as she felt the hot-cool wetness of his tongue against that nipple, too, tracing circles over it until it tingled and ached. His hand was warm against the underside of her breast, pushing it up so that he could better taste it, and then he drew the nipple fully into his mouth, sucking it hard while his hand returned to the other breast and his thumb stroked the hardened peak. Deirdre whimpered with need, her lips clinging desperately to his as his palm skimmed the curve of her waist and flared out over her hip, his thumb nearing that aching, throbbing, burning part of her that was begging so shamelessly for his touch.

His mouth left her breast, and cool air rushed in to take its place. She lay there, her breath coming hard and fast as he eased himself onto his side, resting his weight on his good shoulder while his admiring gaze swept over her.

Deirdre blushed, hotly.

"You," he murmured. "Are beautiful."

She was all too aware of his hand, warm and delicious against her belly, the nearness of his fingers to that part of her that seemed to have caught on fire.

"But Christian, I don't know what I'm supposed to *do*," she said in a little voice.

He smiled. His hand fanned out over her belly, the fingers now spreading to slide against her pubic bone and the soft curls that lay between her legs. "Deirdre, love, you needn't *do* anything ... yet. Next time, maybe, but for now ... for now, just let the captain be in command, eh?"

She took a deep shaky breath and realized, suddenly, that that male part of him that had so fascinated her earlier was pressing hard against her thigh. "Aye, Christian. Ye teach, and I'll do my best to learn." She shut her eyes, stiffened her arms at her sides, and waited.

He gave a little laugh, and spent a few moments dragging his hand through a long, spiraling curl that trailed over her shoulder, encouraging her to relax, allowing her time to get used to the feel of a man's hand and mouth against her virgin flesh.

"Are you sure you want to do this?"

His hand left her hair, roved down over her breast, and she shivered as his thumb circled her nipple and teased it back into a taut peak. "Aye, Christian—after one last, wee request."

He rose onto his elbow, his chest and shoulders filling her vision. "Yes?"

She gazed up at him, and swallowed hard. "Which way ... is Ireland?"

His hand stopped abruptly. *"Ireland?"*

"Aye." Sheepishly she added, "I need to know which direction it's in so that when this monumental thing ye're goin' to do to me happens, I can be facin' it."

He stared at her. A corner of his mouth twitched with amusement. Then his face crumpled and rich, heady laughter tumbled out of his chest. "Bless me, Deirdre, nowhere on this earth is there anyone like you. Ireland lies far beneath the horizon, and at your feet. Precisely where it should be." His laughter faded away and he stared down at her, his eyes becoming soft with love once more. "Now, pray, is there anything else you demand of me?"

"Aye, Christian."

Her hand came up to touch his cheek. "And that is, my dear, homesick little love?"

"I want ye to keep kissin' me."

Smiling, he claimed her lips, drinking of the honeyed sweetness of her mouth. Her arms wound around his neck and he knew, suddenly, that his time was limited and that every fear he'd had about his ability to complete this act had been for naught. The sweet anguish was growing harder and harder to bear, and it was all he could do to slow himself down as he moved his hands over her trembling body, soothing her, calming her, teasing her ... arousing her.

Five long years since he'd had a woman. Five long years since

Emily had been taken from him. He cringed, waiting for his dead wife's face to appear before him and smash his desire to pulp. But there was only the loveliness of this sweet, brave young woman beneath him, only the pale and untried sweetness of her body, only the reverent adoration in her wide purple eyes that drove through his heart and wrapped itself around his hungry soul.

He pressed his face into the curve of her shoulder, burying his nose in her fragrant curls as his hand caressed her belly and his fingers twined in the soft, silky curls at the junction of her thighs. She clamped her legs together, her whole body going tense.

"Open, love," he murmured against her neck. "Open, and let me touch you."

"It ... it tickles, Christian."

He drew back, forcing himself to go slow and easy with her. But his staff was hot and throbbing, driving itself against her thigh and begging for release. *Control,* he told himself. *Just go slow.*

He slid his fingers through the silky triangle between her thighs, seeking her opening. He found her slick and wet and hot, and it was a struggle to get his own breathing under control as she responded to his touch with an answering shiver, the lips of her femininity clamping around his gently questing fingers.

"Relax," he murmured. She did so, and allowed him to gently ease her legs apart ... then she caught her breath as he slid a finger between the soft folds of her womanhood and stroked her gently, back and forth, over and over again. He took a deep and steadying breath and bent his head to her nipple once more, his fingers smearing her dampness through her curls as she pushed herself upward against his hand, seeking a deeper touch.

From somewhere, he heard her soft voice: "Aye, Christian ... it feels good, real good, just like ye said it would."

"It will feel even better, in a moment."

"Oh, Christian, I don't think it *can* feel better—"

And then his thumb, wet with her dampness, found the hard, swollen bud of her womanhood, gently kneaded it—and with a little cry, Deirdre bucked upward on the bed as the first waves of climax began to rush down upon her. Christian kept stroking, his mouth coming down against her own to muffle her cries, his thumb still against her even as he slid his fingers deep inside her wet cleft.

She writhed against him. Panting, he tore his mouth from hers and buried his face in the curve of her shoulder, drawing the last shudders of pleasure from her with his fingers and moving himself into position above her. *May God help me,* he thought, and then, on shaky limbs, he took a deep, steadying breath, abandoning all hesitations, all good sense, and all gentlemanly intentions he'd sought to employ.

With a harsh groan, he leaned back and drove his knee between her thighs. She was still breathing hard, dazed by the force of her first climax; now, she turned her head, her breath feathering against his wrist where it lay alongside her head, her lips moving over his skin, kissing him, loving him, tasting him.

He gazed down at her perfectly formed breasts, her taut belly, the soft indentation of her navel, the wet, silky black triangle between her thighs. Then he stared down at his arousal.

He was ready. By God, he had never been *more* ready.

"Open for me, Deirdre."

His knee pressed harder, and Deirdre, just beginning to recover from the heights to which this wonderful man had brought her, gazed up in wonder at him as he slowly lowered himself down to her. She wound her arms around his back and opened her legs, waiting as he paused, looking at her with dark, hungry eyes in an unspoken question.

She gave him a shy little smile of encouragement.

He smiled back.

Then he bowed his head, the handsome, sun-bleached locks tumbling down over his brow as he grasped himself in one hand and slowly guided it to her entrance. She tensed, waiting for pain, feeling only gentle pressure and exquisite, slippery sensation as the velvet head slid gently between her hot and moist folds. He released himself and leaned forward, favoring his shoulder as he slowly, carefully, began to slide himself inside her, stretching her, filling her with a deep and pleasurable fullness. She felt him give a mighty shudder, as though the effort was too much for him, and his face went rigid with concentration.

And then he stopped, his great body quivering as if on the verge of something tremendous.

"Christian?"

She felt his hot breath against the curve of her neck and shoulder, heard it rasping in her ear. "I can go no further, Deirdre ... without taking your maidenhead."

"I don't *want* my maidenhead anymore. Make me yers, Christian."

He needed no further invitation nor encouragement. He slid his hands up into her hair, anchoring her head as his mouth claimed hers and his tongue plunged between her teeth and desperately sought her own. She moaned, arching upward to meet his kiss. Then he tensed, drew back, and sheathed himself within her.

The pain was searing, a white lance of fire. She drove herself upward, meeting it bravely, boldly, and gratefully. Slowly, the discomfort faded away on waves of dampness that ran hotly between her thighs, and as it left her, she realized that in its place was a depth of feeling so intense, so agonizingly wonderful, that she thought she would die from it.

And now he was moving within her, pulling out, thrusting in, and building a rhythm that made her writhe with sweet agony. His tongue melded with hers, his mouth ground against her lips, his hand gathered her hair and crushed it in his fist. Faster and faster he moved, no longer gentle and slow, no longer able to take his time. His breathing came faster. Harsher. Hotter. Moisture broke out between straining bodies. Breath mingled and mixed, became one—

It started. She felt it in the deepest, darkest, most hidden recesses of her body, her soul, building, pulsing, welling up and up—

"Christian!"

She arched up to meet him, her senses exploding with a violence that shook her to her core. Her hands clawed at his back, her nails sank into his skin, and she clung to him, gasping, as she spasmed uncontrollably and her legs clamped fiercely around him. His body went suddenly rigid, and he drew back and thrust himself one last time into her, impaling her to the hilt of himself. She felt his seed, pulsing and throbbing warmly inside her, and it brought another glorious release, another cresting wave of sweet agony that left her sobbing with joy and wonder.

Exhausted, triumphant, he sank down atop her, supporting his weight on his forearms and breathing hard. Slowly, the burning sensation faded away, and the last waves of pleasure radiated out through her fingertips, her toes, the nerve endings of her skin. After a long moment, he finally moved off her and lay alongside her, one arm thrown possessively over her waist and drawing her close, until she was pressed against his still-pounding heart.

"Deirdre?"

"Aye, Christian?"

A long moment went by in which the only sound was their intermingled breathing, the fading tattoo of their heartbeats.

He raised his head and looked at her, and the depths of his soul were reflected in his eyes.

"Thank you."

Chapter Twenty-One

"I don't know wot the two of 'em are doin' down there, but I think ye might wanna go get the cap'n and tell 'im we've just sighted land off the starboard bows."

"*I* ken what they be doing, Skunk," Ian said importantly. "The same thing they've been doing for the past five days. Let 'em be. A pretty lass to warm his bed is just what our cold and aloof Lord and Master needs to warm up a bit." Ian turned away, shading his eyes as he stared out over the thousands of diamond-like waves, all dancing and jumping in the sunlight. The frigate dipped into a trough, heaved herself up again, and impatiently tossed spray over her bows. But there, it was unmistakable. A thin purplish line penciled atop the horizon of blue, blue sea.

Land.

For a crew that had left England hating its new commanding officer, their change in attitude toward him and their vessel was nothing short of astounding. Ever since the heated engagement in which they'd taken the French corvette, pride in themselves and their ship had run rampant. Men at their watches sang "Hearts of Oak." Hibbert was as likely to be found in a clean uniform as a rumpled one, Skunk no longer grumbled while scrubbing the decks each morning, Teach had taken it upon himself to care for Tildy and her puppies, and Ian diligently oversaw daily gun practice.

But as for their strict disciplinarian of a captain, the idea of him being in love was an endearing and richly amusing one, and there was not a soul aboard the frigate who didn't watch the blossoming romance with a keen mental telescope—and comment upon it daily. Oddly, this rough group of seasoned tars felt strangely protective of what was happening between their commanding officer and his Irish girl, and though most of them were a good deal younger than he, they saw themselves as protectors of those fragile seeds of newfound love.

Of course, such feelings of mutual protectiveness—the Lord and Master watching over them in battle, and the crew watching over his romance with the girl—went far to foster the sort of respect, liking, and loyalty that every captain strives for between himself and his men—and which no previous captain of HMS *Bold Marauder* had ever enjoyed.

Until now.

"Yeah, 'bout time someone thawed the Ice Captain," Teach remarked, crossing his arms and leaning his bulk against one of the boats snugged securely in the frigate's waist. He gave a sly grin. "God knows even Delight couldn't do it."

"Heard she tried, though," Milton Lee put in.

"And failed."

Skunk waved his hand and scoffed, "Delight ain't his type."

"The captain and Deirdre belong together," Elwin snapped. "Any fool can see that!"

"Still, isn't it something, the two of 'em being in love." Ian rubbed his beard, and his eyes grew reflective. "And tae think how much our bonnie Irish lassie hated our very English captain when she first came aboard."

"To think how much we *all* hated him," Teach added, with an expression of mixed shame and puzzlement that was echoed by his companions.

They stared down at their shoes, and even Skunk distractedly kicked at the deck seams. Finally he said, "Ah, but the girl's good for him. She makes him smile. She makes him mad. She makes him anythin' but emotionless."

"Aye, I've actually heard him *laughing*," Rhodes said, craning his neck as he gazed out over the whitecaps toward the distant land. "Can you imagine?"

Ian laughed. "'Bout bluidy time!"

"I say, Ian," Wenham said, "in all seriousness, if you want to make our commanding officer happy, *do* send someone to tell him we just sighted land. By my reckoning," he added, looking down at his chart and tracing the coastline with his finger, "it's Cape Cod. The captain'll want to make the ship presentable for his admiral."

"Presentable?" Ian drew himself up, peeved about being reminded of his duty. "What's wrong with her? I doona see anything amiss!"

Rhodes coughed and raised a mocking brow. "Salutes and all that, Ian?"

Skunk nodded. "*Ceremony* stuff. Things *we* don't know nothin' about."

"Of course," Ian said, flushing and puffing out his chest. "Hibbert!"

Like some of the others, the youth had a spyglass to his eye. However, his was not trained toward the distant land but up at the maintop, where Delight had gone to share a "picnic lunch" with one of the marines.

"Hibbert!" Ian roared, purpling with rage. "'Tis angry ye be making me! Get yer wee tail over here before I thrash ye to within an inch of yer life!"

Flushing hotly, Hibbert snapped the glass shut and came to stand next to his lieutenant.

"Aye?"

"That's 'Aye, *sir*,' and doona be forgetting it!" He glared fiercely down at the boy, his hands fisted against his hips, his red beard blowing in the wind. "Now go rouse the captain. Give him my respects, and tell him we've raised Cape Cod."

Hibbert frowned, snapped off a sloppy salute, and with a last wistful glance up toward the maintop, went below.

"Wot was 'e looking at, anyhow?" Skunk murmured, scowling as he tipped his oily head back and stared aloft. But there was nothing to be seen up there but acres of proudly set sail, all bloated with wind and pushing the frigate on a steady course toward Boston.

❧

"Christian."

He lay beside her, one well-muscled arm thrown possessively over her ribs and anchoring her body to his, his face turned into the mass of spiral-curling black ringlets that toppled over her shoulder and onto the pillow.

She hated to wake him. But the knocking on the door was not going away.

"Christian!" she hissed.

Sweet Mary, the man slept like the dead! She wriggled out from beneath the heavy weight of his arm, let him settle into the space where her body had been, and dipped her head to press gentle kisses atop the hard rise of his shoulder, where a fresh bandage stood clean and white against his skin. Her fingers twined in the hair that curled boyishly against the back of his neck; her palm smoothed it away from his temple. He was warm and heavy and heartbreakingly handsome. Just looking at him made her want him all over again.

The knocking came louder.

"Christian!" She put a hand against his arm and shook him. His heavy, regulated breathing didn't change. She stared down at him, realizing that, for the first time since she'd known him, he had not had the nightmares.

No wonder he slept so deeply.

The knocking stopped. "Captain?"

Hibbert. Desperately, Deirdre leaned down, nuzzled aside the golden waves of hair, and put her lips against his ear. "Christian, my love. Wake up! Yer men be wantin' ye!"

He made an unintelligible noise, reached out, and hauled her close to his body. "Don't leave me, Deirdre...."

"Wake *up!*" she hissed, wishing she could strangle Hibbert for disturbing their newfound happiness.

He groaned and turned over, his gray eyes opening to regard her with lazy adoration. "What is it, dear girl, that you invade my dreams?"

"Yer dreams?" She laughed. "I hope I'm in them!"

He reached up, captured a curl, and pressed it to his lips, his warm gaze holding hers. "Yes, love, you are in them. I daresay you are the mistress of my dreams."

"And ye be the master o' mine. Stop, Christian!" she gasped as he gently pulled her head down to his via his grip on her curl. "Hibbert is outside the door."

The knocking became a downright pounding. "Captain?"

"Damn your bloody eyes, Hibbert, what the devil do you want?"

"Mr. MacDuff's respects, sir, and he's just sighted land off the starboard bows. Mr. Wenham says we're off Massachusetts Bay, and that we'll raise Boston Harbor soon."

Christian sighed and inwardly groaned, suddenly wishing this voyage could go on forever. "My compliments to the first lieutenant, and tell him to prepare the ship as though the king himself is awaiting us. We'll make a fine show for those rebellious colonials, eh, Mr. Hibbert?"

"Aye, sir. We'll show those colonial upstarts we're not a navy to trifle with! We'll show 'em we're a *king's* ship!"

Christian threw back his head and laughed the sleep out of his sluggish body. "Aye, we'll do that, young fellow. Now go, and do not tarry. I'll be on deck shortly."

"Boston!" Deirdre cried excitedly. Impulsively, she threw her arms around her lover's hard body. "Oh, Christian. How can I thank ye enough? Just think, my cousin is there. I haven't seen him in years! He'll help me to find my brother, Christian, ye wait an' see!"

He looked at her soberly. "And so, as God is my witness, shall I, Deirdre."

THE PEOPLE OF BOSTON, which had been closed to colonial trade since the establishment of the hated Port Act, saw her first as yet another royal frigate, sent to quell resistance and restore order. They wasted no time dispatching messengers to let the rebel leaders know of her coming. The nervous governor might rejoice over the arrival of a smart and powerful frigate, but otherwise her appearance was unwelcome by all except the Tory population, the British troops camped out in Boston Common eager for news of home, and of course, the crusty old admiral whose small squadron lay at anchor in the harbor.

The flagship of Vice Admiral Sir Geoffrey Lloyd was a huge, double-decked leviathan boasting a murderous array of seventy-four guns. The admiral himself, a stiff-lipped, cantankerous old salt whose long years of sea service had left him tired, achy, irritable, and dreaming about his upcoming retirement, sat now at a fine table in his day cabin, squinting his eyes and frowning as he read the latest broadside, initiated and distributed by that hotheaded rabble-rouser Sam Adams.

Lately, though, the rebels were not all that occupied Sir Geoffrey's weary mind. Yesterday, he had received the distressing news that the king's frigate *Bold Marauder*—which he'd been expecting for several days now—had encountered the smuggler known only as the Irish Pirate in company with a French freebooter while the pair had been attacking a lone English ship. Although *Bold Marauder* had taken the French vessel, the Irish Pirate had managed to escape and bring the embarrassing news back to Boston, where it had been enthusiastically received—and spread—by the upstarts.

Outside the door, the marine thumped his musket smartly on the deck, interrupting the admiral's musings. "*Halcyon*'s captain to see you, sir!"

"Send him in," Sir Geoffrey said, shoving the broadside away with a tired motion.

The door opened and Captain Merrick entered, his cocked hat held respectfully in his hands, his chestnut hair shining in the sunlight that slanted down through the hatch behind him.

"Ah, Brendan. It is good of you to join me for the midday meal. Do come in."

The young man was tall and handsome, an intelligent, promising young rake with a quick wit and a mirthful grin. Clever and compassionate, the captain of the frigate *Halcyon,* anchored in the lee of nearby Castle Island, had climbed far and fast through the naval ranks. As usual, the young half-Irishman was in high spirits.

"You'll be pleased to know, sir, that His Britannic Majesty's frigate *Bold Marauder* has just been sighted, standing for the harbor."

"*Bold Marauder!*" the admiral exclaimed, the tiredness instantly fading from his sloped shoulders, his aching limbs. "Damme, Merrick, it's about time. I've been itching to ask her captain just what happened between him and that blasted Irish Pirate and why he failed to capture the rogue. And as for the ship herself, why, one can never have enough frigates, eh? *Bold Marauder* will be a welcome addition to our little squadron."

"Faith, sir, that she will," Brendan said hesitantly.

Their gazes met. Both were well aware of the frigate's bad reputation, but a missive written by Rear Admiral Sir Elliott Lord and delivered into Sir Geoffrey's care by a fast-sailing packet had already advised the admiral of the identity of *Bold Marauder*'s commanding officer. The frigate might be the most rebellious ship in the king's fleet—but her new captain was the most principled, disciplined, and upstanding officer the Navy had.

Something, certainly, to raise his spirits after the worsening situation here in Boston!

Sir Geoffrey rose to his feet with rare agility and clapped his subordinate on the back, the matter of the rebel broadside already forgotten. "Ah, 'tis good that she's here, eh? And Captain Lord is a fine officer with a long and distinguished record. A capable, competent, and thoroughly dislikable chap, but one who can be trusted to bring his ship in with a fine show!"

The young frigate captain frowned. "I beg your pardon, sir, but I served with Captain Lord aboard the old *Londoner* and I did not find him dislikable."

"Forgive me, Brendan. I had forgotten his, er, loss. Such things can change a man, and not for the better." The admiral finished the last of his tea, and called impatiently for his steward. Normally cranky and dour, Sir Geoffrey was beaming with boyish excitement. "Ah, *Bold Marauder* is just what these Bostonians need. Captain Lord can be counted upon to put on a fine display of competence, seamanship, and discipline! He'll set an example, not only for our people, but also for these damned rebels who think His Majesty's forces are nothing but a bumbling display of misplaced pomp and arrogance." He beckoned for his steward to enter. "And these bumpkins have grown troublesome enough, have they not? They ridicule our troops, they ridicule our seamen, they ridicule the governor, they ridicule our attempts to maintain order." He raised his arms, allowing his steward to help him into his coat. "No, not that one, Percy, the other one. Yes, the dress coat. And my finest sword, if you please! I will not honor Captain Lord with anything less than perfection!"

From above came excited cheers as the flagship's crew welcomed the arrival of the new ship.

"My flag captain is on an errand ashore, Brendan, so I'm counting on you instead to ensure that *Bold Marauder* is received with highest ceremony. I want every officer in his best uniform, every tar at attention, and a proper, rousing salute from the guns of every ship in the squadron. I want no effort spared, do you understand?"

"Yes, sir."

"Off with you, then, and do not tarry!"

The dashing young captain touched his hat and strode swiftly from the cabin. Still in his twenties, he was as much a part of his crew as he was captain of it, well loved and much respected by his subordinates. As he went topside, the flagship's men joked and traded barbs with him and called him by his first name, privileges that few seamen in His Majesty's Navy would have dared and few commanders would have allowed.

But then, Captain Brendan Jay Merrick was quite unlike most commanders in His Majesty's Navy.

His coxswain, a big, strapping Irishman who'd been his best friend since the days when they'd grown up together in Connemara, grabbed his elbow and pointed out over the sparkling harbor toward the majestic sight of the incoming frigate. "God Almighty, Brendan, she's a sight t' make a lad's heart weep, ain't she? Don't ye just swell with pride, knowin' ye designed 'er?"

The young captain, a modest and humble sort, smiled and shrugged. "If she's lovely, Liam, it is because of her captain's hand, not mine. He deserves the credit for making her look so smart."

The frigate was taking on detail, the tall shadows of her masts falling across the trees of a nearby island as she moved gracefully past it. Her topmasts boasted proud squares of pale, gold-tinted sail, and her yards were smartly angled to make best use of the unsteady breeze. She was a glorious sight, the water curling back from her rakish bow, sparkling in the sun and gleaming upon her stem and despite himself, her young designer experienced a surge of pride.

He felt a presence at his elbow and turning, found the old admiral beside him, his face as bright as a schoolboy's, his eyes crinkling with humor as he gazed out at the approaching frigate. "I see, sir, that you could not resist," Brendan said, grinning.

Impatiently beckoning to a midshipman, Sir Geoffrey snatched a telescope from the boy and raised it to his eye. On the deck behind them, the first lieutenant was snapping orders, and the bosun and his mates were driving the men into a state of order. "I may be an old man, Brendan, but not so old that the sight of a well-run, smartly disciplined fighting ship doesn't bring a tear to my eye. Damme, she's lovely." He handed the telescope to the young captain. "Leave it to Captain Lord to put on a display of seamanship our Navy can be damned proud of!"

Brendan raised his glass to his eye, never flinching as the deck beneath his feet quaked to the might of the flagship's guns as she welcomed the proud new arrival. Answering puffs came from *Bold Marauder*'s gunports, the salute smartly done and as precisely calibrated as a ball to a musket's barrel. Brendan moved the glass, saw the officer who stood rigidly on the quarterdeck, and smiled as he recognized the man who had once been his captain.

On shore, there were already crowds gathering to watch the new arrival.

"This is *just* what we need to show these rabble-rousers what is meant by a *king*'s ship!" The admiral's voice was tight with pride as he stared out over the water at the glorious, majestic frigate. "And, by God, there's Lord himself, the absolute epitome of what a king's officer should be! Damme, Brendan, don't keep the glass all to yourself, man! Have some pity on an old tar who's half blind as it is!"

But the young officer had gone stiff, the color draining from his face.

Impatiently, Sir Geoffrey snapped, "Damme, Brendan, the glass *please!*"

Slowly, the captain brought the telescope down, blinking in shock and then horror. His face was very white. He looked at Sir Geoffrey. He looked back at the frigate and had a sudden, desperate urge to hurl the telescope overboard before his admiral could discover for himself what he had seen through that circular field.

Something that, judging by the sudden, thunderous commotion from shore, the jeering crowds had already discovered.

Something that the flagship's crew were rushing to the rails to see, pushing and shoving in their haste.

Something that the admiral, smiling triumphantly as he raised the glass to his keen and bleary old eye, would be seeing just ... about....

Brendan shut his eyes, wincing.

"Great *GOD* above!" Sir Geoffrey thundered, and the glass dropped from his hand to smash upon the flagship's deck.

Now.

The old man clutched at his heart. "He has a ... a *woman* in the maintop!" he croaked, his face going purple. "And she's totally *naked!*"

Chapter Twenty-Two

❧

"I have never been more *humiliated* in my life!" Sir Geoffrey raged, storming up through HMS *Bold Marauder*'s entry port with Captain Brendan Jay Merrick close behind him. He cringed as the ceremonial trill of pipes, meant as a salute, rang mockingly around him.

Captain Lord, splendidly turned out in his finest uniform and wearing a gold-tasseled dress sword at his hip, stepped forward to receive them. He was smiling, and his shoulders were squared and straight. Solemnly, he doffed his hat. "Welcome, sir, to His Majesty's frigate *Bold Marauder.* I am honored to—"

"Spare me your damned pleasantries, *Captain Lord*! By God, you have made me the laughingstock of Boston, and I'll see you in your cabin *now*!"

"Sir?" the captain said, confused. At his side and slightly behind him, his first lieutenant, a big, ruddy-faced Scot with a shock of red hair, exchanged puzzled glances with the second lieutenant. And coming up from the hatch was a fat white spaniel, who took one look at the enraged Sir Geoffrey—and promptly emptied her bladder in terror.

"*I said now!*" the admiral thundered.

"Yes, sir. By all means," Christian said tightly, grabbing Tildy and wondering what the devil had riled the admiral so. *Bold Marauder* had put on a fine show, one the king himself would have been proud of. She was clean and smart and beyond reproach. Keenly aware of his men's equally confused stares, he turned abruptly and led the way to his cabin, holding himself upright and feeling his shoulder beginning to throb. "Sir, please watch your head—"

"Hold your damned tongue, Lord, I've been on warships a damn sight longer than you!"

They were now beyond earshot of *Bold Marauder*'s crew. Christian swung around, his eyes blazing. "Pray, sir, I don't know what grieves you so. My ship is *faultless!*"

The admiral was a head shorter than Christian but in his rage, his stature was considerably increased. Glaring up into the captain's gray eyes he roared, "There is a *woman* in your maintop, Captain Lord, and *she is not wearing a stitch of clothing!*"

Christian stared at him. Horror drained the color from his face and left it white, then gray.

Dear God, he thought. *Delight.*

Cold sweat broke out of every pore and he turned just outside his cabin door, trying to maintain the last shreds of his dignity. The admiral's rage was a tangible thing, and Christian was keenly aware of not only Sir Geoffrey but also the young Captain Merrick—who looked quite sympathetic, if not a little amused.

Ian MacDuff, his own Scots temper ready to blow, came charging down the short corridor. "Here, now, Captain, 'tis looking right bonnie we be! What the saints has the old fart all riled—"

Sir Geoffrey went purple.

Quietly, Christian said, "Mr. MacDuff, please send someone up to the maintop *immediately* to fetch Delight down."

"Del—" Ian's jaw came unhinged.

"Yes Ian, *Delight.*" He bent his brow to his hand, feeling his career sliding into ruin around his feet. "Pray, do so now ... before the damage becomes irreparable."

Ian left at a dead run.

"My apologies, sir," Christian began. "I had no—"

He couldn't say he had no idea. It would only pound another nail into his coffin. Besides, there was no use trying to make excuses. He was already incriminated. Finished. Doomed to court-martial, disgrace, and the rest of his life spent on the beach. With a defeated sigh, he shoved open his cabin door, forgetting, too late, about—

"Great *God* above, Lord, do you run a goddamned brothel or a fighting ship?" the admiral thundered as the raven-haired girl on the bed, clad in nothing but the captain's shirt and a pair of baggy trousers, flung aside the covers and flew across the cabin.

Christian shut his eyes.

"Brendan!" she shrieked. And with a happy cry, the girl threw herself into the startled arms of Sir Geoffrey Lloyd's next consideration for flag captain.

Christian was too devastated to feel surprise that the two knew each other. He was too devastated to feel jealousy at the way Deirdre was clinging to the dashingly handsome Captain Merrick. He was too devastated to feel the sudden, throbbing agony in his shoulder, the hollow nausea in the pit of his stomach, the numbness that was even now permeating his limbs.

His career was finished.

"Deirdre, please address the captain with the respect he deserves," he said quietly, putting Tildy down with her puppies and already hearing the death knell of a court-martial.

But Captain Merrick had swept Deirdre up in his arms, swung her around, and was now hugging her fiercely. "Nonsense, Captain Lord! Faith, the lass is my *cousin*! How very *good* of you to bring her all the way across the Atlantic just to deliver her into my care!"

Cousin. Brendan. Boston.

Of course.

"What?" Sir Geoffrey snapped, whirling.

Merrick's pointed gaze met Christian's from above Deirdre's shoulder, and Christian was quick to grasp what the shrewd younger captain had so quickly offered.

Escape.

"Yes, yes, of course," he said lamely, feeling the piercing gaze of the old admiral driving between his shoulders. "She had a most trying time of it, but I daresay she made a good sailor."

"She always did, even when I took her up to Mayo in my little sailboat so she could see the castle where her ancestress lived. Never once got seasick, did you, Deirdre?"

"Oh never, Brendan! And remember climbin' Crough Patrick, an' the awful storm that hit us on the way home? Why, if it weren't for yer skill as a sailor, the angels would've collected us that day for sure—"

Sir Geoffrey glared at the two cousins, glared down at the puppies, and glared up at Captain Lord. "You mean to tell me you were merely transporting this—this *girl* to Boston, Captain Lord?"

Christian met the sharp stare unflinchingly. "Yes, sir."

Hastily, Deirdre offered, "Me mam died, ye see, and Brendan's the only family I got left."

"I saw no mention of a female passenger in the dispatches from your admiral back in Portsmouth, Captain Lord!"

"Uh, Sir Elliott has had a lot on his mind lately, sir. Perhaps he forgot."

"Your brother is not the type to *forget!* And this still doesn't explain that—that *female* in your maintop, shamelessly waving a kerchief in greeting to the people of Boston upon your *glorious* arrival!"

A commotion sounded just outside the door as the "female" in question was escorted aft.

"Oh, dear God," Christian began, graying with horror as he realized that Ian was bringing Delight in.

Just then, the door swung open and Delight, clad in nothing but a wool blanket, sauntered in, much to the pop-eyed consternation of Sir Geoffrey.

"Why, Captain Lord, you did so spoil my fun by retrieving me from the maintop! Lo, I got the most awful burn on my *derriere* on the way down," she purred, suggestively rubbing her bottom through the blanket. "Why, hello, sir...." Her eyes gleaming, she sauntered over to the suddenly apoplectic Sir Geoffrey. "You must be the admiral. I just *love* a man with *power*," she crooned, sidling close to him and dragging a fingernail down his seamed, suddenly white cheek. "You'd just love a little romp with Delight here, no? I have the most wickedly wonderful methods of—"

"Ian, *get her out of here*!" Christian roared.

Even Brendan looked shocked, though his eyes were glinting with mirth.

"*IAN!*"

"Uh, aye, sir, 'tis trying I am—"

Delight rubbed herself against Sir Geoffrey's chest, her hand roving down his waistcoat toward his breeches. The admiral's face was going a bright, alarming red, a shocking contrast to the whiteness of his hair.

And then Delight allowed the blanket to slip to the floor.

Christian shut his eyes and groaned. Brendan Merrick gulped and nearly dropped his cousin. Delight Foley touched a hand to the admiral's groin—

And Sir Geoffrey slid to the floor in a dead faint.

"'Twas too much for his heart, sir," Elwin Boyd said matter-of-factly, leaning over the admiral and fanning him with a piece of paper. "But I think he's coming around now."

Sir Geoffrey, who'd been laid on the bed, blinked and tried to sit up, his hand going unconsciously to his heart. "Let me up, you bumbling fools!" he snarled, pushing aside their hands. The blonde doxy was nowhere in sight. Young Merrick stood nearby, his lips twitching with suppressed laughter. His Irish cousin—a comely young thing with striking eyes and an out-of-control mane of wild black hair—sat beside the bed, her worshipful gaze passing between Brendan and the tight-lipped Captain Lord. She held a glass of water in her hand, and seeing that he had recovered his senses, tried to press it to Sir Geoffrey's lips.

"Here, sir. Drink, and 'twill make ye feel better."

"There's nothing wrong with me! The devil take the lot of you, treating me like some blasted invalid! Damn your eyes, Captain Lord, you have much to answer to!"

"Yes, sir." The captain turned to the surgeon. "Please leave us, Elwin."

The Irish girl's hand came up to touch a strange, ornate Celtic cross at her throat. Lifting her chin, she fastened her steady gaze on the admiral. Her eyes were beautiful, stormy, of a brilliant purple shade that reminded him of violets in springtime. "Please, sir, don't be takin' yer anger out on Captain Lord," she said in her gentle brogue. "He's a fine and upstandin' officer, and wouldn't tolerate any shenanigans."

"And what do you call that—that *spectacle* in the maintop?" Sir Geoffrey raged, more to Captain Lord than to the young Irishwoman.

Again the girl answered, unfazed by his anger. "Oh, her name is Dolores. She has a bit of a problem, ye see? She's coming home after living in Normandy for a few years, and got rather ... well, corrupted. Ye know how those French people are, Sir Geoffrey."

The admiral's eyes narrowed, for as a true Briton he had no love for the French. "Yes, I know *exactly* how they are."

The girl looked sadly down into the glass of water. "Well, sir, they ruined her and poisoned her mind. She left Boston as a sweet and innocent woman of virtue, but those awful French had their way with her, ye see, and, well.... She ended up in Portsmouth after her French husband died, and Captain Lord, bein' the gallant naval officer he is, took it upon himself to deliver her safely back to her family here in Massachusetts. He put so much time and effort into makin' somethin' of this crew—a real hard-to-manage one, if ye'll recall—that it wasn't always easy for him to keep an eye on Deli—I mean, Dolores. But she can't help herself, sir. 'Twas the French influence."

The admiral's eyes narrowed. "French influence, you say?"

Bless you, dear girl, Christian thought, shutting his eyes.

"Oh, aye," Deirdre was saying. "French influence. She was there for some time, subjected to their ways and all. No wonder she came out of it as a ... well, changed woman."

Brendan's eyes were dancing with mirth as, behind the admiral's back, he exchanged glances with the speechless Christian. "Quite right, Sir Geoffrey," he said, careful to keep his tone properly sober. "An immoral and lascivious people, you must agree. Faith, I shudder to think of any impressionable young female at the mercy of their carnal ways!" He cast a pointed glance around the orderly cabin and looked up, as though he could see through the great beams to the decks above. "That aside, Captain Lord, please accept my congratulations on what wonders you have achieved with this vessel! The last time I saw her, I was ashamed to admit that I had designed her." He turned to the admiral and said cheerfully, "Really, sir, don't you think that Captain Lord's success at making something of *Bold Marauder*'s crew far outweighs the, uh, little incident with Miss Dolores?"

Deirdre again offered the water to Sir Geoffrey. "Poor Dolores. And oh, think of her father, and how ashamed and distressed he'll be when he sees what has happened to his sweet, innocent daughter." She sighed and shook her head. "But those French are a vulgar people, aren't they, Captain Lord?"

Brendan, caught up in the game, answered before Christian could reply. "Faith! The whole country's a den of iniquity, if I do say so myself!"

His eyes narrowing, Sir Geoffrey snatched the glass of water from the girl's hand, and stared at his young captain. Merrick's logic, as usual, was sound. Captain Lord had managed to work wonders with the finest frigate in the king's fleet and yes, that ought to count for something more than a court-martial. Granted, his pride stung, and he'd have to account for the humiliating incident before Governor Gage, but Brendan was right.

He drained the glass and thrust it back into the Irish girl's hand. "I suppose there's nothing to be done for it then, but to return the woman to her father and let *him* deal with her," he muttered irately. "You say her family lives here in Boston?'

"Well, almost. She tells me her home is on the west side o' Cambridge, wherever that may be."

"Less than ten miles from here," Sir Geoffrey grumbled. "I suppose it falls upon *me,* then, to escort her back."

Brendan cleared his throat and drew himself up, his eyes suddenly eager. "Faith, sir, but I'd be happy to oblige."

"Yes, I'm sure you *would,*" Sir Geoffrey snapped. "But I'll not have my finest officer tarnishing his name and reputation by being seen in the woman's company until a cure can be found for her ... *condition.*" He turned to Christian. "I trust that she has something besides a blanket she can wear, so that she can be escorted from this ship with some degree of dignity?"

Christian paled, thinking of the trunk of gowns—and other *equipment*—that Delight had had hauled up from the brig and now lay close, *too* close, in a nearby cabin. "Er, yes, sir, though I daresay they could use some ... uh, alterations."

"Fine. See to it that your sailmaker has them done. I want that woman off this ship by sundown."

Brendan, fidgeting, persisted. "Will you, then, be escorting her back to her family, sir?"

"You seem quite bloody *eager,* Captain Merrick!"

Brendan flashed a quick grin. "Aye, sir. I wouldn't want *you* to tarnish your name, either."

"Oh, go on with you!" the admiral retorted. "I don't give a king's damn who takes her, as long as she's removed from this vessel before she can cause our Navy any more embarrassment. By the way—"He frowned and turned to Deirdre, his eyes narrowing. "Who is this father in the unenviable position of having sired her?"

"All I know, sir, is that his name is Foley, and that he and his family live outside o' Boston in a place called Menotomy."

The admiral stared at her. "Foley? *Menotomy?*"

"Yes." Her brow furrowed in a frown. "Do ye know the family, then?"

"Oh, I know them, all right." He snatched up his hat. "Captain Merrick, you may have the afternoon to catch up on old times with your cousin, but I expect that girl to be safely delivered into her father's care by sundown. You will receive additional orders shortly. And you, Captain Lord"—his harsh stare settled on Christian—"I shall see you aboard the flagship at eight bells. We have *much* to discuss."

Christian heaved a silent sigh of relief. Then he picked up his own hat and, squaring his shoulders, followed the admiral out the door to see him properly off the ship, his shoulder aching, his head throbbing with suppressed tension.

But at the door he paused to flash his beloved a look of indebtedness and admiration.

No matter what trouble she'd caused him back in Portsmouth, here in Boston she had just saved his career.

SIR GEOFFREY ANNOUNCED an informal dinner for his officers in his cabin aboard the massive seventy-four-gun *Dauntless,* whose dining area alone made the entire cabin of HMS *Bold Marauder* seem small and cramped in comparison. But there was more than enough room in the cabin for Sir Geoffrey, his captains, and the huge array of food brought in by stewards and smartly turned-out midshipmen.

They were a small but diverse group: the cranky, stooped old admiral with his shrewd and piercing eye; his flag captain Stanley Cutler, already well into his cups; Captain Hiram Ellsworth, a high-minded but ambitious prig; Lieutenant Peter Atkins, loud, swaggering, and boastful; a varied array of young officers—and Christian.

He sat at the polished mahogany table, watching the admiral's servants clearing away the rich meal which his stomach, used to the horrors of naval fare, had accepted first with glee, then with hesitation and now, a growing remorse. His queasiness was not helped by the open hostility of the cabin's other occupants.

Cutler raised his glass and downed its contents in a single gulp. "So, Captain Lord," he said, exchanging a sly glance with the others, "I'm told you made something of that worthless rabble you left Portsmouth with."

"I could not make something of them if there was nothing there to begin with."

Ellsworth made a snorting noise. "Ha! *Bold Marauder*'s previous captain is a dear friend of mine. He told me her officers and crew are naught but a bunch of incompetent arses who don't know a stem from a stern."

Laughter rippled around the table but Sir Geoffrey, thanking a midshipman for bringing him a pillow to put between his brittle old back and the unforgiving chair, didn't notice the open insult to Christian's crew.

"I say, they must *still* be a bunch of incompetent arses, Ellsworth!" Cutler said recklessly, sniggering as he poured himself another glass of port. "They've already bungled the very thing they were sent here to do—apprehend that damned Irish Pirate. Can you imagine? Why, *Bold Marauder* had the rascal right under her guns and still the fellow got away! Ah, Captain Lord, I pity you, having to take command of those dolts!"

"My crew behaved admirably and to my satisfaction," Christian said tersely. "And what do you mean, Irish Pirate?"

"Don't tell us you didn't know. All of Boston is abuzz with it."

Christian put down his glass. "Abuzz with what?"

"Why, the news of course. You really don't know, do you? That smuggler you engaged off the Maine coast? He's the Irish Pirate."

More snickers.

No. He hadn't known.

"That will be enough, gentleman," Sir Geoffrey said crossly. "Captain Lord has only just arrived. One cannot expect him to know it was the Irish Pirate he'd engaged, as the scoundrel flies no colors. Finally, do not forget that he had an English cutter to assist, a French corvette to man, and other things to occupy him."

"Aye, such as a doxie in the main top!"

"Would that we *all* had such ... *diversions!*"

"Poor Merrick. He designed your frigate, didn't he, Lord? How ashamed of her he must be!"

"Aye, to think of his masterpiece crewed by a bunch of pillocks with nothing better to do than cause trouble and make their gloriously esteemed *captain,* whose lofty heights *we* shall never aspire to, look terrible!"

Their laughter was abruptly silenced by Christian's fist slamming down atop the table. "My crew behaved gallantly under extreme circumstances and I found no fault with their behavior, none at all!" He threw down his napkin and lunged to his feet. "I will not sit here and suffer hearing them maligned!"

He felt Sir Geoffrey's eyes on him, scrutinizing him, his old mouth beginning to curve in an approving smile.

"Sit down, Captain Lord. And the rest of you, hold your damned tongues. I daresay none of you would've fared any better. Regardless of *Bold Marauder*'s reputation, I have nothing but respect for a captain who will defend his crew even when he knows that some improvement could stand to be had. You have my admiration, Captain, for all you've accomplished with them in such a short time. For the most part, your ship made a fine showing upon entering the harbor today."

"So did the girl in the maintop," Cutler said, sniggering.

"I said *enough*!" Sir Geoffrey said sharply, unwilling to see one of his officers embarrassed, no matter how displeased he was over the incident with Dolores. He leaned forward to adjust the pillow behind his back. "I called you together to share a meal, and to allow you and Captain Lord the opportunity to acquaint yourselves with each other. With tension mounting by the day between our forces and the rebels, we must work together. Dissent will get us nowhere."

The naval officers looked down, exchanged glances, and one or two cleared their throats.

The admiral leaned back in his chair. "As you all know, Lord Dartmouth has sent orders to General Gage, the governor here in Boston, to arrest the rebel leaders of this so-called Massachusetts Provincial Congress. These men—Adams, Hancock, and the physician, Dr. Warren—have no respect for the king's authority, and will stop at nothing in their quest to seed dissent and rebellion amongst the general populace. They have just commemorated that unfortunate event they call the Boston Massacre in a way that nearly set off a war in itself, but that just goes to show the nature of these upstarts with whom we are dealing. They grow bolder by the day, heedless of the fact that the town is filled with our troops and supported by our ships here in the harbor. Now, reports are coming in that they are gathering arms and ammunition and secreting them in the countryside." He paused, and let his hard, penetrating stare rake each of them in turn. "Tell me, gentlemen, *just who do you think they're preparing to use these arms against?*"

Christian said nothing, his shoulder, throbbing more and more the longer he sat, forgotten. He had known, of course, that matters on this side of the Atlantic were bad, but he had not known that the people here were actually taking up arms against the king's forces....

The meal wore on, the situation in Boston was further discussed, toasts to king and country were drunk and eventually the admiral, his tired old face showing the strain of the day, dismissed them to go back to their ships.

Christian rose to his feet.

"A moment, please, Captain Lord."

He paused, absently massaging his wound and waiting until the others were out of earshot. "Thank you, sir, for defending my people's honor. It is most appreciated."

"Nonsense. From what I've observed, you've shaped them into a fine and respectable crew. Sir Elliott advised me in his missives about the exact nature of what you were taking on when he assigned you to *Bold Marauder*, you know." The admiral allowed a hint of a smile. "Not that I hadn't already known. But make no mistake. While I defended you before your peers tonight—who, I might add, are merely envious of your accomplishments—I remain most distressed about the debacle with that Foley woman and so, I'm afraid, is General Gage. However, even the most embarrassing incidents are capable of bearing fruit. As this one did."

"Sir?"

"Please have a seat, Captain. I did not detain you for additional rebuke, but to discuss the Navy's mission for you."

"The Irish Pirate," Christian said, smiling wryly. "My apologies, sir. Had I known that sloop was his, I can assure you—"

"Never mind that, Captain. We will catch the rogue—or, shall I say, *you* will catch him." He leaned forward and poured them each another glass of port, the lights of Boston twinkling in the darkness beyond the great stern windows behind him. "Things have grown tense here over the past several months. Last year's Port Act—which, as you know, was intended to punish Boston for that wretched Tea Party incident—met with anger and rebellion, and while meant to starve and choke the town into submission, all it did was unify and strengthen the rebels."

Christian took a sip of his port.

"This, and other punitive actions meant to clip the wings of Massachusetts's self-government, have only made the rebels even more defiant. General Gage, between you and me, is ineffective. He draws up declarations and refuses to enforce them, pretending ignorance while the bumpkins blatantly defy them right under his nose. We have warships in the harbor, thousands of troops in and around Boston, and London standing on her tiptoes watching the whole damned mess, yet he is loath to enforce his own decrees. As a result, the rebels grow more and more bold." Sir Geoffrey gave a weary sigh. "Their Dr. Warren drew up a set of resolutions declaring that there was no need to obey the Port Act, and implored the people to prepare themselves for a war against England. Last fall, they sent representatives to Philadelphia to partake in a colony-wide assembly of rebels calling themselves the Continental Congress, and have since proceeded to downright *steal* money from the royal collections to fund their treasonous schemes. Altercations break out between our troops and the populace. Things are so damned tense, 'twill only take a spark to blow everything to kingdom come."

"I had not realized the situation has deteriorated to such an extent," Christian said quietly. He looked down at his glass. Suddenly, its contents looked like blood to him.

"I believe war is imminent," Sir Geoffrey continued. "The rebels have established Committees of Safety to oversee a new militia, a motley rabble calling themselves minutemen, so named because they are ready to muster, march, and move at a minute's notice." The admiral made a disgusted noise. "Can you imagine? Bumpkins—farmers, ordinary citizens, merchants—taking up arms against the finest army in the world." He shook his head. "They haven't a bloody chance."

Christian looked down at his port again and, suddenly unable to drink it, slid the glass away from him.

"In any case, Captain, as I mentioned earlier, I was most intrigued to learn the name of this woman you took aboard as a passenger. Dolores Ann Foley LeBrun—it appears she has dropped her married name following the death of her French husband—is the daughter of one Jared Foley, a printer who lives in the western part of Cambridge, in the village of Menotomy. He claims to be loyal to King and Crown, but recent intelligence reveals a suspicious amount of *activity* to and from the Foley home at all hours of the day and night. Activity that is highly suspect for a man purported to be a Loyalist."

"Are you saying that Foley is a rebel?"

"I'm saying we *suspect* he's a rebel. He is most assuredly a printer, Captain, and as such, is in a position to print and distribute inflammatory broadsides."

"I see."

Sir Geoffrey took a sip of his port. "The fact that Gage's spies have seen Foley in company with Adams, Hancock, and Warren is not, of course, the Navy's concern. But I'll tell you what is," he said, pausing and looking hard at Christian. "Foley has also been seen with the Irish Pirate."

Christian raised a brow. Suddenly he remembered Delight, cornering him in the brig and bragging that she was going to seduce and win the notorious smuggler for herself, and began to wonder if there was more here than had initially met the eye.

"And just who is this so-called Irish Pirate?" he asked.

"That's the only name we know him by. What difference does it make? He's a rebel, and he must be stopped. Were he a simple smuggler, I would not be so concerned with him, but the Americans are secretly moving guns into the countryside and they are obviously coming from somewhere."

"And you suspect that source is this Irish Pirate?"

"One of the sources, certainly, and a major one at that. Had the exchange not already been made, you undoubtedly would have found the hold of your French corvette packed with crates of muskets. So you see now why you must apprehend the scoundrel. Gage won't move against the rebel leaders, but the Irish Pirate is *my* responsibility, and I am not content to sit back and watch a bloody war unfold. This rogue is procuring arms from Philadelphia and Baltimore, smuggling them into ports north of Boston, and passing them to the rebels who are, in turn, hiding them in the countryside with the intent of using them against our forces. This, Captain Lord, is why the Irish Pirate *must* be stopped."

The admiral stood up and began to pace. "There is no time to waste. Your mission is to apprehend this smuggler as quickly and efficiently as possible using every resource at your command. He and Jared Foley run in the same circles, so it may be a matter of killing two birds with one stone. You will call upon Miss O'Devir at the Foley home in Menotomy."

Christian stiffened. "Sir?"

"Since the Foleys claim to be Loyalists, they cannot protest a respected officer of the king's Navy calling upon their daughter's friend, now, can they? And speaking of Miss O'Devir—and by the way, that was most gallant of you to deliver her to Captain Merrick, though I am not so old or blind that your obvious *affections* for each other have escaped me—'twould be most unseemly for her to remain upon a man-of-war with one hundred and fifty tars. Especially," he added, wagging a paternal finger, "in light of how you and the girl share such *affections*." He chuckled. "Because she is kin to one of my finest officers, I will do all that I can to preserve her reputation, as well as yours—which I daresay your envious peers would take great delight in tarnishing. To that end —and because she may be of use in reporting the activities of the Irish Pirate to us—I have arranged for her to lodge with the Foleys."

"But—"

"The matter is settled, Christian." The admiral drained his glass, then put it down on the table with an air of dismissal. "Captain Merrick is escorting both young women to the Foley home as we speak."

Christian looked away to hide his dismay.

"I know you don't wish to be separated from the girl, but it is necessary. I believe the Irish Pirate to be a secret friend of Jared Foley, whose own activities are highly suspect. Your courting of Miss O'Devir at the Foley household is perfect for this assignment, and will keep anyone from suspecting your true purpose for being in the countryside, which is, of course, to gather information so we can apprehend this smuggler. *That* is between you and me, and no one else."

Christian took a deep breath, unconsciously pressing his fingers to his throbbing shoulder. "Does Captain Merrick know of this plan? And why was he, a frigate captain himself, not chosen to apprehend the Irish Pirate? Surely he is more than capable."

"Merrick is half Irish himself, Captain, and as you know, the Irish are a clannish race. I would not send him against one of his own. Though I have no doubt that he would do his duty, I would not ask such a thing of him. In fact, I think it would be in *everyone*'s best interest if I send him off to join the frigate *Lively* in patrolling the coast."

With that, the crotchety old admiral got to his feet. Christian did the same, his heart heavy. Poor Deirdre. He hadn't even had the chance to say goodbye to her, or to properly thank her for coming to his rescue this afternoon. And no doubt she was homesick, lonely, frightened, and miserable.

The admiral walked with him toward the door. "Take heart, old boy," he said, clasping his shoulder and missing Christian's wince of pain. "'Twill not be forever. In fact, you might even begin calling on Miss O'Devir tomorrow. Now, that's something to look forward to, eh?"

"Indeed, sir."

But at the door, the admiral gave him a level, warning look. "Just ... watch yourself, Captain, and keep your nose clean in all of this. This assignment could be very dangerous. There are those who would delight in shooting you down, and I would not have the career of England's future admiral jeopardized." He gave a tight smile. "Do I make myself clear?"

"Yes, sir. Very clear."

"Very well then. Now if you'll excuse me? It has been a *most* trying day."

Chapter Twenty-Three

Deirdre hated Massachusetts from the moment she stepped off the wharf, staggered, and nearly fell at the unfamiliarity of solid earth beneath her feet.

It didn't take her long to discover that Boston was cold and ugly, the buildings as bleak and forbidding as the faces of the people who inhabited them. Red-coated soldiers patrolled the streets. Most of the shops were closed, some showing the effects of vandalism. Hungry, mean-looking dogs ran in packs looking for a stray chicken or a heap of garbage, their teeth flashing if one came too close. Drunken seamen were thick along the waterfront; some, upon sighting Brendan, touched their forelocks in a sign of respect. But there was no such respect amongst the out-of-work townspeople who lounged idly about, their expressions sullen and cold as they watched him help the two girls into the carriage he had hired to take them out to the Foley home.

The countryside west of Boston was just as bleak as the port town and no friendlier. Treacherous ruts carved up roads that were muddy and half-frozen. The trees were still bare, their branches gray and skeletal against the cold sky. The earth was carpeted with dead grass that was not green, as it should be, but brown, and flattened to the ground like a head of dirty uncombed hair. Here and there, snow made a tired, dingy crust upon a shaded slope, and fields divided by rambling walls of granite boulders loomed on either side of the road.

With each mile that brought her farther and farther from Christian, Deirdre's heart sank. Blocking out Delight's chatter and Brendan's responsive laughter, she pressed her nose against the window and blinked back tears of homesickness and despair.

"Christian," she whispered miserably, her gaze fixed on the distant hills. "Oh, why couldn't I just have stayed with ye? Why does yer admiral have to be so concerned with my reputation when he doesn't even *know* me?"

The admiral. He had invited, nay, demanded that Christian dine with him aboard the flagship, and as Deirdre had solemnly watched her lover changing into his best uniform and calling for his dress sword, she'd had no idea they were to be separated. Her anticipation of stripping off that dashing uniform upon his return had been hopelessly dashed when, shortly after Christian had left, Brendan had arrived to take both her and Delight out to the Foley home in Menotomy.

Deirdre had protested fiercely, but her cousin had only apologized for having to follow orders that he admittedly agreed with.

Finally, stormy-eyed and angry, Deirdre had gathered up her few belongings, grabbed one of Christian's shirts so she'd have something of his to comfort her, and joining Delight and Brendan, departed the home she had known for the past month.

"Tell Christian where I am!" she had said, desperately taking Ian's hand just before she'd left the ship. 'Tell him the Old Fart's sendin' me away! Tell him to come rescue me as soon as he can!"

"Aye, lassie. Now keep your chin up, and hold tight. The Lord and Master'll not abandon ye."

No, surely he wouldn't, she thought, staring out at a hard blue sky that was strangely naked of cloud. It looked nothing like the misty gray skies of home, reminding her again of how far away her beloved Ireland was. But Ian was right. Christian would *not* abandon her here. In her heart, she knew that as soon as he could get away, he would come for her.

But as they traveled farther inland, she couldn't prevent the mounting despair and homesickness. The sky was not the only feature of this bleak and barren land that was strange. In fact, nothing was the way it *should* be. Back home, the trees would just be starting to branch and bud. Back home, daffodils would be poking up through lush grass that was so brilliant and green it hurt your eyes to look at it. Back home, the weather would be raw and moist, not crisp, dry, and bitterly cold.

She glanced at her cousin for reassurance, but he obviously didn't notice the alarming differences between the two lands, so caught up was he in responding to Delight's subtle remarks and not-so-subtle invitations.

Deirdre turned away to stare out the window once more, her heart sinking with every mile.

"Here we are!" Delight cried as the carriage drew up beside a squarish, two-story house painted a humble shade of brown. "Now Deirdre, you *must* remember not to call me Delight, especially after all the pains I have taken to appear presentable!" Laughing, she indicated her modest blue dress, then yanked her shawl over her shoulders to conceal the tempting swell of her bodice, which had been purposely bared for the benefit of Brendan's appreciative eyes. "And you, Captain Merrick, simply *must* join us for supper! Mama will be most distressed if you do not, and"—she trailed her fingernails down his sleeve and gazed invitingly up into his eyes—"so will I."

"Yes, Brendan, please stay," Deirdre pleaded, unwilling to be left with these people she didn't know, distressed about losing contact with her cousin, terrified about being abandoned in this bleak and foreign land. She gripped his sleeve, her eyes desperate. "'Tis only for supper—"

The door to the house opened and a woman appeared on the

threshold. Clad in brown-and-white calico, she had a white apron around her ample waist and blond hair tucked severely beneath a muslin cap.

"Dolores Ann!"

"Mama!"

Delight leapt out of the carriage, raced across the lawn, and flung herself into the woman's arms. There was much hugging and weeping and cheek-pinching before Delight, dragging her mother back across the muddy lawn, could make introductions. Brendan had already stepped down from the carriage and now stood holding his fancy, gold-laced hat. "Oh, Mama, I have brought guests!" Delight bubbled happily. "My friend is in the carriage— she's from Ireland—and our gallant escort here is her cousin, Captain Brendan Jay Merrick, who was kind enough to accompany us from Boston to ensure that no harm befell us. He's in the king's *Navy,* Mama!"

That last word—*Navy*—was oddly stressed, almost as if in warning. Deirdre, still inside the carriage, saw a fleeting look of alarm cross the woman's face as she looked at Brendan in his handsome uniform; then she allowed him to take her hand and bow over it, a gesture that soon wiped the uneasiness from her eyes and had her cheeks flushing pink, for Brendan was uncommonly handsome and full of Irish charm. "How do you do, madam," he said, grinning warmly. And then, turning to hand Deirdre down from the carriage, "My cousin, Deirdre O'Devir."

Mrs. Foley's eyes widened as she looked at Deirdre, taking in the seaman's jacket that covered her shoulders, the trousers that hid her long legs. Then she saw the misery in her eyes and her demeanor changed. With a sudden smile, she reached out and hugged Deirdre as fiercely as she had her own daughter. "Oh, do come in, poor thing, you must be absolutely frozen! A cup of chocolate will restore you in no time."

"Thank ye, Mrs. Foley. I ... I'm sorry to be intrudin' like this. I'd just as soon have stayed aboard the ship—"

"My, you have the most *delightful* brogue!" She put her hands on Deirdre's shoulders and stood back, admiring her and pretending she didn't notice the tears welling up in Deirdre's eyes. "Why, just listen to her talk, Dolores Ann! And good heavens, don't speak such nonsense; you're not intruding at all. Any friend of Dolores's is a friend of ours. Besides, we were expecting you; the admiral in Boston sent word ahead that my daughter had arrived and was bringing a friend. Come, come, my dear, let's get you out of those atrocious clothes and into something a bit more ladylike. And you, Captain Merrick, do come in and join us for supper!"

"Faith, that's kind of you, madam, but I really couldn't—"

"I insist! Jared is at the shop right now, but he'll be home shortly. Meanwhile, you *must* come in and tell us what our gallant Navy is doing to protect us from these horrible rebels."

"Yes, Captain Merrick, you simply *must!*" Delight echoed, eyeing him appreciatively, suggestively, hungrily, from behind her mother's back.

No man could resist such an invitation, not even a king's officer. And so it was that Brendan found himself ushered into the Foleys' house, a pale and wan Deirdre trailing in his shadow.

HOURS LATER, Deirdre, seated morosely beside Brendan and listening to the effusive Delight babble on, was as miserable and homesick as Christian had feared she would be.

Outside, the night pressed against the windows and the fire in the hearth did little to dispel the sense of loneliness that pervaded her very soul. Wind moaned under the eaves, made the flames waver and jump in the grating. Home had never seemed so far away. *Christian* had never seemed so far away. It was almost as if both belonged to another time, another place.

"Deirdre? Are you all right, lass?"

She glanced up at her cousin, whose mirthful eyes were dark with worry. "Aye, Brendan. Just … just a wee bit homesick, 'tis all."

She looked down, her heart raw and aching.

"Why, I'll bet you're just missing your handsome Lord and Master," Delight chirped, shooting Brendan a bold glance from beneath her lashes. The look went unnoticed by her mother, who had gone to the hearth to ladle more stew from the pot, and her father, who had been subtly studying the naval officer all during supper.

Brendan laughed, ever his cheerful self. "No, she misses Ireland," he said, noting the canvas bag in her lap. "Don't you, Deirdre?"

"Oh, let the poor girl alone, you two!" Mrs. Foley scolded with mock sharpness. She plunked a steaming bowl of beef stew down and reclaimed her seat. "She's been across an ocean, traveled all day, and is probably tired to the bone. No wonder she's feeling poorly!"

Poorly was not the word for it, Deirdre thought, picking up her spoon and trying to pretend she had an appetite. And both of them were right—she missed Christian as much as she missed Ireland.

She took a deep breath and took a spoonful of the stew. It tasted as it should, but the yellow, coarse bread that accompanied it was dry and tasteless. She stared down at it, hating it as much as she did everything else in this awful place.

Beside her, Brendan squeezed her hand. She looked up and saw a reassuring twinkle in his eyes, a mirthful grin on his lips. Imitating her dejected look, he gave her a black scowl, turning down the corners of his mouth and lowering his eyebrows until she couldn't help but smile. But her response was short-lived, and as soon as he turned back to his meal—and Delight—Deirdre was again staring down at her lap, her eyes on her bag of Irish mementos.

Oh, Christian, she thought. *If only I was with ye right now, safely wrapped in yer strong arms and snuggled against yer big, warm chest....*

She poked at her stew, making herself take a few bites so she wouldn't appear rude. Outside it was awfully black, the darkness thick and alien and hostile. The wind shook a loose pane against a casing, and a cold draft whispered across the wide-boarded floor and curled around her ankles.

American stew. American darkness. American wind.

American cold.

Her hand tightened around the bag in her lap, and she took a deep, steadying breath.

I want to go home.

She was able to keep her composure throughout the meal, knowing that the time would soon come when she could be alone, free to feel the misery of her heart without having to put on a brave face. Beside her, Brendan was already beginning to fidget, and she knew that soon he would leave, abandoning her in this foreign, unfriendly land with a family who ate strange food and talked with a strange accent.

"You all right, Deirdre?" Delight asked gently.

Deirdre nodded quickly, too quickly, and tried to smile. Delight's father glanced at her. No doubt he was angry that he had another mouth to feed. He had barely said two words to her all night, instead watching Brendan and her with a look in his shrewd blue eyes that did nothing to make her feel welcome.

Talk went on, with the elder Foleys idly inquiring what the Navy was doing to quell smuggling, and Brendan giving bland answers that disclosed nothing. And all too soon, the steam stopped rising from the stew, the flames began to die in the hearth, and Deirdre caught her cousin glancing repeatedly at the shelf clock standing on a nearby table. Raw loneliness filled her, and she felt a momentary stab of panic.

Don't go, Brendan, she thought desperately. *Oh, please, don't go and leave me here all by myself.*

But the dreaded moment finally came. Brendan gave a great sigh, complimented Mrs. Foley on the meal, accepted a chunk of cornbread wrapped in linen for the "trip back," and picked up his black, gold-laced hat.

Deirdre followed him outside. "Oh, Brendan, I wish ye wouldn't leave me here," she said forlornly. "I can't bear it, truly, I can't."

"Faith, Deirdre, such carrying-on! 'Tis not the end of the world, you know!"

"This place is awful. Everything's different, no one is friendly, and I just want to go home. In fact, the sooner you and Christian can find Roddy—"

"Yes, Roddy." Her cousin reached down and gently grasped her shoulders, his eyes, for once, serious and dark in the pale starlight as he gazed down at her. "I know you told me on the ride out here that you came to Boston to find me so that I could help you locate your brother, but faith, Deirdre, that's not going to be as easy as you may think. He could be anywhere." He sobered further. "Even dead."

"I know that, Brendan. But I promised Mama that I would find him and bring him home to Ireland so she could rest in peace. I've got to at least try."

"Yes, I suppose you must," he said resignedly. "Just don't get your hopes up, Deidre. I'd hate to see you get your heart broken." He embraced her tightly, his arms closing around her shoulders. He had grown taller, stronger, even more handsome since she'd seen him last, but he was still the laughing, beloved cousin she remembered so well—and, he carried the blood of Ireland in his veins, the brogue of Connaught in his voice, the soul of Connemara in his heart.

Home.

She clung to him, unwilling to relinquish him to the night, blinking back tears as their parting grew closer by the moment.

She did not want to be alone out here in this cold and wretched place, with strangers. She did not want him to leave.

And she ached for Christian. Oh, God help her, did she ache.

"Well, Brendan, if anyone can find Roddy, 'tis you and Christian," she said at last. "I have faith in the two of ye."

"Yes, and I'm sure that Captain Lord will be here just as soon as he can get away. He'll help you find your brother, I'm certain of it."

She stared at him. "Aren't ye goin' to help?"

He shook his head. "Sir Geoffrey is sending me back to sea tomorrow to cruise the north shore and make sure things don't get out of hand there." He saw her stricken look and touched her cheek. "But I won't be gone forever, lass. When I come back, I promise to help find Roddy."

"D'ye think he's still alive, Brendan? Do ye?"

A shadow passed over his face. "Thirteen years is a long time, Deirdre."

"He's alive," she declared, raising her chin. "I feel it in my bones. We'll find him, Brendan, ye just wait and see. Christian already promised he would do everything in his power to get him back for me. He feels responsible, as it was his press gang that took Roddy in the first place, but I don't hold him accountable for it anymore. He was just doin' his duty." Fire flashed in her eyes. "Nay, Brendan, 'twas the Navy's fault, and it's up to the Navy to return my brother to me!"

He looked down at her, his eyes affectionate, his face beloved and dear. "Ah, lass, you certainly have the determination of our Grace O'Malley in you, don't you?" He smiled and walked with her toward the waiting carriage. "And now I must go. Can't keep the admiral waiting, you know."

On sudden impulse, she flung her arms around his neck, clinging tightly to him. They embraced each other for a long moment, she wearing her homesickness on her sleeve, he well used to this strange land and uncharacteristically silent as he pondered all she had told him over the course of the afternoon. Finally he stood back and with a reassuring grin, reminded her that Christian was not so far away, and then climbed swiftly up into the carriage.

Moments later, it was fading into the night.

Deirdre stayed out on the half-frozen lawn until the horse's hoofbeats had faded and the carriage's lanterns had shrunk to mere sparks in the distance. At last they were gone altogether, and she was alone.

Her shoulders drooped and she took a deep, shaky breath. Finally, she turned and trudged back into the house and up the narrow wooden staircase to the room that Mrs. Foley had prepared for her. Someone had brought her bag of Irish mementos up and placed it on the little stand just inside the door. The bed was neatly turned down, waiting. She retrieved her bag, pulled a thick, heavy quilt from the bed, wrapped it around herself, and went to the window. After much tugging, she managed to get it open. Cold night air swept in. She sat down on the bare floor and gazed out into the night, imagining her beloved cousin traveling somewhere out there in the darkness, away from her—and toward Boston, where everyone she now held dear in this world seemed to be.

"Oh, Christian," she murmured, staring out into the darkness. Before leaving the frigate, she had taken one of his shirts from his sea trunk and stuffed it into her bag; now, she pulled it out, pressed it against her lips, and breathed deeply of his scent. The heartache that had been building all evening grew unbearable. "Please, come and get me. Please, oh, please, don't let me rot out here."

Stars twinkled above the treetops and low-lying hills. Wood smoke lay heavily in the cold air and wafted through the window. Just cross the road, the windows of a tavern glowed orange in the darkness. Figures in silhouette moved back and forth behind the panes.

Was Christian aching for her as much as she was for him? Had the elderly admiral forgiven him? Was his shoulder causing him pain? What was he doing right now? She hugged the shirt to herself, feeling the tears welling behind her eyelids, in the back of her throat. In her lap was her precious bag of Irish mementos and she touched it, her fingers moving over the odd lumps and bumps and knowing each shape in the darkness.

Far, far off in the distance, a dog barked, the sound lonely and sad in the night.

How far away from her now was Brendan? A mile? Two?

She reached into the bag and found the soft clump of wool from an Irish sheep. That tiny connection with home—so near, and yet so far—brought a piercing ache to her heart, and she bent her head, burying her face against the canvas bag to try and hold back the tears.

Home. Where was it? In which direction did it lie?

She looked up into the night sky. Alarm spread through her when she could not find the North Star. Dear Lord, were the stars that shone over this godforsaken place different from those that stood over Ireland? Shivering with cold, Deirdre clutched the tuft of wool and leaned far out the window, craning her neck and peering up at the peaked roof of the dark house.

There. The North Star, beloved and familiar, like an old friend. Choking relief swept over her, and she shut her eyes in silent gratitude. *Thank God.* That at least was reassuring. She leaned out the window once again, contorting her body at an unnatural angle so that her face was turned homeward.

At that moment a gust of wind came up, tearing the wool from her hand. She cried out and make a mad lunge toward it, but the lonely white tuft drifted off into the darkness, dancing on the wind, fading away until it was swallowed by the night.

Far away, the dog barked again.

Stricken, she pressed steepled hands to her mouth as hot, salty tears finally began to course down her cheeks and over her fingers. "Oh ... oh, dear God, no....

Ireland.

Another piece of it gone.

She wrapped her arms around her knees, bent her head, and clutching Christian's shirt to her heart, wept until she could weep no more.

❧

"HEAVENS, Deirdre, what was all that bumping and thumping going on up there last night?" Delight asked at the breakfast table the next morning. She stuffed a spoonful of strange yellow pudding into her mouth and reached for the pitcher of tree sap—which, Deirdre had been told, was called maple syrup. "I thought the house was going to come down!"

Deirdre raised her head. She had not found much rest last night and she knew it showed in her face. Only when she had made some adjustments to her bed, then fiercely hugged Christian's shirt in her arms and pretended she was hugging *him,* had she been able to find sleep.

Mr. and Mrs. Foley were regarding her curiously. Outside, sunshine was bright across the land, making the low-lying hills in the near distance look as purple as the Twelve Bens back home. Deirdre's cheeks flamed and sheepishly, she murmured, "I'm sorry. I didn't mean to keep anyone awake. I was ... movin' the bed."

"Moving the bed?"

She stared down at her hands, suddenly embarrassed. "I wanted it to ... to face Ireland."

Even the stern and stoic Jared Foley was hard-pressed to keep his lips from twitching in amusement.

"Well, I never!" Mrs. Foley exclaimed. "You have got to be the most homesick young lady I've ever known. You'll just have to meet our Irish friend soon. Perhaps that will make you feel better."

"Irish friend?" Deirdre asked, suddenly brightening.

"A seafarer, just like your man," Delight said, her eyes glinting.

"What?" Mr. Foley asked, peering at Deirdre from over the top of his wire-rimmed spectacles. "You have a suitor?"

"Oh, he is *most* handsome," Delight said. "He masters a ship, is that not so, Deirdre?"

"Aye," Deirdre said proudly.

Mr. Foley put down his fork. "Which one?"

"His Majesty's frigate *Bold Marauder.* Christian is a king's officer. A captain in the Royal Navy."

"I see." Mr. Foley exchanged a quick glance with his wife and, picking up his fork, cast his gaze back down toward his plate.

"Did I say somethin' wrong?"

"No, Deirdre." Mrs. Foley patted her hand. "Not at all." Again she glanced at her husband. "We should like to meet him sometime. Wouldn't we, Jared?"

"Aye," he grunted, attacking his hasty pudding.

Deirdre looked at them, wondering what she had said to upset them. Certainly, the mood around the table seemed to have suddenly changed. She glanced at Delight, hoping to find an answer, but her friend was looking down, smiling and picking a bit of shell from her eggs.

The sudden silence was uncomfortable. Deirdre picked up her fork and, shunning the strange hasty pudding, went for the more familiar eggs instead.

They weren't from an Irish hen, but at least they didn't taste any different.

Perhaps there was hope here, after all.

Despite Sir Geoffrey's assurances, and Christian's desire to race off to Menotomy at the first chance he had, it was two days before he could get away from his duties. Meetings with his admiral and General Gage to discuss rebel movements and the presentation of his bold plan to net the Irish Pirate kept him near his command. But by the third morning, when he awoke bleary-eyed, lonely, and exhausted, he knew he could delay no longer.

Tildy, leaving her growing puppies sleeping in a pile, had climbed into bed with him, but though her presence was a small comfort, no one could take the place of his beloved Deirdre. Every time he'd rolled over and looked at the pillow, he imagined his Irish girl's thick, spiraling black curls spread over it, her innocent purple eyes gazing at him with adoration. He hadn't realized how much he missed her until he was forced to sleep alone.

How had she fared through the nights? The poor mite was probably homesick as hell, out there all by herself in an unfamiliar countryside with people she didn't know. Anger swept through him at the unfortunate circumstances that had separated them. He rose from his bed. There was no sense in allowing her to suffer any longer.

He washed, shaved and dressed. He packed a bag with a few civilian clothes, then chose his finest shirt, his dress coat, and his gold-tasseled presentation sword. He made a handsome picture as he appeared on deck, and could not have been more pleased with the smartness and ceremony with which his men saw him over the side.

They stood by the hammock nettings, watching his gig carry him across the sparkling harbor, threading its way between the other anchored warships.

"Something's troubling our Lord and Master," Hibbert said, as though no one else had noticed.

"Aye, he's in a bad way. The Old Fart must ha'e given him a good setting-down the other day," Ian said, glaring at the huge flagship that shimmered in her own reflection.

"It ain't *his* fault none of us knew Delight was up there," Skunk muttered.

"Elwin says the Old Fart was so mad he was spitting nails."

"Should've let Delight work her charms on *him*," Teach growled, joining them. He held a flintlock pistol in his hand, and was cocking the empty weapon, pulling the trigger, cocking the weapon, pulling the trigger, his annoyance obvious and beginning to become annoying in itself. "Might've done the Old Fart a world of good."

"She tried," Elwin said, scowling at Teach, then picking at a callus on his finger. "But it was Deirdre, not Delight, who got the old crust softened up enough that he finally quit raging at our Lord and Master. Never saw anything like it. Had him eating out of her hand, she did."

Click, snap, click, snap, went Teach's pistol.

Wenham scratched at his great, jutting ears. 'Too bad that young Irish captain had to take Deirdre from us. I'll bet that's what's got our poor Lord and Master in such a sorry state, having her stolen away from him like that."

"That young captain be her cousin, y' know," Ian said.

"Her *cousin?*"

"Aye. Ye can see some resemblance around the mouth. Same smile."

"Same way of talkin', too. Boglander brogue," added Skunk.

Click. Snap. Click.

"Christ, would ye quit with that noise? It's irritatin' as all hell!" Skunk snarled.

Teach merely grinned, and kept on doing it.

Ian cleared his throat. "Well, *I* think we need tae be cheering up our captain. What do ye all think of inviting him tae the wardroom to dine with us tomorrow night? That way he won't have tae eat all by himself. Besides, 'twill show him how much *we're* behind him, no matter what the Old Fart says or does!"

"Aye, good idea, Ian!"

Rhodes melted out of the shadows and seated himself upon the gunwales of one of the ship's boats. His tone was solemn. "When I accompanied him over to the flagship yesterday, one of the lieutenants told me our captain isn't well liked. The other commanders are jealous of his record, envious of what he's accomplished." He swept them with his black eyes. "They'll not make things easy for him here."

"Huh! Piss on *them,* I say!" Skunk said, his eyes flashing. "Sufferin' bastards, I hear *any* of 'em sayin' one bad word about our captain and I'll skin the wrinkles from their hides and stuff 'em down their bloody throats!"

"Aye!" they echoed in unison, their eyes fierce, protective, and angry.

Teach raised his pistol and pointed it at the huge flagship. *Click. Snap. Click.* "And that goes for that old fart of an admiral, too!"

Chapter Twenty-Four

Christian was not sorry to get away from Boston for the day.
The tense and explosive atmosphere of the town made him
uneasy, with red-coated troops spoiling for a fight, bored sailors
lounging along the wharves, and resentful colonists who'd been
out of work since Parliament's Coercive Acts had deprived them
of their jobs, idling about. Now the townspeople had nothing
better to do than taunt the British troops, monitor their every
movement, and report back to the infamous Sons of Liberty, who
were behind this whole wretched mess.

Beneath him his horse, a strapping chestnut stallion he'd
leased from a Welsh major eager to pay off a gambling debt,
sensed his anxiety and began to prance. Christian's hands tightened on the reins. If only Sir Geoffrey hadn't discovered Deirdre
aboard the frigate; he'd give anything to have her safely behind
the protection of *Bold Marauder*'s guns should the inevitable
explosion between colonists and the king's forces occur.

And of course, there was the undeniable fact that he
loved her.

Rico had barged into his cabin that morning while Christian
had been eating his breakfast. "Every man jack aboard the frigate

knows you're pining for the Irish girl," his friend had said as Christian morosely toyed with his boiled egg and ship's biscuit. "Why don't you just marry her and get on with life?"

"Marry her?"

Why not? It was a simple solution to the loneliness that had plagued him for the past five years. He had lived in hell for all that time, but now that he'd had a taste of heaven, thoughts of even one more day alone were suddenly unbearable.

Deirdre. He loved her, yes, he knew that now ... and she, by her own word, loved him. He gazed ahead through the pricked ears of his mount, smiling as he pictured that beloved face, those spiraling black curls, her sometimes stormy, sometimes childlike, but always loving amethyst eyes that had haunted him for the past month.

Eyes that he knew now had haunted him for the past thirteen years.

He shifted in the saddle, nudging his horse into a trot and gritting his teeth against the sudden pain in his shoulder. What would marriage to her be like? She'd already proved she could adjust to life aboard a king's warship; would she be happy as the wife of a king's officer?

And could he, a battle-scarred, sometimes cynical king's officer who'd seen far too much of the world, make her happy? Was he good enough for her?

Holding the reins in one hand, he reached down and checked to be sure the ring he'd put into his pocket this morning was still there. Of purest gold, it was a lion's body, its eyes blood-red rubies, its mouth glinting with diamond chips, its tail the band that would wrap itself around a delicate finger. The ring was exquisite, and as ancient as the title that Christian's ancestors had held for centuries. Upon the death of their father, Elliott would inherit, but Elliott had ardently professed that he would sooner fall victim to a cannonball than matrimony, and so the ring had long ago fallen into Christian's possession.

The fact that Elliott *had* fallen victim to matrimony hadn't changed things.

Christian still had the ring.

Deirdre O'Devir Lord. His heart warmed as he tried out the name on his tongue and he found himself smiling as the horse, skirting the occasional puddle, carried him closer and closer to Menotomy. Yes, he liked the sound of that name. Liked it very much.

Deirdre O' Devir Lord.

He wanted her as his wife.

But would she have *him*?

He was, after all, an Englishman, and not just any Englishman, but the one she'd spent the past thirteen years of her life hating. And despite having made inquiries amongst some of the other naval officers and their men, he was no closer now to fulfilling his promise to find her brother than he had been last week, no closer to righting the dreadful wrong that he—and England—had done to her and her family all those years ago.

By God, he *would* right it. He *would* find her brother if it was the last thing he did and reunite the family that he, in the king's name, had torn apart.

So caught up was he in his musings that before he knew it, he was crossing a bridge over the Mystic River Brook, passing beneath the branches of two old elm trees that guarded the little village of Menotomy, and entering the settlement itself. He looked about with a critical and assessing eye for this was, after all, where Deirdre would have to live until he made her his wife.

A typical New England town, it was tiny and picturesque. Stone walls and fences bordered the road. Fields strewn with a haphazard scattering of granite, sheep, and cows rolled away into the distance, melting into gentle hills of birch, pine, oak, elm, and maple. Yet despite the mildness of the early spring morning, he sensed a tension in the air.

He touched the inside of his elbow to his sword hilt. The day seemed tranquil and serene, but he could feel unseen eyes upon him, eyes that watched him with suspicion and no small degree of hostility.

He slowed the horse to a walk, passing the Black Horse Tavern and Spy Pond, where geese honked loudly and shook the water out of their broad wings. From somewhere he heard the distant sound of fife and drum, and wondered if even now the so-called minutemen were mustering, preparing to practice their futile maneuvers.

The thought both saddened and alarmed him.

The Menotomy minutemen, he'd been told, were a new unit, led by a farmer named Benjamin Locke whose house lay farther west along the Concord Road. Christian gazed at the peaceful fields and the humble dwellings that spilled smoke from their chimneys. Why had things come to this? Why couldn't Englishmen live in harmony with one another? Why couldn't Parliament be more sympathetic to those who lived across the sea, and all those in power back in England be more understanding about the concerns of the colonists? God help the poor bumpkins if and when things came to blows between them and the king's forces.

They wouldn't have a chance.

The haunting music was disturbing and depressing. Christian urged his mount faster, wincing with each jolt to his shoulder but preferring the sound of the beast's hooves over that of fife and drum. Mud splashed up and splattered the animal's belly, its forelegs, and Christian's gleaming boots, but the horse shook its head, wanting more speed. He tightened his hands on the reins, keeping the stallion's pace contained. The traffic was heavier here, the other travelers staring at him as he passed. Seeing an open carriage with a pair of women in it, he touched his hat in polite greeting. Their eyes raked him with disdain. A youth no older than Hibbert glared at him with open hostility from behind a stone wall and a group of farmers, leading a milk cow, spat on the ground in open contempt. Disturbed and feeling increasingly ill at ease, Christian continued on.

He passed another tavern, where movement at the windows indicated his presence was not unobserved. By God, was the whole village watching him? He wondered if people had seen him coming and spread the news of his arrival long before his horse had even neared the place. But then, perhaps they had reason to be suspicious. There was no reason for a naval officer to be this far inland.

Ahead was an intersection, a store, and a church, beyond which lay a small graveyard, its headstones bleak and forbidding even in the bright sunlight. He passed several more houses, another tavern, and there, directly across the road, stood the simple brown house that, according to Sir Geoffrey's roughly drawn map, belonged to Jared Foley.

At last.

He pulled his horse to a halt, content just to sit for a minute in the sunshine and gaze upon the girl who stood at a well in the front yard, toiling with a rope and what must have been a rather heavy bucket at its end. Instantly, he forgot his throbbing shoulder. Her bent back was toward him, her bottom outlined in a plain skirt of green linsey-woolsey, her muslin petticoats barely clear of the mud in which she stood. Her hair, black as pitch and caught in a loose braid, followed the curve of her spine and brushed her hips. He saw her shoulders working as she wrestled with the heavy rope.

Vaulting from the saddle with an ease that was rare amongst mariners, Christian strode quietly across the lawn, his boots squishing in damp turf. But she didn't hear him. He came up behind her, grasped the rope and began to pull.

"Need some help?"

"*Christian!*"

She flung herself against him, squealing with surprise and delight and burying herself against his coat. His arms closed around her and for a long moment he could only hold her, burying his face in her hair while a fierce sense of love and protectiveness welled up in his chest. His heart constricted, making it hard to breathe, impossible to think. But it was a good feeling. It was an even better one to see how happy his appearance had made her. How different she was in every way from how Emily had been.

Closing his eyes, he held her close, wishing with all his heart he could take her back to *Bold Marauder* with him. Tonight. Now. Forever. She smelled of road dust and spring sunshine, clean wind and freshly baked bread. She was soft and warm, utterly feminine, totally guileless. He liked that. He liked the feel of her in his arms. He liked everything about her.

By God, there was nothing he *didn't* like.

"Oh, Christian, ye don't know how lonely I've been without ye! I hate it here, I do! The birds are different, the animals are different, the people are cold and unfriendly, and they talk funny, act funny. The air is cold, the grass is brown. Thank God ye came to take me back t' the ship, because I'll surely die if I have to stay here another day!"

"Deirdre, I did not come here to take you back to *Bold Marauder*." He took a deep breath and looked down into her eyes. "I came here to ask you to—"

The front door of the house banged open. "Deirdre?"

A girl stood there, clad in a blue woolen gown and a cloak of linsey-woolsey. She had blond hair, not bleached and silvery like his own, but rich and tawny and yellow, worn severely braided and entwined around her head. Her face was plain, fresh, and unpainted; her eyes, smiling and knowing.

The eyes, bold and brimming with raw prurience, were what gave her away.

"*Delight?*" he gasped, shocked.

She picked up her skirts and hurried across the lawn, her finger laid across lips that he'd last seen red and painted. "Don't call me that in front of my mother—she'll have my hide!" Nervously, she glanced back toward the house. "It's *Dolores Ann!*"

Stunned, he peeled Deirdre off his chest just as the woman in question appeared on the threshold.

If Christian had any doubts as to where the Foleys' true loyalties lay, they were instantly abolished by the woman's reaction to the presence of a king's officer on her front lawn. Her face drained of color. Her eyes went wide, and a wet dishcloth fell from her hands and splashed into a mud puddle at her feet.

Just as quickly she regained her composure and stepped forward, only her darting eyes and high, jittery voice betraying her nervousness. "Why, sir, 'tis not often we receive naval visitors out here in Menotomy! First Captain Merrick, now you ... I assume you must be, uh, Deirdre's suitor?"

Stepping forward, Christian tucked his hat under his elbow and bowed gallantly over the woman's hand. It was, he noticed, trembling. "Captain Lord, at your service." He straightened up. "Forgive me for not sending word ahead, but I was desperate to see Miss O' Devir. And, of course, pay my respects to your lovely daughter and her family, from whose hospitality my dear Deirdre has obviously benefited." He regarded the woman, his gray eyes steady and keen. "Given the hostility my presence seems to have elicited from your neighbors, I can only thank God that my beloved has found sanctuary with a family that is loyal to king and Crown. I hope I have not come at an inconvenient time?"

"Oh—oh, no, n-not at all!" Mrs. Foley said too quickly, her skittish manner as condemning as if she'd blatantly admitted that she and her family were anything *but* loyal. "Why don't you come in for some refreshment? A cup of chocolate, perhaps?"

"I would enjoy that, madam. And if I may allow my horse a drink of water before I join you?"

"Yes, yes, please do! You may tie him up there beside the watering trough. Dolores Ann? Please stop gaping and come with me—*now!*"

Christian smiled wryly. It was all too obvious that the woman had no desire this side of Hades to have him there, but to be anything less than hospitable, especially toward a decorated and respected officer of the king's Navy, would cast suspicion on the Foley name.

Had she been this skittish around Brendan? He wished he'd had the chance to speak to the other frigate captain before Sir Geoffrey had sent him back off to sea.

He watched Delight's mother hurry back to the house. In typical New England fashion, the structure faced south, its roof steep and sloping to rid itself of winter snows, its big chimney set squarely in the center. Five windows reflected the sunshine from the top floor; four more, with a door between them, looked out from the bottom. A barn stood a short distance away from the house, ringed by a fence containing two horses sleeping in the early spring sun.

"I see you've got yourself a steed, Captain Lord." Delight's gaze roved over the stallion whose coat, glinting in the sunlight, was the color of rich cherry. She quirked a brow. "But then, there are many activities besides *riding* that one can do upon a horse, no?"

Christian started to deliver a sarcastic comment, but just then the door banged open. "Dolores Ann! You come in here this instant!"

Delight sighed and rolled her eyes. "Oh, I really *do* wish I'd stayed in France sometimes. You'd think I was still a blushing miss of seventeen, the way they're both treating me." Still muttering, she sauntered off across the lawn, hips rolling. As she reached the door, Mrs. Foley yanked her inside. The woman's mouth was moving, her hands gesturing angrily, and Christian wished he could hear what she was saying to her daughter. Feigning indifference to them, he looked at Deirdre as she caught his sleeve.

"Oh, Christian, I'm so happy to see ye. I'm so lonely, and

missed ye so much last night, I thought my poor heart would break!"

She looked up at him, smiling. Her fingers rested against his lapels; her slim, lithe body pressed against his. Her heart was in her eyes, brimming with love and joy, and again he felt his chest swell and threaten to burst. She was *his.* She had given herself to him and in her innocence, had made him a man once more, in all senses of the word.

And soon, she would be his in name as well as in heart. He couldn't wait to give her the ring, couldn't wait to see her reaction.

By God, I love her.

Knowing that Mrs. Foley was probably observing them from her window, he gently pried Deirdre's hands from his lapels. "Come, dearest. Let us go in and behave ourselves for a bit, shall we?"

"Oh, Christian. Please don't ask me to be behavin' myself for too long. I want to be alone with ye and show ye how much I've been missin' ye!"

His loins tightened in instant response. As she took his hand and led him to the house, he wondered how he had ever thought he might be impotent. "Well, then," he said, smiling down at her walking beside him, "perhaps you can borrow a horse from the Foleys and we can go, er, *riding* afterward?"

"Oh, Christian, can we?"

It would be the perfect time to ask her to be his wife. His heart fluttered in excitement, but he managed to maintain his composed demeanor. "Aye," he said, tipping her chin up and gazing into her wide purple eyes. "Now let us go and be sociable."

But as they entered the house Deirdre, with Delight trailing in her wake, fled up the stairs with an excuse about having to change her clothes and Christian was left standing all alone just inside the door.

He looked around, his hat in his hands. The house was small, plain, lived-in. He walked into the main living area, which appeared to double as a kitchen, feigning casual interest while his keen gaze searched for anything that would further boost suspicions that the Foleys were anything but Loyalists. But there was nothing incriminating. The house smelled of herbs, cooking, and years of fires burned on the huge hearth that dominated the room in which he stood. They were strange smells to his mariner's nose, just as the room itself, a palace compared with the size of his cabin aboard *Bold Marauder,* was strange to his seafarer's eyes. Wide-boarded floors were scuffed smooth by years of shoes. The massive, soot-blackened hearth was framed by cooking utensils of various sizes, shapes, and forms. He smelled baking bread, peered into a stewpot and saw a pudding boiling in a cloth. Herbs hung from overhead rafters, and a set of chairs surrounded a rough-hewn table spread with clean linens.

He looked at the chairs. In which one had his Deirdre taken her supper? Sat and talked to her hosts? Pined inside with home-sickness?

By God and all that was holy, she would not be out here for long. As soon as he gathered the evidence Sir Geoffrey needed to brand the Foleys as rebels of the Crown, as soon as he himself found and chased down the Irish Pirate—who was, as Sir Geoffrey had put it, "putting weapons in the hands of babes"—he would marry her and get her out of here.

That day couldn't arrive soon enough.

Mrs. Foley came bustling around the corner, absently patting her hair, her lips drawn tight, an anxious frown creasing her brow. Her hand flew to her chest at the sight of him.

"Oh! I hadn't realized you'd already come in—"

"My apologies, madam. I did not mean to startle you."

She hastily indicated a chair. "No matter, Captain. As you know, things are so tense I suppose we are all in a state of agitation, what with those awful rebels whipping up the countryside as they are!" She turned away, unable to meet his eyes, and quickly changed the subject. "Dolores Ann tells me you took extraordinarily good care of her during the passage, and that your crew was most obliging to her *every* need."

Christian swallowed the wrong way, coughed, and out of the corner of his eye caught Delight's amused gaze as she entered the room in time to hear her mother's comment. "They were, uh, quite attentive," he said slowly, grabbing the cup of hot, steaming chocolate that was set before him.

"I'm glad to hear that," Mrs. Foley said. "Of course, one can never be too safe nowadays, what with such riffraff as that awful Irish Pirate terrorizing the seas! Why, I'm told that he struck again just last week ... engaged himself in battle with an English frigate!"

Christian nearly scalded his throat at the woman's reckless taunt. He set the hot chocolate down. "Battle? There was no battle, madam. The English frigate in question was under *my* command, and any damage she sustained was dealt by a Frenchman, not an overgrown brat playing at being a smuggler."

His remark, carefully delivered with just the right amount of anger and righteous British indignation, had the desired effect. He saw his hostess's eyes gleam before she quickly set a slice of pork pie before him. "Is that so, Captain? I don't think the Irish —I mean, the scoundrel—is 'playing.' In fact, I hear he's become quite successful at his *game*."

"I wouldn't know," Christian said mildly, carefully sipping his chocolate and pretending a blithe disregard for the subject. "He didn't have the courage to stay and fight. Not that it matters. My admiral views him as a paltry inconvenience, and so do I. The Navy has better things to be doing than chasing after vermin, and I certainly wasn't sent across three thousand miles of stormy North Atlantic for the sole purpose of apprehending this nuisance who seems determined to get himself hanged."

The woman took the bait. "You mean, you've been sent all the way from England *just* to catch the Irish Pirate?"

"Ridiculous, is it not?" Christian gave a benign smile. "Of course, one cannot blame me for my lack of interest in the assignment. I have far more important matters on my mind."

"Such as?" she prompted, trying to conceal her inquisitiveness.

Christian picked up his knife and fork and cut a piece of the pie. He allowed a smile to touch his mouth. "Oh, such as the pursuit of other, more ... shall I say ... *romantic* interests."

She stared at him.

"Really, Mrs. Foley," he said, smiling patiently. "After that display on your front lawn, is there any doubt in your mind as to what brought me to Menotomy? I have fallen in love with Deirdre and wish to marry her at the earliest convenience. Have you never been in love, madam? Do you not know, or remember, what it is like to be unable to think of anything but the object of your affection?" That much, at least, was true. "My beloved Deirdre consumes my attention, my dreams, my every waking moment. I have little thought for this Irish Pirate, and even less care for what bit of glory I might earn by catching him."

Bit of glory indeed, Christian thought to himself. He had been tasked with apprehending the scoundrel and he would do just that. But first and foremost, he had to gain the Foleys' trust—and fool them into thinking he did not take his assignment seriously.

Apparently his plan was working; his hostess had visibly relaxed, and it occurred to Christian that marrying Deirdre, and thereby removing his excuse to visit the Foley household, would be quite welcome in Mrs. Foley's eyes indeed.

"Well, then," the woman said brightly, "I shall not detain you in your courtship of the girl. Personally, I think you make a striking couple! In fact—"

At that moment, Deirdre came flying down the stairs, her cheeks pink with excitement. "Ye like it, Christian?" She made a quick, childish pirouette, the skirts of her new riding habit flying to reveal shapely ankles. "'Tis Del—I mean, Dolores's. She gave me some clothes to wear 'til I can sew some of my own."

Judging from the tailored fit of the bodice, and given the superior size of Delight's bosom, Deirdre had already been at work with needle and thread.

"You are beautiful, my love." His eyes warmed. "I am undone."

He was also growing impatient. Pushing the plate of pie away, he drained the last of the hot chocolate and got to his feet. "Mrs. Foley, may I have your permission to take Deirdre riding?"

"Yes, yes of course, Captain Lord. In fact, take one of our horses for Deirdre. Oh, would that we could all be young again, and in love!"

Christian nodded, took Deirdre's hand, and bending to kiss it, led her from the house, secure in the knowledge that Delight's mother thought him nothing more than an arrogant and smitten fool who had little interest in actually apprehending the Irish Pirate.

But as the Foley women stood on the porch, watching the tall and handsome officer escort their houseguest across the yard, Mrs. Foley was anything but calm. She waited until they were out of earshot, then turned frantically on her daughter.

"I don't like this one bit!" she cried, wringing her hands. "That's all we need, to have a king's officer sniffing around here!"

"*Really,* Mama, he's a naval captain," Delight purred, forgetting to use her normal tone of voice and earning a sharp glare from her mother. "And naval officers concern themselves with the affairs of ships and sea, *not* with patriot gatherings such as those that you and Papa have become involved in."

"Still, the man makes me nervous! He's too polished. Too controlled. And those eyes ... they discern too much! He *knows,* Dolores Ann!" She gripped her daughter's arms, her fingers biting into the soft flesh, her eyes wide with fright. "He *knows!*"

"Pooh, Mama. He knows nothing. He's merely in love with Deirdre, that's all." Delight smoothed a lock of golden hair and tucked it under her mobcap. "Why, if you'd seen the utterly scandalous way those two behaved aboard ship, you'd know *just* what I'm talking about."

"Dolores Ann, everyone knows he was sent here to apprehend the Irish Pirate!"

"And by his own admission you heard how little the task means to him." Delight laid a hand on her mother's arm. "Really, Mama, you worry too much. Captain Lord is a brave and steady man and he will do his duty, but he is not cunning and clever like our Irish Pirate. Why, Roddy will run circles around him. In fact, he already has. Now come. Let us go and see to supper, no?"

Taking her mother's arm, she led her into the house.

Chapter Twenty-Five

They rode side by side, he gazing hungrily at her trim form, she admiring the way the sunlight picked out the gold in his hair where it lay caught in a queue between his broad shoulders. He smiled over at her, his eyes dark beneath the shadow of his hat, and she felt suddenly giddy with happiness. Despite the hostile looks some of the townspeople were giving him, she was proud to be at his side.

They rode onward, gazing at each other so much that it was left to the horses to choose their path. To Deirdre, America suddenly did not seem so bleak. She had been too homesick to appreciate her surroundings, but now, at the side of the man she loved, the sunlight looked brighter, the chickadees and cardinals and jays more colorful, the water of a nearby pond cobalt with brilliance, the scents of springtime—mud, melted frost, running water, fresh air— sharper.

And trees? She had never seen so many in her life, for the moors of Connemara were bleak and barren and empty of such thick woods.

"Christian?"

"Aye, my love?"

She was looking at a V of geese winging high overhead, their brash honking drifting down in waves of sound. "D'ye ever miss England?"

He smiled gently. "All the time."

"The same way I miss Ireland?"

"Perhaps. Though I confess I don't carry a bag of trinkets with me to remind me of it."

She frowned. "Are ye teasin' me?"

"Who, me?" His lips twitched. "I simply find it a most charming trait, your sentimentality for home. But someday you will learn that home is not where you happen to be living at the moment, or even where you hail from—but where your heart is. Home can be any place, as long as the one you love is there with you."

"If that's true, Christian, then I am home now."

He urged his horse closer to hers and reached out across the short distance to take her hand. "Was it hard for you, being alone these past nights?"

"Aye," she said, the misery of those lonely hours nearly forgotten now that Christian was there with her. "But I managed."

"Oh?"

"I took yer shirt," she admitted. "It wasn't much, but holding it in my arms, I felt as if I had a part o' ye there with me. And ye know what else I did, Christian?"

"Pray, do tell."

"I sat at my window and figured out by the stars just where Ireland is—then I moved my bed so I can fall asleep every night with my face toward it."

He laughed in high amusement and leaned over to kiss her cheek.

"Christian, d'ye think all the Englishmen who are here—I mean, all the men in the ships, and all the men of the general's troops—want to go home, too?"

"I am sure they do."

"I don't know why anyone would want to live here, Christian. The land is ugly. And everyone's so cold and unfriendly."

"The people are unhappy with England's policies right now, Deirdre. When things are resolved, and agreements reached between the colonists and Britain, then you will find America a very beautiful place."

"'Tis nothin' like Ireland," she declared huffily.

"No, it is not. It has its own beauty."

"I see nothin' beautiful about it. The birds look different, the animals look different, the people talk different, and the grass is brown. Whoever heard of brown grass? In Ireland right now, the grass'd be green and pretty!"

He slanted her a grin. "In Ireland right now, it would be raining."

She clamped her lips shut.

"And," he pointed out with another gently taunting smile, "New England gets heavy snow in the wintertime—unlike Ireland—which is why the grass turns brown. But you wait. I daresay in two or three weeks, it will be as green as it is at home."

"Ye promise, Christian?"

There was such a look of childish hope in her eyes that he was nearly undone. "I promise, Deirdre."

She looked away, and they continued for some time before she spoke again. "Christian?"

"Yes, my dear?"

"Have ye been thinkin' of yer other promise? Yer vow to help me find my brother?"

"Aye, Deirdre, I've been thinking of it. And so, apparently, has your cousin. I have not had opportunity to speak with him directly and will not for some time, as Sir Geoffrey has sent him out to patrol the coast. However, he did send me a note, pledging to do all that he can to help us." Christian did not add that locating her brother would be akin to finding a minnow in the

Atlantic, for that would only crush her. "In the meantime, I will do everything in my power to restore your brother to you, so help me God."

"If anyone can find him, *you* can," she declared, her eyes reverent and full of childish trust in what she obviously considered to be his godlike abilities. He knew he could never live up to her expectations of him, and swiftly changed the subject.

"Are the Foleys treating you well?" he asked.

"Aye."

"You are managing, then?"

"Aside from losin' my wool the first night, aye."

He gave her a puzzled, sidelong glance. "Losing your *wool?*"

"'Twas from Ireland," she said defensively. "It blew out the window when I was tryin' to figure out in which direction Ireland was."

"I see." He hid a private grin.

"But I still have my Irish air left," she said, her face very serious. She patted her horse's neck. "And my pebble and my sand and shells. And of course I still have my cross, which I *can't* lose because I never take it off."

"Never?" he teased.

"Never!"

He laughed, his eyes glinting with amusement as they left the village behind them. The horses plodded along, their ears flicking back and forth, their hooves thudding dully against the road. In the distance, purple hills rose against the horizon and here and there a farmhouse, spouting a tuft of smoke from its chimney, made a splash of color against the landscape. Eventually they found a small path that led off the road and down through the trees. The horses slowed, slipping a bit in the mud as they descended, and Christian ducked beneath low-hanging branches. Deirdre was right behind him, admiring the way his shoulders stretched the fabric of his uniform coat.

So intent was she in studying him that she almost allowed her horse to plow into his when he stopped.

He turned then, smiling, his eyes dark with unspoken desire. "Do you find this spot as pretty as any in Ireland, Deirdre?"

She looked around. A stream, swelled with spring thaw and rain, tumbled over a bed of brightly colored pebbles and wound away into the woods. Sunlight shone down through a stand of evergreens, dappling a carpet of pine needles and dead leaves from the previous autumn. High above, a bright blue sky shone through the trees and here and there large granite boulders, their color that of Christian's eyes, rose out of the leaf-strewn forest floor.

Deirdre shut her eyes, listening to the happy babble of the brook. "I think it might be," she admitted slowly.

"Do you find it a place that is suitable to ... being *alone* with each other?"

"Oh, aye, Christian. I wouldn't care if I was sittin' in a mud puddle, long's I was with ye."

He grinned and swung down from his saddle. Her eyes hungry, she watched as he tied his horse to a nearby tree, loosening the girth so the big stallion could relax. She started to dismount but he was there, his hands around her waist. She gazed happily into his face. Since when had that face, this man, become so dear to her? A shaft of sunlight slanted down through the trees, falling over his gray irises and picking out a hint of green there. "Please, love," he said, smiling up into her eyes. "Allow me the pleasure."

"Christian, ye don't always have to be playin' the officer and gentleman, ye know."

"I am not playing," he said seriously, plucking her from the saddle as though she weighed no more than the tuft of wool she had lost. She fastened her arms around his neck and gazed up into his eyes, sighing with delight as he carried her to a sunlit spot a short distance away. "And though I intend to stretch the limits of the word 'gentleman,' I shall always behave with your interests uppermost in my mind."

With that he set her down, took a rolled blanket from behind the cantle of his saddle, and spread it out over the ground. Somewhat shyly, Deirdre helped him straighten the corners and stood looking up at him. Dear God, she had never thought an Englishman could be so utterly, achingly, handsome. And she had never thought she could love someone as much as she did him.

He took off his hat, hung it on a nearby tree branch, and removing his sword, came to stand beside her. She was suddenly aware of the muscled strength of his thighs, the heat of his powerful body, his fierce need for her and her alone. He reached out and cupped her chin in his hands, his thumbs warm against her cheekbones as he gazed down into her eyes for a long, intense moment. "Do you love me, Deirdre?"

She returned his stare unblinkingly. "I love ye more than I love life itself, Christian."

"Do you love me enough to become my wife?"

He couldn't have stunned her more if he had grown a third arm. Her eyes widened, her jaw went slack, and her lips moved several times before she could form the words. "Ye mean ... ye want to ... to marry me? Ye mean I wasn't just hopin' against hope that ye'd ask?"

"You had hoped I would ask?"

"I *prayed* ye'd ask, Christian. But I didn't think ye would, you being English, and me bein' Irish 'n' all."

"English, Irish, it makes no difference. I love you. You love me. I'd marry you tomorrow if I could, so eager am I to get you out of Menotomy and back with me—where you belong."

"I know, Christian," she said gently, her hands coming up to touch the hard planes of his cheeks. "Brendan already explained it to me, that Sir Geoffrey wouldn't like it none if ye kept a woman aboard yer ship who wasn't yer wife. He told me it might look bad for ye when it comes to promotin' time. I don't like to be away from ye, Christian, but I understand now why I have to be." She shrugged. "Besides, the Foleys are treatin' me well. I know I won't be out here forever."

"Indeed, you will not be. As soon as your cousin returns, I will ask him for your hand."

"Oh, Christian...."

He slid his hands around her waist and drew her close, claiming her lips in a deep and passionate kiss that burned away all memories of her loneliness. She melted against him, her hand coming up to slip beneath his queue as the kiss deepened, their tongues touching, tasting, his hand warm against the small of her back and pressing her hips against his arousal. After a long moment the kiss ended, and he reached into his pocket and drew something out. Looking down, Deirdre saw that his palm was turned upward and a ring, as ancient and beautiful as Grace's cross, rested on its hard and callused surface.

Her hands went to her mouth, her gaze flashing up to his.

"This has been in my family for hundreds of years," he explained, gently prying her hands away from her mouth and tenderly grasping her left one. It was shaking so violently he had to close his fingers around it to still it.

"Marry me, Deirdre O' Devir?"

"I'll marry ye, Christian Lord."

He smiled and slid the ring onto her finger.

She stared at it, holding her breath and unable to speak. There it was, proclaiming to the world that she belonged to this brave, handsome, battle-scarred sea warrior. Tears filled her eyes and he lifted her hand so that the sunlight caught the rubies of the lion's eyes, the diamonds of its teeth.

"You are mine," he declared.

"Christian, this is the happiest moment of my life." She knuckled her wet eyes and stared at her hand for a long moment, then hugged it to her breast, mating the ring with the cross. It appeared to be a spontaneous gesture but he guessed, knowing her penchant for sentimentality, that it was a purposeful melding of Irish and English, one heart to its mate, one proud ancestry to another.

His heart swelled within his chest, aching with love for her.

And then, impulsively, she threw her arms around his neck. He responded immediately, crushing her in his embrace, one hand coming up to cup her nape and draw her close in a kiss that was desperate, savage, and hard.

"By God, I've missed you," he murmured, resting his chin on her shoulder and breathing hard. "I doubt I can wait until you are well and truly mine."

"Do ye *have* to ask Brendan, Christian? Can't we just get married and be done with it?"

"As your closest living relative, Deirdre, it would be wrong *not* to ask him."

Deirdre was already loosening his neckcloth, drawing it away from his throat, rising on her tiptoes so she could press her lips against his skin. She breathed deeply of his unique scent, a heady mix of shaving soap, his wool coat, the sea. Her pulse began to beat a little faster and she spread her palms beneath the coat and began to push it off. It was a mild day and he had left the garment unbuttoned, but the waistcoat was not so. Her fingers fumbling, she pushed each gold anchored button through its hole until the waistcoat was open and his fine white shirt was all that lay between his chest and her hand.

He looked down at her, his eyes dark with desire, a little smile playing about the corner of his mouth as Deirdre pared his waistcoat from his shoulders, taking care to be gentle where the musket ball had been lodged. As she slid her hands up beneath his shirt, drawing it up and over his head, her eyes went soft with wonder at the magnificent display of male power and beauty that was his sculpted, well-muscled chest. Only a fresh bandage marred its perfection, and when it came off, yet another scar would mark where his strength and courage had seen him through another battle.

"The sight of ye makes me burn for wantin' ye, Christian," she breathed, her eyes and hands devouring his body. She touched his strong corded arms, the sparse golden hair that roughened his chest and torso, then reached up and untied his queue, letting the thick silky hair slide between her fingers. He let her look and touch her fill, then pulled her close to him and kissed her long and hard and thoroughly.

She melted against him, her hands drifting up his torso, down his back and around to the hard planes of his belly as she lost herself to the kiss. Her fingers found the flap of his breeches and boldly, she slid each button through its hole until the garment gapped open and slid a little way down his hips. As she took him in her hands, she found him hot, hard, and ready. Gently, she stroked him, rubbing her thumb over the velvety head and taking pleasure in each soft groan that came from him, the way he filled her hand, the increasing desperation of his kiss.

And then Deirdre sank to her knees, her lips whispering down the flat slab of his belly, and kissed him.

He caught his breath, driving his fingers into her hair to anchor himself.

Holding him in one hand, she put an arm around the back of his thighs and held him close, brushing her lips along the hot, swollen length of him until his breathing grew hoarse and unsteady and she felt tremors moving through his great body as he fought to keep himself under control. She looked up at him, saw that his eyes were half shut, his expression almost pained; then, Deirdre rubbed him against her cheek, against her lips, and gently took him into her mouth.

His knees buckled and within moments they were both down

on the blanket, her short-jacket discarded, her stays loosened and removed, her body, clad in nothing but her shift, petticoats, and stockings, lying beneath his as he kissed her hungrily, one hand drifting down to pull up the hem of her petticoats. She felt the warmth of his hand against her bare leg; the brush of his knuckles as he dragged the skirts up, exposing her thighs to the cool air, and then his hand was against her cleft, parting it, gently stroking her until her own dampness bathed his fingers.

"Christian ... oh, how I want ye," she murmured.

"Not half as much, Deirdre, as I want *you*," he responded, and pulling back, kissed a trail down her throat, over her collarbone, and down to the neckline of her chemise, where she felt his tongue against the rise of one breast, gently nipping, tasting, licking. Then, cupping the soft globe in his hand, he brushed his thumb over the muslin-clad nipple, back and forth, over and over until she was moaning in delight.

"Ohhh...." she said, sighing.

He lowered his head and began to suck on the taut, hardened nipple through the thin muslin, drawing both it and the fabric deeply into his mouth.

It was agony. Sweet agony.

Through the wet fabric she now felt his tongue, licking the pebbled nipple, stroking it into an even harder peak. Deirdre writhed beneath him, her body suddenly too hot, her heart beating like a drum beneath his relentless tongue, his masterful mouth.

He pulled back only long enough to gaze down into her face. "You, my love ... are the most beautiful woman I have ever known. Thank you ... thank you for consenting to become my wife. My lover. My very best friend. I am the most blessed man on earth."

He drew up her skirts. And then he pulled back, slid his hands under her hips, lifted them like an offering, and buried his face between her legs.

The first scrape of his chin against her inner thighs nearly sent Deirdre over the edge, but when she felt his breath against her wet folds, then his thumbs as he spread the damp, intimate flesh wide, she sobbed and in a growing frenzy, caught at the edge of the blanket, the dried leaves beneath, her fingers digging into the earth as her body began to writhe and twist beneath him in its headlong flight toward release.

"Christian—"

He only spread her further and as she began to gasp and keen, his tongue moved against her wet slit, tasting, licking, stroking, before pressing against the engorged little bud in which her passion was centered; he drew it into his mouth and sucked it hard, and Deirdre came against him with a fevered cry, her body arcing upward and convulsing on shattering waves of pleasure that left her gasping in tears of joy.

He moved up, cradling her between his forearms, seeking her lips once more, and she tasted herself upon him as his hand moved down between them to himself, guiding the velvety tip to her entrance. Deirdre reached down, helping to position him, and as slick and wet as she was he slid easily into her, stretching her wide, wide, wide, filling her until she thought she could take no more.

He paused there, the corded muscles of his arms standing out in relief as he balanced himself.

"I love you, Deirdre," he murmured.

And then he began to move within her, drawing back, pushing forward, sheathed in her wet, hot core as he built the timeless rhythm of love. Her eyes drifted open, watching the concentration in his face, the way his eyes, heavy with desire, had darkened. His hair tumbled over his brow. The veins on his arms stood out, thick with blood. Faster, stronger, deeper ... passion built once more, and her legs came up to wrap around his hips as she sought even deeper closeness, the slick friction unbearable, exquisite, joyous. And here it came again, that soaring pleasure-pain that was building in her belly, building, building, until her world splin-tered apart and her cries rent the air; he gave a final, mighty thrust, stiffened, and with a hoarse groan, buried his face in the curve of her neck, his seed pulsing hot inside her as he found his own release.

They clung to each other long after the last tremors faded, he taking his weight on one arm, the other reaching down to find her hand and hold it as they drifted slowly back to earth. Then, moving slightly, he wrapped his mighty arms around her, rolled onto his back, and heartbeat to heartbeat, held her protectively, lovingly, fiercely, against himself.

Nearby, the brook splashed happily over stones and sand. Overhead, the wind sighed through the pines and a chickadee flitted from branch to branch, its distinctive song clear and bright. The sun grew stronger, and beneath the blanket the ground was earthy, springy, and warm.

They slept, two people caught up in love, and when they awoke some time later, they came together again ... and again ... until the sun began to dip below the trees and the shadows grew long.

They washed in the chilly waters of the brook, dried them-selves with the blanket and slowly dressed each other, their hearts heavy at the thought of parting. It was nearly dark by the time they rode into the Foleys' yard and after a short apology to their hostess about keeping Deirdre out for so long, Christian led his young love back out under the stars and taking her arms, looked down into her eyes.

"This won't last forever, Deirdre."

She laid her cheek against his chest and stared out into the darkness, holding him tight. "Will you be back, soon?"

"Within the next day or two, if the admiral can spare me."

They clung together, neither willing to say goodbye; but finally the moment came for Christian to leave. Slowly, reluctantly, he set her away from him, his hand lingering on hers, his eyes dark and sad as he gazed down into her upturned face.

"I love you, Deirdre."

"I love you, too, Christian. Be safe."

Then he mounted his horse and touching his hat to her, rode off, leaving her standing there on the darkened lawn until his shadowy figure had disappeared into the night.

Chapter Twenty-Six

Christian did not get very far down the Concord Road before turning back. The feel of Deirdre's body still burned in his memory, and he ached for want of holding her. Soon now, they would be together forever and he would ache no more. But he had not been sent here for pleasure; he had been sent here to apprehend the Irish Pirate—known enemy of the Crown, brazen supplier of arms to the rebels—and as a good and dutiful officer of his king, he intended to do just that.

Acting upon a tip from his own spies, General Gage had informed him of tonight's meeting at which several known rebel leaders—Samuel Adams, John Hancock, and Dr. Joseph Warren— were supposed to gather. No doubt the Irish Pirate would make an appearance, too. The whereabouts of the meeting had not been known, but Gage had had his own suspicions as to where it would be.

Christian halted his horse beneath the branches of a sprawling oak and rummaging in his saddlebags, found his wig, a bit crushed but otherwise perfect for his disguise. He donned it, replaced his hat, and traded his naval coat for the shabby green frock coat that, along with the blanket, had been rolled up behind the cantle of his saddle.

Back down Concord Road he went, a slightly rumpled traveler on a tired horse, nothing about him indicating he was a proud and decorated sea warrior in the service of the king. As he came around a slight bend in the road, he saw the lights of the Foley house; a single candle glowed orange behind the curtains of an upstairs window, and his heart gave a painful lurch as he thought of Deirdre up there getting ready for bed—and probably missing Ireland with all her young heart.

Did she miss him, too? When she blew out the light, would she go to the window, pull back the curtain, and gaze out into the night, thinking of him as he had thought of her from the lonely darkness of *Bold Marauder*'s cabin?

He sighed and turned away, focusing on his mission. He might not be *with* her tonight, but at least he would be *near* her.

Just across the street from the Foley homestead was the tavern he had noted earlier, and here, he pulled the horse up and dismounted. Though his plan was sound and carefully conceived, he was still alert for danger. Surely the same villagers who, hours earlier, had glared with such hostility at a British naval officer, wouldn't recognize this road-weary traveler as the same man. He hoped they wouldn't recognize his horse, either. But chestnut was a common color, and the night was dark. Leading his horse, he cleared his throat and pounded a fist against the tavern's door.

Several moments went by, long moments in which the only sound was the wind moaning through the trees above. Then he heard footsteps, and the click of a latch being cautiously lifted. The door was cracked, then opened wide. A woman stood there, her dark hair covered by a mobcap, her eyes suspicious. She held a candle in a tin holder, and this she lifted, shining it fully into Christian's eyes until he blinked.

"Good evening, madam," he said wearily, inclining his

bewigged head. Behind him, the horse gave a deep sigh, as though in full cooperation with his ruse. "Have you a room for a sore and weary traveler, and perhaps a meal to warm his cold bones?"

The woman lifted the candle higher, her shrewd eyes taking in his slightly unkempt appearance. At last, satisfied, she lowered the light and glanced quickly up the road from whence he had just come. "Aye, we've room for ye. Nice clean chamber upstairs, and some leftover stew still bubbling over the fire."

"I am much obliged, madam."

"There's a barn out back. Put your nag away and then join us for a bite to eat. We're plain and simple folk, but you'll not find us lacking in hospitality."

An hour later, Captain Christian Lord, hero of Quiberon and pride of the Royal Navy, sat in darkness on the bare floorboards of his room, the door locked behind him, his body well fed and wide awake. The bed was turned back, waiting for him. The embers of a fire glowed in the hearth. The window was open to the night, and he had a small spyglass balanced against the sill and trained on the Foley house directly across the road.

He doubted he'd have long to wait.

He thought of Mrs. Foley's sudden panic when he had appeared, unexpectedly, at her door this afternoon, and her prevailing skittishness throughout his visit. He thought of Delight Foley admitting her desire for the Irish Pirate when she had cornered him aboard the frigate, and her plans to seduce and win him to her bed. He thought of the open hostility the villagers had shown him, and the suspicious way the tavern owner's wife had studied him before finally letting him in. He thought of Foley's reputation as being loyal to king and Crown—and he thought of the broadsides Sir Geoffrey had shown him, broadsides most likely printed by Jared Foley and meant to inflame the rebels toward inevitable bloodshed.

Bloodshed that must, at all costs, be prevented.

Christian's mouth hardened. The Irish Pirate must be caught

before he could supply the rebels with any more arms and ammunition

It was a matter of life and death.

Shifting his weight to a more comfortable position, he raised the glass once more, trained it at the dark house across the street, and sat back to wait.

IT WAS SOMETIME around midnight that Deirdre awoke.

Her eyes came slowly open as sounds permeated her consciousness. Low tones of men talking. A voice, heavy with an Irish brogue ... not Brendan's, but somehow familiar ... as familiar as the devil-may-care laughter that followed it.

She stared up at the dark rafters above her head, wondering if it had been a dream. But the house was quiet. Hugging her arms around Christian's shirt, Deirdre sighed, turned over in bed, and let her eyes drift shut.

Again that reckless laughter.

Her eyes shot open.

It had been no dream.

She peeled back the blankets and shivering, rose from the bed. The floor was cold, even under her socks, and she hugged her arms to herself as she padded silently to the window. Outside, several horses stood tethered, dark shapes in the gloom. Deirdre's eyes widened and this time, she knew the voices downstairs were no dream—and neither was the one that was hauntingly familiar, agonizingly unplaceable, and as Irish as hers.

"He's nothin' but a buffoon, Foley! Christ Almighty, ye think I'm afraid o' some vain, out-for-glory, trophy-huntin' Englishman? Bah! Yer own wife just said he's more interested in this Irish guest o' yers than he is in the business of his bloody king!" A tankard banged boastfully down upon a table. "And don't ye be forgettin', I've already tangled with him once and showed him me heels. Our naval captain may have 'imself a swift and powerful frigate, but that bumblin' crew o' his can barely figure out a shroud from a sheet, let alone how t' use her guns!"

Deirdre, her heart beginning to pound with the feeling that she was about to stumble upon something that was going to change her life, crept across the room and, reaching for her robe, wrapped it around her. Slowly, she opened her door and slipped quietly down the stairs, hearing the voices getting louder and louder.

"Your swagger will be the death of you, man," she heard Mr. Foley say sharply. "Captain Lord is no buffoon, but an officer of unqualified skill and tenacity, highly respected by his admiral and his king. No doubt he has drilled that *bumbling* crew into one as smart as any in the king's Navy—"

"You mean there are some in the king's Navy that are smart?" another, mocking voice joked.

"Very funny, Hancock," Foley snapped. "And you, my fine Irish friend—you'd do well to cover your tracks and have a care about becoming too cocky."

Deirdre, just outside the parlor in which the men were speaking, flattened herself against the wall, her fists clenched in anger. How dare they talk about Christian like that! And who was this Irishman who boasted so recklessly, whose voice was so familiar, but whose face she could not place?

"Really, Papa," came a woman's voice, "you are as skittish as Mama. Our Irish Pirate will run circles around Captain Lord. Why, there is no comparison between their skills, their intelligence, the quality of their crews. Besides, as I told you, the good captain is, shall I say, *otherwise occupied* of late—too much so, in fact, to be placing much attention on his task of apprehending the Irish Pirate."

Deirdre's eyes widened with shock. *Delight!* And if her friend had just called the speaker *"our"* Irish Pirate, then was the infamous smuggler, whose rich, melodic voice evoked vivid images of home, right there in the very next room?

She stood frozen, hardly daring to breathe. No wonder Delight's restlessness during supper ... the pains she'd taken over her appearance earlier ... the renewed interest in her *manuals* and her continued glances at the small shelf clock on the mantel. Lord above, if Delight was in love with a rebel, then wouldn't it stand to reason that *she* was a rebel, too?

Along with her whole family?

"Oh, sweet Jesus," Deirdre whispered, suddenly terrified. It was all she could do not to flee the house and run all the way back to Boston and the protective safety of Christian's arms.

"I met Captain Lord some time ago," came another, steady voice, "and he did not strike me as a buffoon, but a capable, clever, and unbending disciplinarian, entirely devoted to his king, his duty, and his command. I would not pass him off so lightly, my friend. Your English nemesis is not a man to be trifled with."

"Pshaw," the Irishman said with reckless laughter, "if ye'd only seen that frigate o' his takin' a beatin' beneath the guns of a little French corvette, ye'd feel as I do! 'Twas pitiful, I tell ye, to see a fine ship like that so poorly fought and sailed! So quit yer worryin', eh? The lovely Dolores Ann here crossed the Atlantic aboard her. She knows her captain better than any of ye! Tell 'em, love! Would ye say the man is single-minded and determined? Obsessed with bringin' me down?"

"He is clever and tactical, but any single-minded determination he possesses is not directed toward capturing you, but winning the love of our guest. As long as he is so ... *occupied,* I do not think him to be a particular threat."

"Regardless," Foley said harshly, "the man is well decorated, highly respected, and dangerous."

Another voice, thoughtful and educated, came through the ajar door. "You seem to have an active dislike of Captain Lord, my friend. Mind that such personal animosity does not dull your own keen edge and land you within range of his guns."

"Aye, you do seem to harbor a ripe hatred of the fellow!" cried the man called Hancock. "Why is that?"

"As Dr. Warren just said, my reasons are personal, and none o' yer concern." *Oh, where had she heard that voice?* Deirdre shut her eyes, trying to place it and wishing she dared to pry open the door and have a peek at her countryman's face. "But I tell you this. I'll not enjoy a better revenge than makin' the king's captain look like the fool he is. He'll not catch me, by Christ's blood!"

"Enough, then." came another voice, hard with authority. "Let us get down to business. Our minutemen companies have been drilling tirelessly, preparing for the worst. Captain Locke here has done an exceptionally fine job with his Menotomy lads, but all the training in the world is useless without more guns." A chair creaked, and there was the splash of liquid into a glass. "My merchant friend in Philadelphia is sending us two hundred French muskets, which we can expect by week's end. Since it's too risky to try and bring the shipment into any of our nearby harbors, my plan is to have our Irish Pirate here meet the vessel off Marblehead under cover of darkness. The transfer must be done quickly and efficiently. Not only is Captain Bishop's *Lively* patrolling these waters, but now, so is the frigate *Halcyon*."

This was getting worse by the minute, Deirdre thought. And then she felt a high, itchy sensation in the back of her nose. *Dear God, don't let me sneeze now!* Panicking, she pinched her nostrils shut.

"Child's play," the Irish Pirate boasted.

Adams continued. "Waste no time in pleasantries. Land the guns in Salem, where they will be met by the Sons of Liberty. Our men will transfer them to wagons, cover them with hay and vegetables, and send them directly to Concord."

"It's too dangerous," Delight said. "The British have stepped up their patrols."

"I don't like it, either," said Jared Foley. "You get caught in that sloop under the guns of one of those frigates and it will be all over for you."

The Irish Pirate's laughter rang out. "Bah, I'll not get caught. There are scores of small fishing and trading vessels all up and down the coast. Mine is not so different as to arouse any suspicion."

"And we *could* use those muskets," Hancock proclaimed. "I say let's do it."

"Are you up to it, my fine Irish friend?"

"For the love o' God, o' course I am!"

"Very well, then. The Philadelphia ship is due to arrive on Saturday night. She will flash two lanterns at her bow, three times in succession. Your signal of acknowledgment is to be the same."

"Should he learn of it, Gage will move to stop us," came the steady voice of the one who'd been addressed as Dr. Warren. "You may be sure of it."

Deirdre's nose was burning, and she felt the sneeze building. She stepped backward, wondering if she'd have time to make it back upstairs before it hit. Involuntarily, she sucked in her breath—

"And when he does we will be ready for him, you may be sure!" A fist pounded against the table. "The time has come to make a stand against tyranny, oppression, and the cruelties imposed upon us by a dispassionate monarch grown fat on—"

At that moment, Deirdre sneezed.

It was not a small, feminine burst of sound. It was a full-blown, silence-shattering roar that seemed to shake the walls, the ceiling, the door that suddenly burst open to reveal a room of shocked faces.

In the space of a heartbeat she saw them. Delight, sitting beside her parents and staring at Deirdre in horror; several men dressed in the decent clothes of merchants and the well-to-do, some in powdered wigs, others with their hair worn natural and clubbed at the nape; and dominating the room, a tall, forbidding man with a wildly curling mane of black hair that lay loosely about his broad and muscled shoulders. He had a rogue's smile, eyes the color of her own, and a face of hard planes and sharp angles.

A face whose memory thirteen years could not dim.

The blood drained from Deirdre's face. She swayed and clutched at the door for support. The occupants of the room suddenly reacted, some cursing, some blanching with fear, some looking to the one who was obviously their leader—this Sam Adams—who stood, at a loss for words, beside the black-haired Irishman.

"Oh, dear," Delight murmured, finding her voice.

And then Deirdre, frightened and shivering in her nightshirt and robe, was dragged forcefully into the room.

She stood staring into the eyes of the legendary sea smuggler. Her hands came up, purposely drawing out from beneath the closure of her robe, the gleaming cross that had belonged to another Irish pirate. She let it rest proudly at her bosom, seeing the rebel smuggler's eyes widen in shock as recognition swept the color from his cheeks.

There were no secrets left.

Christian, unwittingly, had fulfilled his vow to her after all.

"Roddy?" she whispered, the faces of everyone else in the room dropping away into nothingness, until there were only those darkly fringed violet eyes looking down at her. "Is it really *you*?"

He stared at the cross, then at her.

"Aye, 'tis me," he murmured, still in shock.

Foley grabbed at his shoulder. "Tarnal hell, she knows your identity, man!"

But the Irish Pirate turned and laid a hand on Foley's arm. "Fear not that she'll betray me to her fair-haired Briton." He gazed down into Deirdre's face, and reached out to touch one long black curl.

"What do you mean, 'fear not'? You're as good as dead!"

"Nay," Roddy said quietly. "The lass is me sister."

SITTING CROSS-LEGGED BEFORE THE WINDOW, Christian's legs and feet had long since fallen asleep but his mind was alert, wide awake and sharp. He had not moved from his position since sitting down and the spyglass, trained with a marksman's aim at that single glowing square of light that was the Foleys' parlor, had not wavered so much as an inch over the past hour.

He had seen it all. The first horse, its rider in a dark jacket, materializing out of the night and turning into the Foleys' yard; another and still another, until it was clear that Gage's suspicions about the whereabouts of the rebel meeting were correct.

That these men were indeed the rebel leaders, Christian had no doubt. He had viewed descriptions and drawings provided by Sir Geoffrey and General Gage, and one or two of them he had even seen on the streets of Boston—the outspoken Sam Adams, and the tall, handsome Dr. Joseph Warren.

Adams's face, at the moment, was dead-center in the circular field of his spyglass.

Other faces came into view as the rebels moved across the room. John Hancock, pompously dressed, wealthy, much given to laughter. The silversmith Paul Revere, middle-aged and a bit overweight. Jared Foley with his ink-stained hands, and his daughter Delight. Her eyes had been following the black-haired rogue whose face Christian immediately recognized.

The Irish Pirate.

His hand tightened around the spyglass. How he wished he could go over there and arrest the bloody lot of them. But no. With the exception of the Irish Pirate, the rebel leaders were in Gage's hands. His task was to apprehend the seafaring smuggler— something he could not do until he caught the rascal at his game.

As for Jared Foley being a rebel, Christian had all the proof he needed.

He lowered the glass, rubbed at his eyes, and raised it once more. Suddenly, the breath caught in his throat. A woman had come into the room. A slim, fair-skinned woman with a spiral-curling mane of raven curls, a woman who, as he watched, flung herself into the arms of the man he had been ordered to apprehend.

It was Deirdre.

The spyglass fell from his hand. Shock tore through him and he could only stare, blinking, at that square of golden light, seeing the small figures within through the fog of disbelief and denial.

No.

She was embracing him. Standing within his arms and laughing up at him.

Kissing his cheek.

Christian stumbled to his feet, reeled against the wall, and nearly went down. His hand flashed out and grabbed the bedpost, gripping it so hard his knuckles went white. This couldn't be happening. This *wasn't* happening. He put the back of his hand to his brow and found it cold and clammy.

But the effort of standing was too much. He felt suddenly sick and sat down heavily, numb with shock and beginning to tremble.

No.

But the awful truth was right there across the street. Unmistakable. Undeniable. He bent his head to his hands, his shock giving way to logic, logic giving way to grief, grief giving way to anger, anger giving way to blazing, white-hot fury.

She had betrayed him. She—his sweet Irish girl—had betrayed him.

I love ye, Christian. His heart convulsed in grief, and he clenched his hands as he tried to get himself under control. *God help me, I love ye."*

"I trusted you," he bit out, his fist slamming into the wall.

Blood sprayed from his knuckles but he never felt the pain, for it was insignificant in the face of the crushing blow he'd just been dealt. "Damn you, I trusted you, believed in you, *loved you.*" He stumbled back to the window, seeing the Foleys' door open to spill pale yellow light upon the barren lawn. "How *could* you? Oh, Deirdre, *how could you?*"

People were moving out onto the lawn as the meeting broke up. Riders were mounting their horses and disappearing into the night, until there were only two people still out there in the darkened street.

Deirdre.

And the Irish Pirate.

Her lovely, traitorous face was pale in the gloom as she turned it up toward that of her lover. He wanted to shut his eyes but he couldn't. He wanted to turn away but, sickened, found he could do nothing except stare as Deirdre pulled something out of a bag he recognized as the one containing her Irish mementoes and pressed something into the smuggler's hands. Then her arms came up to wrap themselves around the man's neck.

Betrayed.

He heard snippets of her laughter. Heard the smuggler's deep voice and again, Deirdre's happy giggle. The sounds drove another nail into the coffin that contained his dying heart, then another, until everything inside of him went dead.

For him, there was nothing left. No feeling, no pain, nothing. Just—emptiness.

He stood there watching them until at last the smuggler mounted his horse and with a flourish rode away. Deirdre remained all alone in the road, the wind blowing her dark tresses around her shoulders, her face turned toward the east.

Toward where her lover had gone.

Christian put his head in his hands. Now he knew the real reason Deirdre O'Devir had been aboard his ship, and it wasn't to find her long-lost brother. Pain filled him as he realized how foolish he'd been. She had only wanted free passage to America so she could reunite with her Irish lover—and, no doubt learn every secret of the Royal Navy, and of Christian's own mission, that she could pass on to him.

Mouth tight, he stood staring down at the lone figure out in the road outside. "Two can play at your game, dear girl," he gritted through clenched teeth. "So help me God, you will rue this day, and so will your bloody lover."

Chapter Twenty-Seven

The decks of HMS *Bold Marauder* were lonely and dark, with only a few lanterns hung in the shrouds to make a stand against the fog that blanketed the harbor. A few idle seamen swilled their grog and bemoaned the absence of Delight Foley. A marine stood leaning against his musket, his eyes scanning the mists and his thoughts far away. Ian MacDuff was the officer of the watch and to relieve the boredom, had brought out his bagpipes, much to the dismay of those who happened to be on deck with him. For a short time the pipes had honked and croaked and moaned, until the accompanying curses and protests from his shipmates had sent Ian storming off in high Scottish rage.

Now, he stood sulkily beside Skunk on the empty quarterdeck, seeking shelter beneath the dripping tarp that had been rigged against the earlier, drenching rain. Lantern light caught the glimmer of moisture as it trickled down masts and tarred lines, pooled upon booms and yards, and dripped relentlessly upon the decks. Skunk pulled his cap down over his grimy forehead and wiped a cheek with the back of his hand. "Quiet night out there," he muttered. "Hibbert says the Lord and Master's still up."

Ian, shivering in the cold, damp rain that fell from the black sky above, cast a quick glance aft. Sure enough, a glow from the skylight confirmed Hibbert's observation. "Aye, I'd say he is."

"Somethin's up, Ian. He's been silent and keepin' to himself since he got back from visitin' the Irish lass. Ye don't think somethin' happened between 'em, do ye?"

"I doona ken, Skunk. But 'tis right you are about something being in the air. The Old Fart came aboard this afternoon and he and the captain met in his cabin for over an hour. Evans was eavesdroppin' outside the door, and said that tomorrow night we'll see action."

"Action?"

"Well, I know I shouldnae be tellin' ye this, it probably being highly confidential and all, but we *are* shipmates...."

Skunk swung around, his eyes eager. "Aw, Ian, just tell me!"

The big Scotsman shrugged. "Well, Gage has his own system of spies, sprinkled throughout Boston and the surrounding countryside. Ye ken, in taverns, inns, pretending tae be friends of the rebels."

"Go on," Skunk urged, glancing over his shoulder even as Teach and Hibbert, his uniform dull and drooping in the mist, joined them.

"Aye, tell us, Ian!"

The Lord and Master would be furious if he found out that Ian was divulging secrets, but peer pressure overruled Ian's misgivings. Besides, the crew had long since abandoned their animosity toward the man who treated them with a respect and humanity not often seen in the Royal Navy. They would stand by him, no matter what.

"Well, these spies of Gage's have learned that the rebels are planning tae smuggle a whole shipment of guns ashore. 'Tis tae happen tomorrow night, off the coast of Salem." He glanced over at the nearby *Halcyon*, her riding lights dim in the foggy darkness.

"Ye ken how Captain Merrick returned from his patrol earlier this evening? Well, apparently he spied a large merchant vessel in the waters off Cape Ann. He tried tae hail the ship, but she took advantage of the dusk and fled. Kind of suspicious behavior, don't ye think? Sir Geoffrey thinks her presence only confirms the rumors of an exchange tomorrow night. He wants us to be there to nail the smugglers and catch 'em in the act."

"I wonder if it'll be the Irish Pirate," Teach mused, swinging his tomahawk.

"I doona ken. But a dangerous mission 'twill be, whoever the rebels send. I canna imagine they'd entrust the job tae anyone but their best—the Irish Pirate."

Skunk's smile was wry. "And I can't imagine the admiral entrusting our job to anyone but *his* best."

As one, they glanced toward the dim glow of the captain's skylight.

"The Lord and Master."

❧

THE SHIP WAS NEARLY EMPTY, for Christian was one of the few captains who trusted his company enough to allow them shore leave. Given the harsh life of the Royal Navy, many seamen deserted ship given the slightest opportunity, but Christian's humane efforts had earned him the loyalty of his subordinates— men who, not a month past, had wanted nothing more than to make his life hell.

It was a triumph, yes, and so was his success in linking Jared Foley and the Irish Pirate to the rebel leaders. But Sir Geoffrey's praise for both accomplishments meant nothing to a heart that had stopped beating when Christian had seen the woman he loved in the arms of another man.

He got up and walked across the cabin to the open stern

windows, absently rubbing at his sore shoulder. Beyond the glass he could see nothing but darkness and fog, punctured here and there by the fuzzy glow of lanterns hung in the shrouds of neighboring ships, and, off in the distance, the lights of Boston. There were no stars. There was no horizon. Encased as the area was in a lonely cloak of mist and fog, it was hard to believe that thousands of British troops inhabited the town, trying to keep peace in a situation that was ready to explode into war. It was hard to believe that far beyond the fog, the shoreline, and Boston itself, rebels were secreting stores of arms in the countryside. It was hard to believe that out to sea a merchantman waited, carrying a vast shipment of arms—and it was hard to believe that the rebels would entrust anyone but the Irish Pirate to receive that shipment when the exchange was made tomorrow night.

Christian knew in his heart that he would succeed in apprehending the notorious smuggler. He knew it as surely as he felt the damp tendrils of mist seeping through his clothes, chilling his skin, and dampening the back of his neck. But the assurance brought him no triumph, just a hollow, empty feeling of loneliness.

How would *she* react when he brought down this man who obviously meant the world to her? Would she come to him, begging for his release? Would she practice another form of deceit upon his scarred and wounded heart?

Christian stared out at the soupy blackness beyond the stern windows. His fingers brushed the bench seat where Deirdre had sat, touched the blanket that had once been wrapped around her shoulders. His throat constricted and he closed his eyes, feeling dead and empty and alone. But from behind him came the whines of the puppies as they snuggled together for warmth, and the gentle sounds of Tildy's tongue as she washed the tiny, furry backs.

No. Not quite alone. Christian turned and went to them, his eyes sad as he looked down at these babies that Deirdre had helped bring into the world. Bending down, he scooped up the runt of the litter, so small that it fit in the palm of his hand, and, tucking the animal beneath the lapel of his waistcoat to warm it, carried it back to his desk.

The puppy nuzzled against him, mewing like a kitten. Its small mouth fastened around his finger. Closing his eyes, Christian laid his cheek, stubbled now with bristle, against the tiny head. The fur was soft beneath his lips, sweetly scented and warm.

Like hers.

Emotion rose in his throat. He swallowed hard and reached for his inkwell and pen. First Emily, and now Deirdre. Both had betrayed him and sought the arms of another. Why? He cuddled the puppy and shut his eyes against the sudden pain. *Why?*

The puppy licked his chin. Thank God for animals. At least they were faithful and true.

It was too bloody bad that the same couldn't be said for women.

SEVERAL MILES away in the little village of Menotomy, the night was cold and raw. Rain fell from the blackened sky and wind drove the dampness into one's very bones. But Deirdre, wrapped in a quilt and sitting on the floor beside the open window of her bedroom, rejoiced in it. If she closed her eyes, she could almost imagine she was back in Ireland. About the only thing missing was the pungent scent of peat fires wafting in the damp air.

Her bag of Irish mementos was at her side, though now it was nearly empty. The miniature of her mother and the old sliver of wood that had been part of her papa's boat were carefully arranged on the little stand beside her bed. But apart from them, there was not much left from home. She had given the bag of sand and shells from the Connemara beach to Roddy, and even now her heart warmed at the memory of how his eyes had misted over for the briefest of moments out there in the starlight at her simple but generous gesture. Of Ireland itself, she had only the pebble from the pasture, and the flagon of air left.

Her fingers came up to touch the Celtic cross that never left her neck.

And the legacy of Grace O'Malley.

She gazed off into the darkness, thinking of Christian. Missing him. She had not seen him since he'd given her the ring, but just having it on her finger assured her of his love, and was a promise in itself that she would never again be alone.

But oh, what should she do about the awful predicament in which she now found herself?

She touched the ancient cross, trying to draw strength and guidance from it. Should she send word to Christian telling him that her own brother was the Irish Pirate? How would he react? What would he do? Christian was a king's officer; would he choose his duty to apprehend Roddy over the vow he had made to restore him to her?

No. Surely not. After all, he had promised that he would find her brother and make right the wrong he had done to her family. There was no question in Deirdre's mind that Christian would do the right thing.

Still ... to think that Roddy, of all people, was the Irish Pirate. Deirdre was still dazed over the discovery—and very, very frightened. Her brother had not changed much in the years since she'd last seen him; he was still rash and reckless, still full of bravado, still hot-tempered and volatile, but just as easily given to laughter. Such traits could, as the rebel leaders had warned, bring about the downfall of a man whose successes against the British had apparently gone to his head.

Deirdre's worry increased. Christian was not one of the village lads with whom Roddy used to delight in getting into fist-fights. He was no puffed-up and swaggering braggart who couldn't see past the tip of his nose. He was no bumbling idiot, no incompetent idler. Christian was one of the finest officers in the king's Navy, and he commanded a mighty frigate that was fully capable of smashing the little sloop that Roddy would captain tomorrow night when the arms transfer was made.

Only Delight seemed to feel no trepidation over the impending exchange. "Roddy knows what he's doing, Deirdre," she'd said when she'd come to explain why she hadn't revealed her family's rebel sympathies. "This is just one more mission. The Lord and Master knows nothing of it, just as he knows nothing of our involvement with the patriot cause. You just watch. Roddy will get the guns, Adams and Revere and Hancock will meet him on shore, and the cargo will be safely transported to Concord. There is no need to be so scared."

"I love my brother," Deirdre had murmured, twisting the ring that weighed so heavily upon her finger. "But I love me future husband, too. And here I am, unable to protect either one of 'em, and stuck in the middle of hostilities between two lands that aren't my own. Dear God, what a mess."

"You're not angry, then, that I never told you we're rebels?"

"No. But please, don't try to draw me into yer quibbles with England. I can sympathize with yer plight here in the colonies, for Britain treats yer people no better than she does mine—but the truth of the matter is that I love an Englishman, will marry an Englishman, and to help ye in any way would be to betray the man I love."

"You'll have to choose a side," Delight had said quietly. "Your betrothed may be a king's officer, but your brother is a rebel, Deirdre."

"Aye, and that creates a bit of a problem." Deirdre had raised her head, and her eyes had shone with pride as she met the gaze of her friend. "But I am *Irish*. And as such, I'll stay true to my own heart."

Her heart—which lay ten miles away in the cabin of a mighty frigate, in the care of the most wonderful man in the world.

Drawing the quilt around her, she laid her forearms over the damp windowsill, rested her cheek against her wrists, and closed her eyes. Moments later she was asleep, her little bag of dwindling Irish mementos at her side, Christian's shirt against her skin, and her face turned toward Boston.

Chapter Twenty-Eight

The dreary weather continued late into the following afternoon, and it did nothing to dispel the worries of those who stood in the Foley yard bidding good-bye to the Irish Pirate.

Rain had darkened his tricorne to a shade very near the inky blackness of his curls, caught in a thong of leather and hanging over his turned-up collar. Water dripped from the brim, trickling down his back and soaking his wool coat. His mare's hide was wet and steaming, and as Roddy swung up into the saddle, he gave her neck a fond slap and gazed down at the two girls who had braved the raw weather to see him off.

"Godspeed, my handsome smuggler," Dolores Ann murmured. She tilted her face up to his, her tongue suggestively touching the corners of her lips, then tracing their perimeter in a way that caused his eyes to darken and his blood to burn through his veins. A delight, was the widow Dolores, Roddy thought, remembering their "walk" of this morning. That walk had given them both plenty of exercise—but not in the manner in which the elder Foleys might have been led to believe....

He saw his sister, her eyes dark with worry, standing just behind Dolores. She was still the same gentle, sweet sibling he'd known and loved in Connemara when he was a mere lad and she barely out of swaddling clothes. And she still wore that ancient cross, the first thing she touched when fear overcame her.

She was touching it now. Not just touching it, but gripping it with such ferocity it was a wonder the metal didn't bend.

Reining his horse around, Roddy went to her, leaned down in the saddle, and embraced her. "Please understand, Deirdre. I know ye don't hold with the rebel cause, but 'tis important to me. Yer foolish English captain doesn't even know I'm sailin'. So wipe that frown off yer face and send me off with a smile, eh?"

"That *foolish English captain* is to be my husband, Roddy," she reminded him, the rain wet upon her cheeks. Her mouth was tight. "Please don't talk of him like that."

Roddy's jaw hardened. He had no love for Captain Lord, and the rocks would be gone from the fields of Connemara before he'd allow the Briton who had pressed him into the English Navy to wed his little sister. He'd see the bastard dead, first! But for now he would keep his silence, trusting that separation from the Englishman, as well as the Foley's gentle influence, would bring Deirdre around to the rebel sympathies.

"'Tis sorry I be, Deirdre," he said, touching his thumb to his sister's cheek and wiping away a trickle of rain. Beneath him the mare fidgeted, eager to be off. "But ye'll forgive me if yer Englishman is not on me list o' favorite people. Perhaps someday I can forgive him, as you have—but not now."

Straightening up, he tipped his hat to the two girls, blew Delight a kiss and galloped off, his cloak billowing behind him.

HMS *Bold Marauder,* cruising slowly through the dark, wind-ruffled seas a league off Cape Ann, had just completed another long tack when the lookout's voice came down through the mists that smothered the tops and yards so high above.

"On deck! Lights blinkin' two points off the starboard bow!"

On the quarterdeck, Christian turned to stare off into the night. It was the signal he'd been waiting for.

"Beat to quarters," he said quietly, "but no drums and no bosun's whistles. I want everything done in complete silence."

His voice was barely above conversational tones but so quiet was the ship, so eager and tense was every man in the crew, that everyone heard his command—and indeed, had been expecting it.

Anxiety instantly gave way to action. With hushed urgency and brisk efficiency, men darted through the darkness to their stations, some running to the huge guns that had already been loaded and run out. Others gathered near the pinrails, ready to grab sheets and braces in preparation to change tack while others scrambled aloft with the nimble ease of monkeys. They needed no urging from their superiors to keep silent, no direction as to what to do, for the Lord and Master had had them rehearsing this moment from the time the frigate, unseen under the cover of night and fog, had slipped quietly out of Boston Harbor several hours before.

He was a clever one, their commanding officer. He'd ordered all lanterns doused before they'd even left their anchorage and ensured that every man knew his task. Now they worked in darkness that was blacker than Hades, but they knew their ship so well that they needed no light to traverse decks that were now slick with rain and mist and spray.

"We'll get that smuggler, you just watch," Skunk said to Hibbert, who had just come up from below. "Cap'n's had us rehearsin' this moment all bleedin' day."

"Aye," Teach murmured from close by. "He's out for blood. Pity the poor rogue who dares tangle with *our* Lord and Master!"

Christian, standing beside the wheel on the pitch-black quarterdeck, heard their comments as he stared off into the darkness, and those who saw his smile thought it as cold as the wind that made his heavy boat cloak billow around him. The mists made it nearly impossible to see anything off the starboard beam, but high above the deck in the maintop he knew it was clear, and the lookout had no such encumbrances to hinder him.

Forward, he saw a ship's boy dart out of the shelter of the bulwarks, but the lad was stopped by Skunk's meaty paw before he could ring the ship's bell to signal that another half hour had passed. No noises must penetrate the eerie silence to give them away. One wrong move and the Irish Pirate would escape them.

"Eight bells, sir," whispered Ian, coming up beside him.

Christian nodded. Midnight. He sensed the anxiety in Ian's voice and saw it mirrored in the barely visible faces of those who surrounded them. "Very well, Ian." Rain dripped down from an overhead yard, and his shoulder throbbed with pain. Ignoring both, Christian walked to the quarterdeck rail and peered down into the gloomy darkness of the ship's waist, where a hundred faces were all turned toward him, eagerly awaiting his command. Twin rows of dark, hulking shapes made up the batteries of the frigate's big guns. He heard the hiss of spray at the bows, the soft drum of rain on the decks, and the hum of the westerly wind high up in the tops. Water creamed softly along the sides, and aft, their wake was lost in fog. *Bold Marauder* was ready. The guns were ready. His men were ready, and he had the element of surprise.

Tonight, he vowed, the Irish Pirate would pay the price of treason against the Crown.

Suddenly Ian gripped his arm and pointed out into the darkness. "Lights out to larboard now, sir! Looks like an answering signal from another ship."

The Irish Pirate.

The fog had begun to thin, and now Christian could see out over the black seas and into the night, where the wink of a distant lantern pierced the darkness. Then the mists closed in again. He glanced at the compass, estimated the vessel's position, and looked at his officers, all awaiting his command. They were a formidable lot, and he harbored as much trust in this formerly motley crew as he had in any other he'd had the pleasure to command; Ian, his beard wet with rain, his eyes fierce and determined; Rhodes, quiet and competent and sinister; Wenham, chewing on the stem of a pipe he dared not light; and Hibbert, dressed in a uniform that was desperately in need of a wash.

"Mr. Hibbert!" he snapped, and the midshipman made his way to his captain's side.

"Aye, sir?"

Christian's eyes raked the middie's unkempt clothes with mock severity. Then he grinned, for his attempts to make the youth look the part of an officer had become a ship-wide joke. "For God's sake, go change into a clean uniform! This is a *king's ship*!"

Hibbert smirked and bolted below. His captain shook his head and opened his spyglass. Some things would never change. But this crew was a far cry from the one he'd left Portsmouth with. They had quit England in disgrace; soon, now, they would make both their Navy and their country proud.

He gave the order to change tack. Moments later, *Bold Marauder* was heeling over in the wind, slipping like a great, predatory hawk through the black mists of the night.

"EASY WITH THOSE CRATES THERE, LADS," the Irish Pirate said, anxiously watching as the men, toiling in the rain, struggled to load the heavy crates aboard the sloop as quickly as possible. The transfer was happening swiftly, silently, competently, as it had been done countless times before, as it would be done countless times again. Boats, struggling in the swells, moved back and forth between the hove-to merchantman and the little sloop, their crews cursing and damning the wind and the rain. Above, the flapping topsail sent down a continual shower, and rigging banged noisily in impatience. A single lantern, set in the shrouds a foot above Roddy's head, provided the only light and now it shone upon the dark, bearded faces of men grown hard by living just beyond the reach of the law.

"One more trip and that'll do it, Cap'n," said a seaman, grinning up through the darkness as his boat nudged against the rocking hull. He reached up and caught the wet line one of his mates tossed down, then hauled himself up the side.

"Good," Roddy said, glancing nervously out into the night. A feeling of doom weighed heavily in his bones, and he would be happy when the exchange was done and he was safely back in Menotomy. "Just hurry the bleedin' hell up, would ye? 'Twill be dawn by the time ye laggards've finished."

His good humor spurred them into even more haste, and a half hour later the boats were back aboard, the merchantman was slipping away into the mists, and the crates of guns were being transferred to the hold.

Roddy wiped the rain from his face with the back of his hand, envisioned Delight's silky thighs spread beneath him, and accepting a hot mug of buttered rum, went aft to join his first mate by the tiller. Already his spirits were on the rise, and he breathed a sigh of relief as the staysail was backed, the sloop turned, and wind began to swell the big mainsail. The mists were clearing, filing away out to sea as though being towed by an invisible force, and he could see stars beginning to shine dimly through the lingering vapors and sliding in and out of the fuzzy haze.

"'Twill be a fine mornin', eh, Stubs?" he said to the one-eyed, scar-faced thief who'd escaped debtors' prison only to find his fortune at sea.

"Aye, Cap'n. Stars are comin' out."

"In more ways than one, lad, in more ways than one!" Roddy said, thinking of the woman he had once known as Dolores Ann and now knew as Delight. He grinned, his teeth flashing white in the gloom.

"Should I douse the lantern, Cap'n?" asked a seaman just coming up from below.

"Nay," Roddy said with an impatient wave of his hand. He gazed out into the darkness. More stars were crystallizing through the fading mists now, growing sharper and brighter as the night cleared. "There's no one out here but us."

"Adams is going to be singing our praises for sure," Stubs said, accepting a mug from a passing seaman. "Christ, this is getting easier and easier. The Royal Navy just ain't what it used to be."

"Well, with such incompetent dolts as Captain Lord to head it, what d'ye expect? He's probably out combin' the seas off Cape Cod, the fool!"

Several nearby seamen hooted with laughter. Stubs slapped his thigh, and Roddy raised his mug in a mocking toast.

"To the Royal Navy and its ships o' fools!"

"Aye! A pox on the whole bloody lot of 'em!"

Harsh guffaws rolled out over the decks. Pipes were passed. More rum was poured; some was spilled.

And aft, the stars began to go out as a tall, dark shape rose menacingly out of the darkness behind them.

But no one saw the giant squares of canvas blotting out the heavens.

No one heard the increasing roar of water as the bows of a mighty frigate swallowed the little sloop's wake.

And no one happened to look around to notice.

"I'll drink to that!" Roddy said, his eyes dancing. "A pox on England, a pox on its ships, and a pox on Captain Christian Bloody Lord, whose inability to capture the dreaded Irish Pirate will land him straight in the annals of history as the biggest fool the Royal Navy ever bred!"

At that very moment, the night blew apart in a deafening roar of thunder and flame as the Royal Navy's finest—which had been silently trailing its quarry for the last quarter hour—opened fire. In one deadly salvo from her bow chasers, the mighty *Bold*

Marauder smashed the mast from the little sloop and left her staggering helplessly in the water.

In disbelief, Captain Roddy O'Devir picked himself up from the deck where he'd been thrown and watched as the powerful frigate slid out of the darkness, her guns glinting in the starlight. He saw men behind their big muzzles, waiting for their captain's signal to fire. He saw marines gathered along the rail, their muskets trained down upon his shattered decks. And he heard the clipped voice of the English commander and knew that he had just made the most grievous error of misjudgment in his career as a mariner—an error that would probably cost him his life.

"This is His Majesty's frigate *Bold Marauder*! In the name of the king, heave to and prepare to receive boarders! You are all under arrest!"

A grievous error indeed.

The voice belonged to that same *fool* whom Roddy had just scorned, a man who, he realized with a sinking heart, had turned out to be no fool at all.

Captain Lord.

Chapter Twenty-Nine

"*D*eirdre!*" Delight's voice, shrill with panic, cleaved the darkness. "Deirdre, wake up! Oh, God, the Lord and Master caught Roddy! *He caught Roddy!*"

Instantly awake, Deirdre sat up just as Delight, crying bitterly, threw herself into her arms. Outside, dawn glowed upon the horizon and gray light filled the room. "Paul Revere just brought the news, Deirdre! Your Englishman caught him after he made the trade and saw the whole thing. Roddy'll hang for this, Deirdre! He'll *hang!*"

Deirdre began to swing herself out of bed, but Delight was hysterical. "Oh, Deirdre, you have to do something, anything, *everything* in your power to get the Lord and Master to release Roddy! There's no one but you he'll listen to, no one but you who can persuade him to let Roddy go!" Her fingers bit into Deirdre's shoulders. "The man loves you, Deirdre! He'll do anything you ask!"

Deirdre embraced the other girl, trying to calm her. "Aye, Delight, he will. Now stop yer cryin'. Christian made me a promise that he'd find my brother and return him to me to make up for press-gangin' him all those years ago." She smiled, serene in the face of her friend's panic. "So see? 'Twill be no problem a'tall. I'll just go to Boston, tell Christian who Roddy is, and he'll let him go."

Deirdre crawled out from beneath the covers and padded across the room to stand at the window. The floor was cold beneath her bare feet, the dawn vibrant upon the eastern horizon. *Ah, Christian,* she thought, hugging her arms to herself. There was no reason to be upset, no reason to fear that he wouldn't honor his word to return Roddy to her. Thank God, actually, that it had been him and not some other Royal Navy captain who had apprehended Roddy!

"Oh, Deirdre, how can ye be so sure?" Delight wailed. "Captain Lord is a king's officer! He values nothing as much as duty, loyalty, and service. What if he won't listen to you?" She burst into wild sobs. "Oh, God, what if he won't *listen?*"

Deirdre's head came up, and she touched the ring. "He is to marry me, Delight. He will listen." She turned confident eyes upon her friend. "I promise."

THE PUPPIES WHIMPERED in their box, tiny blobs of white fur that crawled over each other and pushed against their mother's belly as they suckled greedily at her milk-swollen teats.

Christian sat backward in a chair watching them, his chin resting upon his wrists, his wrists resting on the top rung. His coat was slung carelessly over a neighboring chair, and his fancy gold-laced hat rested atop one of its posts. Stripped down to waistcoat, shirt, and breeches, he gazed sightlessly at the puppies, trying to glean some small sliver of joy from their antics.

To no avail.

He had been working on a report to Sir Geoffrey all morning, and sheer exhaustion had forced him to take a break. He had not slept in two days, and his body was crying for rest. But he was afraid to close his eyes and give in to the sleep his body craved, for in his heart he knew that the nightmares would return.

Somewhere beneath him and deep within the frigate's hold was the man who was his Irish girl's lover. That he had succeeded in outsmarting and apprehending the rascal brought Christian no sense of triumph. Revenge had been empty, hollow, meaningless. There hadn't even been any action, for the Irish Pirate's sloop had mounted only a few swivel guns that would have been ridiculously ineffective against the strapping might of a king's frigate. The tall, defiant-eyed sea rogue had surrendered without a fight, knowing that any attempt to defend his ship against *Bold Marauder* would only result in needless bloodshed.

Now the rebel crew was in a Boston gaol, the Pirate himself locked in what had once been the playground of Delight Foley. Christian was taking no chances. He dared not send the notorious smuggler ashore for fear that the angry mobs would storm the gaol and free their hero. But those same people who might storm a gaol would think twice about approaching a king's frigate.

His chin on his wrists, he stared dully down at the puppies, not seeing them, but Deirdre. He thought of how she had dug the musket ball from his shoulder, how she had loved him with her body, how her eyes had shone so brightly when he'd given her his ring.

To think that her actions had been false; to think that it wasn't him she loved, but another.

The pain that ravaged his heart was a hundred times worse than anything he'd endured at the hands of Elwin Boyd's surgery. It hurt such that he could not sit here and think about it. He rose from the chair, picked up a puppy, and returned to his desk. There he sat, carefully positioning the baby in his lap so it would not fall, and retrieved his pen. Exhaustion made his movements forced and mechanical. He dipped the quill in the inkwell and willing the weariness from his brain, tried to continue with his report. In his lap the puppy fell asleep, contented and warm.

Christian's head drooped, the fair hair falling over his brow. His eyes flickered shut, opened again, and jerking his head up, he dipped the quill in the inkwell once more. He was just starting the next page when he heard the stamp of a musket against the deck outside his door. A moment later it opened, and Ian MacDuff, with Evans standing grim-faced behind him, stepped inside.

"Prisoner's asking tae see ye, sir."

The lieutenant held his hat respectfully in his hands, and the scent of his damp clothes permeated the confines of the cabin. Christian looked up and blinked, his eyes heavy and aching with exhaustion. In his dazed, numbed state, it took a moment for him to realize that someone had spoken to him.

Cradling the sleeping puppy, he got to his feet and moved across the cabin to place the baby with its mother. Ian took a step forward, thinking to assist his captain, for the Lord and Master looked to be in a sorry state indeed.

"Are ye all right, sir?"

"Aye, Ian. Never felt better."

"If there be anything ye want tae talk about, doona hesitate tae ask...."

Christian paused. He stared dumbly at the bulkhead, his throat working. Then he raked a hand through his hair and looked at the lieutenant. "Thank you, Ian. I shall remember your kindness, but I fear that talk will not aid me in the slightest."

"The Irish lassie, sir?"

Christian said nothing.

"I know ye be missing her, sir, but ye'll be back together soon, now that ye've accomplished yer mission—"

"You do not understand!" Christian's eyes were suddenly blazing. Then his voice softened, became dead and lifeless once more. "Forgive me, Ian. I have no right to be sharp with you, none at all." He put his hands on the back of a chair and looked down, his eyes bleak. "After I went to Menotomy to call upon her—and ask

for her hand in marriage—I—I saw her in the arms of another man."

Ian's mouth fell open and his hat dropped from his hands. "Another man, sir?" His face went slack with shock. "Why, she loves you. She wouldnae do such a thing—"

"It was the Irish Pirate, Ian. And the memory of her standing in his arms shall go with me to my grave."

He looked at Ian, his eyes raw with anguish. But the big Scot had no words of comfort, nothing from his own vast experience with the bonnie sex to relieve the pain of his commanding officer. "'Tis sorry I be, sir ... I had no idea."

Christian turned away. "Thank you, Ian. Your concern will not be forgotten."

"I'll let ye be, then, sir," Ian said, quietly, sensing his captain's need to be alone. "But please do think about getting some sleep before ye have tae face the Old Fart. And I'm sorry for disturbing ye. I just thought ye'd want t' know the prisoner's demanding tae see you."

"Damn the prisoner. He can bloody well rot for all I care."

"Aye, sir. I'll tell 'im that."

"Please do, Ian." Christian was aching with fatigue, his heart a raw wound whose pain was rivaled only by the incessant throb of his shoulder. Dimly, he was aware of Ian moving away and down the passageway, roaring for Skunk and Teach as he went.

Soon the news would be known throughout the ship. Soon every man aboard would know that he'd been neatly deceived by a lovely Irish girl with innocent purple eyes. But he found he was too tired to care. Too tired to fight the anguish, the pain, the pity that would surely come his way.

And the nightmares.

Too damned tired.

He stumbled to his bed and swayed on his feet with exhaustion.

Sleep.

He sat down and slowly bent to take off his shoes.

Sleep.

He was out before his head hit the pillow, and sure enough, the nightmares found him.

Only this time, the treacherous dream-woman who betrayed him was not the woman he had once wed, but the one that he had hoped to.

Deirdre.

THE SUMMONS TO repair aboard the flagship *Dauntless* came shortly before noon, and Christian was shaken awake by a hand on his shoulder. He clawed his way out of the fog of oblivion, opened his eyes, and saw Rhodes standing there, the silver wings of his black hair shining in the sunlight coming in through the stern windows.

"Sorry to wake you, sir. Sir Geoffrey just sent his flag lieutenant across with orders to come aboard *Dauntless*. He wishes to speak to you before dinner about the Irish Pirate."

"Dinner?" Christian said, sitting up and rubbing his eyes.

"Aye. He's throwing a big celebration aboard the flagship in your honor. Gage will be there, and so will a host of other dignitaries."

Christian swung out of bed, alarmed to find himself in clothes that were now on a level of unkemptness with Hibbert's worst.

Rhodes added, "Gage wanted to give the party at his residence in Boston, but Sir Geoffrey thought it unwise, given the, er, present state of the townspeople."

"State?"

"Aye. The people are in an uproar, sir. You caught their hero. Adams and Hancock are stirring up the rabble with rousing speeches. Warren is demanding the prisoner's release. A fight broke out between one of our majors and a crowd of rebels, and there was a near riot in the streets. Our troops are doing all they can to contain the situation, but the people are screaming for your head on a platter, and that's putting it mildly."

Christian sighed. "Very well, then. I shall be up shortly."

Rhodes's eyes grew uncharacteristically sympathetic. "I'm sorry to hear about the girl, sir."

"Thank you, Russell. You'll understand if I do not wish to discuss her."

"Of course, sir."

His face solemn, Rhodes went out. An hour later, Christian had bathed and dressed. He left his cabin and went on deck, clad in his finest dress uniform and carrying his gold-tasseled presentation sword.

The sight that greeted him nearly did him in.

Seamen clung to the rigging, holding their hats to display their respect for him. Officers lined the rail, standing stiffly at attention. Even Hibbert had taken pains over his appearance. Whistles shrilled, drums rolled, and *Bold Marauder*'s people saw their captain over the side with a smart and moving salute that swelled his troubled heart. He blinked to cover his emotion, for he knew that they were trying their best to cheer him in the only way they could.

Even the gig's crew was smartly turned out, the oars rising and falling in perfect unison as the seamen rowed him through the harbor toward the towering hulk of the flagship.

Christian kept his eyes straight ahead lest someone see the anguish there—and thus missed the tiny rowboat that passed him just off to starboard, carrying a young woman with spiral-curling black hair toward the proud and mighty *Bold Marauder*.

"Christian!" she yelled, standing up in the boat and waving her hat before Jared Foley or Delight could pull her back down. *"Christian!"*

She saw his back go rigid, but the handsome sea officer never turned.

"Christian!"

The rowboat tipped dangerously in the water as Deirdre fought to keep her balance. He did not turn to acknowledge her, and sudden worry filled her. What was wrong? Why was he ignoring her? Dazed, she sat back down and stared at Delight. "He went right by me," she whispered. "Sweet Mary, he didn't even turn around, and I know he heard me!"

"I fear we're too late," Jared grunted as he saw the admiral's side party preparing to welcome the naval captain aboard the flagship with all the fanfare due a hero. The shrill of whistles cleaved the air, mocking their hopes of securing Roddy's release. "Your fine, upstanding sea officer has done what he came here to do, Deirdre—apprehend the Irish Pirate. It appears that he has no further use for you, or for anything but the glory such an accomplishment will bring him."

"But no, he wouldn't *do* that to me, Mr. Foley! He has no reason to ignore me like that! He loves me!" she cried, indicating the ring on her finger. "I *know* Christian, and he loves me!"

"But he loves his country more," the man said, resting on the oars and watching as the blue-and-white-clad officer scaled the great tumble home of the mighty flagship.

"No! He wouldn't cast me aside like this, Mr. Foley! He just wouldn't!"

"I beg to differ, Deirdre." The printer's eyes gazed hopelessly into hers. "He just did."

Chapter Thirty

The elaborate dinner that Sir Geoffrey threw to celebrate Christian's success had been more fitting for a king than a mere naval captain whose latest accomplishment was just one more in a series of triumphs that marked a long and decorated career. Despite Sir Geoffrey's praise and General Gage's pleasure, Christian was glad to see the evening finally come to a close.

Tired, weary, and wanting nothing more than the solitude of his own cabin, he left the flagship to the piercing shriek of the side party's salute and the stamp and clatter of Sir Geoffrey's marines. Now, with the sea wind driving the unpleasant scent of pipe smoke from his uniform, he stared longingly toward the glimmering lights of the frigate he called home.

In the darkness he saw figures moving on her decks, along her gangways, gathering at her rail. His coxswain called up to the frigate to alert the watch to his arrival, and the decks became a flurry of activity. The gig moved into the orange reflection that sheeted the water around the ship's hull, passing beneath the long bowsprit and the figurehead crouched just beneath it.

The crew hooked onto the frigate's main chains, and he leapt the short distance. But as he made his way up the black, forbidding side, he suddenly wished he were back aboard the admiral's flagship, where there were no memories to haunt him—and no nightmares waiting to torture him the moment he closed his eyes.

Christian pushed open the door to his cabin, and was not in the least bit surprised to find *her* waiting for him.

She was sitting on his bed, her thick curls scattered over her shoulders. Tildy's puppies were cradled in her lap and all but lost in the voluminous folds of her skirts. Lantern light framed her face and hair in a soft, heavenly glow.

"Christian," she whispered brokenly.

"Get out."

She didn't move.

"Did you hear me?" he snarled. "I said, *get out!*"

They stared at each other, his eyes blazing, hers wounded and sad. She made no move to leave, and he didn't trust himself to touch her. A tantalizing bit of ankle peeped above her mud-spattered shoes, and he turned away, furious that she could still arouse his interest after the treacherous way she'd treated him.

The silence stretched on, until her eyes filled with tears.

"Why?" he asked, his voice tortured. He slammed his fist against the bulkhead and felt pain explode in his wounded shoulder. "For God's sake, Deirdre, *why?*"

She stood, carefully put the puppies back with her mother, and turned to face him. "I might ask the same of *you,* Christian." Her eyes were tragic. "Does glory mean so much to ye that ye'd abandon those who love ye?"

"What?"

"Ye gave me yer ring, asked me to become yer wife— then ye pretended I didn't exist. I didn't do anythin' wrong, but you ignored me when I called to ye in the harbor, treated me like I wasn't even there."

He glared at her, his eyes blazing. "Why the bloody *hell* should I have acknowledged you?" he roared, ripping off his hat and hurling it to the table. "After what you did to me!"

"I did nothin' to ye! 'Twas *you* who treated me like I didn't exist!"

"Oh? And who's the one already cuckolding her future husband, eh?" he snarled, frightening her with the intensity of his anger. "Who was the one who professed to love me when all the time her heart belonged to someone else? Who was the one who worked so damned hard to win my trust, then betrayed it with no care for the consequences?" Her face went white with shock, confusion. "Don't sit there and pretend you don't know what I'm talking about! You came here to try to save your damned lover, didn't you? *Didn't you?*"

"My ... my *lover*?"

"A plague on you for your bloody deceit! The game is up, Deirdre! I *knew* you'd come to me today with some wicked plea to release him, and that's the only thing you haven't disappointed me in, so help me God!"

"Christian," she whispered, her eyes brimming with tears, her voice trembling with hurt, "I have no lover except you."

"How dare you stand there and *lie* to me!" He clenched his fists at his sides, his mouth a slash of anguish. "I *saw* you in the bugger's arms, by God! I bloody well saw you, Deirdre, so forget trying to tell me there's naught between you and him! I know now why you came to America. I know now why you finally consented to stay with Dolores or Delight or whatever the cursed hell her name is. You did it so you could be close to *him*! I should have figured it out before—you're Irish, he's Irish—by God, you even *look* alike—"

"Christian."

She walked slowly across the cabin toward him. Her face was very white, her eyes very purple, her lower lip very red and swollen where she'd caught it between her teeth. The cross glittered from the folds of her shirt, a shirt, he saw now, that was achingly familiar because it was one of his. Damn her. Damn her to hell and beyond.

She came right up to him and stopped. He caught the scent of her soap, her damp woolen waistcoat, her rain-washed hair. Tentatively, she reached out and placed one hand upon the gold insignia of his sleeve, the other against his thundering heart. His jaw hardened and he clenched his fists at his sides, every ounce of will straining to hold his temper in check.

"The Irish Pirate is not my lover," she said levelly. Her eyes held his, beautiful, brilliant, and brimming with unshed tears. "How could ye even *think* I'd betray ye like that, Christian?" Her throat worked, and big, fat droplets began to roll down her cheeks. "'Tis you whom I love. *You.* And it hurts me that ye have so little trust in me that ye'd think I'd do anythin' to ever hurt ye."

"I—*saw*—you," he gritted out, shutting his eyes and turning his head so he wouldn't have to look at her. "Damn you, Deirdre! I didn't go back to Boston after I left you the other night! I turned around and took a room in the tavern across the road so that I could spy on the Foleys' activities." He ignored her widening eyes. "Sir Geoffrey had intelligence that they were rebels. Gage's spies learned there was to be a patriot meeting that night, and given that it was *my* task to apprehend the Irish Pirate, and that he was suspected to be in league with the rebels, I felt it prudent to learn all I could." He tilted back his head, unable to look into her eyes, unable to stand the soft pressure of her palm against his heart. "But never did I expect to see *you,* of all people, standing out in the road embracing the bastard. I *saw* you, Deirdre. I saw you hug him, kiss him, give him one of your precious Irish mementos." His eyes darkened with anguish. "Damn you, I *saw* you."

For a long moment she said nothing. Then she gave a heavy sigh and trembling, bent her head until her brow rested against his crisp lapels. "Aye, that ye did, perhaps," she said slowly. "Ye saw me in the arms of the Irish Pirate, I'll not be denyin' it. And I'll not deny that I love him, too, but not as a lass loves her man, as I do you."

"What other bloody way *is* there to love a man?"

"A moment ago," she whispered, "ye said that the Irish Pirate and I look alike. Did ye ever stop and consider that I might love him not as a lover ... but as a *brother?*"

He stared at her for so long his heart seemed to stop beating. The breath caught in his chest, and speckles of darkness danced across his vision. Her words hung heavily in the room, and her eyes were steady, unwavering, questing.

"Did ye ever stop an' ask yer prisoner what his real name is?" she asked gently.

"Dear God...."

"And did ye ever stop and recall the face of the lad yer press gang took from Connemara all those years ago, Christian?"

He shut his eyes.

"Did ye?"

"No," he murmured, kneading his forehead. "Oh, dear God, Deirdre—"

More tears were tumbling down her cheeks. "I would never, ever do anythin' to hurt ye, Christian," she whispered, reaching up to knuckle her eyes. "But to think that ye trusted me so little as to think I would, breaks my heart."

He collapsed into a chair, his eyes anguished. "Why didn't you *tell* me, Deirdre? By God, why didn't you tell me the Irish Pirate was your brother?"

"I didn't *know* he was my brother until I saw him at the Foley house," she confessed. "And I haven't seen *you* since ye left that evenin'. How was I supposed to tell ye?" She came closer to him, her hands clenched together, her lips white with pain. "And would it have made a lick o' difference if I had?"

"What do you mean?"

"Would ye still have gone after him, Christian?"

He stared at her, then looked away.

"Would ye?"

He set his jaw. "I am a king's officer, Deirdre. I had no choice but to go after him."

The breath left her chest in a ragged sound of defeat and despair. Slowly, she said, "And does that mean that, as a king's officer, ye can do nothin' to free him?

Emotion warred in his face, and he raked a hand through his hair. Then he lunged to his feet and began to pace. "I must abide by my duty to king and country, Deirdre." At the windows he turned, his eyes dark with torment. "I cannot release your brother. He is an enemy of the Crown and therefore must be punished for his activities against it."

She raised her chin. The hope was fading from her face, and terror began to fill her eyes. He turned away, unable to look at her. "They will hang him, Christian."

He whirled. "By God, Deirdre, what am I to do about it? I can do nothing to help him, not now!"

"Ye could just let him go."

"And face a court-martial?"

"No one has to know about it."

"I am a king's officer, Deirdre! You don't understand, damn you!"

"Oh, I understand, all right," she said bitterly, her wounded eyes flooding with fresh tears. "Ye speak of duty and gallantry and being an officer and a gentleman. Aye, ye're an officer, all right, and a fine one at that—*but ye're no gentleman.* Yer word, yer honor, are as hollow as a rotten oak."

She moved toward the door, her face tight, her chin high. His hand flashed out and caught her arm. "What do you mean?"

"Ye're no gentleman," she said. "A gentleman always keeps his word. Ye *promised*, Christian, that ye'd help me find me brother. Ye promised to return him to me, but now ye're goin' back on yer promise. Ye're goin' to stand mutely by and let him hang, just so ye can gather all the glory yer Navy can bestow upon ye. Another medal for that fine and decorated chest, another step up the ladder to promotion. Aye, ye'll be an admiral someday, I've no doubt. But if it's men like you who make admirals, then I pity England."

"Deirdre—"

She pried his ring from her finger and held it in the palm of her hand, lamenting all that it had meant, all that it *could* have meant. "I've no wish to marry ye now, Christian. I'll not have a man who lacks honor, a man who breaks his word to the woman he wants for his wife."

"Deirdre, please let me explain—"

"There's nothin' to explain, Christian. Ye made me a promise to help me find me brother. Ye found him, all right. But if he is hanged and put to death for believin' in a cause that in his heart is righteous and just, then ye've taken him from me not once, but twice."

He stood paralyzed, only his eyes moving as they flickered to the ring.

She turned and walked slowly to the door, choking on tears while she ached for him to say the words that would bring her back to him, the words that would keep her from walking out of his life, the words that were the only thing standing between Roddy and a hangman's noose.

The words that, once uttered, would mean a lifetime of happiness for both of them.

She paused, her hand on the door latch while her eyes beseeched his. "Let my brother go, Christian. Please say ye will. I beg of ye...."

He set his jaw and turned away.

Taking a deep, shaky breath, Deirdre plucked the ring from her palm, laid it on the table, and quietly left the cabin.

Chapter Thirty-One

"Captain, sir?" Midshipman Robert Hibbert stood in the doorway, his gaze probing the cabin's gloomy darkness until he spotted his commanding officer sprawled in his chair. The Irish girl had left a week ago, and the Lord and Master had been down here ever since; now the captain stared dejectedly at a half-empty bottle of brandy, one arm cradling Tildy, who sat in his lap and regarded Hibbert with sad eyes.

In their box, the puppies whined pitifully.

"Captain?" Hibbert repeated, stepping into the cabin.

Slowly, Christian raised his head. His eyes were lifeless, bleak, his untouched breakfast congealing on a plate near his elbow. "Pray, what is it, Hibbert?"

The young midshipman frowned at sight of the brandy bottle. "Uh, Mr. MacDuff's respects, sir, and says to tell you a barge is setting off from the admiral's ship and heading this way. Sir Geoffrey is in it, sir."

"Thank you, Hibbert."

The Lord and Master remained unmoving, staring dejectedly out the stern windows at the gray, rain-pocked sea.

"Uh, begging your pardon, sir, but don't you think you might want to, uh, maybe make yourself look, uh ... presentable?"

The gray eyes remained fixed on the sea. "Have a care to whom you're talking, Hibbert."

"I am, sir." The midshipman drew himself up and smoothed his own smartly pressed uniform. "But this is a *king's ship*," he said pointedly, "and we wouldn't want our captain taken aback."

Christian turned his head and stared at the boy. Then he looked down at his own uniform. He wore only his shirt and breeches, and both were badly rumpled and in need of a wash. A large spot of spilled brandy—or was it rum? he couldn't remember—stained his shirt front, and his hair was rumpled and unqueued, lying loose and untidy around his shoulders. He swallowed hard and looked down at his hands. "Thank you, Hibbert."

Drawing himself up, Hibbert swelled with pride. "I'd be happy to help you buckle on your sword and clean up the cabin," he offered, with a pointed glance at the brandy bottle. "Ian says we have maybe ten minutes before Sir Geoffrey reaches us. It's windy out there, and his crew's having a hard row."

"Yes, of course," Christian said woodenly. He got to his feet, swaying a bit unsteadily. He could feel the midshipman's worried eyes upon him. He was not making a very good role model for the young officer, or for any of his men.

And he didn't give a bloody damn.

Topside, he heard the side party being mustered as the crew prepared to receive the admiral. Shaking his head to clear it, Christian set Tildy back down with her puppies, and pouring a pitcher of water into his basin, plunged his hands into it and scrubbed at his bristled face.

Hibbert saw his predicament immediately. "Would you like me to shave you, sir?"

The tired smile was answer enough. Christian sat down and closed his eyes, allowing the lad to lather his face. From above, he heard Ian's gruff voice coming down through the skylight as he ordered the side party into position.

"I know you're feeling poorly about the girl," Hibbert said suddenly, bravely, as his captain's eyes opened to regard him with anger. "And we're all proud of you for outsmarting the Irish Pirate and bringing him to heel." The razor moved over Christian's chin. "But don't you think you might just consider letting the man go? I mean, I've talked to him, and we've been playing cards with him every night—"

"*What?*"

"He's really a nice fellow, Captain O'Devir. Not a criminal at all, sir, but a man who believes as strongly in his ideas as—and pardon me for saying so, sir—you do in yours."

"He is a treasonous rebel and traitor to his king," Christian snapped, "and do not forget it!"

"Aye, sir." The razor scraped over Christian's cheek, but the youth's hand was surprisingly steady. "I know you think you can't let Captain O'Devir go, because *we* might be angry with you, but we held a meeting, sir, and we don't want to see him hang."

Christian seized the midshipman's wrist. "Why the hell does everyone on this bloody planet seem to think I can just release the scoundrel? Such decisions are not mine to make! And, by God, this is a king's ship. I have a code of honor and duty to uphold, and so do the bloody lot of you." He shut his eyes, cringing as he heard the bosun's whistles shrilling on the deck above. "Besides," he added in a gentler tone, "I can't just *release* him. You know that, Hibbert."

"I know, sir. But you've got to do something.... We know you're loyal to the king; we know you're loyal to this ship and the flag that flies above her decks. But in the end, who wins if the Irish Pirate is hanged? No one. The rebels are still going to transport arms to Concord, and everyone knows that Gage will soon have to move against them."

"Hibbert, you show a devilish amount of wisdom for one so tender in years."

"And pardon me, sir, but you show a devilish amount of stubbornness for someone as advanced in yours."

"Pray, go to hell."

The midshipman laughed, wiped the razor clean, and toweled the streaks of lather from his captain's austere face. "Well, sir, I just wanted you to know that *we* won't think any less of you if Captain O'Devir ... *escapes*. And—" He paused, looked away, and then met his captain's hard gaze with unflinching resolve. "I know this has been a long time in coming, sir, but I have to say it. You're the best Lord and Master we've ever served under ... and we only want to see you happy."

Christian looked down. "Thank you, Hibbert. That ... that means a lot to me."

"It's the truth, sir. Now, if you'll just stand up, I'll help you into your dress coat. I do believe I hear the Old Fart's voice outside now—his barge must be bumping our hull, I'd say." Christian rose and allowed the young midshipman to help him into the heavy blue coat. He pulled his sleeves free of the cuffs and buttoned the coat to conceal his stained shirt. Then he tied his hair back, picked up his hat, and raised his arms so that Hibbert could buckle on his sword belt.

"You will make a fine captain someday," he said as the midshipman stood back to survey his handiwork.

"Thank you, sir. I have had a good example to follow."

For the first time in days, the Lord and Master's severe face broke into a grin; then he abruptly turned and exited the cabin. Hibbert stood there for a moment, his eyes moving almost reverently over the captain's family coat of arms that hung on the bulkhead, the painting of the king, the crossed swords, the set of fine pistols.

Then he walked to the table, picked up the bottle of brandy, and throwing the stern windows wide, flung it into the sea.

"I SAY, Christian, Gage cannot stop singing your praises," Sir Geoffrey said, his shrewd eyes raking *Bold Marauder*'s decks for signs of laxity and finding none. "He toasts you at every meal and has written letters to the king commending your apprehension of the Irish Pirate."

"I am flattered, sir."

"Don't be—you earned it. Damme, you're a fine candidate for flag rank, Captain Lord, a fine candidate indeed." Aware of the frigate's crew watching him, the crusty old admiral straightened his back and followed *Bold Marauder*'s captain below. "D'you know, my flag captain is proving to be most incompetent, and I must choose another. Captain Merrick comes immediately to mind, as he is a fine young officer, but I've already been accused of showing favoritism where he is concerned. But then, he's earned his laurels, too."

Christian pushed open the door to his cabin and let out a relieved breath. Young Hibbert had done a fine, albeit hasty, job of tidying it up.

The admiral's words suddenly hit him. "What are you saying, sir?"

Sir Geoffrey clapped Christian between his shoulders. "I'm offering you the position of flag captain, my good man."

Christian stared at him. He'd carried the flags of admirals before, but still, it was an honor. Another step toward raising his own broad pennant. Another way the Royal Navy had of thanking those who were loyal to the Service.

Loyal.

There, that word again. He fisted his hands, the force behind the unseen gesture causing fresh pain to burst in his shoulder. He hadn't felt very loyal these past few days.

Ye speak of duty and gallantry and bein' an officer and a gentleman—
He swallowed with difficulty.

—but ye're no gentleman. Yer word, yer honor, are as hollow as a rotten oak.

"Well, my good fellow?" Sir Geoffrey said, grinning. "What d'you say, eh, Christian?"

Another medal for that fine and decorated chest, another step up the ladder to promotion.

Christian turned bleak eyes upon Sir Geoffrey. To be asked to carry the flag of his admiral was the greatest honor that could be bestowed upon a captain. There were those in the fleet who'd give their eyeteeth to be in the position he now found himself.

.... yer word, yer honor are as hollow as a rotten oak.

He met the admiral's gaze. "I am deeply honored, Sir Geoffrey," he said quietly, knowing, even as the words left his mouth, that the decision he had made—and was about to carry out—did not entitle him to carry the flag of any admiral, let alone wear the coat of a king's officer.

But it would allow him to live with himself.

To spend the rest of his days knowing that he had done what was morally right. To be able to face himself in the mirror every day. To know that he had made his decision, based not on the decree of the Navy to which he had devoted his life, but on the code of honor that he—as an officer, as a gentleman—lived by.

Honor. It went far beyond the service a man gave for his king and country; it encompassed his very thoughts and deeds in dealing with his fellow man. Long ago, he had committed an unpardonable sin against an innocent family when, in the name of the king's Navy, he had taken young Roddy O'Devir from his homeland.

It was time to atone for that sin.

"Well, Christian?"

The Lord and Master's eyes were steady, resigned, proud. "Thank you, sir ... but I'm afraid I must decline."

IT WAS cold and damp in the tiny space in which the Irish Pirate found himself. He lay on his back, shackled and staring up into the darkness, a wool blanket draped over his body and a small pouch of Irish seashells clenched in his hand.

Down here in the depths of the frigate, sounds were distant and muffled. Thrice a day, a young midshipman brought him a meager meal of bread and cheese and salt pork. He was afforded a small jug of water, a few blankets, and all the privacy he could possibly want. But for the past few hours, the ship had been as quiet as a tomb.

Roddy's fingers curled around the felt pouch, feeling a shell that his sister had plucked from a beach that he would never see again in this lifetime. Emotion clogged his throat, and he suddenly wished he could turn back the clock and make up for those lost years with her. Caught up in the patriots' cause here in America, he had used it as a sort of revenge against the English for what they had done to him. Now he lay moldering in the orlop of a king's frigate, and the only reward for his actions was the hangman's noose.

Roddy had had many days to think about his life, his plight, the foundations and workings of his own heart. His hatred for Captain Lord had faded to grudging respect, for the man had outwitted and outsmarted him. The English captain lived by a strict code of honor and duty honed by many years in the Royal Navy. Just as he'd been merely following orders when he had pressed Roddy so many years ago, so he was only doing his duty in apprehending the notorious Irish Pirate.

A man could not be hated for doing his duty.

But Roddy, too, had done his duty. He had smuggled food to the hungry, out-of-work people of Boston after the British had closed the port down as punishment for the Tea Party incident. He had worked side by side with Adams, Hancock, and Warren to bring about fair treatment for his adopted land. He had done his duty, and followed the decree of his heart.

He would die with a clear conscience, and perhaps someday he would be remembered as a hero.

Outside, he heard footsteps detaching themselves from the weighty silence, and his stomach rumbled in hunger. It would be young Hibbert, bringing him his supper. Pork and bread and cheese, or maybe dried peas boiled into edibility. It mattered naught. He would eat it. And later, perhaps, some of the English lads—who really weren't such bad fellows after all—might sneak down with a tot of rum and a deck of playing cards.

The door opened and a slice of light cleaved the darkness. "Hello, Hibbert," Roddy said, still staring up at the deck beams above his head.

There was no sound but the closing of the door.

Roddy shut his eyes. "What is it tonight, laddie? Boiled beef and hard tack? Dried peas and hard tack? Cheese and hard tack?"

"Leg of lamb," a voice said quietly.

The Irish Pirate's eyes shot open. His head turned on the pillow and he sat up, staring at the man who stood there, a tray in one hand, a lantern in the other.

"Christ Almighty!"

The English captain gave a tired smile. "No. Merely Captain Lord, come to bring you your last meal."

Roddy's jaw hardened and he clenched his fists, feeling the chains biting into his skin. "Are ye mockin' me, Brit?"

The gray eyes regarded him steadily, taking in Roddy's filthy shirt and breeches, his unkempt hair, his eyes that were so much like those of the girl Christian loved. "No, my good fellow, not at all. I merely thought you might appreciate something a bit more bracing than our normal fare."

He set the tray down on the deck flooring, because there was no table in the tiny room. Roddy's mouth watered. On a fine plate of what had to be the captain's china was a sizzling slab of roast lamb, running with juice and sprinkled with mint and an assortment of fragrant herbs. A wreath of boiled potatoes surrounded it, and there was a steaming chunk of fresh bread that looked suspiciously like the type he used to enjoy back home in Ireland, so many years ago.

"Is this some sort o' joke?" Roddy snarled, his temper flaring as he saw the bottle of fine wine set on the tray.

The English officer reached into his pocket and drew out a key. He moved slowly across the small space between them, the lantern picking out the gold in the lace of his coat, the thick waves of his hair. He grasped Roddy's chains, fitted the key into the lock, and snapped it free. "No joke, my dear fellow," he said quietly. "As I said, this is your last supper aboard *Marauder*. Sentence has been passed upon you ... tomorrow it shall be carried out."

"Hangin'?" Roddy asked nonchalantly, lifting a proud chin that was now heavy with beard.

"I am afraid so."

Roddy swallowed, a prickle of fear shooting up his spine. He eyed the plate of hot food. The English captain eased himself to the decking, leaning his broad back against the bulwark and letting his hands dangle over his bent knees. "Pray, eat it before it grows cold," he said, motioning for Roddy to sit down as well. "My cook went to considerable effort to prepare this for you."

Warily, Roddy slunk down from the bunk and lowered himself to the decking across from his nemesis. His stomach growling, he picked up the fork and knife and sawed into the juicy slab of lamb. "Looks like the fare my mam used to make back home," he muttered, brushing his errant, dirty hair off his brow with the inside of his elbow.

"I am glad."

Roddy took a bite of meat and shut his eyes in bliss. "It's been many a year since I've been in the Navy, but I know this isn't customary, a king's captain goin' to all this trouble on behalf of a prisoner."

"'Tis a humane thing to do, I should think. And my methods have never been regarded as ... customary."

Roddy sawed off another piece of lamb. He raised his gaze to the other man's and found the gray eyes regarding him steadily. Between swallows, Roddy said, "I'm not goin' to waste time in pleasantries, seein's how I don't have very much of it left to waste. But the two of us go back a long way, and I've had a good many hours down here t' think about things. I hated ye, truly I did, for every one of these past thirteen years. I lived for the day I could cross swords with ye and run my blade through yer heart." He took a bite of bread and washed it down with a long swallow of the wine. It was an expensive wine, and had no doubt come from the English captain's private stores. "But now I find I've lost all me taste for revenge."

The gray eyes regarded him quietly.

"I know, too, that ye fancy my sister," Roddy said, waving his fork. "She's a fine lass, a bit on the sentimental side but a warm-hearted girl who'll make ye proud." He cut a piece of potato and put it into his mouth. "If ye give me yer word ye'll treat her as a lady, and honor her for the rest of yer days, I'll be consentin' to let ye have her hand in marriage."

The Englishman smiled a sad, private smile. "Thank you, Captain O'Devir. That is most generous of you."

"I mean it. I told ye I hated ye, but I don't any longer. Besides, any lad who can outwit and outsmart the Irish Pirate deserves to win the hand of his sister."

For some reason, the innocent remark seemed to distress the other captain. He looked away, and for the first time Roddy noted the deep lines of strain and sorrow etched into his austere features.

Long moments went by. In the awkward silence, neither man spoke, and Roddy returned his attention to the food, his mind a thousand miles away.

Abruptly, the Englishman said, "I have allowed all of my crew a well-deserved shore leave."

No wonder the ship was so quiet tonight. "All of 'em?"

Captain Lord began to pluck at the gold insignia on his sleeve. "Yes, all of them."

"Never heard of such a thing, a captain lettin' his entire company go."

The gray eyes lifted to regard Roddy. "Again, Captain O' Devir, my actions have never been considered *customary*."

Roddy stared at him. If he didn't know better, he would swear the Englishman was trying to tell him something, but damn him if he knew what it was.

"Yes, Captain O'Devir, I let them all go, with the orders that they are to be back by midnight. It does a crew good to have time away from their ship, would you not agree?" He continued to be markedly interested in his sleeve. "Of course, that leaves just the two of us aboard."

Roddy took another bite of lamb.

The Englishman did not look up, frowning now, as he smoothed a bit of thread on his sleeve. "Just you and me ... Roddy. Two captains with none but the other for company." He glanced at the shackles, now lying slack across the bunk. "Why, you could rise up, knock me in the head, and be away from here with no one the wiser for it."

Roddy stopped chewing. Slowly, he put his fork down and wiped greasy fingers on his breeches. "Aye ... that I could."

"Of course, you would have to make neat work of it. My admiral would not take kindly to the fact that the Irish Pirate has escaped. Nor, for that matter, would General Gage." He gave a heavy sigh and continued to pick at his sleeve, his hair glinting in the lantern light, his pale lashes throwing shadows across his cheeks as he took a marked interest in what he was doing. "To overpower me and render me senseless would be the only faintly acceptable excuse, I should suppose … but I'm talking nonsense, am I not?" He looked up then at Roddy and grinned, and the simple gesture transformed his face—the face of a man who had known much pain and suffering in his own right—into that of a youthful lad on the eve of discovering something wild and forbidden.

"Aye, you are indeed," Roddy agreed gravely.

"But still, 'twould be an easy matter," the Englishman mused. "We are of like height and build, and therefore a fair match of strength. Why, you would only have to get in a lucky blow in order to make your escape.... Of course, I would have the devil of a time explaining the incident to my admiral, but then, I have had difficult times explaining worse things to both him *and* other superiors."

Their gazes met, deep purple against flinty gray. Roddy picked up the bottle of wine, drank long and hard from it, and passed it to the other captain. He did the same, and passed it back to Roddy, until it was empty.

Again their gazes met.

The unspoken bargain was sealed.

The sins of the past had been forgiven.

Captain Lord got to his feet, tall and strikingly handsome. He reached up and removed his fancy cocked hat, baring his hair to the shimmering glow of the lantern. Then he looked at Roddy, and the shadow of a smile touched his hard mouth.

"And, of course, not a soul shall ever know the truth," he warned.

He turned, presenting his proud shoulders, his broad back, and moved toward the door.

The Irish Pirate wasted no time. Raising the bottle, he brought it crashing down on the back of the fair head and caught the English captain under his arms as he fell, gently lowering his heavy, sprawling body to the deck.

He knelt there for a moment, looking down at the uncon-
scious officer and silently thanking him for giving him back his
life. "God love ye, Cap'n Lord," he said, and then, without further
pause, was on his feet and racing topside.

Chapter Thirty-Two

War broke out two days later.

On the previous Friday a warship from England had arrived in Boston, carrying orders from Lord Dartmouth, Secretary of State for the Colonies, to General Gage, directing him to waste no further time in breaking up the rebel network. Gage, fearing for his position as military governor, was quick to act. Intending to arrest Adams and Hancock, and to seize the stores the rebels had reportedly secreted in Concord, he chose the fateful night of April 18th to make his move.

Though he took every possible pain to keep his plan secret, telling no one but his wife and Hugh, Lord Percy, of the impending march on Concord, Gage had unwittingly alerted the watchful eyes of the rebels during the preceding days by activities that were suspiciously suggestive of an impending military activity on the grandest of scales. Spies, mounted messengers, and intuition on the part of the rebels guaranteed advance knowledge of Gage's plans, and days before the British troops began their fateful march, the patriots had already transferred their arms stores in Concord to other secret sites. They hid sacks of bullets in nearby swamps, melted their pewter plates down into musket balls, and devised a set of signals so that, when the king's troops made their move, the information could be quickly passed on to Concord and other outlying towns.

By the time Gage's select troops of grenadiers and light infantrymen, numbering some eight hundred, stole quietly out of Boston on the night of April 18th under the command of Lieutenant Colonel Francis Smith, and were ferried in the warships' boats across the Charles River to begin the sixteen-mile march to Concord, rebel messengers were already galloping from Boston to spread the midnight alarm.

The American War of Independence had begun.

DEIRDRE WAS awake and sitting at her window, staring out into the crisp, moonlit night, when Paul Revere galloped through Menotomy, shouting at the top of his lungs.

"The regulars are out! The regulars are out!"

The hoofbeats rose in crescendo, growing louder and louder, peaking, and then fading away into the distance. In their aftermath, she saw lanterns being lit in the windows of the neighboring houses, the tavern across the road. People began to wander outside, staring off toward where Revere had gone and milling about in confusion.

It was finally happening.

Deirdre shut her eyes, bent her head, and, with the cross clasped between her hands and its chain wrapped around her fingers, prayed.

For the safety of Roddy, whom she had not seen or heard from since that rainy afternoon when he'd left on his final mission as the Irish Pirate and who, according to Jared Foley, was hiding at the Boston home of Dr. Joseph Warren following the brief scuffle with the captain of HMS *Bold Marauder* during which he'd made his escape.

For the safety of her adopted family, who had spent the night preparing for war, cleaning, oiling, and rolling cartridges for their two muskets, and maintaining a state of watchfulness.

And most of all for Christian, whom she missed with every beat of her lonely, aching heart. If only he had released Roddy and honored his promise to her. But how could she have expected him to forsake the values and traditions by which he had lived the past twenty years of his life, turning his back on his own principles of what was just and right?

He was a king's officer.

Sadness weighed heavily in her heart, and she pressed her lips to the spot on her finger where his ring had rested for so brief a time. How stricken he'd looked when she'd taken it off and laid it on his desk, then turned her back and left him. Anguish filled her. At least he would be safe behind the frigate's mighty guns should the worst happen.

She raised her head and looked out into the night. Figures moved in the darkness, their voices hushed and excited. More and more people, alerted by the night messenger, were trickling from their houses and standing in the road, some staring fearfully toward the east, from whence the regulars would soon be coming.

Deirdre shut her eyes once more. Her lips moved against the hard edges of the cross, and she suddenly felt cold all over.

"Please, God, watch over all those I love, and those I do not love, those I know, and those I do not know. Please, dear Father, keep everyone safe, especially Roddy, wherever he may be, and my beloved Christian. I love him, Father, I love him so very much—even if he *did* put duty before me. And please, oh, Father, don't let the minutemen have to take up arms against the regulars, for there are good and decent men on both sides."

She paused, shivering in the night air that wafted in through the open window. The scent of wood smoke hung in the air and a faint breeze rustled the trees. It was early springtime, and soon, everyone said, the leaves would be on the trees, just like they were back home in Connemara. She saw the grass shining silver in the moonlight, and felt a pang inside at the memory of Christian's promise, for that grass—so brown and dead and ugly when she had first arrived in America—was now growing every bit as green as any field back in Ireland.

Downstairs, she heard Mr. Foley snapping orders, instructing his wife and daughter what to do when the troops came. Soon, she knew, someone would be coming up to get her, but she had a few moments left. Precious moments before she had to leave the sanctuary of her little bedroom.

Her gaze lifted to the eastern horizon beyond the trees. She thought of the king's soldiers, making their way even now through the moonlight toward them, and a prickle of doom made the hairs rise on her neck and shivers dance the length of her spine.

She bent her head once again, and squeezing her eyes tightly shut, prayed, "And oh, Father, please, oh please, please, please— don't let anyone get killed...."

"Deirdre?" It was Mr. Foley calling from the foot of the stairs. "Get dressed and come downstairs. The regulars are out!"

As though she didn't know.

"Aye, Mr. Foley, I'll be right down."

She stood up, her muscles cramped from sitting at the window for so long. She put on a green jacket, a thick, quilted petticoat and a pair of boots. She had gone to bed in Christian's shirt—and she left it on beneath her stays, keeping the only part of him she had close to her heart. Then she picked up her canvas bag, nearly empty now except for the flagon of Irish air. That little bag had traveled the vast Atlantic. It had never left her person since she had said good-bye to her beloved Ireland. It would not leave her now.

She was just descending the stairs when the first dogs began to bark wildly in the distance, piercing the quiet of the night. Fear rose within her and a deep rumbling began to sound from the east. The Foleys raced to the front window and peered out into the moonlit night. And in the little cupboard, the plates began to vibrate. Louder and louder and louder—

"Dear God above," Mrs. Foley breathed, paling with fright.

For just outside the window, the measured tramp of their feet shaking the very floor upon which the Foleys stood, was a vast, unending river of red-coated soldiers marching past, their bayonets gleaming in the moonlight. Here and there an officer rode, his steed's hoofbeats like the knell of doom. The dark line stretched as far as the family could see, and the rattle of wagons, the stamp of the war-horses, the measured thunder of booted feet were enough to send Mrs. Foley reeling back from the window, closing her eyes in terror.

"Dear God," she repeated, and leaned heavily against her husband. "Dear God, have mercy on us all...."

They dared not light even a candle. Some of the troops broke rank and darted across the lawn, stopping to drink from the well before racing to catch up with their comrades. It seemed to take forever for them to pass, and it was a long time before the frightened Foleys dared to leave the safety of their house and venture outside to join the neighbors milling about in the road.

They found people streaming from their houses, standing in the moonlight and pointing toward the west, toward Lexington, where the soldiers had gone. Lights began to glow from windows, and somewhere a baby wailed. Then Solomon Bowman, the lieutenant of the Menotomy minutemen, went racing from door to door, summoning his men and ordering them to assemble on the Green at the crack of dawn to march to Concord and Lexington.

Jared Foley wasted no time. Gathering the powder cartridges they'd been making ever since the first rumors of Gage's planned raid on Concord had reached them, he laid them on the table and turned to his wife. "Throw all of the pewter and silver into the well," he told her, gripping her trembling shoulders to steady her. "Gather up everything of value, then take the girls and go to the Prentiss house with the other women."

"Oh, Jared," she said, on the verge of hysteria, "please do not ask me to leave my home!"

"I do not ask it, Joanne, I demand it!" He lowered his voice. "There will be bloodshed this day," he murmured. "I feel it in my bones. You will take the girls and go to the Prentiss house with the other women and children, out of sight and away from the road when the regulars pass through on their return to Boston. Do no defy me in this, Joanne." He turned away, missing the mutinous set of his wife's jaw, and the exchange of glances between Deirdre and Delight, both of whom knew she had no intention of carrying out her husband's wishes. He picked up the rolled packets of black powder and began to stuff them into his cartridge box. "If blood is shed today, then I pray that those who die will not do so in vain. This moment has been a long time in coming, Joanne." Straightening up, he folded her quickly to his chest. Then he set her back, and looked deeply into her eyes. "Whatever happens, keep the girls safe. I will leave you with one of the muskets in case, God forbid, you are called to defend yourself."

And then dawn began to glimmer on the horizon, and the urgent beat of a drum rolled across the fields, calling the brave minutemen of Menotomy together. Grim-faced fathers and eager-eyed sons bade good-bye to wives and children and sisters, and toting muskets and ammunition, raced to the town Green to answer the call to duty, never knowing that for some of them, it would be the last farewells to their loved ones that they would ever make.

Shortly thereafter, the farmers were marching toward Lexington under the command of Captain Benjamin Locke.

For the people of Menotomy, it would be a day of bloodshed and death.

❧

ON THE QUARTERDECK of HMS *Bold Marauder*, Christian paced in agitation. His face was hard with tension, his eyes bleak and worried. The nightmare had come to him last night, more intense, more vivid, more frightening than ever before. A nightmare of blood and fighting and death, only this time the victim was not the woman he had once married—but the young Irish girl whom he loved.

And he, bound to the frigate by the command of duty, was unable to save her.

Several hours earlier, eight hundred troops under the command of Lieutenant Colonel Francis Smith had left Boston under cover of darkness with the intent of seizing the rebels' military stores in Concord. And now, reinforcements of some twelve hundred more, under the capable command of Hugh, Lord Percy, had just left to join them.

Deirdre was out there. Alone. Unprotected. In the middle of it, should that spark explode into flames.

He shut his eyes against the memory of the nightmare and tried to shake the overwhelming sense of doom. The nightmare was meaningless, merely a product of his own worry—surely, things wouldn't go that far, would they?

By now Smith's select troops, tense and eager for action, would have reached Concord. They would already have long since passed through the little West Cambridge village of Menotomy. Had the awesome and terrifying might of nearly a thousand armed soldiers awakened Deirdre as they'd marched through in the moonlight? Had she looked out her window and trembled in fear? Where was she now? What was happening?

And oh God, what the deuced hell was he doing here aboard his ship when he ought to be with her?

Keeping her safe?

He leaned his brow against a shroud, anchoring a hand in the stiff ropes that supported the mainmast. *Go to her. Tell her you* did *release her brother, after all. Damn your pride, man, just* go!

Footsteps sounded on the ladder that led up to the quarter-deck and turning, he saw Rico Hendricks approaching. He frowned, and the bosun yanked off his hat and belatedly saluted the quarterdeck.

"Sorry, sir."

Christian merely gave a tight smile and gazed off to the west, feeling Hendricks's eyes upon him. The big Jamaican cleared his throat. "Er, how're you faring this morning, Captain?"

Distractedly, Christian reached up to touch the lump on the back of his skull. "Fine, Rico," he murmured, staring off toward Boston. "'Tis my heart that worries me, and the dread that darkens it."

Hendricks joined him, his face grave as he let his hands dangle over the rail. He had been the one to discover his friend and captain out cold on the deck flooring of the brig, the prisoner long gone. But he knew of the inner war Christian had been fighting in the days immediately preceding Roddy O'Devir's escape. He knew his captain was not so careless as to turn his back on a dangerous prisoner, and that it was no coincidence that the entire crew had been ashore when the Pirate had gotten away. And he knew that pride would never allow his commanding officer to admit that maybe, just maybe, he'd had a hand in that escape....

Yes, there was more to it than that, and every man aboard the frigate knew it. Sir Geoffrey had been enraged to learn of the Pirate's escape, and only the persuasiveness of his favorite captain, Brendan Merrick, had saved Christian from a court-martial.

Abruptly, Christian said, "The nightmare returned last night, Rico."

Rico said nothing, merely looking down into the harbor below.

"For five years, I was tormented by the fact that I was unable to rescue Emily from that burning house. For five years, I have gone to bed every night knowing I would see her standing in those flames once again, screaming as they consumed her ... *burned* her." His voice was harsh. "For five years, I have lived with the anguish and guilt of not being able to get her out of that house."

Rico looked down, pretending to study the calluses on his broad hands.

"Now the nightmare is back, Rico, but this time it is not Emily who is trapped and afraid ... it is Deirdre." Christian took a deep, ragged breath, the shadow of his hat falling over his hands as he bent his head. "And again I stand here, helpless."

Rico said nothing, watching the morning light glittering on the sea below.

"I shall not remain helpless this time, Rico." The shadow fell away as Christian's head came up. "I must go to her, get her out of there, keep her safe, tell her I love her. And—" he looked away, his features contorted with anguish—"I must confess the truth. About ... about the other night."

"Aye, sir. Perhaps you should."

Christian looked at him sharply, but Hendricks only gave a reassuring smile. "Have no fear, sir," he said, "Your secret is safe with us."

A voice boomed out behind him. "Well sir, if ye're going, ye'd best be off. Word has it that Lord Percy and his reinforcements are long gone. But if ye hurry, you should be able tae catch up tae them."

Christian turned. Ian MacDuff stood there and he was not alone. Behind him, the entire crew had gathered, ready to support their captain in any decision he made whether it be good or bad, wise or unwise. He had won their trust, their loyalty, and, perhaps, even their love.

He straightened up, the strain easing from his face.

"You're going, then, sir?" asked Rico, smiling.

"Of course I am." Christian turned to face the big Scot. "I may return as your commanding officer," he said quietly, "or I may return in irons for disobeying my admiral. Either way, Ian, I leave *Bold Marauder* in your hands."

He strode resolutely down the quarterdeck stairs. Hibbert, who'd been eavesdropping, was standing there holding his captain's boat cloak. Already the crew was assembling, organizing themselves into tight lines of discipline and respect. The sight caught at Christian's heart, for he knew it might very well be the last time he was ever honored so.

His gaze moved over these men who had come to mean so much to him. Teach, huge, and bristling and formidable, his belt strung with weapons of every size, shape, and kind. Hibbert, trying hard to emulate what he thought a good officer should be, his uniform fresh and clean. Ian, his red curls glinting like fire and Skunk, his pungent scent enough to give him a private standing space of several feet. Wenham, sad-eyed and hulking. Rhodes, tight-lipped and unsmiling. Evans, standing at the forefront of his grim-faced marines, and Rico, his dark eyes shining with pride as he came forward to present Christian with his sword.

The boat had already been lowered, and far below the oarsmen waited.

Slowly, Christian passed the carefully formed lines of seamen and officers, smartly returning every salute. At the rail he paused and looked up at the giant, billowing flag—the flag that he had spent his life defending, the flag whose honor he had sworn to uphold, the flag that would always swell his heart with pride.

Then Rico was handing him his sword and Ian was touching his hat as he accepted command of the king's frigate *Bold Marauder*.

"Godspeed, sir. I hope ye find her, and may the both of ye return to us safe and sound."

Christian returned Ian's salute. Then he turned, climbing down the side of the ship and into the boat that waited below.

HUDDLED in their homes and in the crowded rooms of the Prentiss house, the women and children of Menotomy paled at the first distant boom of gunfire to the west.

The alarming reports had come trickling in as horsemen raced through the village shouting the news. Fighting had broken out at dawn in Lexington, and colonists and soldiers had been killed. There had been a skirmish at the north bridge in Concord. The regulars had failed to find the stores of munitions and ordnance and were now headed toward Menotomy on their way back to Boston.

Earlier in the afternoon, a twelve-hundred-man relief force under the command of Lord Hugh Percy had marched past on its way to aid Colonel Smith, their bayonets glinting in the sun, their mighty field pieces rumbling along on giant carts made especially to carry them. And no one would ever forget the sight of a little girl, attending her mother's cow as it grazed by the side of the road, looking up to see the oncoming redcoats. As the animal plodded through the ranks the child, heedless of the danger, followed it fearlessly. The regulars left her alone, and one or two even paused to ruffle the child's hair. Then the main column of Percy's men had passed, their measured footsteps sounding like the tread of one monstrous leviathan. They were flanked by mounted officers and trailed by carts and wagons laden with supplies. It seemed to take forever for the road to empty, and still stragglers came galloping by in their wake for hours.

In Concord, Colonel Smith's exhausted troops, failing to find the rebel stores and growing increasingly alarmed at the sight of minutemen pouring in by the thousands from all over the countryside, had turned and headed back toward Boston. Incited by the earlier bloodshed, the rebels began to fire on them from behind stone walls, fences, and trees. Soldiers fell, dying. Order began to dissipate. The troops returned the minutemen's fire, but it was impossible to hit men who fought like Indians, hiding behind trees and stone walls, only to pop up and pick them off.

Panic took over, and what had begun as an orderly march back toward the safety of Boston and the warships anchored there, soon became a downright flight. By the time the soldiers met up with Lord Percy's relief force outside Lexington, all semblance of order had been lost. After a brief rest, the regulars resumed their hasty retreat, taking fire from all sides.

As Smith's weary forces fled east, desperate to reach still-distant Boston, Major Pitcairn, knowing the men needed an outlet for their fear and frustration, cunningly sent Percy's fresh troops ahead and outside of the main column with permission to burn and pillage everything in their path. By the time they hit Menotomy, they had carved a path of violence and destruction.

And Menotomy was not to be spared.

Deirdre, huddled at the window with Delight, Mrs. Foley and several neighbors, felt her companions' hot breath stirring her hair, warming her neck; she smelled the sweat of their fear and heard their sobs of terror, a terror that was reflected in her own heart as the sharp crack of gunfire and the boom of cannon heralded the approaching arrival of the fleeing British forces.

With a sound like rising thunder, they came around a bend in the road, nearly two thousand men running as fast as their legs could carry them. Officers galloped past, their coattails flying, shouting desperately for order. Wagons toting the dead and wounded rumbled by, their wheels lodging in mud and spinning free once more. Musket fire cracked around them and Deirdre saw a soldier fall, only to be trampled by the river of red-coated regulars. A horse reared up and plunged over backward, crushing the officer who had been so proudly mounted on its back. Minutemen, mere shadows in the haze of gun smoke, darted from behind trees, their muskets spurting flame and smoke.

Mrs. Foley cried out as she saw her husband and Captain Locke dive headlong over the stone wall that bordered the house, popping up to train their muskets on the fleeing troops. Gunshots cleaved the air and more redcoats fell, some wounded, some dying, some already dead. Flames and roiling black smoke burst from the windows of a nearby house as the soldiers ransacked the building and then set it afire. People ran screaming out into the road. Minutemen raced into the nearby house of Jason Russell, and Deirdre saw the old man die on his front steps as a wild-eyed redcoat cut him down, savagely bayoneting his body.

"Lock the windows!" Joanne Foley cried, and sobbing, they slammed the shutters shut against the carnage outside. Deirdre and Delight clung to each other. The windows rattled in their casings with each thunderous reverberation. One blew apart as a musket ball burst through, flinging the shutters wide and slamming into the mantel just above their heads. Fists pounded on the door and angry curses rent the air. Joanne Foley hefted the musket, swung it toward the door and fired, the thunderous blast exploding in their heads. Outside, a man screamed in agony and another hurled himself through the open window, only to be brought down by the musket of an old man who took careful aim at the redcoat from his place on the stairway. Blood exploded against the wall. Flashes of red drove past the window. Horses screamed in fright, bellowed in agony. Smoke tainted the air and the cries of those who had been shot, those who had been bayoneted, those who were dying, pierced the walls of the little house.

Gunfire roared from the house of Jason Russell, where the minutemen had made their stand, and with each hollow boom, each crack of a musket, the women sobbed and cried and huddled together. The horror seemed to go on forever. Then the thunder began to fade as the fleeing soldiers raced on toward Boston, leaving the wounded and dead in their wake.

Like a land savaged by storm and just opening its eyes, Menotomy began to stir. The fields were strewn with bodies, some clad in the king's colors, some in the ragged wool and homespun of local farmers. Outside, in the muddy road where puddles of water were now stained crimson with blood, the dead and dying lay. A few last shots rang out as minutemen fired upon straggling British troops who, carrying their wounded and dead, were too exhausted to fight back.

Long, keening wails came from the townspeople as here and there someone recognized the corpse of a loved one. Women comforted screaming babies and sobbing children, began to stagger out of the houses in which they had barricaded themselves. The wounded and dying lay in the road, in the fields, draped over fences and walls. A red-coated figure stirred in the yard outside and reached for his musket, only to fall back, his legs jerking, as a single shot cracked out.

And then, from the east, Deirdre heard the hoofbeats of a single, approaching horse.

She knew. She knew, even before she ran to the door and flung it open, who it was. She knew, even before she saw him, that he had come looking for Roddy. And she knew, even before her mouth opened in a desperate scream of warning, that it was already too late to save him.

The glistening, foam-flecked hide of the big chestnut stallion swept around the bend and burst into view. And though a cloak covered his fine uniform, it was all too obvious that the figure who sat so tall and straight in the saddle was a military man, no less an enemy than those who had slashed a murderous swath through the village a mere ten minutes before.

"Christian!"

The horse kept coming, the rider's cloak billowing in the wind.

"Christian, *no-o-o-o-o!*"

She was racing across the lawn, her skirts flying, before anyone could stop her. She stumbled once, fell, picked herself up and kept on running even as his alarmed gaze found hers, even as she saw a minuteman rise up from behind the shelter of a stone wall and carefully, deliberately, bring his musket up to bear on the lone rider.

"No-o-o-o-o-o-oooo!"

The explosion seemed a thousand times louder than the mightiest of *Bold Marauder*'s broadsides. In horror, she saw smoke and fire burst from the gun in a brilliant cloud of color. She saw the minuteman raise his fist in triumph. She saw the rider jerk in the saddle, a streak of blood ripping along his thigh, his hand going for his sword a moment before another shot sent his cocked hat spinning away into the mud.

He tumbled from the horse, his bright hair glinting in the sunlight.

Screaming, she raced to him and plunged to her knees in the mud where he had fallen. The big stallion bolted, thundering back down the road, the irons of the empty saddle slapping his sides. Somewhere behind her Jared Foley was yelling, and the boom of cannon and gunfire was far off in the distance now.

Christian lay still and unmoving. Blood seeped from the hair at his temple.

"*No!*" Deirdre screamed, grabbing his hand and falling over his body. "No, no, no, you can't die!" Sobbing bitterly, she pressed his hand to her heart, to the cross, her tears dropping upon the insignia on his sleeve that marked him as a king's captain. "Please, Christian, don't die on me. Oh, dear God, don't take him from me, *please,* God, don't take him...."

Shadows stamped out the sunlight. Concerned hands grasped her shoulders, tried to gently pull her away. She heard Delight's voice, saw someone poke a musket at Christian's chin and, satisfied that he was no threat, move away.

"Don't die, Christian ... oh, please, don't die." She crushed his hand to the cross, never seeing the drops of blood that the sharp points raised, never feeling them trickle down her wrist to stain her own sleeve as she bent over him. "Dear God, please don't take him, he was just doing his duty, oh, God, oh, God, *please*—"

Jared Foley was there beside her. He knelt down and grasped the captain's other wrist, his thumb pushing up the sleeve to find a pulse. "He's alive," he said, straightening up. "Merely a flesh wound. Lucky he is, too, for *he* will live to see many tomorrows."

"Don't know what the tarnal hell a sea officer's doin' way out here," muttered another, peering down at the gold lace of Christian's coat where the cloak had fallen open.

"Aye, 'tis rather strange, eh?"

But Deirdre, clutching his lifeless hand, knew why he had come. In that brief, awful moment when their gazes had met just before the minuteman's musket had felled him, she had seen the truth.

He had come for her brother.

Her throat constricting, she took off her kerchief and pressed it to the blood that trickled through the pale hair where the bullet had grazed his temple. Bitter shame coursed through her. She had tried to make him choose between his promise to her and the principles by which he lived his life. How could she have thought he would abandon his values? How could she have thought he would turn his back on the Navy, on his duty to king and country? In his eyes Roddy was a traitor, an enemy of the Crown.

It was unfair of her to expect him to abandon his principles, just for the sake of love. It was unfair to think that the two of them would ever have a chance to be happy together.

But the fact that she loved him would never change.

Slowly, Deirdre O'Devir reached up and removed the chain that had kept Grace O'Malley's cross against her heart for so many years.

The cross that she had sworn never to take off for as long as she drew breath.

She shut her eyes, her lips moving in silent prayer. Then she closed it in her palm and pressed it to her lips for a long, tremulous moment. It was warm with the heat of her body, and before it could cool, she lifted Christian's lolling head, drew the chain over his hair, and carefully eased his head back down, her lips lowering to touch his skin, his parted lips, in a final kiss of farewell.

"I love ye, Christian," she said brokenly. "Dear God, I love ye...."

There the cross lay, against his heart, against the proud buttons and lapels of his coat. Deirdre got to her feet, her hand coming up to touch the strangely empty area at her throat. But she had done the right thing. She had given him a symbol of her love, a precious part of herself so that he would never forget her. Her eyes streaming, she turned to Jared Foley, knowing that he and his family would take care of her captain until he recovered.

There was nothing left in America for her, and the colonists' fight was not her own. If she and Roddy stayed here any longer, her brother would surely be caught and hanged—if not by Christian, then by someone else.

She had come here to find her brother, and she had found him. She had come here to fulfill a vow to her dying mother—and now it was time to honor that promise.

Find my son, Deirdre, and bring him home to Ireland.

It was time to go home.

"Mr. Foley?"

He was kneeling down beside the captain, helping his daughter try to staunch his bleeding. He looked up at Deirdre.

"Please take me to me brother," she said quietly, her proud Gaelic face shining with courage and misery beneath her tears.

"What?"

At her feet, Christian was beginning to stir. She looked down at him through the blur of tears, her heart breaking. "Christian will only hunt him down again, ye see? He's smart and determined, Mr. Foley. He's the finest officer in the king's Navy. He'll find Roddy and take him from me only this time, 'twill be forever."

"What are you saying, girl?"

She looked up, turning her face toward Boston—and Ireland

beyond. A gust of wind came up, carrying the smoke of battle and tugging at her hair.

Brokenly, she murmured, "That it's time for me to go home."

❧

SHE STOOD on the shore at Boston Harbor, her eyes seeking the British men-of-war anchored there. Her gaze moved over each of them until it finally settled upon the one that was different from the rest ... leaner, lither, somehow more beautiful than the all the others. The one with the pointer crouched beneath its bowsprit, the one that had brought her here to America, the one that she would never, ever forget.

HMS *Bold Marauder*.

The wind blew from the east, making the frigate's pennants snap. It continued on toward shore, dancing over the waves and making them crest with merriment, playing across the glistening blue waters of the harbor, pulling at her hair and tugging at her clothing.

She threw back her head and opened her arms, embracing the wind for a final time.

And then she uncapped the glass flagon, letting the Irish air escape to be forever mated with its American cousin. She allowed the flagon to fill with wind, then tightly capped it once more.

Her brother stood nearby, uncharacteristically quiet and solemnly waiting to take her out to the little brig he had hired to bring them home. His face was a mix of conflicting emotion, his heart in turmoil, for only he knew of the unspoken promise he had made to the man who had once been his enemy.

A promise he now considered breaking.

Roddy stepped forward, biting his lip.

And then he stopped, his eyes tragic.

He couldn't do it. For he had made a promise, and Roddy O' Devir always kept his word.

Chapter Thirty-Three
CONNEMARA, IRELAND

The press gang was in.

One could tell by the way a thick pall had come over the land, like mist snuffing out the noonday sun. One could tell by the way the little village that clung to the sea's edge grew quiet and seemed to huddle within itself, the people slamming shut the doors of their whitewashed cottages and watching the roads from behind slitted curtains. One could tell by the way the taverns emptied and the young lads fled into the hills that climbed toward the majestic purple ridge of the twelve mountains, where they would hide until the threat was past.

And one could tell by the big, three-masted men-of-war that filled the harbor.

This time, England was at war with America ... and not everyone wanted to fight.

It was an infrequent threat, the Royal Navy seeking its unwilling recruits from this bleak, storm-tossed area of western Ireland that even God seemed to have forgotten. No able-bodied young man was safe from the press gang. And so it was that Deirdre O'Devir solemnly watched her brother sigh with exasperation and leave, grumbling as he headed into the hills where the others had already fled.

Then Deirdre locked the doors and waited.

So many years ago, this same scene had enacted itself, just as it was happening now. She pulled a chair up to the fire—a good, Irish peat fire that glowed warmly in the hearth—and sat staring into the flames.

A flagon sat in a revered spot on the table before her and she reached out, touching the cold glass, staring into its seeming emptiness and remembering that last day in Boston, so many months past.

She would never uncap the flagon and let the American air out.

Just as she would never empty the vial of American water scooped from that same harbor, toss away the felt pouch containing Boston sand and seashells, discard the tuft of hair combed from the Foley's plow horse, or eat the bread—made of corn grown in Massachusetts pastures and milk gleaned from the Foley's cow and baked over a good, American wood fire—that was carefully wrapped in a square of linen and tucked away in her bedroom.

Home was where the heart was, Christian had once said. Home could be any place on earth, as long as it was with the one you loved. And it wasn't until Deirdre had returned to her beloved Ireland that she realized the place of her birth was no longer her home. It wasn't until her heart began to pine for a handsome Englishman she could never have, that she realized her heart belonged not to Ireland, but to Christian.

The fire had grown too warm, and she stood up, the heat fading instantly from her face to leave her cheeks cold and empty. She hugged her cloak to herself and stared morosely into the smoking fire. There was a decided nip in the air, and in America, or so Roddy had told her, the leaves would be starting to take on glorious colors of scarlet, orange and gold ... colors unknown to the trees of Ireland.

She walked to the window and looked off toward the sea, where she could see the towering masts of the men-of-war silhouetted against the western sunset. Over thirteen years ago she had seen masts very much like these, from this same window, and had gone to see for herself just what was so terrible about the English and their Navy that everyone so hated and feared.

Now she knew there was nothing terrible about the English, nothing terrible about their Navy.

She had learned a lot in these thirteen years.

Outside, the wind began to rise, moaning around the little cottage as it had done for centuries. The clouds grew thicker, heavier, darker. She thought of Roddy, hiding up in the hills with the others. She thought of her neighbors, terrified of losing their loved ones to the dreaded press gang. And she thought of the new horse in the barn, a gift from Roddy that she had named Booley in honor of Christian's pony from his childhood.

A desire to relive painful memories finally got the better of her. Huddled in the cloak, she hurried across the garden, saddled the horse, and, once away from the cottage, sent him galloping off toward the sea.

Night was coming on; mist was filing in from the ocean, and the shadows of dark clouds trailed over the land. Recklessly, Deirdre urged the horse faster, not pulling him up until they had crested the last rocky hill.

There she sat, a pale, ethereal beauty, her hair whipping around a face dominated by the haunted eyes of a grieving soul. Far below, the sea swapped kisses with the base of the hill, thundering and booming and sending up great sheets of spray. She licked her lips and tasted salt, and drew her cloak more tightly around her.

Then she clawed the wild snarls of hair from her eyes and gazed out over the ocean.

A half mile out in the bay, a British warship lay, majestic in all its dread, frightening in all its beauty. And another, its pale sails furled upon its yards, its anchor cables stretching down into the sea. And still another, sloop-rigged and nimble, and all but dwarfed where it lay in the shadow of the fourth and final ship, a mighty, towering wall of wood pierced by the snouts of what had to be a hundred guns.

Its mastheads seemed to scrape the bellies of the low-hanging clouds themselves, and from one of those masts flew the colors of a rear admiral.

Not just a single warship this time, but a squadron.

Behind her a stone, loosened by the horse's hooves, skittered down the hill, the sound cleaving the stillness. Deirdre gave a start and spun around, her skin crawling with the uncanny feeling that she was being watched.

But there was no one there and the wind, peppered with rain, was suddenly cold and damp.

Beneath her, the horse began to fidget. Then his ears pricked forward, his head lifted, and Deirdre's breath caught in her throat, for a boat had been lowered from the flagship and was plunging through the breakers toward shore.

She forgot the oncoming storm. She forgot the approaching darkness. She forgot the feeling that she was being watched.

The boat—not just any boat, but a smartly painted one that was surely the pride of some high-ranking officer—was nearing shore now, its crew having a rough time of it in the heavy seas. Oars rose and fell in perfect rhythm, and every so often the boat's bow would nose up as it plowed a wave, drenching the men and the tall officer in the stern with spray.

She shut her eyes, emotion choking her throat. A drop of water splashed upon her hand, another upon her wrist, and Deirdre never knew if it was rain or her own tears, for as she edged the horse toward the edge of the cliff she saw that the officer—some thirteen years older than he had been that other time, but no less handsome, no less proud—had a telescope to his eye and was training it on *her*.

She flew from the horse and dashed down the cliff path, her skirts flying, the tears streaming down her cheeks. The officer leaped from the boat, and before the seamen could even pull the craft up onto the beach, Deirdre had plunged into the surf and flung herself into his arms.

His brows were blond and haughty, and his fancy, gold-laced hat covered richly gilded hair that was caught at the nape with a black ribbon. He had long, pale eyelashes, eyes the color of fog, and a profile that reminded her of a hawk.

He clasped her to him, nearly crushing the breath from her. And then he drew back, his heart in his eyes. She had expected cold fury, but there was only love.

"Really, dearest, you lead me a merry chase."

Behind him the seamen, grinning, exchanged happy smirks as they drew the boat up onto the beach. She saw familiarity in the rumpled unkemptness of a midshipman's uniform, the stench of a huge, barrel-chested body, and the fearsome countenance of a piratical fiend.

In the midshipman's arms were three mostly-grown puppies.

Deirdre began to sob uncontrollably. "Oh, Christian, there's nothin' for ye here! Let my brother alone, I beg of ye! He'll not be goin' back to America. He'll not be causin' any more trouble—"

He laid a finger over her lips.

"I did not come here for your brother, Deirdre."

She stared at him.

"I did not come here to press more Irishmen."

She couldn't move.

"I came here, dear girl, for *you*."

He took her hands and gazed solemnly down at her. She felt her heart swelling, melting, bursting, and saw her emotions reflected in his eyes. "Ah, Deirdre ... I thought you had deserted me—until I found *this*." He reached up and drew out the cross, still hanging from its chain around his neck. "I may have wagered all in coming here, but I took this to mean that you really *do* love me."

"Christian, I never *stopped* lovin' ye. 'Tis just that—"

He silenced her with a kiss. "Dear girl, I did not go to Menotomy that day to recapture your brother, as you believed. Delight told me, you see? No, I went there to find *you,* to keep you safe, and to make a confession — one that I should have made long ago, but one that I refrained from making because of my foolish pride."

She swallowed hard, searching his face.

"Regarding that, er, *scuffle* your brother and I engaged in when he made his escape?"

"Yes... ?" she said slowly.

"Well, 'twas no accident. I *allowed* him to overpower me." He looked a bit sheepish, and had a sudden interest in his sleeve. "In fact, I confess that I asked him to."

Her eyes widened with shock. "But I thought—"

He laid his lips against her brow. "I know, love, what you thought. And if Roddy made no mention about what really happened between us, 'tis because he was more attentive to his promise to *me* than I was with mine to *you*." Tears spilled down her cheeks, and he wiped them away with his thumb. Then he reached into his pocket and slowly drew something out, looking at it for a long, reflective moment. "I ... I hope you still want this."

It was the ancestral ring of the Lord family.

"I love you," he said quietly. And then he took her hand and slid the ring onto her finger.

Behind them, the seamen erupted in wild cheering, and even the puppies yapped with excitement.

"Oh, Christian...."

He smiled down at her, tall and beloved and achingly handsome.

She reached out to touch his lapel. Then she looked beyond him to the harbor, her eyes widening at the sight of the huge, magnificent warship.

He noted her confusion. "Sir Geoffrey was so angry that I'd abandoned my command, he kicked me out of Boston and sent me back to England, vowing he hoped never to set eyes on me again."

"But that big ship out there—"

"Yes, my dear ... I've been promoted."

"Promoted?"

"'Twas Elliott's doing." He smiled. "You see, love, when I returned to England, I learned that my manipulative brother had gone to great lengths to amuse himself by giving me command of *Bold Marauder*. No one could make something of the frigate, and the Navy had all but given up on her. Unbeknownst to me, Elliott made a bet with the first Lord of the Admiralty that I could succeed where the others had failed. A bet that, if he won it, would earn me a certain promotion."

"Ye mean t' tell me they made ye a rear admiral for straightenin' out *Bold Marauder*?"

"Aye, but lest you think Elliott is one to show favoritism, do know that our family relationship has never stopped him from disciplining me in the past. In fact, he made quite a public display of doing so the day I tried to leave Portsmouth."

"But I don't see *Marauder*."

"No, she is at Spithead, being refitted for a voyage to the West Indies. She will join us shortly, under Captain MacDuff's command."

"Captain MacDuff? The *West Indies?*"

He smiled, and touched her cheek. "I will not fight the rebels, Deirdre. Had Sir Geoffrey not kicked me out of Boston I would have handed in my resignation, for the Americans have my sympathies. No, my squadron will be deployed to the Caribbean, there to monitor French activities. They are sure to throw in their lot with the Americans sooner or later, and one can never trust the French, you know!" He sobered and stared down at her, taking her hands in his own and raising them to his lips. "As soon as *Bold Marauder* is ready, we shall be away. But I will not leave here until I have all the crew that I need."

"And how many d'ye lack ... Admiral Lord?"

"One."

She stared up at him, her heart bursting with love and pride and joy. He was all that she could ever want. He was all that she would ever need. The tears rolled down her cheeks as he reached up and drew off the cross. Slowly, he settled the heavy chain over her head, positioning the ornate cross back where it belonged, between her own breasts, against her own heart.

She swallowed tightly. The rain clouds were moving away, and late sunlight stabbed down through them now, kissing the harbor with the promise of a golden tomorrow.

The promise of a lifetime of golden tomorrows.

"What do you say, dearest?"

She smiled up at him, twisting the ring around her finger, unable to speak for a long, long moment. The big flagship waited. The three accompanying vessels waited. The seamen waited, the puppies waited, her future waited—

He waited.

"Just let me pack a few things, Christian," she said, "and leave a note fer my brother."

Leading the horse, he walked with her back to the cottage, and shortly afterward, she was being rowed ceremoniously out to the big man-o-war that flew the proud pennant of a rear-admiral.

Around her neck was Grace's cross.

In her lap was a little chest containing the miniature of her mama, the wood from her papa's boat, and a square cut from Roddy's shirt.

But there was no canvas bag, for this time there was no need of any Irish mementos.

Deirdre O'Devir was finally going home.

Keep reading for a special sneak peek of the next book in the Heroes Of The Sea series, Captain of My Heart! (Brendan's story!)

A Heartfelt Thank You!

Thank you from the bottom of my heart for reading my book. If you enjoyed it, please consider posting a review. Reviews don't just help the author, they help other readers discover our books and, no matter how long or short, I sincerely appreciate every review.

Would you like to know when my next book is available? Sign up for my newsletter:

Also, please follow me on BookBub to be notified of deals and new releases.

Thank you again for reading and for your support.

PREVIEW TAKEN BY STORM

Get your copy of Taken by Storm today!

Prologue

The fire started as a spark set to hay, a twisting viper of black smoke before a draft from the stable's open door blew it into life.

With a savage, whooshing roar, the hay burst into flame.

Satisfied, the man tossed the lantern into the loose straw and stepped back as the fire's hot breath hit him. He stood watching the hay blacken, crackle, and disintegrate, mesmerized by the flames, feeling their heat pressing against his face and sucking the moisture out of his pores, drying out his eyes, searing the inside of his nose, and crawling into his lungs with deadly malice.

Take this, you bastard. Teach you to go breaking agreements. If I can't have the Weybourne fortune—and the horses—no one can.

Acrid smoke blackened the air, banked down from the rafters. Coughing, he whipped out his handkerchief, covered his mouth, and stepped back, toward the safety of the door and the coolness of the night beyond. Already, the fire was out of control, a frenzied demon swallowing up stacks of hay, leaping up the partitions that separated the empty stalls, and charging toward that one, single box at the end that was not empty at all.

A shrill whinny pierced the night, and then, hooves ringing desperately against wood.

The stallion was the most valuable horse in England, if not the world, but the man made no effort to save it. He heard its whinny become a terrified scream, felt the fire growing hotter, louder, angrier, pressing hot clothing against his skin, beginning to scorch, blister, and suffocate him. Smoke began to choke him, and he tasted burning wood and hay, turpentine, leather and dirt. Eyes watering, his lungs constricting in the searing heat, he retreated from the stable, the fire raging at his back.

From behind him came the stallion's frightened scream, piercing the hellish clamor of fire and heat. It was a horrible, ghastly sound of pure terror and he pictured the flames reaching for the proud animal, engulfing it, burning it.

Such a waste.

It could've been otherwise, Weybourne. You old fool.

Outside, the night air engulfed him like a cool blanket, and he sucked huge gulps of it into his lungs to rid them of smoke and heat. At his back the inferno roared, and he heard the great timbers of the stable caving in upon themselves, a last distant battering of shod hooves meeting wood...

And then, a crescendo of thunder rising behind him.

He whirled and saw the stallion.

Wild-eyed with fury and terror, its tail streaming smoke and fire, the horse came charging out of the flames like a winged specter of death. It made straight for him; he saw the fire reflected in its savage black eyes, against its burnished coat, in its wide, flaring nostrils that burned an unholy red—

He threw himself out of the way just in time.

The great beast galloped madly off into the night, its mighty hooves making the earth tremble beneath him.

Shaken, his trousers smudged with dirt, the man pulled himself to his feet. Sweat poured down his hot face and sheets of fire snapped and popped and reached for him. Flames danced within the collapsed building like legions of angry devils. And now, faintly, he heard hoarse cries, and turned to see Weybourne himself running from the house, trailed by servants who were trying in vain to catch up to him.

"Shareb!" the old man cried. "Shareb-er-rehh!"

Silhouetted in the conflagration's bright light, the fire-starter moved backwards, and behind a stately elm whose leaves were already curling in agony against the intense heat. Smiling, he watched as the earl came rushing toward the stable, arms waving, old legs pumping, his night cap trailing from his head.

"Shareb!" the old man cried, and then his voice rose in a desperate scream of bleak agony: "*Shareb-er-rehh!*"

"Stop him!" shouted one of the servants, running as fast as he could. "My lord, no!"

Another section of the stable roof imploded, spouting a fountain of sparks and churning black smoke toward the stars above.

"*Shareb!*"

"No, milord! Don't go in there, *it's no use!*"

"Shareb-er-*rehhhhhhh*—"

The old earl ran blindly through the sheets of flame and into the burning stable; the servants charged toward the back of the building in the hope of gaining a safer entrance; then, there was only Weybourne's horrible screams as the fire caught him. His clothing ablaze, he came staggering out, gaining fifteen, maybe twenty feet, before he fell, clutching his chest.

The arsonist moved out from behind the elm and stood staring coldly down at the dying man.

"You..." the old earl gasped, the flames glowing orange against his face as he dragged open his eyes and saw who stood over him. "Knew it was you... did it for revenge, didn't you... should have trusted my instincts about you..."

The fire crackled and sighed. Pungent billows of black smoke enclosed them, cut them off from the shouts and screams and calls that pierced the darkness.

The arsonist knelt down to the old man's level. "Pity, pity, Weybourne. I suppose young Tristan told you all about me, did he not? Is that why you wanted to break the agreement?" He arched a brow, a faint smile touching his mouth as the earl stretched a wizened hand toward him, fingers clawing the glowing earth in a spasm of agony. "Well, *I'm* in debt, too... and I'll be damned if I let you break your promise to me. Good-night, Weybourne. May you rot in hell."

He stood, still looking at that pitiful old hand reaching toward his boot. Above the fire's roar, he heard Weybourne's wheezing gasps, watched the feeble hand jerk and stiffen, saw, in the unholy glow from the burning stable, the skin going ashy and gray.

And heard, off in the distance, the thunder of hoofbeats.

Hard, fast, and furious.

The stallion was returning.

This time, the man slithered off into the night, while behind him the stable burned...

And burned.

Also by Danelle Harmon

Introducing

The Bestselling, Award-Winning, Critically Acclaimed

DE MONTFORTE BROTHERS SERIES

"The bluest of blood; the boldest of hearts;

the de Montforte brothers will take your breath away."

 # 1 Kindle Store bestseller: The Wild One

The Wild One

The Beloved One

The Defiant One

The Wicked One

The Wayward One

The Admiral's Heart

The Fox & the Angel

My First Noel

The Homecoming

OFFICERS AND GENTLEMEN

Captain of My Heart

My Lady Pirate

Wicked at Heart

Lord of the Sea

Heir to the Sea

Never Too Late for Love

THE NOBLE LORDS

Master of My Dreams

Taken by Storm

Scandal at Christmas

My Saving Grace

Pirate in My Arms

About the Author

New York Times and *USA Today* bestselling author Danelle Harmon has written many critically acclaimed and award-winning books. A Massachusetts native, she has lived in Great Britain, though these days she and her English husband make their home in New England with their daughter Emma and numerous animals including three dogs, an Egyptian Arabian horse, and a flock of pet chickens. Danelle welcomes email from her readers and can be reached at Danelle@danelleharmon.com or through any of the means listed below:

CONNECT WITH ME ONLINE!
Danelle Harmon's Website
Danelle Harmon's Blog

Want to know when the next new title from Danelle is released?
Click here!

Even more ways to connect: